HARRY TURTLEDOVE

THROUGH DARKEST EUROPE

A TOM DOHERTY ASSOCIATES BOOK **TOR** NEW YORK

THROUGH DARKEST EUROPE

Copyright © 2018 by Harry Turtledove

A Tor Book
Published by Tom Doherty Associates
175 Fifth Avenue
New York, NY 10010

www.tor-forge.com

Tor® is a registered trademark of Macmillan Publishing Group, LLC.

The Library of Congress Cataloging-in-Publication Data
is available upon request.

ISBN 978-0-7653-7998-6 (hardcover)
ISBN 978-1-4668-7132-8 (ebook)

Our books may be purchased in bulk for promotional, educational, or business use. Please contact your local bookseller or the Macmillan Corporate and Premium Sales Department at 1-800-221-7945, extension 5442, or by email at MacmillanSpecialMarkets@macmillan.com.

First Edition: September 2018

Printed in the United States of America

0 9 8 7 6 5 4 3 2 1

To L. Sprague de Camp once more,
this time for *The Ancient Engineers*.

THROUGH
DARKEST
EUROPE

I

Khalid al-Zarzisi had the window seat as the airliner flew from Tunis to Rome. The senior investigator peered down at the blue, blue water of the Mediterranean. When he studied at the madrasa in Cairo, one of his instructors said Homer had a special word for that special color. But he'd been out of the madrasa more than twenty years now. Homer's word was on the tip of his tongue, but it didn't want to come off. It was . . . It was . . . Khalid muttered in frustration.

Then he found it. "Wine-dark!" he blurted, and felt better.

"Huh? What's that?" his partner asked. Dawud ibn Musa looked like an unmade bed, as usual. His robe was wrinkled. His keffiyeh sat on his head at an angle no doubt meant to be jaunty but in fact sloppy. He should have taken time to shave, too. It was an early-morning flight, but al-Zarzisi had.

"The wine-dark sea," Khalid said. The whole phrase made him even happier than the word had.

"Huh," Dawud repeated. He leaned forward and to his left so he could see out past Khalid to the Middle Sea. Being junior to Khalid—and being a Jew besides—he always got the middle, where his boss sat by the window or on the aisle. He looked out for a few seconds, then shrugged broad shoulders. "Just looks like water to me."

"You don't have a poet's soul," Khalid said.

"Oh, yeah? And you do?" Dawud retorted. Khalid prudently didn't answer that. A senior investigator needed a poet's soul the way a camel needed a fountain pen.

A stewardess pushed a tray of refreshments down the aisle. Her robe stopped a palm's breadth above her knees. A perky cap did a token job of covering her hair. "Sherbet? A fizz? Wine? Spirits?" she asked, first in the classical Arabic educated men and women all over the world understood, then in the Maghrib's Berber-flavored dialect, and, finally, in Italian.

"Wine," Dawud ibn Musa said, and then again, in case she hadn't heard: "Wine!"

"Yes, sir," she said. "Three dinars, please." From somewhere inside his robe, he pulled out a rumpled five-dinar note. The stewardess' smile looked pasted on as she gave him his change. It brightened again when her eyes lit on Khalid. "Anything to drink, for you, sir?"

"I'll take one of those little bottles of wine, too," he said. He had exact change ready when she handed it to him. She sent Dawud a look that said *See?* He ignored it. He'd been ignoring looks like that for as long as he'd worked with Khalid, and probably for a lot longer than that.

Dawud poured his wine into the plastic glass that came with it. He looked at it, then leaned left and forward again to peer at the Mediterranean. He shook his head. "They aren't the same color."

Khalid unscrewed the cap on his own bottle of wine. As he poured it, he answered, "I don't think they're supposed to be. Homer meant the sea was as dark as wine, that's all."

Maybe he was right. Maybe he was wrong. It *had* been a long time since he graduated from the madrasa. He sipped the wine: a thoroughly ordinary red from somewhere outside of Algiers. Yes, the Qur'an said you weren't supposed to drink alcohol. Khalid worried about that no more than most Muslims had for centuries. If you wanted to drink, you drank. If you didn't, no one would grab you, ram a funnel down your throat, and pour wine into you.

Some people Khalid knew enjoyed drinking more *because* it was *haram*—forbidden. He glanced over at Dawud. Jews could drink alcohol as they pleased. His partner's glass was already empty. Dawud didn't seem to miss the extra fillip.

Christians could drink as they pleased, too. Back in Khalid's father's day, whenever you saw a Christian in a movie, he'd be lying dead drunk in a gutter. Directors didn't do that so much any more. It was . . . what did high-minded people call it? Annoyed at himself, Khalid groped for a word again.

This time, he found it without having to shout it out loud. Insensitive, that was what they said. He snorted softly. You couldn't offend anybody these days. Christians, blacks, Eskimos . . . They all started screaming their heads off. And the Eskimos were insisting that you call them Inuit.

He snorted again. He wasn't worried about Eskimos, even under the name they'd decided they liked better. Christians, sadly, were a different story. His eyes flicked this way and that. About a third of the passengers on this flight were Christians. Instead of the robes and keffiyehs that were standard for well-dressed men from Cairo to Tangier, from New Damascus to Seattle in the Sunset Lands across the Western Ocean, from Shanghai to Jakarta to Delhi—yes, and from Rome to London, too—they stubbornly clung to their short tunics and tight trousers.

And the women . . . Khalid al-Zarzisi sighed. Their tunics were baggy, so as not to display the bustline, and had sleeves that reached their wrists. Similarly, skirts dragged the ground. A devout Christian woman was more dismayed to show her bare ankle than a worldly Muslim woman would have been to get surprised naked. Not all Muslim women were so very worldly, nor all Christians so very devout. Altogether, though . . . *Altogether, what is one to do with such people?* Khalid wondered.

Dawud produced a cigar and stared at it longingly. "No smoking on this flight, sir," the stewardess said, her voice starchy with disapproval.

"Yes, yes. I was just reminding myself I still have it." Dawud put it away with the air of a man saying farewell to a love lost for-ever—or at least until he could light up again.

"Those things aren't good for you, you know," Khalid remarked.

"I do know that, as a matter of fact. Everyone says it so often, I suppose it must be true," his partner answered. "What I didn't know was that someone told you you were my mother."

Ears burning, Khalid subsided. To his relief, the pilot announced that they were starting their descent into Rome then. The brassy, amplified voice booming out of speakers made the silence between the two investigators seem less oppressive. Khalid hoped it did, anyhow.

He peered out the window as the airliner came in for a land-ing. Rome had been a great city once. Monuments from ancient days still poked out from the houses and shops and businesses surrounding them. The ancient Romans hadn't been Muslims, of course. Till late in their history, they hadn't been Christians, either. Some people—even some otherwise cultured people—still thought of everything before Muhammad's day as part of the *Jahiliyah*, the time of ignorance. How anyone could look at the remains of the Colosseum and reckon the Romans ignorant was beyond Khalid. You had to keep a sense of history, a sense of proportion. Didn't you?

The airliner bounced once when the landing gear hit the run-way. A Christian woman sitting on the other side of the aisle from Khalid and Dawud crossed herself in gratitude that they'd made it. Khalid didn't like open displays of piety. They made him ner-vous. He had his reasons, too, but he doubted any of them would have made sense to the Christian woman.

Along with everybody else, he and Dawud filed off the airplane. Signs inside the airport were in Arabic and, in the blocky, backwards-running characters of the Roman alphabet, in Italian. He followed them to baggage claim. There he stood and waited . . . and waited . . . and waited. He began to fume.

Dawud was fuming, too—literally. As soon as he'd got inside, he'd lit up that cigar. Now he puffed happy clouds of smoke. Muslims and Christians had proved equally fond of the weed from the Sunset Lands. Several Christian women smoked pipes. Khalid thought that made them look even more out of touch with the main currents of the world than they would have otherwise, but they doubtless cared not an olive pit for his opinion.

After much too long, the baggage carousel started spinning. One by one, bags trickled out. "I know we're on the wrong side of the Mediterranean," Khalid grumbled, "but this shouldn't happen anywhere."

"I've got mine," Dawud said, grabbing his suitcase as it came by. He kept an eye on it once he had it; Italians had earned their reputation as a light-fingered lot.

More and more bags emerged from behind the scenes, but not Khalid's. He swore under his breath. He and his partner had checked their suitcases in Tunis at exactly the same time. They would have gone into the airplane together. Why hadn't they come out together, dammit?

Had one of those light-fingered Italians lifted his bag before it got to the carousel? That would be just his luck. He was growing more and more glumly sure of it when the suitcase bounced out. "About time!" he exclaimed.

They went on to customs. "Passports, please," the inspector said in a bored voice. But the boredom fell away when he got a look at the documents. His bushy eyebrows jumped up toward the edge of his olive-green uniform keffiyeh. "Oh! You're them!"

"That's right," Khalid said. Nobody'd told him the customs officials on this side of the Mediterranean knew he and Dawud were coming. Because nobody in Tunis had told him, he'd assumed these Italian officials wouldn't know. Which only went to show what assumptions were worth.

The customs official stamped his passport. Then the man brought the rubber stamp down, much harder, on Dawud ibn Musa's. He shoved the passport back at Dawud. "Nobody said you'd be a . . ." His voice trailed off, not quite soon enough.

"Yes?" Dawud said blandly.

"Nothing," the customs man said. "Go on. You're clear. Just go." He made a noise down deep in his throat, but he didn't—quite—spit on the concrete floor.

Whistling a tune that had been popular the year before, Dawud went. Now, somehow, the angle at which he wore his keffiyeh did look jaunty, not sloppy. Or maybe that was Khalid's imagination.

He hurried to catch up with his partner. "I'm sorry you had to go through that," he said.

"If you worry about every single idiot and asshole in the world, you'll go crazy," Dawud answered. "So I don't."

But he did, as Khalid knew from experience. He just didn't let it show. Even in Muslim countries, Jews didn't always have it easy. They had to pay extra taxes. Those were only token fees most places these days, but they were there. And, even in this tolerant age, if a Jew and an equally qualified Muslim were up for the same job, the Muslim would land it nine times out of ten. Plenty of Muslims still looked down their noses at Jews for refusing to accept Muhammad as the Prophet of God. The saying was that a Jew had to be twice as good as a Muslim to get half as far.

Every bit of that was true. All the same, Khalid couldn't think of any Muslim emirate or sultanate or republic where mobs rampaged through the streets murdering every Jew they could catch. Christians, by contrast, blamed the Jews for killing Christ. That might have happened almost two thousand years ago now, but their hatred was as fresh and fiery as if it were yesterday morning. Even when they weren't rioting, they had no use for Jews. They especially had no use for Jews in positions of authority.

"I'll tell you what really pissed off the customs man," Khalid said. "He knew you were good, that's what."

"Screw him—not that any woman in her right mind would want to," Dawud said. Yes, the Italian bigot had got under his skin.

They were going to have to work with more Italians. They would have to work with other Western Europeans, too. Khalid al-Zarzisi hoped they wouldn't have any problems. He shook his head. No—he hoped the problems they were bound to have wouldn't be too big.

Once they cleared customs, they could go out to the meeting area. A blue-eyed man with a neatly trimmed sandy beard held up a cardboard square with Khalid's name written on it in Arabic and Roman letters. When Khalid and Dawud came up to him, he greeted them in musically accented classical Arabic: "Peace be with you, gentlemen. I am Major Giacomo Badoglio, of Grand Duke Cosimo's Ministry of Information." He displayed an identity card with his photograph, then almost shyly added, "Please forgive my bad Arabic."

Khalid had seen a copy of that same photograph in Tunis. It matched the man holding it. "And to you also peace," the senior investigator replied. Then, haltingly, he switched to Major Badoglio's language: "Your Arabic are—uh, is—better than my Italian, to believe me."

Badoglio's eyebrows jumped. "You've learned some, anyhow. That's more than most people from the south coast would do." He stuck to Arabic; aside from the accent, he spoke it well, even if he was modest about it. He bobbed his head to Dawud ibn Musa. "I'm sorry—I wasn't given your name."

"Of course not. You were given your own," Dawud replied. Major Badoglio blinked. After a moment, Dawud relented and told him who he was, sticking to Arabic while he did it. Khalid knew Dawud spoke fluent Italian—far more fluent than his own. Not letting Badoglio know that might prove useful, so Dawud didn't. A lot of men wouldn't have been able to resist the temptation to show off.

If the prospect of working with a Jew bothered Major Badoglio, he didn't let on. All he said was, "Come with me, both of you. I'll take you to the Ministry, and then to your hotel."

He had a car and driver waiting outside. The car was a little gray Garuda, from the Sultanate of Delhi. Only thick-rimmed spectacles and a false mustache could have made it more anonymous. The driver . . . The driver scared the piss out of Khalid. He wasn't very tall, but he had wide shoulders, scarred hands, blunt features, and eyes as dark and opaque and deadly as a cobra's. If he wasn't a hired killer, he could have played one in the movies.

He drove like a hired killer, too—if the killer also intended to murder himself. Traffic in Tunis was frantic. Traffic in Rome . . . The large majority of people here were Christians, of course, and they drove as if they were so sure of heaven that they didn't care whether they died right this minute. Little cars, motorcycles and scooters, bicycles: they all dodged one another, and pedestrians, and the massive, snorting trucks that kept Rome fed and supplied. Everyone who had a horn leaned on it. Everyone who didn't yelled instead.

After one of the longest hours Khalid had ever lived through, the Garuda pulled up in front of the Ministry of Information: a large, massive pile of reinforced concrete that conveniently stood between Saint Peter's and Rome's Aquinas Seminary, the mother of all such places. "Well," Dawud said. "*That* was fun."

Concrete barriers made sure no automobile could jump up onto the curb and set off a big bomb right in front of the building. Fanatics had done that—and worse—here and there in Europe these past twenty years, trying to weaken and destabilize governments that favored friendly relations with the rest of the world.

That was why Khalid and Dawud had crossed the Mediterranean. The Maghrib didn't want the Grand Duchy destabilized. The first thing a new, hard-line regime in Italy would do was start making noise about who ought to own Sicily and Malta. The next thing . . . The Sultan, the Wazir, and the Wazir's cabinet didn't want to find out what the next thing was.

The barriers had gaps between them. People did need to get by. Somebody determined might squeeze a motor scooter—and as much in the way of explosives as a scooter could carry—through one of those gaps. The guards at the top of the steep marble stairway carried Persian assault rifles. They looked very alert. They needed to. Their lives were on the line, and they had to know it.

Major Badoglio climbed the stairs with Khalid and Dawud. The driver took the little gray Garuda wherever he took it and did whatever he did afterwards. He was only an underling, the kind of person his superiors forgot as soon as he'd done whatever they needed from him.

At the top of the stairs, one of the guards inspected with meticulous care the major's identity card, and those of the two Maghribis. At last, reluctantly, as if afraid he might be missing something, he nodded and said, "Pass on."

Another guard opened the door for the newcomers. He didn't have to tug very hard, but the door must have worked on uncommonly smooth hinges. It was three times as thick as Khalid would have expected, and the edge had the dull sheen of steel.

"You take security seriously," al-Zarzisi remarked.

"My dear sir! We would be in a sorry state if we didn't," Major Badoglio said. "I know you have problems on your side of the sea. Believe me, I do. But, meaning no disrespect, ours are worse."

"Yes. I know." Khalid started ticking them off on his fingers: "Too many young people. Not enough jobs. Not enough money. Not enough hope. And all your preachers pouring gasoline on the fire with this talk of a new crusade."

"You will understand, Inspector—I am a Christian. I am proud to be a Christian," Badoglio said. "But those people . . ." He shook his head. "This is not what Jesus preached. Not what I understand Him to have preached, anyhow."

"'I came not to send peace, but a sword,'" Dawud ibn Musa quoted.

Major Badoglio winced. Then he sent Dawud a look that mingled surprise and respect. For a moment, Khalid didn't understand what was going on. Then, suddenly, he did. Dawud had quoted a saying of Christ's that contradicted what the Italian security man thought about Him. Khalid was surprised, too. Dawud was a man of parts, but Khalid hadn't known he could spout sayings from the Christians' part of the Bible.

Stiffly, Badoglio said, "People can quote out of context from the Qur'an, too."

"Oh, no doubt." Dawud stayed polite, as he commonly did. Khalid nodded agreement. The Muslims who still denied the possibility of evolution did exactly that. So did the handful of Muslims who still denied that the Earth went around the Sun.

But that wasn't the point. The point was that the people who quoted the Qur'an out of context did so to make an argument. The people who quoted the Christians' part of the Bible out of context did so to inspire fanatics to martyr themselves. That was what they had in mind—and, all too often, what they got.

"Well," Khalid said, breaking the awkward silence that followed Dawud's deadpan, perhaps too-polite, agreement, "let's see what you've got here."

"I'll be glad to show you." Major Badoglio sounded perhaps too eager. "Come with me, gentlemen, please." He hurried down the corridor. Khalid and Dawud followed. Khalid smiled at Dawud. The Jew soberly looked back. Maybe he didn't find any of what had just happened amusing. But Khalid had known Dawud a long time. His guess was that the Jew did, but that he wouldn't let his own face know, let alone anyone else.

A few of the men in the Ministry of Information were Muslims. The large majority, though, were Christians like Major Badoglio: intelligent, well-educated men who should have been able to separate their reasoning faculties from the religion in which they'd been raised. One of them, a man of about Khalid's age, boasted of how proud he was to have been educated at the Cairo madrasa. Khalid didn't remember seeing him there, which proved exactly nothing. Several of the other Italians had studied at other famous centers of learning throughout the Muslim world.

They were bright, yes. They were capable, certainly. But Khalid had trouble warming to any of them, though he hoped it didn't show. They should have been able to separate their reasoning from their religion. They should have, but could they really? What *was* going on in their heads?

Khalid sighed silently. You worked with what you had, with the people you found. The world being as it was, what else could you do? Not a thing. And, if you feared the people you found might prove imperfectly reliable, what could you do about that?

You might not want to tell some of them some of the things you knew. Of course, they might not want to tell you everything they knew, either. If that turned out to cause problems . . . Well, the world was as it was, and it wasn't any other way.

Or they might try something else. They might tell you everything they knew all at once, hoping to drown you. If that wasn't what the men from the Ministry of Information were up to, they had more enthusiasm than they knew what to do with. They sat Khalid and Dawud down in a windowless room lit by fluorescent lights: a room that could have belonged to any bureaucratic outfit anywhere in the world. They gave them strong coffee and surprisingly good sweet rolls.

And they gave them papers that covered the table in front of them more than half a cubit deep. Some of the papers were reports they'd compiled themselves on the multifarious groups that roiled the peace in the Grand Duchy of Italy these days. The rest had come from those groups themselves. Some were propaganda posters and broadsheets and flyers. The rest the Ministry of Information had captured in raids up and down the peninsula. Those were the ones the fanatics didn't want the outside world to see—unless, of course, they were plants. Were the Aquinists and their friends devious enough to do something like that? Probably.

Waving at the sea of paper, Major Badoglio said, "You begin to get an idea of what we're up against."

"Well," Khalid said, "yes." If he didn't sound happy, that was only because he wasn't.

Some of the documents were in classical Arabic. Those were the ones the fanatics wanted the world to see. Some, Khalid noticed at a glance, were in bad classical Arabic. Quite a few, though, could have been written in the Maghrib or Egypt or any other country where all educated men used the tongue that bound the world together.

Other papers—both for local consumption and private documents—were in Italian. Khalid read it better than he spoke it. He carried a little dictionary to help him out. With patience, he could extract meaning, which was what he needed to do. He didn't think he would ever get fluent enough to judge literary quality.

And still others were in Latin. Latin served the Christians of Western Europe, and especially the fanatics among them, the way Arabic served the rest of the world. It let them communicate with one another regardless of what their birthspeech might be. And it seemed holy to them, because it remained the language in which their priests conducted their services.

Latin was a closed book to Khalid. Oh, he could recognize a word here and there, because he read Italian. But Latin's beastly grammar made it far more different from Italian and its other daughter tongues than modern Arabic dialects were from their classical source.

He glanced over at Dawud ibn Musa. Right this minute, the Jew was examining a poster of a stern, steel-jawed Saint Thomas Aquinas with the Arabic legend GOD IS NOT MOCKED! Since he hadn't let on that he knew Italian, he probably wouldn't look at any documents in that language till Badoglio went away. Did he read Latin, too? Khalid wasn't sure, but he thought so.

Dawud passed the poster over to Khalid. "He knew what he thought, all right."

"He sure did," Khalid agreed. "That's . . . a big part of the problem we're facing now."

He picked his words with care; he didn't want to offend Giacomo Badoglio. But he couldn't help wondering when Western Europe would recover from what seemed to him the malign influence of Saint Thomas Aquinas. Back in the seventh century (the thirteenth, by the calendar the Christians still used), Aquinas had pondered the relationship between God and man's pursuit of scientific knowledge. No doubt he was spurred on by new Latin translations of Aristotle. They came into Latin from Arabic, of course; the Muslim world had known Aristotle for many hundreds of years, even if not in the original Greek.

It wasn't just that Aquinas concluded that studying science corrupted religion because it reduced man's faith in God's omnipotence and omniscience. No: what really mattered was that he set forth his conclusions in an enormous Latin book, the *Summa Theologica* (one bit of the arcane language Khalid did know). So overwhelming were his arguments that he carried almost all his fellow believers with him. And intellectual pursuits in Christendom had languished ever since. *Better surety of the next world than useless knowledge of this one*, Aquinas had declared, and most Christians agreed with him to this day.

Strangely, a century and a half earlier, a Muslim philosopher named al-Ghazali examined exactly the same question—and reached exactly the opposite answer. Al-Ghazali was convinced that Muhammad and Aristotle could be reconciled. *God has created nothing man may not investigate*, he wrote in his greatest work, *The Revival of the Science of Religion. The more man learns, the better he may glorify God.*

As Saint Thomas Aquinas' view was accepted by Christians, so al-Ghazali's was in the Muslim world. And so reason and science advanced and then exploded in the *Dar al-Islam*, while Christendom stagnated for centuries. Christians still kept reacting to what their more inventive, more creative neighbors did. They lost war after war. They lost chunks of land and bigger chunks of pride. Now, still in the name of religion, they were looking for new ways to hit back.

The real irony was that, in the real argument between Aquinas and al-Ghazali, the Christian had the right of it. The centuries that followed the time of the two philosophers proved that science and reason *did* tend to corrode faith. Whether their benefits in this world outweighed that was a matter of opinion.

Khalid al-Zarzisi thought they did. He'd been inoculated against childhood diseases. He'd drunk clean water growing up, so he never caught diphtheria or typhoid. When his appendix started aching like a rotten tooth, he'd been etherized while a skilled surgeon cut it out of him. The dentist numbed his mouth before working on his teeth.

He used the telephone and telegraph. He watched television and movies, and listened to the radio and recorded music. He could drive a car. He flew in an airplane when he needed to. He took electric lights and air-conditioning for granted. When he lay down with a woman, he didn't need to worry about leaving her pregnant unless she wanted a baby. He'd met a Turk who'd walked on the moon.

All those things—and so much more about the modern world—would have struck both al-Ghazali and Aquinas as miracles. The difference was, al-Ghazali would have applauded them. To Aquinas, with his thought always firmly fixed on the soul and the world to come, they wouldn't have mattered. They had nothing to do with what was really important.

A phrase in one of the pamphlets on the table leaped out at him. It was from Matthew, one of the books in the Christians' part of the Bible. *For what is a man profited,* Matthew wrote, *if he shall gain the whole world, and lose his own soul?*

That was the question, all right. Khalid didn't spend much time—waste much time?—worrying about the state of his soul. He was comfortable enough in this world that he didn't see the need. Not every Muslim would have agreed with him: far from it. But more would have than not. Scholars and scientists and doctors and engineers all across the vast sweep of the realm of Islam had made the world a different place—a better place, he thought.

Thomas Aquinas' modern disciples had a different view. They were convinced all Muslims were bound for hell. (They were also convinced all Christians who presumed to disagree with them would head in the same direction.) But they thought Satan saved his hottest fires and sharpest knives for secular men. And they thought their duty was to send such men to the Devil as fast as they could.

Idly, Khalid wondered what the world might have looked like had al-Ghazali decided against reconciling God and Aristotle and Aquinas in favor. He shrugged. The notion struck him as unlikely. Islam was a supple, rational faith, while Christians had always been proud to think of themselves as drunk with God.

As if to underscore the point, Dawud pulled out another poster. This one showed Aquinas with a Persian assault rifle like the ones the guards here carried clutched in an upraised fist. In the background, demons wearing robes and keffiyehs scuttled for cover. DRIVE OUT THE FOREIGN DEVILS! the poster screamed. ITALY IS FOR CHRISTIANS!

"Charming," Khalid murmured.

"Isn't it?" Dawud said. "Well, one thing's certain, anyway."

"What's that?"

"We've got our work cut out for us."

Pigeons strolled the sidewalks of Rome and stepped out into the streets to cross as if all the traffic had nothing to do with them. It was as if they thought flying was beneath their dignity.

Sometimes—most of the time, even—people and birds on foot managed to get where they were going. Most of the time, yes, but not always. Khalid watched a dog nuzzle a crumpled ball of gray feathers in a gutter. After a moment, the dog picked up the prize and trotted away with it in his mouth. One pigeon had bucked the odds and lost.

Badoglio's driver honked at a man crossing against all common sense. The man stopped right in front of the car. He was going to swear, maybe to use some of the Italians' expressive gestures, to let the world know what he thought. He was going to . . . till he got a look at the driver. Then he scuttled for the curb as fast as he could go.

Standing in the pedestrian's place, Khalid would have done the same thing. With a small, satisfied grunt, the driver stepped on the gas and went on.

Not far outside Saint Peter's, the Garuda stopped. Guards in gaudy medieval uniforms came up to check documents. The Pope was a secular prince as well as a spiritual lord. Just how much of a secular prince he was at any given moment depended on a lot of things. His personality and that of the reigning Grand Duke made good starters.

Marcellus IX, the current occupant of the Throne of Saint Peter, was a modern man, a progressive man: as much as he could be when he headed a two-thousand-year-old institution that had spent most of the second half of its existence trying to believe the world, and ideas about the world, hadn't changed. If Marcellus died an un-timely death, his successor was much too likely to be an Aqui-nist. That could prove unfortunate for all kinds of reasons.

It was also a major cause of Khalid and Dawud's trip to Italy.

However medieval the Papal Guards' uniforms, their weapons were businesslike submachine guns. They studied Major Badoglio's ID and, with more interest, those of his companions from the Maghrib. One of them spoke into a walkie-talkie. He waited for an answer, then clicked the set off. "They're expected, all right," he said.

"Somebody should have told us, then, dammit," another guard said.

The fellow with the walkie-talkie spread his hands, as if to say *What can you do?* He nodded to Badoglio's driver. "Go ahead."

Khalid had visited the Church of the Holy Sepulcher in Jerusa-lem: a side trip, because he was really there to see the Dome of the Rock. The Christians' shrine there was ramshackle and ancient. It had gone up three centuries before the Hijra calendar opened: in the fourth century of the Christian era. No one would have said it didn't look its age, either.

But Saint Peter's made the Church of the Holy Sepulcher seem well maintained by comparison. Both buildings were about the same age, but Saint Peter's had seen harder use and far fewer repairs. At its heart was a five-aisled basilica. Other buildings or rooms or whatever you would call them adhered to the sides of the basilica the way mussels and barnacles adhered to a pier.

Once upon a time, the Papacy had been rich. Once upon a time, a Pope had launched a war that took Jerusalem out of the *Dar al-Islam* for years. But no more. These past few hundred years, the Papacy and Christendom in general had fallen on hard times. Half a terra-cotta roof tile lay by one of Saint Peter's outbuildings. Khalid craned his neck, trying to see from where it had fallen. Yes, there was the spot. If they didn't fix it pretty soon, the roof would leak.

Another guard waved the Garuda to a parking place: in Rome, something more precious than rubies. Two more escorted Major Badoglio and the investigators from the Maghrib into Saint Peter's.

The first thing Khalid noticed was a nondescript little pot sitting on the mosaicwork floor. It almost seemed to be trying to pretend it wasn't there. He soon spotted other shy little pots and bowls. Sure as Shaitan, the roofs here did leak.

Incense filled Khalid's nostrils. Bishops and cardinals stared curiously at the newcomers. Their gaudy vestments put him in mind of the long-downfallen Byzantine Empire (a Seljuk Sultan still reigned in Constantinople, though for the past two centuries he'd had to answer to an elected parliament and a cabinet of ministers from the most popular faction).

At first glance, the prelates' costumes shone and sparkled in the mix of candlelight and electricity inside Saint Peter's. When Khalid took a longer look, he saw how threadbare and worn the silks and satins and cloth-of-gold had grown. Had any of the surplices and chasubles and albs and other pieces of clothing with improbable names been new when these venerable men's grandfathers were boys? Impossible to say for sure, but Khalid would have bet against it.

That thought made him look at the interior of the church in a whole new way. The ornamentation seemed very rich. Gold gleamed everywhere. But how much of what looked like solid gold was only leaf or gilt? How much was polished brass masquerading as its better? How much of what had once been gold had the Popes had to sell off over the years to pay their bills? Again, Khalid didn't know, but he knew what his guesses were.

"This way, gentlemen," one of the gaudy guards said, leading Badoglio, Khalid, and Dawud through a maze of narrow, winding corridors that left Khalid wishing he could unroll a string behind him, the way Theseus did in the Labyrinth. Would he ever find his way out of here again? He had to hope so. The guard opened a door with creaky hinges. "His Holiness the Pope awaits you."

II

Marcellus IX, servant of the servants of Christ, was a little, wrinkled man somewhere around seventy years old. He looked like an Italian—which is to say, not too different from someone from the Maghrib. His beard was white, his bushy eyebrows still dark. Behind the magnifying lenses of his spectacles, his brown eyes were keen and clever.

"Your Holiness," Major Badoglio murmured. The Pope held out his hand. Instead of kissing it, Badoglio kissed the large, heavy ring the Pontiff wore. How many lips, over how many centuries, had kissed that ring? Khalid had no idea. Irreverently, he wondered how many diseases the insanitary thing had spread.

"Who are your colleagues?" Marcellus asked in Italian. His vestments were in better shape than those of most of his prelates, but still far from new.

"Your Holiness, I present to you Senior Investigator Khalid al-Zarzisi and Investigator Dawud ibn Musa," Badoglio replied in the same language.

The Pope's head bobbed up and down. Questions were easy when you already knew the answers. Marcellus nodded to each of the men from the far side of the Mediterranean in turn. "I am pleased to make your acquaintance," he told them in excellent classical Arabic. With a thin smile, he added, "One from the younger dispensation, one from the elder."

"Yes, your Holiness," Khalid said in the same language. He found himself smiling back. That he might like the Pope hadn't occurred to him when he got on the airplane bound for Rome.

"And the two of you are here to protect me from my overzealous coreligionists—is that right?" Marcellus went on smiling. Khalid didn't think he could stay amused with the threat of the Aquinists hanging over his head, but Marcellus kept to himself any worries he might have had.

Khalid was a beat late answering the question. He was looking around the chamber in which the Pope worked. Marcellus' crowded bookshelves held volumes in Arabic, Latin, Italian, and some other languages that used the Roman alphabet but that Khalid couldn't read.

One of the Arabic texts, he saw, was a Qur'an printed in Cairo. Another was a copy of Abdallah ibn-al-Zubayr's *Concerning the Development of Natural Creatures Through Time*, which had incensed Christian, Muslim, and Jewish theologians when it appeared almost two centuries earlier. Officially, the Church still condemned it. Officially, the Church was still reluctant to admit the Earth went around the Sun and not the contrary.

"If we can, your Excellency," Khalid said, looking away from the bookcases.

"And what can the two of you do that all my guards cannot?" Yes, Marcellus *was* amused. Khalid admired him for it.

"What can we do, your Holiness?" Dawud spoke for the first time. "Maybe nothing."

Major Badoglio hissed. That wasn't the way you talked to a Pope, or to any of the sovereigns who held secular power in Western Europe. You told them what they wanted to hear. If you didn't, you wouldn't get the chance to tell them anything else. Muslim advisors, some well-meaning, others perhaps less so, had found that out time and again. In the old days, their rulers had held near-absolute power, too. No more, not in most of the Muslim world.

Trying to make amends, Khalid said, "You may be sure of our loyalty, your Holiness, even if some of your guards, unbeknownst to you, prove . . . overzealous was your word, yes?"

"Yes," the Pope said placidly. He steepled his fingertips. The Fisherman's ring shone in the lamplight. His gaze swung back to Dawud. "Why may I be sure of a Jew's loyalty?"

"*You* never persecuted my people, your Holiness, even if the Church did," Dawud replied. "Who knows what an Aquinist would do in your place, or in Cosimo's? Who wants to find out?"

By the way Giacomo Badoglio fidgeted, he was almost ready to piss himself. How long had it been since such straight talk was heard in this tradition-choked office? How many times might it have done some good? However ruffled the major might be, the Pope kept smiling. "Better the devil you know, eh?"

"If I thought you were a devil, your Holiness, I wouldn't be here," Dawud answered. "I'm here because I'm pretty sure you're not."

"A small compliment from a stranger is worth more than a grand one from a courtier," Pope Marcellus remarked.

"You would have a hard time finding a smaller compliment than that," Major Badoglio said, acid in his voice.

"I think not," Marcellus said. "Plenty of Jews would call me a devil, or even the Devil, and they would have their reasons, too. Finding one who does not—is worth something, anyhow."

"May I ask you a question, your Holiness?" Dawud said.

"Ask. I don't promise to answer," the Pope replied.

Dawud pointed to ibn-al-Zubayr's volume. "Into what sort of creature is the Church developing now? Into what sort of creature do you want it to develop?"

"The world has changed," Marcellus said—sadly? Khalid thought so, but he wasn't sure. The Pope went on, "The Church needs to evolve to keep any kind of place in the world we have now. If the Church does not evolve, we will be left behind and forgotten. This is my view, you understand. You would find other believers who feel differently. To them, any kind of change is . . . we use the word *anathema*. Do you understand this?"

"Muslims would say *haram*, I think." Dawud managed a smile of his own, a crooked one. "And here we both are, talking about what they would say."

"So we are," Pope Marcellus agreed, irony freighting his voice. He, at least, headed a community that formed a majority over a broad swath of land. Jews were a minority everywhere, and probably always would be. But, as Dawud noted, both Jews and Christians had to recognize Islam's cultural dominance. Marcellus continued, "*Anathema* is stronger than *haram*. It is condemned, not just forbidden. Still, the ideas are close enough."

Khalid found a question of his own: "What would happen if the Aquinists took control of the Church?"

Marcellus' long face got longer yet. "My view is that they would use the scientific and engineering advances of the fifteenth century to drag the world back to the fifth." Even he used the Hijra calendar unless he was calculating the dates of the festivals of the Church.

"Yes, I think so, too," Dawud ibn Musa said. "That's why I will keep you and the Grand Duke alive if I can, your Holiness—and if you let me."

"How can I say no?" the Pope asked dryly.

"Oh, I think it would be easy enough, your Holiness," Dawud answered. "After all, what else has the Church been saying for the past seven hundred years?"

Surveying himself in the hotel room's full-length mirror, Khalid shook his head. "This has to be the least practical, least comfortable outfit in the history of the world," he said. "It's squeezing me everywhere."

Dawud ibn Musa contrived to look just as sloppy in Christian garb as he did in the clothes he usually wore. Half to Khalid's surprise, Dawud did notice he'd buttoned his tunic wrong and fixed it. His trousers remained rumpled and baggy in the seat. His shoes had scuff marks on the toes. They were brand new, so Khalid didn't know how they'd got them, but they had. Dawud was not without talent . . . of a sort.

And yet, he might attract less attention on the streets of Rome than Khalid did in his scrupulously correct outfit. No one wearing a disguise would wear it so badly as Dawud did. So an Aquinist was likely to reason, anyhow. Aquinists were great ones for reasoning. They claimed they followed in their namesake's footsteps. What Aquinas himself would have had to say about that . . .

"None of this is liable to matter at all if somebody from the Ministry of Information has already fingered us," Dawud said, and Khalid started worrying about things more immediately relevant than Saint Thomas Aquinas' opinions.

If there were any things more immediately relevant than Saint Thomas Aquinas' opinions. In the Christian world, the old turned new again. Sometimes it never even got old to begin with.

"We wouldn't just have to worry about Aquinists in our regular outfits," Khalid said. "Any tough guy who didn't like the way we look could decide he felt like messing with us."

"Well, I'm a pretty tough guy, or I like to think I am, and I sure don't like the way we look," Dawud said.

"That's not what I meant, and you know it," Khalid said. Dawud had the grace to look sheepish. Sometimes Khalid could embarrass him by calling him for being difficult. Sometimes not, too.

They walked down the hall to the elevator. They might have been anywhere in the world as they did. The hotel was one of dozens, maybe hundreds, owned by an anonymous society based in Arkansistan, one of the larger republics in the Sunset Lands. About the only difference between this hotel and one in, say, Qom was that the kitchen here served pork, though it also had a *qadi-*inspected *halal* section to prepare food for observant Muslims.

A sweeper in the lobby snickered as Dawud sauntered by. Dawud might attract attention, but not because he looked like a Maghribi slumming in Christian clothes—only because he always looked like a clothes donkey instead of a clothes horse. He smiled benignly at the sweeper, which left the fellow scratching his head.

As soon as he and Khalid got outside, he lit up a cigar about the size of a banana. That didn't make him conspicuous, either. Just the opposite, in fact. Far more people in Christian countries puffed cigars and pipes than was true south of the Mediterranean.

Khalid wondered why that should be so. Did Christians mistrust the research of Muslim and Jewish doctors on what tobacco did to you? Or were they so confident of heaven that they smoked regardless, reckoning all the nasty things that might happen to their bodies in this world of little account?

Of course, Dawud puffed away, too. He couldn't very well not know what a lifetime of smoking did. And Jewish notions of heaven were far murkier than those of either Islam or Christianity. He smoked anyway. He liked the taste. He liked the aroma. And he liked the little nicotine buzz. Khalid gave a mental shrug. His colleague was an adult. If he wanted to exercise free will, he could—no matter how stupid it seemed to Khalid.

Rome brawled around them. Locals paid less attention to them now than they would have to a couple of men in robes and keffiyehs. Some travelers from Muslim countries and some modernist Italians did wear the international style. People hooted at them from across the street and from upstairs windows. No one did anything worse than jeer . . . not where Khalid saw, at any rate.

Every street corner was a miniature souq. Men and women with carts and baskets sold fruit, flowers, religious medals, counterfeit antiquities, equally counterfeit watches, pills to enhance masculinity, bootleg videotapes, and anything else they could get their hands on. Whatever they had, they hawked it stridently and insistently. Getting past them meant running the gauntlet again and again.

They were deaf to *No, thank you*. They were just as impervious to a simple *No*. Before long, Dawud was doing as the Romans did. He'd yell *"Vaffanculo!"* and accompany it with a graphic pumping gesture of his forearm. That got the message across. The street sellers didn't get angry. They just laughed and swore at him and Khalid in turn.

"How friendly," Khalid remarked after someone peddling sausages called him something he didn't fully understand. Whatever it meant, it sounded electrifying.

"You know what's funny? It *is* friendly, or a lot of it is. Read stories about what the markets in Tunis and Cairo and Damascus were like a couple of hundred years ago. They were like this, that's what," Dawud said. "Too many laws, too many regulations, take the starch out of life."

"Well, it could be." Khalid reflected that in those days, if a street vendor had called him something like that, honor would have compelled him to try to murder the man. Or maybe not. Maybe it would all have been a game. If you couldn't watch polo and endless backgammon tournaments on television, you had to make your own fun.

An obvious traveler with a map came up to them and spoke in halting, Persian-flavored Italian: "Excuse me. Can you tell me where is the Mausoleum of Augustus, please?"

Khalid was pleased to be taken for an Italian. But he didn't know where the mausoleum was, and he didn't know Italian well enough to fool even a tourist. None of which turned out to matter. Dawud launched into an elaborate explanation, again complete with gestures. He turned the little Persian man around and gave him a shove in the right direction, as if he were launching a ship.

"My, my. I'm impressed," Khalid said. "How do you know where Augustus' mausoleum is?"

"Oh, I don't. Haven't the slightest idea," Dawud said blithely. "But I didn't fall out of character. And if I'm wrong, someone else will set the poor fool straight sooner or later. Or he'll figure out how to read the map for himself."

"You're hopeless!" Khalid exclaimed. "No. You're shameless!"

"Well, I love you, too," Dawud replied. "But I have fun—not like that poor gal."

He pointed to a young woman whose red-brown complexion argued that she came from the Sunset Lands. She was crouched at the edge of the sidewalk, vomiting into the gutter behind a parked car. The car had a big, glittery bumper button for Dawud al-Buwayhidi, a popular singer from Iraq.

"I hope she's not sick," Khalid said.

"Chances are she's just toasted." Dawud ibn Musa sounded matter-of-fact, not reproving. "Arkansistanis and Oregonis and people like that have trouble holding their liquor—everybody knows it. They come to a place like this, where people have taken drinking for granted for—what?—three thousand years now, and they go a little crazy."

Despite yelps from traditionalists, drinking alcohol had been legal for everyone over sixteen in almost all Muslim countries except the Sharifate of Mecca and Medina for anywhere from fifty to two hundred years. But, even though it wasn't against the law, many people remained uneasy about it. In Christian Western Europe, there was no uneasiness. If you felt like drinking, you drank, and, if you felt like getting drunk, you did that, too.

Some Muslim tourists came to this part of the world for tavern crawls, not for antiquities or scenic views unmatchable closer to home. Some touring firms catered to that crowd. As Khalid knew better than most, if someone had a vice, someone else would try to make money off it.

Not at all by accident, before too long he and Dawud found themselves walking past the front gate to the Aquinas Seminary. The building—an enormous concrete pile that might have gone up anywhere in the world over the past fifty years—was at least as heavily fortified as the Ministry of Information. Concrete vehicle barriers and razor wire kept away unwelcome visitors. Anyone who did want to go inside had to clear at least two checkpoints manned by armed, alert-looking guards.

Grand Duke Cosimo's gonfalon did not fly over the seminary. Neither did the Pope's banner, gold and white and adorned with the crossed keys of Saint Peter. The Aquinists had their own flag: a red cross on a black background, with the words DEUS VULT!—*God wills it!*—below, also in red.

That had been the Crusaders' motto in days gone by. The Aquinists preached that Christianity needed a new crusade, or a wave of them. They wanted to turn back the clock, to bring the struggle between their faith and Islam to something like even terms again. Most Muslims were willing to let them believe as they pleased, as long as they left other people alone. But that didn't satisfy the Aquinists. They wanted the whole world to believe as they did, and they were convinced God willed it should be so.

How anyone could presume to know what God willed was beyond Khalid. Saying as much would not have endeared him to the Aquinists. Come to that, he couldn't think of anything he might say that would have endeared him to them.

"I wonder what's going on behind those windows," he remarked. He knew he sounded uneasy. Even the windows made the seminary look like a fortress. They were small and narrow, more like slits for archers than anything else. It was as if the architect hadn't wanted to let light from the outside world into the Aquinists' stronghold. Was that choice deliberate or subconscious? Only a mind-healer would even be able to make a good guess.

"Just what you think," Dawud answered. "They're training people not to care whether they live or die, as long as they do what God—and their superiors—tell them to do. And how many of these places are there in Western Europe?"

"Nineteen big ones like this. I don't know how many little hole-and-corner places there are, and I don't think anybody else does, either," Khalid said. "Plus the hole-and-corner places in our countries."

Being a Christian was easy enough in Muslim lands. Like Jews, Christians had to pay a yearly tax for the privilege of practicing their religion in peace. These days, the tax was about what a pita full of falafel cost. Human-rights advocates urged getting rid of it altogether, but it didn't inconvenience anybody.

There had always been Christians in the Muslim lands that stretched from the Maghrib to Iraq, even to Persia and India. Christianity got there first, after all. The longstanding followers of Jesus were as loyal to their states as any Muslim or Jew. But the immigrants . . .

People went where the jobs were. If that rule wasn't as old as the world, it came close. Christians from Western Europe worked in manufactories in much of the Muslim world. And they dug ditches and hauled trash and repaired roads and did all the other jobs richer, better-educated Muslims weren't interested in doing. They formed their own little isolated communities inside the states where they lived: communities centered on their homelands and religion.

Tunis, for instance, had a Little France and a Little England. Each one sponsored a polo club. Hooligans bashed heads whenever the two teams clashed. That was nothing the watch couldn't handle. Muslim polo enthusiasts sometimes went over the line, too.

But the Europeans also brought their own religion with them. Aquinism flourished among them. Looking back, Khalid could see how that had happened. European workers were in but not of the states where they lived. Most of them were poor. They looked around and saw that Muslims and Jews and even native Christians had more than they did. How could they not resent it? And if Aquinism fed on anything, it fed on resentment.

The French worker who'd lived in Tunis for twenty years before blowing himself up in the showroom of a Garuda dealership that wouldn't sell him a car because his credit was bad . . . The Swedes who'd plotted to steal an airplane and fly it into the Ka'bah during pilgrimage season . . . They might have pulled it off if one of them hadn't got drunk and blabbed. There were too many others like them.

"What are we going to do?" Khalid asked.

"Keeping Marcellus alive would make a good start. Cosimo, too," Dawud answered. "And staying alive ourselves might be nice, if we can manage it."

"It would, wouldn't it?" Khalid agreed—wistfully?

A woman whose tunic was cut low in front and whose skirt was tight through the haunches sidled up to the two of them and said, "How about it? Are you interested?"

"No thanks, sweetheart. Maybe some other time." Dawud tried to let her down easy.

"Fairies!" she snarled, and swiveled away.

"So much for that." Khalid had a hard time not laughing. "You should have just told her *'Vaffanculo!'*, too."

"I was hoping I wouldn't have to. I always like to start at the polite end and go downhill from there, if you know what I mean," Dawud said.

"She was in the gutter from the start," Khalid said, remembering the other young woman losing her breakfast behind the car with the bumper button.

"Afraid so. Turning tricks will do that, I suppose. If you ever had any illusions that human beings are the way God meant them to be, I can't think of anything likely to cure you faster," Dawud said.

Khalid hadn't looked at it from that angle. Dawud always had a different slant on things—that was one reason he made a good investigator. But Khalid's gaze went up to the black flag with the red cross and the defiant motto flying atop the Aquinas Seminary. If those people were the way God meant them to be, He had a really nasty sense of humor.

And maybe He did. Given the way the world worked, the odds He did were pretty good. When Khalid said as much, Dawud nodded. "This surprises you because . . . ?" he asked.

"It doesn't surprise me. It just makes me sad." Khalid glanced over at the black flag again. "A few hundred years ago, they would have strung us up for making cracks about God's sense of humor. And if the people in there get their way"—he pointed toward the seminary—"they'll start doing it again."

"One more thing to look forward to," Dawud answered.

There didn't seem to be much to say after that. They walked away from the fortresslike building. A spot between Khalid's shoulder blades itched, and it wasn't the unfamiliar tunic he wore. Was somebody watching him from one of those windows? Was somebody drawing a bead on him from one of them? Or was his imagination working too hard for its own good?

He hoped it was just his imagination. He wished he had an easier time believing it.

The guards outside the Ministry of Information were every bit as careful checking Khalid and Dawud's IDs the second time the Maghribis visited the building as they had been the first. Khalid recognized one of the men from the first time. "You see us before," he said—he wasn't quite stuck in the present indicative in Italian, but he came close. "Why so, uh, worried now?"

"Routine," the man answered. "I may have seen you, but the rest of the boys here haven't."

"All right," Khalid said. It wasn't really, but what could you do? Routine was a powerful god, one with many worshipers all over the world. Plenty of people bowed before him in Tunis, as Khalid had reason to know.

An underofficer with an assault rifle escorted him and Dawud to Major Badoglio's office. People who didn't work for the Ministry of Information weren't allowed to wander around with no one watching them. Strangers ambling through a similar establishment in Tunis would soon have had somebody keeping an eye on them, too.

"Good day, my masters," Badoglio said in his trilled classical Arabic. "You will have seen the Aquinas Seminary by now?"

"Oh, yes," Khalid replied. Speaking the language he used most of the time felt good. "An impressive place—maybe for the wrong reasons, but impressive all the same."

"I would not argue with you," Badoglio said.

"How can the Pope let the Aquinists get away with what they do and what they teach?" Khalid asked. "He is like a Caliph in the old days, only he can pronounce on doctrine, too—is it not so?"

"That is our tradition, yes," Badoglio replied: not the most ringing agreement Khalid had ever heard.

He pressed ahead even so: "Then if he says to the Aquinists, 'Your doctrine is bad, and you cannot get to heaven by blowing yourselves up,' they have to listen to him, don't they?"

The Italian security man looked up at the fluorescent lights set into the ceiling. "In theory, yes," he said, picking his words with obvious care. "But theory is not always real. There is religion, you will understand, and then there is politics. And there is . . . passion, I suppose you would call it. If a man believes something strongly, and you tell him he must not any more, what will he do?"

"Try to kill you," Dawud ibn Musa said at once.

That also struck Khalid as likely. But he said, "The Aquinists already want to kill Pope Marcellus. How could this make matters worse there?"

"There are other possibilities. The Aquinists might stop recognizing that his Holiness has any authority over them if he orders them to do something they believe to be wrong," Major Badoglio said. "They may bring many believers with them if they do, too. The Church has seen too much schism and heresy these past few hundred years. Christians cannot afford to fight among themselves, not when—" He broke off. He was swarthy, but he flushed all the same.

"Not when you'd rather be fighting Muslims," Khalid finished for him.

"I was not speaking for myself. I was talking about the Church," Badoglio said with as much dignity as he could muster.

"Of course," Khalid said. Christians often came unmoored in these modern times. Not many felt as comfortable in the secular world as Muslims did. Christianity had to try to assimilate in a generation or two what had developed over centuries in Islam. No wonder even people who most wanted to be modern often found themselves betwixt and between instead. They couldn't stay the way they had been, but they couldn't turn into what they wanted to be, either.

"God will sort things out in His own time," Badoglio said. "I truly believe that."

"Maybe He will. But don't hold your breath waiting," Dawud told him. "And trust me, my friend—you'll never get better advice from a Jew."

Christians were convinced Jesus was the Messiah. Jews didn't believe it. Muslims proclaimed Muhammad as the Seal of Prophets. Jews didn't believe that, either. They went on waiting . . . and waiting . . . and waiting longer still. They'd started the monotheistic faiths that now sprawled over more than half the world, and by all appearances they intended to finish them, too.

Major Badoglio eyed Dawud. By the look on his face, he wasn't used to getting any advice from Jews. There weren't many in Italy to get advice from. The handful who stubbornly stayed on had far fewer civil rights than their coreligionists enjoyed in Muslim lands. But the major prided himself on being modern. He couldn't tell the Jew in front of him what he thought. He might be embarrassed, even ashamed, to think such things.

In the end, all he did say was, "Well, you may be right." He seemed astonished when Dawud grinned at him. That polite put-down was common in the Muslim world. Khalid wouldn't have been surprised if Major Badoglio had found it all by himself.

"Can we get back to business?" Khalid asked.

"That might be nice," Dawud said.

"Yes. It might," Giacomo Badoglio agreed primly.

"All right. There are two of us here. We are not miracle workers," Khalid said. "How can you use us so we do the most good? I don't think we can storm the Aquinas Seminary by ourselves."

"Neither do I," Dawud said. "We'd need four or five men for that—maybe even half a dozen."

Just for a moment, Badoglio took him literally. Then the major realized the Maghribi was having him on. He wasn't used to foolishness from a Jew, either. "Heh," he managed, and then, "You will understand, I hope, that I do not quite know what to do with the two of you. I was told you were coming, and I was told to make the best of it. That is what I am trying to do." He spread his hands in resignation, or perhaps despair.

Khalid looked over at Dawud. His partner was glancing toward him. Before they'd set out from Tunis, their superiors told them the Italians were screaming for any help the Maghrib could send. The right hand and the left hadn't been talking to each other again. What a surprise!

"We'll help any way we can," he said. "It's in the Pope's interest, and the Grand Duke's, to keep the Aquinists from getting any stronger than they are already." And it was in the Maghrib's interest, and that of the secular Muslim states all over the world, and, as far as Khalid was concerned, that of civilization in general. He didn't want to offend Badoglio, so he didn't say anything about that.

By the Italian's raised eyebrow, he could read between the lines. "No matter how you think of us, my master"—he packed the polite Arabic phrase with reproach and resentment—"we are not barbarians. We have our own past, our own heritage, and we are proud of it. It is older than yours. In some ways, it is wiser than yours."

Khalid was tempted to throw *Well, you may be right* in his face. People who weren't satisfied with having all their material needs met went on and on about the spiritual wisdom of the ancient West, as they did about that of the Far East. If they didn't do a stretch in a Buddhist stupa in Siam, they would visit a monastery in Ireland— one not associated with the Aquinists, needless to say.

"A long time ago, we said something like that to Christian kings," Dawud said before Khalid could speak. "They didn't want to listen. To be fair, Muslims didn't want to hear anything like that from us, either. When it's not *their* worry, people don't care about other people's problems."

"Indeed," Major Badoglio replied. "Then what are you gentlemen doing here, if I may make so bold as to ask?"

"Oh, that's simple, Major," Khalid said. "The Aquinists are our worry, too. The Aquinists are everybody's worry."

"Oh, yes, my masters. When we say beef, we mean beef. When we say veal, we mean veal. You may rely on it." The waiter in the hotel restaurant spoke classical Arabic at least as well as Major Badoglio. He probably—no, certainly—used the language more than Badoglio did. Not without pride, he added, "The *qadi* examined the *halal* part of our kitchen just last week. No pork comes near it."

Khalid had heard those assurances from the hotel staff ever since he and Dawud checked in. He believed them; he didn't think any *qadi* could be bribed into approving a kitchen that harbored forbidden food. Sipping from a glass of grappa, he asked, "And if we should care to eat from the Christian side of the menu?"

The waiter's face lost its professional blandness. All at once, he might have been a man selling filthy pictures, or even his "virgin" "sister." "Well, then, my masters, you can do that, too," he said, his voice cloyingly sweet. "You wouldn't be the first fellows from across the sea who wanted to find out what the pork roast tastes like. No, indeed—not even close."

Yes, there were tours where Muslim travelers roistered through the taverns in Europe's big cities. Were there also tours where Muslim travelers—and maybe Jews, too—gorged themselves on pigs' feet and ham and the pork roast proffered here? There would be if a tour booker thought he could turn a profit from them.

Across the table from Khalid, Dawud drank Italian white wine. That was permitted him, even if pork wasn't. Khalid took another sip of grappa. Liquid fire slid down his throat. Alcohol was every bit as *haram* as pork, of course. But drinking alcohol didn't feel anywhere near as transgressive—no, be honest: as dirty—as a fat slice of pork roast would have.

Why not? Khalid wondered. He suspected it was because you could do without pork more easily than you could do without alcohol. Odds were there'd never been a human being born who couldn't use a drink now and then. But the lure of pork for a Muslim or Jew could only be the thrill of the illicit.

"*Would* you care for the pork roast, my master?" the waiter asked. "People from your side of the water like it fine. A little something you can't get at home, eh? Why else would you travel, if not for that?"

Christians said Shaitan had tempted Jesus. Now Khalid knew exactly how the Devil would have sounded. He had a pretty good notion of the oily gleam that would have been in Shaitan's eye, too. He looked back at the man standing there expectantly, pencil poised above notebook. "The veal and artichoke hearts will do very well for me, thanks."

"However you please," the waiter said, writing it down. *You don't know what you're missing!* every line of his body proclaimed. When Khalid didn't change his mind, the waiter turned to Dawud. "And you, my master?"

"I'd like the clams and mussels in cream sauce, with linguine," Dawud said.

"I will take your orders to the cooks." The waiter bustled off.

Muslims could eat any kind of seafood they pleased. Jews . . . Khalid wagged a finger at Dawud. "What are you doing? That's as *haram* for you as pork would be."

"I know," Dawud said placidly. "But I like clams and mussels, and I can't get all that excited about how pork tastes. If I'm going to break a law, I may as well have a good time doing it."

At the madrasa in Cairo, Khalid had eaten pork. He'd broken a law for the sake of breaking the law. Wasn't that part of being modern?—shoving aside the outmoded ethics of the past? He'd been sure it was when he was twenty. He wasn't so sure any more. He took another respectful pull at the glass of grappa. Yes, he was enjoying himself breaking a law, too.

In due course, the waiter came back with a tray on his shoulder. He ceremoniously set Khalid and Dawud's meals before them. "May your appetites be good, my masters," he said. "Do you require anything else?"

"I think we're all right," Khalid said, and Dawud nodded. With a stiff little bow, the waiter went away. The two men from the Maghrib dug in. The veal was tender and tasty. "How's yours?" Khalid asked after a while.

"Just fine," Dawud answered. He didn't seem to take any perverse delight in eating shellfish barred by his faith. Their taste pleased him, so he chose them.

Italian desserts were not to be sneezed at, either. Khalid patted his belly as he and Dawud walked to the elevator. "If I keep eating like this, you can roll me here tomorrow."

"We can roll each other," Dawud replied. Grappa made that seem funnier than it was.

They'd just opened the door to their room when the telephone rang. Khalid picked it up. "Yes?" He wondered if he'd forgotten to sign the chit in the restaurant.

But it wasn't the waiter, or even the man's boss. "You saw the outside of the seminary," an unfamiliar voice said. "Come in, if you please. Give your names to the guards at the third hour. They will know what to do." The line went dead.

III

"Are you sure we should be doing this?" Dawud asked as he and Khalid walked up to the guard post in front of the Aquinas Seminary. "Someone could be setting us up."

"Someone could be, but I don't think so," Khalid said. "The timing on that phone call was just too good. Somebody—that pimp of a waiter?—was keeping an eye on us. The fellow on the other end of the line *knew* when we'd get back. Or the snoop could have been someone from the Ministry of Information."

"If Major Badoglio doesn't have somebody watching us, he's missing a trick, and he's too sharp to miss many," Dawud agreed. "So they might have tipped off the Aquinists. Isn't that a cheerful thought?"

"All kinds of interesting possibilities," Khalid said.

"One of which is that the guards shoot us as soon as we tell them who we are," Dawud said.

"We're about to find out," Khalid said.

The checkpoint was very close now. One of the guards stationed there, a pimply youth with a submachine gun, looked at the newcomers with gray eyes as chilly as the glaciers of northern Europe. "Who are you? What do you want?" he asked in Italian. If ever there was a place where classical Arabic was unlikely to be heard, this was it.

"I am Khalid al-Zarzisi. This is my friend, Dawud ibn Musa. Last night a man call us and invite us here. We come." No, Khalid's Italian wasn't good. He hoped it was good enough to get the job done.

Then he hoped he lived through the next few seconds. The gun swung sharply toward his chest. But the guard caught himself. He went back and forth with one of his comrades, an older man with four hashmarks on his left sleeve. The senior man listened, then gave forth with a magnificent gesture of contempt. The young guard with the icy eyes quailed before it. Khalid didn't blame him; he would have, too.

"Please excuse Luigi here," the man with the hashmarks said to Khalid. "The only thing wrong with him is, he's an idiot. We are expecting the two of you."

"He isn't—uh, wasn't." Khalid nodded toward Luigi.

"I told you—he's an idiot. What, they don't have idiots in your country?" the older man replied. "Come on. Show me your papers so I know you're really you, and we'll get on with things."

He might not care to speak Arabic, but the way he inspected the ID cards made Khalid pretty sure he read it. And, after carefully patting down the Maghribis, he ordered Luigi to escort them into the seminary to meet . . . whomever they were supposed to meet. He named no more names. In his position, Khalid wouldn't have, either.

"Well, come along, then," the young, acne-spotted guard said roughly. He didn't apologize for almost plugging Khalid. As far as he was concerned, that was all part of the day's work.

He did lead Khalid and Dawud past the other checkpoints in front of the fortresslike seminary. Some of the guards there gave them hard looks, but no one tried to stop them. Khalid wouldn't have wanted to attack the place with anything short of an armored regiment. Even that might have run into trouble: one of the checkpoints had rocket-propelled grenade launchers ready to grab.

As soon as the guard passed the threshold of the seminary, he crossed himself. He paused, plainly waiting for his charges to do the same. When they didn't, he muttered "Heathens" under his breath, as if reminding himself. He waved, urging them to follow.

Khalid didn't, not right away. He was looking at the two images just inside the entrance. That they were there didn't offend him; only very pious Muslims still objected to pictures of human beings—and, in Persia and India, not even those. But they certainly gave him pause.

One was of Christ: Christ stern in judgment. The somber dark eyes in that long, harsh face captured and held Khalid's. He could easily believe he stood before Someone Who knew everything and forgave nothing. Who could hope to pass into heaven if it had such a Guardian as this?

And beside that image hung one of Saint Thomas Aquinas. Muslims said that, if there could have been a Prophet after Muhammad, al-Ghazali would have been the man. Plainly, Christians—or at least Aquinists—thought the same about their leading theologian. This Aquinas wasn't the jut-jawed street fighter of the propaganda posters. If anything, he was more frightening. That round, proud face said he knew . . . oh, maybe not so much as Christ, but as much as a man could know. But however much he'd learned, he approved of none of it.

Dawud touched Khalid on the arm. How long had he stood there, half hypnotized by those images? Too long, evidently. He shook himself like a dog scrambling out of a cold stream and followed the impatient-looking guard.

He didn't have to follow him very far: only to a bank of elevators a third of the way down the long central hall. The elevators came from Abd-al-Latif and Sons, a reputable firm from one of the countries in the Sunset Lands—Khalid recognized the logo. That made him easier in his mind as he got into the car; he might not have cared to trust his carcass to some rickety European model. Evidently the Aquinists didn't care to, either.

This elevator was modified for European use, though. Like everyone else, the Christians of Western Europe did use Arabic numerals—the Roman ones they'd had before were impossibly cumbersome. But, just as they clung to the Roman alphabet instead of the more widely used Arabic script, so their numbers had different shapes from the ones most of the world knew. Abd-al-Latif and Sons had numbered the buttons for the various floors with European-style numerals. Anyone who didn't know them was out of luck.

The guard punched 14: the top floor. The elevator rose as smoothly as it might have in a building in Damascus or Isfahan. It stopped several times on the way up. Some of the men who got on and off were in ordinary European clothes. Others wore black or brown monk's robes. The lights in the top of the elevator car gleamed off their tonsured pates.

None of the Aquinists paid any special attention to Khalid or Dawud. They assumed that anyone who got into the seminary belonged there. Khalid could see circumstances where that might be used against them. Riding this elevator didn't seem likely to be one of those circumstances, though.

When the elevator stopped on the fourteenth floor, the guard got out ahead of his charges. He gestured to the left with the barrel of his gun. To the left Khalid and Dawud went. "Never argue with a man who wants to shoot you," Dawud remarked in Arabic.

"I wasn't going to," Khalid replied.

"Talk so I can understand you!" the guard snapped in Italian.

"*Vaffanculo!*" Dawud told him. "There. Happier now?"

Khalid would have thought insulting a man who wanted to shoot you was as bad as arguing with him—as bad or worse. The guard's expression might have shown any of several different emotions, but happiness wasn't one of them. He growled like an angry bear, down deep in his throat. The gun barrel jerked, then steadied again. The guard said not another word till he got to a door warded by two much smarter-looking fellows with assault rifles. Then he snarled, "Here are the heathens. You're welcome to them."

"You are Khalid al-Zarzisi and Dawud ibn Musa?" one of the men in front of the door said as the fellow from outside stomped back toward the elevator.

"That's right," Khalid replied.

"Your papers." The guard held out his left hand to take them. The right stayed on his weapon.

"We showed them before," Dawud said. "Why do we have to do it again?"

"Because we haven't seen them yet," the guard said. "*We* are the people responsible for protecting the Corrector. So if you'll please show them . . ."

Every Aquinas Seminary was headed by a Corrector. Add them all together and they were the most dangerous dozen and a half men in Europe—probably in the world. Khalid hadn't expected to talk to the Rome Corrector. He'd thought getting inside the seminary would be interesting enough, if he and Dawud could even manage that. If he had to show his ID again to meet one of the great foes of Muslim civilization, he'd do it. Dawud followed his lead.

The guard examined the cards with a jeweler's loupe. He compared photos to faces. It was routine, but not the lazy kind of routine that often turned slipshod. Then he handed back the cards. "Yes, you're you. They patted you down outside, too, right?"

"Right," Khalid said.

"Well, we're going to do that one more time, too. Nothing personal. We do it with everybody." The guard was good at it. Had Khalid been carrying anything nasty, it would have been found.

"Why don't we just take off all our clothes out here?" Dawud asked.

"You aren't pretty enough to be interesting naked," the guard answered. For once skewered instead of skewering, Dawud shut up. The guard finished searching him. "You're clean. I figured you would be, but you never can tell. Go on in." He stepped aside.

FATHER DOMENICO PACELLI, said the nameplate on the Corrector's desk. The man behind the desk looked like neither the stern Christ nor the dyspeptic Aquinas portrayed downstairs. Khalid also had to admit that he bore not the slightest visible resemblance to Shaitan. He was about sixty, with pinched cheeks, a thin, sharp nose, and pale eyes behind gold-framed spectacles.

"*Buon giorno, Padre,*" Khalid said. As long as he stuck to set phrases, he was fine.

But Father Pacelli surprised him by replying in classical Arabic: "Peace be with you, my master."

"And to you also peace," Khalid answered automatically. Then he said, "I did not think you would know this language."

"Why not?" Father Pacelli said. "We need to know it. It is the world's language of commerce. It is the world's language of scholarship. It is the world's language of lies—about us and about many other things. Oh, yes, we need to know it."

"Not everything the world says about Aquinists is a lie," Dawud ibn Musa said.

"Not everything the world says about Jews is a lie, either," the Corrector answered. "Does that make you happier to hear the lies that do get said?"

"I haven't killed anyone on account of them. Not lately, anyhow—I would remember," Dawud said.

Father Pacelli's nostrils flared. His nose was so bladelike, Khalid hadn't been sure they could. How long had it been since someone talked back to him? Years, unless Khalid missed his guess. But the priest's voice remained mild: "Nor have I."

He looked like a scholar. Meeting him in a Muslim land, Khalid would have figured him for a professor of mathematics, or perhaps a doctor. It wasn't easy to imagine him carrying a grenade launcher or an assault rifle. But you didn't have to do it yourself. Khalid thought of Faruq al-Ghaznavi, at whose orders four million Tamils had died in the wars that roiled India a lifetime earlier: not because they were enemy combatants, merely because they were Tamils. In photos taken before he himself was beheaded for crimes against mankind, Faruq looked like the chicken farmer his grandfather had been. You never could tell.

Dawud's mind must have been going down the same path, for he said, "I haven't told anyone else to kill on account of them, either."

"Nor have I," Father Pacelli repeated. "The Aquinist movement is not what you imagine it to be. That is why you were asked to come here: so I could begin to set the record straight."

"That will . . . take some doing," Khalid observed. The three simultaneous truck bombs that destroyed the Majlis Hall in Alexandria and left Egypt essentially without a government . . . The blast that shattered a dam in Arkansistan, flooding a hundred square parasangs and drowning thousands . . . The false pilgrims who blew up not only themselves but those who came to Mecca with nothing but prayer and fasting on their minds . . . The filmed execution of hostages for the greater glory of God . . . The list was long, but those were some of the examples that sprang to mind.

"We seek equality. We want the right to live our lives according to our principles, and not to have yours rammed down our throats," the Corrector said. "Your filthy, leering music, your brazen films, the garbage—there is no other word—on the television at every hour of the day and night . . ." His hands, long and thin and pale, twisted in a gesture of disgust.

"I haven't heard of anyone holding a gun to Europe's head and making you watch the movies and the TV or listen to the music," Khalid said. His own opinion of some of what his civilization produced wasn't far from Pacelli's, but that wasn't the point. That it wasn't the point went to the heart of this dispute. He asked, "Don't you believe everyone has the right—has the duty, even—to choose for himself? We call that freedom."

"Sticking a name on it does not make the name true," the priest snapped, showing asperity for the first time. "We call it license."

"Which doesn't make what you call it a true name, either," Dawud said.

Father Pacelli glowered at him. Khalid always found light eyes unnerving because they were so uncommon on the other side of the Mediterranean. He didn't know whether Dawud felt the same way. More than a few men found fair-haired, light-eyed women exciting—not a word that would ever have applied to the Corrector. Right now, Pacelli was trying to make Dawud afraid.

If he succeeded, Dawud didn't let on. "I don't know what you're waiting for, looking at me like that," the investigator said. "I won't turn red. I won't grow horns and cloven hooves and a barbed tail. And I'm sure I can't fit batwings under this tight tunic."

"No, you are not Satan," Father Pacelli said; even speaking Arabic, he pronounced the Devil's name in the hissing European fashion. "You are only a Jew who thinks he is funny. But Satan inspires your shameless culture all the same. And we will fight him wherever we find him."

"Freedom is—"

"Overrated," Father Pacelli finished for him. "You Muslims will not eat swine, but you act like them. You coddle your lusts. And the worst of it is, you provoke us to coddle ours—and you expect us to pay for the privilege. God will not permit you to proceed with your wickedness."

"And you know this because He told you?" Dawud suggested.

"I know this because I have studied the Bible. You might do well to try it," the priest said. "We will spread God's word any way we can—and we will make our voices heard round the world."

"Believe whatever you please. That's freedom, too," Khalid said. "But you have no right to impose your beliefs on people who don't share them."

"You misunderstand," Father Pacelli said sadly. "We are not imposing our beliefs. I agree with you—that would be wicked. We are carrying out God's will. If I have to choose between the word of God and the word of man, I choose God's. And we will see in the world to come who made the better choice."

He and Khalid looked at—looked through—each other in perfect mutual incomprehension. Khalid wondered if the Corrector had ever read the *Apology* of Socrates. It was probably too secular for him. The Greek philosopher had said something similar, but in a very different context. Socrates meant he would keep looking for truth even if people told him to stop. Father Pacelli was convinced he already had it, and aimed to shove it down everyone else's throat.

"Have we anything more to say to each other?" Pacelli asked.

"Only this: we will stop you if we can," Dawud said.

"I am trying to stop everything your world has been doing to mine for the past five hundred years," the Christian priest said. "You learned from us, you stole from us, and then you decided everything we knew was old and out of date and of no account. And now you laugh at us behind our backs, and even in our faces. Well, the day will come when you laugh out of the other side of your mouth. God wills it, Jew, and God's will *shall* be done."

"Of course it shall. How could it be otherwise?" Dawud answered. "Where you're making your mistake is, you think you're the ones working it." He turned to Khalid. He would have been more impressive heaving his bulk out of a chair, but they hadn't been invited to sit down. "Come on, boss. He's right about one thing, anyhow: we've said everything that needs saying."

Khalid took a small boy's pleasure in turning his back on the Corrector. Out in the corridor, one of Father Pacelli's guards held up a hand when he and Dawud started to walk toward the elevators. "We know what you are," he said, and signed himself with the cross to show what he thought of what they were. "You don't go wandering around without an escort." His gesture might have been medieval, but the little radio on his belt was as modern as next week. He spoke into it, then nodded to the investigators. "Wait here. Someone is coming up for you."

In due course, the somebody arrived: the pimply youngster who'd brought Khalid and Dawud up to Father Pacelli's sanctum. Luigi gave them a dirty look as he marched them away. Khalid would have bet he hadn't been back at his post long when his superior got the word they needed somebody—and sent him back up to the fourteenth floor. A senior underofficer in the Muslim world would have done the same kind of thing. Some bits of business didn't change much from one culture to another.

The guard muttered a few unpleasantries in Italian as he took them down the elevator and out of the seminary. Khalid wasn't sure whether they were aimed at him and Dawud or at the underofficer. Since Dawud held his peace, Khalid suspected the latter.

Once they'd made their way past the last checkpoint on the way out, Dawud remarked, "If they were only a little looser in there, I'd feel like I was getting out of jail."

Khalid looked back over his shoulder at the massive concrete pile. "Now that you mention it," he said, "yes."

After the Aquinist Seminary, even the Ministry of Information seemed a lighthearted, carefree place the next day. It also seemed small to Khalid. The Aquinists were training hundreds—no, thousands—of young men in their rigid theology and in who could say what all else? Far fewer people here seemed to have the job of dealing with (or, better, preventing) the trouble they caused.

He was not surprised to learn that Major Badoglio knew where he and Dawud had gone the day before. He would have been surprised and disappointed if the major hadn't.

"You should be honored," Badoglio said. "Father Pacelli doesn't invite just anyone into his lair."

"I don't think he meant it as a compliment," Khalid said.

"No. He wanted to frighten us." Dawud ibn Musa paused meditatively. "He knows how to get what he wants, too."

"Imagine how frightened we would have been if he'd let us see more of what they're up to in there," Khalid said. Dawud mimed a fit of the shivers. Khalid snorted.

"He might have done it," Major Badoglio said. "Making people afraid is one of the things the Aquinists do best."

"Why does the Grand Duke put up with them? They're a state within his state," Khalid said. "They fly their own flag. They have their own soldiers and their own weapons. I'm surprised they don't mint coins with the Corrector's face on them."

"You just answered part of your own question, my master," Badoglio replied. "They have soldiers. They have guns. Putting them down would mean civil war."

"Sometimes you have to do those things, or else your country isn't yours any more," Dawud observed. "It starts to belong to the people who have the guns and don't worry about using them."

"You have a point," the Italian security man said. "But the only thing worse than starting a civil war is starting one and then losing it."

Dawud winced. So did Khalid. No one who'd briefed them in Tunis had thought that was even a possibility. If Major Badoglio did . . . "What do you think the chances are?" Khalid asked.

Badoglio spread his hands in a gesture an Arab might also have used. "To tell you the truth, I don't know. I don't want to find out, either. Neither does the Grand Duke. His Supreme Highness will stay cautious as long as he can—and then, it could be, a little longer than that."

"What would happen if the Pope ordered the Italian people to back the Grand Duke if there is a civil war?" Khalid inquired.

"You keep asking questions I have no answers for," Major Badoglio said. "But, as I told you a few days ago, I would be surprised if Pope Marcellus were eager to find out. The Aquinists might proclaim him an Antipope and elevate someone else in his place. No one except maybe the Aquinists wants to see another civil war in the holy Catholic Church."

In Islam, Sunnis and Shiites had had their quarrels. These days, nationalism drove people harder than religion through most of the world. To imagine a religious dispute inflaming a big part of a continent . . . It seemed so medieval, Khalid had trouble believing in the possibility. Or he would have, if he hadn't just had a visit—an audience—with Domenico Pacelli.

"They want what they want with all their hearts and with all their souls and with all their might," Dawud said. "If you don't want to stop them just as much as they want to go forward—or backward—you'll lose."

"I do," Major Badoglio said simply.

"I believe you," the Jew said. "But you're only one man. If Grand

Duke Cosimo and everyone he works with don't want it as much as you do, you still have a problem."

"Of course we have a problem." Major Badoglio sounded testy. He made a small production out of lighting a cigar. "If we didn't have a problem, and if we didn't take it seriously, would we have asked for you?"

Instead of answering, Dawud fired up his own large, odorous cigar. Khalid thought he understood how meat felt in a smoker. All the oxygen seemed to have left the room, or, more likely, to have been used up. Eyes watering, Khalid said, "It depends. If you called us because you really want us to accomplish something, that's one thing. But if you called us because calling somebody from the Maghrib makes you look good—well, that's a different story."

"One without a happy ending: for us, for you, for anybody," Dawud added.

"I assure you, my masters, we truly do oppose the Aquinist madness," Major Badoglio said.

Khalid nodded. Showing he didn't trust the major's assurances would only cause trouble. Christians had been giving assurances like that ever since the radicals in their midst became a problem—for more than a generation now, in other words. Sometimes they seemed to mean them. More often, they wanted nothing more than to keep states that had reason to be angry from taking revenge. So it often looked to exasperated Muslims, at any rate.

"Would it be possible for us to confer with the Grand Duke?" Khalid asked.

The request seemed reasonable enough to him. But Badoglio got touchy about it. "If two men from the Ministry of Information came to Tunis, would the Sultan grant them an audience?" he asked.

"Probably. It would give him something to do besides watch horse races and look official," Khalid answered. Major Badoglio blinked. Khalid went on, "Chances are you'd have more trouble getting in to see the Wazir. He rules—as long as he keeps his majority, anyhow. The Sultan only reigns."

Badoglio muttered under his breath. Strongmen thrived in Europe. They always had, all the way back to the days of the Roman Empire. More recently, the Europeans had justified their penchant for one-man rule by what they called "the divine right of kings." To Khalid, that seemed as foolish as the Chinese "mandate of heaven." The Chinese didn't believe in the mandate of heaven any more. Europeans still clung to the divine right of kings—and of other rulers, too. The people were there to give them what they needed, nothing more.

When the major didn't say yes or no, Khalid asked him again: "Can we?" You had to be firm with these people, not let them sidetrack you.

"I'll see what I can arrange," Badoglio said, which might have meant anything—or nothing. Promises on this side of the Mediterranean were too often written on water.

All the same, Khalid said, "Thank you." Here even more than in the busy lands to the south and east, politeness mattered.

Dawud kept trying to accomplish something: "If you can't close down the seminary, can you arrest that Father Pacelli? He can't spend all his time in the building, and if he's not a dangerous man I've never seen one."

Major Badoglio looked delicately distressed. "That might also touch off the strife we fear," he said. "And, even if we were to seize Father Pacelli, the Aquinists would only choose another Corrector. Besides, there is no guarantee the father would not be able to keep on conducting his affairs from inside a jail cell."

That shouldn't happen. Khalid didn't say it. Such things *did* happen, even in places like the Maghrib. There'd been a scandal a couple of years ago, where a felonious olive-oil merchant went right on planning how to adulterate his firm's stock in trade after he went to prison for six years. And if he could do it there for profit, someone like Father Pacelli could do it here for the greater glory of God.

Something else occurred to Khalid. "Please believe me, Major, that I mean no offense when I say it seems as though you and the Grand Duke are looking for excuses *not* to antagonize the Aquinists."

"I take no offense. How can I, when what you say is true?" Badoglio answered. "But I mean no offense when I say you want us to solve your problems for you on our soil, and to pay the cost in blood and trouble."

"Hmm. That could hold some small bit of truth," Khalid said. Beside him, Dawud's cough had nothing to do with the tobacco smoke in his mouth and throat. What the Italian major said held a great whacking lot of truth. The advanced nations to the south and east were no more immune to self-interest than anyone else. Of course they wanted the Christian countries to solve their problems for them. That way, they wouldn't have to spend money or lives themselves.

Badoglio's raised eyebrow argued that he understood the facts of political life at least as well as the Maghribis. "If you were to give us more assistance than you have been in the habit of contributing, my masters . . ."

"I doubt that would change things much," Dawud ibn Musa said. "What would the Aquinists do then? They'd start yelling 'Infidels! Heretics!'—that's what. And then you'd end up with the rising you don't want."

"It could be," the Italian said. The long and short of it was, nobody wanted to do anything serious about the Aquinists. Everybody hoped somebody else would do something serious about the fanatics.

Everyone wants to go to heaven, but no one wants to die. Khalid shook his head. Even that wasn't true, not in Italy, nor in most of Western Europe. The Aquinists had shown that they had plenty of young men—and women—ready to head for heaven (or maybe for a warmer clime) right away, so long as they could hurt their foes in the dying.

The meeting with Major Badoglio petered out a little later. No one tried very hard to keep it going. No one seemed to have much left to say.

For the next couple of days, Khalid and Dawud might as well have been tourists in Rome. They looked at ruins and antiquities. No one bothered them: not the Aquinists, not the Ministry of Information, not the Pope's partisans, not even the greasy waiter in the hotel restaurant. Maybe he worked for one of the Italian factions; maybe he worked for all three of them.

"They were a great people once," Khalid said, looking up and up at the Arch of Septimius Severus. The Maghrib had its share of Roman ruins, too—many from Severus' reign, as he came from the province called Africa—but those of the imperial capital outdid them. This was where all the tax money from the outlying provinces came in, and where most of it got spent.

"They were," Dawud agreed, "but this isn't what they remember when they think of that. They keep this going for the tourist trade. Otherwise, they'd tear it down and build over it."

Sure enough, most of the people ambling through the Roman Forum were travelers from far-off lands. A couple from somewhere in the Sunset Lands argued in an Arabic dialect Khalid could barely recognize, much less follow. A local guide lectured a group of Egyptians (whose country had ruins and antiquities of its own). An Asian man snapped pictures relentlessly, one after another, *click! click! click!* He might have come straight out of a comedy bit on a bad TV show—Korean shutterbugs were always good for a laugh, or at least a tired smile. A nearby Italian constable, one of many around the Forum, looked bored. Only the assault rifle slung on his back argued that the scene might be less peaceable than it seemed at first glance.

Signs and maps in Italian and bad Arabic directed the curious from one site to another and explained what they all were. Trajan's Column, off to the northwest, commemorated a war that would have been nineteen centuries forgotten without it. After studying a map, Dawud pointed east across the Forum toward another arch. "If I ever felt like not being a Jew any more but I didn't want to say the *shahada* three times and become a Muslim, all I'd need to do is walk under that."

"Huh?" Khalid said brilliantly.

"That's the Arch of Titus," Dawud said. "Five hundred years before Muhammad was born, Titus captured Jerusalem, destroyed the Second Temple—it sat right where the Dome of the Rock is now, you know—and brought the loot back to Rome. The arch shows him parading through the streets here with it. And to this day, some rabbis say that any Jew who walks under it stops being a Jew because he did."

"Really? You aren't pulling my leg?" Khalid asked.

"Not this time." His partner spoke with unwonted solemnity.

"Well, that's a new one on me," Khalid admitted. It was a pretty peculiar one, but he didn't say that for fear of offending Dawud.

He might as well have, because Dawud seemed to pluck the thought right out of his head. "Every religion has some strange bits in it. They're easier to spot when they belong to somebody else's, eh?"

"Mm—yes," Khalid said. Then he too busied himself with a map. If he was studying, he didn't have to dwell on Dawud's . . . thought-provoking comment. He could have denied that Islam had any strange bits—but not with a straight face. He'd made the *Haj* to Mecca, more because of what it had meant to his great-grandfathers than because of what it meant to him. And he'd stoned Shaitan, just as other pilgrims had stoned him for 1,400 years. He hadn't thought that was peculiar till this moment, but he would have bet Dawud ibn Musa did.

Then, suddenly and unexpectedly, he jerked as if a bee had stung him. "Oh!" he said, or maybe it was more like "Ooh!"

"What is it?" Dawud asked. "Except for Titus' arch, I didn't see anything to get that excited about."

"It's the Column of Phocas!" Khalid exclaimed. "It's right over—there!" It couldn't have been more than sixty cubits away. It wasn't anything special to look at, not in this square of architecture magnificent even in ruins: a single column about thirty cubits high standing all by itself. All the same, Khalid hurried to it and read the sign at its base: "'In 608 AD, Pope Boniface presented this column to the Byzantine Emperor Phocas to honor the Emperor for permitting him to convert the pagan Pantheon into a church.'"

He was practically jumping up and down. Dawud followed him over much more slowly and eyed him as if wondering whether he'd gone out of his mind. "And this excites you because . . . ?"

"Because it's Phocas. Because it's 608 in the Christian calendar. Muhammad was alive then. Alive and still an ordinary man, I think—wouldn't that have been a few years before God started giving him revelations?" Khalid pointed to the column. "If he were here, he could have seen this going into place!"

"If he were here, he never would have founded Islam back in Arabia, and then where would the world be?" Dawud answered his own question: "Upside down and inside out, that's where. Not where it is now, for sure. And I don't know whether 608 is before or after he said he started hearing God. I don't care, either, to tell you the truth. Who but a Christian would keep track of the old-time Christian calendar that closely?"

"But he was here—he was on the earth—when this went up." Khalid was a secular man. To him, religion was for weddings and funerals, not for swallowing up your whole existence. He hadn't had even a taste of the wonder, the awe, it could inspire for many years. Now he did, but Dawud, not being Muslim, didn't understand it and couldn't share it.

Khalid felt like grabbing the first obviously Muslim traveler he found and dragging him over to the Column of Phocas to see if it thrilled him, too. No, thrilled her: that black-haired beauty with a tunic that displayed her dimpled knees and shapely calves was no priggish European. The Italian cops were leering at her and making what Khalid thought were rude, lewd comments. And if he himself did drag her over here, she'd think he was thinking of his own risen column, not Phocas'.

Life could be very frustrating sometimes.

"Why aren't you a beautiful woman who appreciates what the Column of Phocas means?" Khalid demanded of Dawud.

"Oh. Her." The Jew must have been watching her stroll through the ancient ruins, too. "For all you know, she's a Copt."

"You're no fun!" Khalid exclaimed. Like Jews in the Muslim world, Egypt's native Christians were far more emancipated than their coreligionists in the Old World's isolated north and west. They didn't bow before Saint Thomas Aquinas and his doctrine of piety and forgetfulness. Unfortunately, millions of people did—and the world was still facing the consequences.

IV

When the telephone in the hotel room rang, Khalid had just come out of the shower. Dawud was just going in. They stepped past each other, one wearing a towel, the other his drawers. Khalid's pace picked up as he hurried to the nightstand to answer the phone. Dawud paused at the bathroom door in case it was for him.

"*Pronto*," Khalid said in Italian. *Go on—speak!*, it meant. Italian was a more direct language than Arabic.

But the answer came back in good classical Arabic: "Are you one of the gentlemen from the Maghrib, my master?" It was a woman's voice.

"That's right. I'm al-Zarzisi. Who's this?" he said in the same tongue. Dawud raised an eyebrow. Khalid shrugged at him, which almost dislodged the towel.

As he grabbed for it with his free hand, the woman said, "My name is Annarita Pezzola. I have the honor to serve his Supreme Highness, Cosimo III, Grand Duke of Italy, as administrative assistant."

"*Do* you?" Khalid hoped he didn't sound too surprised. In the Muslim world, a woman in a position like that wouldn't have been so startling. Several women had served their states as Wazir, and some of them had done quite well. But this Pezzola woman had to be uncommonly talented (or, perhaps, uncommonly beautiful) to rise so high in a retrograde Christian country. No more than a beat slower than he might have, Khalid went on, "What does his Supreme Highness want with us?"

Dawud raised that eyebrow again, higher this time. Khalid gave back another shrug. Annarita Pezzola said, "He has asked me to invite you to an entertainment at his palace tomorrow at the second hour of the evening. He hopes to meet you there—informally and unofficially, you might say."

"Please thank him for us and tell him we'll be there," Khalid said at once.

"Just as you say, so shall it be," she replied, and the line went dead.

Khalid whistled softly as he hung up. "What was that all about?" Dawud asked.

"The Grand Duke. We're invited to his palace tomorrow, the second evening hour," Khalid told him. "An entertainment, his aide called it. A woman, by the way."

"That's interesting," Dawud said. "And so is the other. Major Badoglio didn't think he'd want anything to do with us." Before Khalid could say anything, the Jew added, "Of course, Badoglio doesn't think anybody wants to do anything. Something might— God forbid!—happen if somebody did."

"You're not being fair," Khalid said. "He has more problems than he knows what to do with."

"You said it. I didn't." Dawud closed the bathroom door, giving himself the last word.

When he came out, Khalid asked him, "What do we wear to an entertainment at the Grand Duke's palace?"

"Clothes would be good, I expect," Dawud said helpfully.

"Thank you so much, O wisest of the wise!" Khalid exclaimed. Arabic was often most sarcastic when it sounded most flattering.

Dawud bowed as if Khalid meant the compliment literally. "I am your servant," the Jew said. "The way it looks to me is, we can either look like white crows if we put on our robes and keffiyehs while everyone else is in European garb, or we can look like jackasses if we wear the European stuff ourselves and find out everyone else has the international style on."

"Rrr." Khalid made a rumbling noise down deep in his throat. Either one of those things could happen. The Grand Duke was a progressive European. If he hadn't been, he never would have invited investigators from the Maghrib to come to Italy to begin with. He would have backed the Aquinists instead. But he *was* a European, progressive or not. If he wanted to wear native styles, or wanted his henchmen to do the same, no one could blame him for it. Khalid did some more rumbling and muttering. "His assistant didn't tell me what we were supposed to do."

"Well, why don't you call her back and ask her, then?" Dawud said. "Or if that's beneath your dignity, my master, I'll take care of it for you. After all, what else is a Jew good for? What's her name?"

Khalid laughed. "What's a Jew good for? Making trouble, that's what. Her name is Annarita Pezzola, and I'll call her myself."

"That means you think she's pretty," Dawud said.

"I think you're pestilential, is what I think," Khalid said. "Where's the damned phone book? It's not in my nightstand. Nothing but the Christian Bible in there, in Latin and Arabic. They could at least have put a Qur'an in there, too, couldn't they?"

"That's in the nightstand on my side of the bed, actually," Dawud said. "So is the phone book. How long do you think you'll need to get through to her?"

"Good question," Khalid said. "She's close to the Grand Duke, so there are liable to be half a dozen layers of flunkies between the switchboard and her." He eyed Dawud. "Maybe I should have had you do it after all. Your Italian's a lot better than mine, and heaven knows if the flunkies speak Arabic."

"I'll take care of it if you want."

"Never mind. If you've been hiding the phone book, give it to me."

Dawud did. Khalid looked up the number for the Grand Duke's palace. He checked it carefully. European versions of Arabic numerals still seemed strange to him. When he dialed, he asked to speak to *Signora* Pezzola. "*Signorina*," the man on the other end of the line corrected. Then he paused for close to half a minute. "Who's calling? How do you know to ask for her?"

"I am Khalid al-Zarzisi. I just speak—ah, spoke—to her on telephone." He hoped he was making himself understood.

Another pause, this one even longer, made him wonder all the more. At last, the Grand Duke's hireling said, "Please hold the line." Music replaced his voice. Through most of the world, it would have been something popular and disposable—maybe a song by Dawud al-Buwayhidi. Here, it was a sonorous Latin chant: a chorus, perhaps of priests or monks, singing Christian hymns. Progressive or not, the Grand Duke had given ground to the backward-looking Aquinists here. Khalid wondered if Cosimo III realized as much.

The chant held a certain grim grandeur, even if Khalid couldn't understand a word of it. As soon as it finished, another began: dozens of deep voices rising and falling together. That one went silent halfway through. There was a click, and then a woman's voice: "This is Annarita Pezzola."

"Oh, good!" Khalid said in glad surprise: he hadn't expected to reach her so soon. And good for another reason—now he could go on in Arabic. He did; he wasn't sure he could have framed the question in Italian.

"You may wear whatever you please," *Signorina* Pezzola answered, with something that might have been amusement in her voice. "The Grand Duke himself sometimes chooses national attire, sometimes international."

Khalid wasn't sure that helped. "Would he take it for a compliment if we wear your styles, or would he think we look like buffoons?"

"It depends," she said judiciously. "If you *do* look like buffoons, you might do better to stay with your familiar clothes."

"Er—thank you," Khalid said, and hung up. The Grand Duke's aide had never seen Dawud ibn Musa in robes and keffiyeh. The Jew could look like a buffoon no matter what he wore.

"What did she say?" Dawud inquired now.

"We can wear whatever we want."

With his jowls and heavy eyebrows, Dawud's frown seemed fiercer than it was. "I'm not sure I can stand that much freedom."

"Don't worry," Khalid said. "This is Italy. That's about as much as you'll find."

In the end, Khalid and Dawud decided to keep to the international style when they went to Grand Duke Cosimo's entertainment. They were from the Maghrib, after all. It wasn't as if Cosimo and his associates didn't already know as much. And it wasn't as if the Aquinists didn't already know, either.

The cab that took the Maghribis to the Grand Duke's palace dropped them off at the base of the Palatine Hill. A long walk up still awaited them. "Sorry, friends," the driver said. "I can't get any closer."

Khalid sighed—the man was obviously right. Cosimo's security arrangements were even more comprehensive than the Aquinas Seminary's. He didn't want anyone with a weapon getting close enough to the palace to use it. After Dawud paid the driver, the man zoomed away. Khalid and Dawud presented themselves at the lowest checkpoint. "Yes, my masters," a lieutenant said in decent Arabic. "Your names are on the list of invited guests. Now if you will let me see some identification, so I may be sure the faces match the names. . . ."

Resignedly, they displayed their documents. He gave them the same careful scrutiny the guards at the Ministry of Information and the Aquinists had. When he was satisfied, he returned the IDs. That didn't let them advance toward the palace—not yet. It only won them a patdown and scrutiny from a metal detector.

"Do you want me to turn my head and cough?" Dawud asked the man who was searching him. Khalid's patdown was also that intimate; he wasn't sure his doctor felt him so attentively.

"Won't be necessary," the Italian answered, grinning. "And I do believe you're clean, so you can go on." A moment later, Khalid also passed muster. The Grand Duke's men now knew exactly how much change he carried. What they would do with that knowledge, he hadn't the faintest idea. He didn't think they did, either.

Spotlights and floodlamps lit the grounds as brightly as the sun would have. Up toward the palace at the top of the Palatine Khalid trudged, Dawud huffing and puffing beside him. If the Jew were thinner—and if he didn't smoke—the climb might have seemed easier to him. But that thought slipped from Khalid's mind as a couple of Italian words resonated there. *Palazzo. Palatino. Palazzo. Palatino.* He whistled softly. This was the place from which all palaces took their name.

Grand Duke Cosimo tried to mix Roman notions of elegance with modern notions of security. The results were . . . well, mixed. Splendid brickwork veneered the outwalls of the Grand Duke's palace—unfortunately without disguising the massive reinforced concrete from which those outwalls were made. By the same token, towers didn't adequately conceal the quick-firing guns and antiaircraft missiles they housed.

As for the spinning radar dish atop the palace, it was the latest model from Arkansistan. The Maghrib had tried to sell Cosimo *its* newest version, but he'd got a better deal from the republic in the Sunset Lands. Khalid suspected Cosimo might have gone with the Arkansistani radar even if the Maghrib's price were lower. He wasn't the sort of man who wanted to put too much of his safety in his next-door neighbor's hands.

"What would Augustus have thought of all this?" Dawud asked, waving toward the overwrought splendor they were approaching.

Khalid tried to remember what he knew about the founder of the Roman Empire. If ever there'd been a canny ruler, Augustus was the man. "He would have admired the strength, and he would have thought Cosimo was foolish to put it on display," Khalid answered after a moment.

Dawud grunted. He walked on for another couple of paces, then nodded. "Yeah, that sounds about right."

Some Christian cathedrals from after Aquinas' time had bronze doors with splendid reliefs on them. The Grand Duke's doors had splendid reliefs, too. But his proclaimed the greater glory of Cosimo, not of God. And, when the doors swung open after Khalid and Dawud passed another search, the bronze exterior proved as much a façade as the brickwork on the outwalls. The doors were even thicker than those at the Ministry of Information, and made of layers of steel and ceramic like a bank vault—or the skin armoring a main battle tank.

From whom did he buy this? Khalid wondered. From one of the modern countries of the Muslim world, surely. Grand Duke Cosimo wouldn't have trusted his safety to something the Italians made themselves. The doors should have thudded when they closed behind the men from the Maghrib, or so it seemed to Khalid. But they made not even a whisper of sound.

Musicians played in the courtyard, sometimes on instruments you might have heard anywhere in the world, sometimes in traditional European modes. Violins and a harpsichord sounded respectively screechy and jangly to Khalid, but he was no connoisseur of such matters. He'd read articles claiming a place for European music right alongside the classical canon. Then again, only a fool believed everything he read.

A prominent servitor came up to him and Dawud. No one except a prominent servitor would have had the amazing bad taste to wear a keffiyeh with European-style clinging trousers and short tunic. "You gentlemen are . . . ?" he inquired in Italian. They gave their names. "Oh. You're them," the man said, switching to fluent classical Arabic. He waved. The musicians paused. He loudly announced the newcomers. The musicians resumed. He spoke again, in lower tones: "Please come with me. The Grand Duke wants to make your acquaintance."

Whatever the Grand Duke wanted, the Grand Duke got. That seemed to be the unspoken assumption in the servitor's eyes. Whether the Aquinists would agree was something else again.

Like the musicians, Cosimo's courtiers and their ladies paused as the Maghribis walked by. That was not mere politesse on their part, though; they wanted to size up the prominent strangers. Most of the Grand Duke's men wore robes and headcloths that wouldn't have looked out of place on wealthy men from Zanzibar to Canton. The rest—nearly all of them graybeards—clung to local fashions. Only the one servitor so disastrously tried to mix them.

There stood Cosimo, chatting with a Christian priest. The holy man's somber black costume reminded Khalid he was on the other side of the Mediterranean. Cosimo's well-tailored robe and shining white keffiyeh would have been at home all over the world. The Grand Duke's looks certainly wouldn't have seemed out of place in Tunis. Cosimo was in his fifties, and looked younger at first glance because he touched up his hair and his whiskers. He had bushy eyebrows, a prow of a nose, and the watchful eyes of a man who knew he had plenty of things to be watchful about.

"Ah, the Maghribis," he said when the servitor presented Khalid and Dawud. His classical Arabic was even better than his man's. "I hear you stuck your heads in the lion's mouth the other day."

He was well informed. A man in his position who wasn't well informed probably wouldn't hold his position long. "That's right, your Supreme Highness," Khalid said.

"And what do you think of the Aquinists?" Cosimo asked.

"They seem more . . . capable than I expected them to," Khalid answered after a couple of heartbeats groping for the word he wanted.

The Grand Duke nodded. Medals and rosettes and ribbons gleamed on his chest. Like the reliefs on the door, they were dedicated to the greater glory of Cosimo. He might be—indeed, Khalid knew he was—a Christian, but he wanted his subjects to revere him. "I know what you mean," he said. "You expected them to roll their eyes and foam at the mouth and maybe thrash a little"—he jerked spasmodically, but without spilling the drink in his hand—"too, didn't you?"

"Well . . ." That exaggerated, but not by a great deal. Khalid also found himself nodding. "Yes, your Supreme Highness. I suppose so."

"They'd be less dangerous if they did," Cosimo said. "They can act like modern men and use all the tools modern men have come up with—to serve ideals a thousand years out of date."

"I think that's true," Khalid said slowly. It was also one of the pithier ways of summing up the Aquinists' challenge he'd ever heard. Cosimo might worship at the shrine of Cosimo along with his subjects, but he was nobody's fool.

"A lot of grandeur in those old notions. A lot of glamour, too," he said. "If you're doing something for God, you don't need to worry about the right or wrong of it. You don't need to worry at all—you're heading straight to heaven. You just do what you do, and everybody else had better look out."

As he spoke to Khalid, his dark eyes darted now left, now right. Every so often, he would glance over his shoulder. In another man, that would have been rude. Cosimo just seemed cautious.

Dawud ambled back, carrying a murky-looking drink with a candied cherry in it. "Yes, yes, the Jew," the Grand Duke muttered, as if reminding himself. "Your people have even more to lose than Christians or Muslims if the Aquinists get their way, eh?"

"Who, us? Christ-killers? The old dispensation, too blind to see that Jesus was the Son of God or that Muhammad was the Prophet of God?" Dawud's mouth twisted into a sour grin, like a white-haired father eyeing two proud, strapping sons who'd both outgrown him and wished he would dry up and blow away. "Yes, they love us, all right. Even more than other people do."

"You have an odd way of using the word *love*," Grand Duke Cosimo said.

"I have all sorts of odd ways, your Supreme Highness. I *am* a Jew," Dawud answered easily.

"Yes." Cosimo's one-word agreement spoke volumes about what he thought of the old dispensation. One of Dawud's eyebrows lifted, ever so slightly. Khalid noticed, because he was looking for that kind of response. He didn't think Cosimo did. Voice suddenly brisk, as if he was deciding he'd given these people enough time, the Grand Duke went on, "Maybe you'll come up with something other people have missed. Here's hoping." He turned away.

"Well, *that* was interesting," Dawud said. A stranger listening—and some stranger was bound to be listening—would have found nothing amiss in words or tone. Khalid was no stranger, and heard what Dawud didn't say. It came down to something like *We're supposed to be on his side? I'd almost rather work for the Aquinists.*

Khalid might almost have rather worked for the Aquinists, too. But *almost* was a word that covered parasangs and parasangs of ground. Your friends weren't always the people you wished they would be. They were the people you disliked less than your enemies, and sometimes you had to make the best of it.

Such cheerful reflections made Khalid ask, "Where did you get that drink?"

"Right over there." Dawud pointed. Sure enough, a burly Italian in a gaudy medieval-style tunic of crimson-and-gold-striped velvet stood behind a bar, mixing drinks with a quickness nearly magical. The cheroot he puffed damaged his authenticity, not that he seemed to care.

"What would you like, sir?" he asked when Khalid stood before him.

"Gin and quinine water," Khalid said.

"With lemon juice?"

"Please."

"Coming up." The barman's hands were building the drink even as he spoke. He gave it to Khalid. The Maghribi slid a coin across the bar. With a nod of thanks, the barman made it disappear as fast as he'd fixed the drink. Khalid sipped and then smiled. The fellow hadn't stinted on the gin.

A man in military uniform eyed Khalid. "You are a Muslim, yes?" he asked in slow Arabic.

"Yes," Khalid said. "And so?"

The officer pointed toward the gin and quinine water. "You sin by your own faith's rules, yes?"

"That is between me and God, sir. Not between me and any-one else," Khalid answered pointedly.

"What about your priests? Your *qadis*? Your *mullahs*!" Cosimo's henchman groped for the word he wanted.

"What about them?" Khalid said. He and the officer eyed each other. They might both use Arabic, but they didn't speak the same language. To Khalid, religion was a cloak, not a straitjacket.

Plainly, the Italian had different notions. He started to say some-thing else, but waved instead, as if to give it up as a bad job. Then he asked the barman for a fresh drink of his own. His principles intact, he gulped it down.

Dawud was talking to the priest who had been speaking with the Grand Duke. Khalid couldn't make out what they were say-ing, not through the noise of the crowd. He could see the priest's face. The man looked interested, then suddenly astonished. He threw back his head and guffawed. Whatever Dawud had come out with, he liked it.

The officer, perhaps fortified by his drink—and it wouldn't have been his first, oh, no—approached a pretty girl carrying a tray of little sandwiches. Alcohol always made you think you were suave and debonair. The trouble was, it didn't really make you that way. The girl took herself off as fast as she could. The officer stared sadly after her. He had to wonder what had gone wrong. Khalid could have told him, but he didn't think the Italian would have appreciated it.

Plenty of pretty women strolled through the palace. Some of them carried food. Some had wineglasses on their trays. And some were just . . . there. Like a sultan in days gone by, the Grand Duke could and did call out beauties to please his guests.

One of those beauties, Khalid realized, he had seen before. He needed a moment to remember where. She'd been walking through the Forum at the same time as he and Dawud had. He wasn't the most forward type with women, and never had been. His one ven-ture into matrimony, almost half a lifetime earlier, had been brief and unhappy. All the same, that visit to the ancient Roman square gave him a perfect approach now. And maybe the alcohol emboldened him, as it did with the Italian officer.

He made his way through the crowd toward her. When their eyes met, he dipped his head. *"Salaam aleikum,"* he said—*Peace be unto you.*

"Aleikum salaam," she replied—*To you also peace.* The greeting and response were old as time. Any two people could exchange them and be polite. Polite still, she waited to see what he would say next.

He nearly flubbed it. Even from her first two words, he realized she was Italian, not Muslim at all. And he'd been so sure! Nothing for it but to go ahead anyhow: "When you were in the Forum a few days ago, did you see the Column of Phocas?"

Her black eyebrows jumped like a raven's wings when the bird was taking flight. "How did you know I was there?" she demanded. She waited again, warily now. If she didn't like his answer, he knew he would never get the chance to ask her anything else.

"I was, too, with my friend," he said. "I saw you then, and now I have met you."

"So you have." She seemed anything but sure the idea pleased her.

Pretending he didn't notice that—and doing his best not to notice it in truth—Khalid pressed on: "May I ask your name?"

This time, her hesitation was too long for him even to try not to see it. At last, she said, "I am Annarita Pezzola." She gave him her first smile, a very small one. "And if you are who I think you are, we have spoken before, even if we have not met."

"Why, so we have! I should have known your voice." Khalid formally introduced himself. He raised his glass in salute to her. Then he asked, "Why wouldn't you have wanted me to know you were in the Forum? This is your city, your country, after all."

"Because I went as a worldly woman, not like—this." She gestured. By European standards, her dress was stylishly cut. But it covered almost all of her. In most of the world, it would have seemed a hundred years behind the times, likely more. Most of the women here wore modern clothes. But they were wives or mistresses or decorations. She was the Grand Duke's administrative assistant, and dressed for business in Western European women's fashion.

"Why did you do it?" Khalid asked.

"Because I wanted to feel free for a little while," she answered. "To feel like a proper person, a person who doesn't have to hide herself in a tent." She gestured again.

Even before, Khalid hadn't thought she would be connected to the Aquinists. Cosimo would have thoroughly vetted her. And educated, talented Christian women were the least likely of their faith to love the doctrine that came out of the seminaries. To the Aquinists, women were good for bearing children, for cooking, for praying, and not for much else.

"I admired what you didn't hide," Khalid remarked.

"Thank you. A woman wants to be admired. You didn't make rude remarks, the way those stupid policemen did," Annarita said. "You and your partner were civilized about it." She frowned a little. "Why didn't I notice you there?"

"Where you were dressed like a Muslim woman, to fit in my partner and I were dressed like European men," Khalid said.

"That's right—your partner. The *Ebreo.*" The Italian word slipped into her Arabic. "He's here, too, of course?"

"Yes." What was Dawud doing right now? A glance found him: he was talking with a statuesque blonde with a tray of fine cigars from the Sunset Lands. By the way she was laughing, the Jew's chances were probably better than Khalid's. The senior investigator nodded. "Over there."

"Ah. I see." Annarita Pezzola sounded tolerantly amused. "Well, he's not the first fellow to like Luisa." That she would know the name of a cigar girl didn't surprise Khalid, but did tell him she was bound to be good at her job. She went on, "And how is the Ministry of Information?"

Her eyebrows drew down and together: not much, but enough to say she didn't care for the Ministry or a lot of the people who worked there. Khalid didn't care for some of the people there, either. That didn't mean they didn't do a necessary job, though.

Later, he thought he should have reacted more when the serving girl with the exalted look on her face walked by. But that was later, and later was, as usual, too late. They always told you to look for that kind of thing, or for anything else in your surroundings that seemed out of place. But he wasn't on duty, he was talking with the first woman who'd interested him in a long time, and part of him casually assumed a lot of Europeans would be religious fanatics—and would look it.

He waited for what Annarita would come out with next. She seemed to be weighing her words. That let Khalid look away, in the direction the serving girl had gone. He couldn't see her any more; she must have walked into the next room.

Through the rest of the chatter that made up the background at a function like this, he heard Grand Duke Cosimo rumble, "Hello! You're new here, sweetheart. When did they take you on? You're cute!"

Annarita's face went white. "We don't have any new people at this function. We—"

She and Khalid both took one step in the direction of the other room. A woman's voice, softer, answered the Grand Duke as they both filled their lungs to shout. If that wasn't the girl whose face had seemed to shine, he would have been astonished. And if it was . . .

Khalid yelled just as the bomb went off.

Next thing he knew, he was on the floor. Someone else—a gray-haired woman—was on top of him, and thrashing like a goose that had just met the chopper. Something warm and wet splashed his face. Tasting salt, he realized it was blood. The blast had stunned his hearing, but the matron's shrieks drilled through the thick cotton wool that seemed to have been stuffed into his ears.

He shoved her off him. One of his arms complained, but he didn't think it was broken. The gray-haired woman was all over blood. Dimly, dully, he realized she'd shielded him from the worst of the blast. He did what he could for her. He tore a strip from her tattered gown and used it and a fork lying nearby to make a tourniquet. He hoped it would do some good.

Then he looked around for Dawud, and for Annarita. The young woman was just sitting up, a few cubits away. She had a cut over one eye, and another on the side of her jaw. But she could move both arms and both legs, and seemed in possession of her wits. She said something to Khalid—he saw her lips move. He couldn't make out what it was, though.

He cupped a hand behind one ear. When he did, he discovered the ear was bleeding merrily, as ears have a way of doing. Not all the blood on him came from the matron, then. At the moment, a tattered ear was the least of his worries.

"The Grand Duke!" Annarita said, loud enough for him to understand her.

"It is with him as God wills," Khalid answered. After what had just happened, that couldn't mean anything but *He's dead, and there may not be enough of him left to bury.*

Khalid struggled to his feet. One of his ankles hurt, too, but he could walk. Now, where was Dawud? There lay the cigar girl, her gown blown half off her so Khalid could see her shapely legs. They weren't worth admiring, not any more. Something had smashed in the side of her head. Her blood pooled on the carpet. She would never get up again—that was all too plain.

Dawud ibn Musa sprawled behind her. Even as Khalid limped over to him, the Jew groaned, stirred, and sat up. He cradled one wrist in the crook of his other arm. The grimace on his blood-spattered face argued that he had broken something. But he said the same thing Annarita had: "The Grand Duke?"

"*Kaput.*" That wasn't Arabic or Italian. Khalid didn't know where he'd picked it up. Dawud got it, though.

As Khalid had before him, he heaved himself upright. He said something in very colloquial Arabic when he tried to put weight on his left leg. His limp was worse than Khalid's: he walked like a sailor with a peg leg. Each step brought a couple of more pungent colloquialisms. All the same, he stayed with Khalid as they made for the room where the blast had gone off.

Four of Grand Duke Cosimo's guards rushed past them. The guards had started from farther away, but they could move much faster than the two Maghribis. They almost bowled Khalid over. He said not a word. Complaining to trigger-happy men with assault rifles struck him as a losing proposition.

The guards skidded to a stop. That wasn't because even more blood puddled in the other room, though it did. One of the dark-uniformed men crossed himself. A moment later, two others made the same gesture.

They weren't shoulder to shoulder. Coming up in their wake, Khalid had no trouble seeing between them. There lay what was left of Cosimo. Khalid recognized the Grand Duke by his clothes and decorations, not his face; not much of that was left. A few cubits away from him, a cut-glass punchbowl, miraculously unbroken, had fallen on the floor. In it sat the serving girl's head, face up. She still looked exalted. Her features hadn't yet relaxed into death's blankness.

One of the guards said something in Italian so electrifying, it made Dawud's Arabic curses sound like endearments. Khalid hadn't dreamt Italian could do that. You learned something new every day.

"Who succeeds?" Dawud asked.

That hadn't occurred to Khalid yet. As soon as his partner posed the question, he wondered why not. *Because you just came much too close to getting killed?* part of him suggested. That was a reason, true, but it didn't seem reason enough. The main reason Khalid and Dawud had come to Italy was to try to help keep the country stable. Well, Italian stability lay as dead as the Grand Duke. Along with the reek of cordite, the stenches of blood, burnt flesh, and shit said that was very dead indeed.

"Who succeeds?" Dawud asked again, more insistently, and Khalid realized he hadn't answered.

Slowly, he said, "Cosimo has a son." His wits weren't working well at all. "Two sons," he amended. "I think one of them is of age."

"I think you're right." Dawud sounded anything but reassured. Khalid wasn't reassured, either—nowhere near. Republics had ways to carry on when they lost a head of state. In lands like Italy, everything depended on the strongman's character. If the next strongman wanted to take the country in a new direction, what could stop him?

For that matter, if the Grand Duke's heir didn't turn out to be a strongman, how many ambitious marshals and ministers would try to overthrow him? Which of them would look for backing from the Pope? Which would look for backing from the Aquinists? Would rivals play the game of coup and countercoup, or would Italy dissolve into civil war?

Those were all interesting questions. Khalid had answers to exactly none of them. He feared no one else did, either.

The assassin's face stared up at him from the punchbowl. She still looked preternaturally serene. The expression of total certainty her remains bore filled him with certainty of his own. "Aquinists," he said, his voice harsh.

"Astounding, Tariq. What leads you to this astonishing conclusion?" Dawud replied. Battered though Khalid was, he almost hit the Jew. Dawud had the presence of mind—if that was what it was—to impersonate a popular detective's dim-witted sidekick.

Before Khalid could say anything—or swing on his colleague—a doctor in a white tunic pushed past him. As the guards had before him, the man stopped short and crossed himself. "Jesus, Mary, and Joseph!" he burst out. "Why did anyone bother calling me? I can't raise the dead."

"Plenty of living wounded." Khalid automatically spoke Arabic. He wasn't surprised when a physician trusted by the Grand Duke proved to understand the language. Pointing to Dawud, he added, "You can start with my friend here."

Dawud and the doctor both shook their heads. "I'm standing

up," the Jew said. "I don't think I'll keel over right away. Let him take care of the people who are down."

"Yes," the doctor said, and then, "*Dio mio*, how did one of those maniacs get through the security checks? Whoever let that happen . . ." He didn't go on with words. Instead, he sliced a finger across his throat. Then, without waiting for a reply from the Maghribis, he bent down over a writhing man with a shattered leg. Before long, blood splashed and splotched that immaculate tunic.

One of the Grand Duke's guards turned toward—turned on—Khalid and Dawud. He might have been a watchdog, still snarling outside a house that had burned down. "Who the devil are you people? What are you doing here?" he growled.

Carefully—so the guard could see he wasn't reaching for a weapon—Khalid took out his wallet and showed his ID. Dawud did the same with his good hand. His other arm hung at his side like a dead thing.

"Oh. The infidels." Disdain clogged the guard's voice. But then he said, "Well, you'd've wanted to keep his Supreme Highness breathing, anyway."

"*Sì. È vero*," Khalid said, glad the fierce man could see that much. And it *was* true. The only worse disaster would have been the murder of the Pope. That would have thrown all of Christian Europe into chaos, not just Italy. Then Khalid realized he had no idea whether Marcellus IX was safe. The Aquinists might have succeeded with two murders, not one alone. "Is his Holiness all right?" Khalid asked the guard.

The man's scowl got fiercer. Khalid hadn't dreamt it could. "As far as I know, he is, but I don't know very far. He's in God's hands."

That came closer than Khalid would have liked to the Aquinists' defiant cry of *God wills it!* He went into the room where he'd been talking with Annarita Pezzola. She wasn't there any more. Was she looking for Cosimo's son and heir, or would she have decided there'd be no place for her in the government without the man who'd placed her at his side? Khalid had no idea. He wondered if Annarita did.

Another doctor worked on more wounded, and a servant was spreading a tablecloth over the body of the cigar girl Dawud had been chatting up when the bomb went off. "Such a waste," Dawud said. "Such a damned waste."

"Well, yes," Khalid agreed. "But when did that ever stop anybody?" He hoped Dawud would be able to name a time when it had. All the Jew did, though, was shrug a small, sad, painful shrug—which was just what Khalid himself would have done in his place.

V

Muslims put their dead into the ground as quickly as they could. So did Jews. As far as Khalid al-Zarzisi was concerned, that was not only custom—it was also a mercy to those who mourned. Once they got the funeral behind them, they could start picking up the pieces of their own lives.

"They have closure," he said to Dawud ibn Musa.

Dawud raised one of his bushy eyebrows. "Such a pretty word," he murmured. "Wouldn't it be wonderful if it actually meant anything?"

Khalid felt a flush rise and hoped he was too swarthy to show it. "You know what I'm trying to say." If he sounded defensive, well, he was.

"Oh, sure." The Jew nodded. "I just wish you'd found some better way to say it."

"Such as?"

"Don't make me think so hard. It's too early in the morning." Dawud waved at the alarm clock and the lamp on his nightstand and the curtain rod about the hotel-room window—all good places to plant a bug. "If the Aquinists are listening in, or the nice folks from the Ministry of Information, maybe they'll come up with something."

"I doubt it," Khalid said.

Dawud nodded once more, this time mournfully. In death customs as in so many other things, the Christians of Western Europe went their own way. They delayed burial to give themselves more time to grieve, and to make a show of grieving. They did that even when the deceased was a postman or a seamstress. When he was the ruler of one of their most powerful nations . . .

More than a week would pass between Grand Duke Cosimo's murder and his funeral. Part of that was to allow for the usual weeping and wailing, the rest to allow foreign dignitaries to gather in Rome. Whatever the reasons behind it, it struck Khalid as barbaric.

Not that he could do anything about it no matter how it struck him. Cosimo's elder son had been crowned as Lorenzo III, Grand Duke of Italy, as soon as the Grand Duchy's security services made sure he was safe. Pope Marcellus anointed and blessed him. No one wasted time on any of that.

But Lorenzo hadn't asked for Khalid and Dawud to come from the Maghrib to Italy. His father had, but that seemed to mean little to him. He was going to do things the way *he* wanted to do them. He was as headstrong as any other European despot, in other words.

After a couple of days of getting brushed off whenever he sought an audience with the new Grand Duke, Khalid tried the only other ploy he could think of: he telephoned Annarita Pezzola. He did it from a kiosk a good distance from the hotel, one chosen at random. If anyone could listen in on that call . . . maybe that line was tapped from the other end.

He had more than the usual trouble getting through to her. He'd expected as much, and kept feeding coins into the slot. At last, he reached a flunky of a level high enough to have heard his name. That worthy put him through to the late Grand Duke's aide.

"I hope you are well," she said in her fine Arabic after Khalid stumbled through greetings in Italian.

"I was going to say the same thing to you," he answered, relieved to return to the wide world's language.

"Cuts, bruises, scrapes—my ears still ring," she said. "Nothing salves and time won't fix."

"I'm about the same," Khalid told her. "But time is what I wanted to talk about with you. Can't the new Grand Duke see how dangerous it is for him to wait so long before burying his father? He gives the killers more time to plan an attack on the funeral."

"I have told him this. So have his generals and his spies. He may be more inclined to listen to them," *Signorina* Pezzola said. "But the choice is his. He wants a state funeral, to show what an important man his father was on the world stage, and Grand Duke Cosimo was very important indeed. No one can doubt that."

As Khalid dropped more money into the pay telephone, he wondered if she was someplace where she could be overheard. Cosimo had been a strongarm man whose importance, such as it was, lay in backing the moderate Pope and keeping at least a small check on the Aquinists. Whether Lorenzo would manage even so much . . . Everyone could doubt that.

Everyone could, and Khalid did. He realized he couldn't say so straight out. That would have landed him in hot water even in the more easygoing Maghrib. He did say, "Doesn't he realize the fanatics will be gunning for him, too?"

"If he doesn't, it's not because no one has told him," Annarita Pezzola replied. "He has taken certain precautions. I happen to know"—she lowered her voice—"he has taken Corrector Pacelli into custody."

"And the Corrector went?" Remembering Domenico Pacelli's stern, brave features, Khalid had trouble believing it.

But Annarita said, "Oh, yes. He went. The new Grand Duke told him that if he refused the army and air force would level every Aquinas Seminary in the Grand Duchy, regardless of the cost."

The cost would be civil war—civil war mixed with the terror the Aquinists favored. If the new Grand Duke showed he was willing to risk it, or at least convinced Domenico Pacelli that he was, he had more steel in him than Khalid would have looked for in an untested young man. Or he might. "When I met the Corrector, I didn't think he was a man who feared death."

"I . . . said the same thing to Grand Duke Lorenzo," Annarita said slowly.

"And?" Khalid asked when she didn't go on.

"And he thanked me for my view of the matter, and told me he would use his own judgment," she answered.

She was bound to have more experience than young Lorenzo III. That would have been true even if Cosimo were carefully grooming his son for the succession. As far as Khalid knew, Cosimo hadn't been. Like so many tyrants in modern Europe or in the old days in the Muslim world, he'd surely had trouble imagining that he might pass from the scene.

Worse, Annarita Pezzola was a woman. Even a sophisticated Muslim leader might have had to remind himself she owned a brain as well as a pleasing shape. Cosimo had listened to her, yes. But she was, Khalid thought, several years older than the new Grand Duke. That was all too likely to make Lorenzo think she was no more than a lover with a jumped-up job title to give her a veneer of respectability.

Even on brief acquaintance with her, Khalid didn't believe that. She was as sharp as Grand Duke Cosimo had judged her. But to a European man—especially to a young European man—women were most likely to be for making supper or making babies.

Sighing, Khalid said, "Dawud and I will still do everything we can to keep Lorenzo safe. So will our government. We need stability in the Mediterranean."

"Thank you," Annarita Pezzola said. "I will pass that on to his Supreme Highness." She paused again. "Although I don't know how long I will be able to continue in his service."

"If he dumps you, he's a fool," Khalid said bluntly.

"He is the Grand Duke. He has the right to advisors who suit him," she said.

"What would you do then?" he asked.

"I don't know. Teach, perhaps. A convent school is not like a madrasa, but it might be better than nothing." She sounded like someone trying to convince herself and not having much luck.

"You could come to the other side of the sea. People there would be more likely to judge you for what you can do, not for what kind of clothes you wear," Khalid said.

"I don't think I would want to do that," she answered. "I would be a foreigner, an immigrant, a Christian immigrant. I know the kind of work most Christians do in the Maghrib—the kind your people don't care to."

"You wouldn't be like that. You have the language, the skills—"

"Thank you, but no thank you. This is my country. This is my world, for better and for worse. I will live in it. And now I had better go."

Khalid had been about to put another coin into the telephone. He didn't bother, because the line was dead.

Rome filled with dignitaries. Helicopters buzzed around the airport like angry bees, making sure no one attacked incoming airliners. The Maghrib sent its underwazir for foreign affairs. So did Egypt. The Wazir of the Seljuk Sultanate came. More distant Muslim countries sent less senior officials. Representatives also came from China and Nippon and the Hindu states of southern India.

The European lands, though, went further yet. One of their own had perished, and the surviving rulers came to Italy to honor his passing. The King of Aragon and the Queen of Castile flew in on the same plane, which was bound to set gossips' tongues wagging. The Crown Prince of Portugal arrived by himself, except for a contingent of stone-faced bodyguards.

Several German princes came. The Emperor who claimed to rule them all did not. His cash-strapped almost-government couldn't afford to send him. France sent its Dauphin, England the Prince of Wales, and Scotland the Thane of Cawdor—a title whose

importance Khalid couldn't gauge. Several Irish kinglets flew in.
Two of them had hair as coppery as the Thane's.

The hotel where Khalid and Dawud were staying filled with foreign dignitaries and their protectors. An English guard who spoke
only his own language tried to keep the two men from the Maghrib
from getting off the elevator at their floor. Khalid finally showed
the pale-eyed human hound his passport. That got enough of the
message across to the Englishman to make him grudgingly step
aside.

"Did you see his face?" Dawud asked once they were inside
their room.

"I kept trying not to look at him," Khalid said. "He must have
been all over spots when his whiskers started coming in."

"Those weren't scars from pimples." Dawud sounded uncommonly grim. "Those were smallpox scars."

"*Allahu akbar!* In this day and age?" Khalid exclaimed.

"Afraid so," Dawud ibn Musa said. "You'll still see them every
once in a while on Europeans and Africans. The Africans are too
poor to get vaccinated. Some of the Europeans are, too, but some
of them talk about not wanting to disturb God's will."

"Those are the ignorant fools the Aquinists use," Khalid said.
"If it weren't God's will that we didn't have to catch smallpox, He
never would have let that Persian healer notice how men who
worked with cattle hardly ever got sick from it."

"You can see that. I can, too," Dawud said. "Some of those
people, though . . ." He shook his head. "I'm sorry, but sometimes
I wonder if they'll ever really be civilized."

Christians here looked down their noses at Jews. Well, here was
at least one Jew looking down his nose at them, Khalid sympathized with Dawud. If he patronized him a little, too, well, he was
a full member of the richest, most progressive society in the world.
Dawud was also a member, of course, but not one in quite such
good standing. He had a few more dues to pay.

"They say you shouldn't judge," Dawud went on. "They say you shouldn't make comparisons between societies. Before they start saying stuff like that, they should take a look at that bodyguard's mug. At least he lived through it. I wonder how many in his town or wherever he caught it weren't so lucky."

Khalid began to worry that no one would remember to give him and Dawud places in the funeral procession, leaving them to watch it on television like countless others around the world. To try to make sure that didn't happen, the two men from the Maghrib called on Major Badoglio.

The major had dark, weary shadows under his pale eyes. He and his service would have to adapt to a new overlord, too. Pestering him about their places, Khalid felt rather like a small boy tugging at a grown-up's robe. Surely Badoglio had more important things to worry about.

But, as a matter of fact, he had already made arrangements for the men from the Maghrib. "If it pleases you, my masters, you will ride in the car immediately outboard of the one carrying your land's underwazir for foreign affairs," he said.

"By outboard, you mean between his car and the crowd?" Khalid asked.

"Yes, that's right." Major Badoglio nodded. "You will be part of his security detail."

"We'll be in the way if anyone tries to blow him up, is what you're telling us," Dawud ibn Musa said.

"That's about it," the Italian agreed. "I shall have a similar position myself, in a car outboard of his Supreme Highness and the other heads of state and princes marching behind the late Grand Duke's casket."

"Marching?" Khalid said. "Through Rome? Now?"

"So Grand Duke Lorenzo would have it," Badoglio answered stolidly. "They will be as well protected as we can arrange. The Corrector and the Pope will be among them, which . . . may prevent incidents."

"Or, of course, it may not, in which case everyone's in the soup," Dawud put in.

"It will be as God wills," Major Badoglio said, almost as if he were an Aquinist himself.

Before Dawud could come out with any more pungent sarcasm, Khalid said, "Major, if we're going to be in his Excellency's security detail, would you issue us a couple of pistols? We didn't try to bring weapons on the flight from Tunis. That would have been more trouble than it was worth."

"I am your servant," Giacomo Badoglio replied. "Come down to the armory and choose your own."

By what its armory held, the Grand Duchy of Italy's Ministry of Information was ready to fight a small, or maybe not such a small, war. Khalid picked a ten-shot Egyptian automatic, a model also widely used in the Maghrib. Dawud chose a large-caliber revolver.

"Less to go wrong with mine," he said. "And if I hit somebody with a slug from this, I know he'll fall over."

"However you please," Khalid said. "I'd sooner have the extra rounds, and I can reload faster."

Major Badoglio guided them through the paperwork that came with the pistols. Khalid was glad for his help. He read and wrote Italian, but not well—a script that ran from left to right felt unnatural to him. Dawud let himself seem ignorant, too. He held his cards close to his chest, and didn't show the major how fluent he was.

They also got ammunition and holsters, which took more paperwork. The armory sergeant said, "You think these forms are bad? Wait till you see what you've got to fill out if you really do plug somebody."

I'll say God made me do it, Khalid thought irreverently. But that wouldn't do. The Italians' Roman ancestors had been dedicated bureaucrats long before there were Muslims, much less before Islam discovered the need for clerks. And the discovery of that need came to the Muslims after they swallowed big chunks of the Roman Empire (even if it was ruled from Constantinople by then).

"Well," Badoglio said after the last *i* was dotted and the last *t* crossed (Khalid hoped they were all dotted and crossed, anyhow—with that funny alphabet, he might easily have missed a few). "Now all we have to do is get through the procession in one piece."

"If you're going to worry about every little thing . . ." Dawud said. He and Khalid and the Italian major all laughed. It was that or bang their heads against the wall, and laughing hurt—a little—less.

"Here we are again," Khalid said as he and Dawud took their places in the Grand Duke's funeral procession at the base of the Palatine Hill.

"Let's hope they do the security a little better than they did at Cosimo's banquet," Dawud answered. A moment later, he added, "I wish I could smoke."

"Too many cameras around. This is a dignified occasion," Khalid said. There were almost as many still photographers and men with video gear as there were troops with assault rifles, and that was saying a good deal.

"It looks more like a costume drama," Dawud said.

Khalid couldn't even tell him he was wrong. The European kings and princes and noblemen wore their court dress, which made him want to giggle. Velvet and cloth-of-gold trimmed with furs? Tights under it all? Heavy, gaudy headgear? How could anyone in a getup like that *not* look ridiculous? Somehow, the Prince of Wales managed. Few of the other grandees, though, could come close to his natural dignity.

Christian clerics added their own splashes of color to the scene. Khalid was more used to their regalia. Bishops served the European immigrant communities in the Maghrib and other labor-hungry Muslim lands. So did priests and monks, but their robes were as somber as those of imams and *qadis*.

Grand Duke Cosimo's coffin lay on a black wagon drawn by six black horses with tall black plumes sticking up from their head-stalls. The gonfalon of Italy, scarlet with a large polychrome emblem in the center, draped the casket. In a normal Christian burial, it would have been open, to allow a last glimpse of the departed. Khalid thought that uncommonly barbarous. Here, though, the coffin remained closed. The undertakers hadn't been able to make Cosimo at all presentable.

Pope Marcellus wouldn't actually march. He sat in a small half-track with a bubble of bulletproof glass. Corrector Pacelli, in his far more somber robes, walked among soldiers who looked ready to gun him down at any excuse or none. He had to understand he was a hostage for the Aquinists' good behavior. Even so, he seemed as self-possessed as he had in his office at their fortress-seminary.

"Here we are." Dawud pointed to an armored limousine flying the Maghrib's star-and-crescent-moon banner from a radio aerial. Another similar car flew a bigger Maghribi banner. That would be the one carrying the underwazir for foreign affairs.

Khalid and Dawud showed their identification at one of the dark-tinted windows. The men inside must have been satisfied, because a door opened. The two investigators got inside. The limousine, a massive Pontiak from one of the countries in the Sunset Lands, boasted air-conditioning. That was a relief.

One of the security men already inside was named Hisham. The other called himself Muhammad. They both had assault rifles on their laps. "You carrying?" By the way Muhammad asked it, he was ready to throw the investigators out again if they said no.

"Pistols," Khalid answered. Muhammad looked scornful, but grudged a shrug.

A man who could only be Grand Duke Lorenzo gestured imperiously. He looked like a younger version of his dead father. He wore black velvet blazoned with the Italian emblem. His younger brother, Duke Giuseppe, was not in the parade. That, Khalid had heard, was at Lorenzo's orders. If anything *did* go wrong here, Italy would not stay rudderless long.

Responding to the Grand Duke's gesture, a band dressed even more bizarrely than the European royals struck up mournful music. They had to be playing at full blast, because their sorrowing tune penetrated the Pontiak's thick windows and armored sides in spite of the thutter of helicopters overhead.

Following the musicians, the wagon bearing Cosimo's coffin moved forward at a slow walk. Grand Duke Lorenzo came next, flanked by bodyguards whose main duty was to shield him from the crowd. Khalid had seen Italian riflemen in modern camouflage uniforms on every other rooftop. He had to hope their commanders had done a good job of vetting them.

After the Grand Duke marched the European grandees. Centuries ago, Saladin would have confronted lords dressed this way. The Muslim world had moved on since then. Here, time might as well have stood still . . . except for the weapons the guardsmen who stayed between them and the crowd carried.

Pope Marcellus' protective vehicle came next. The lesser Christian prelates followed on foot. The Papal Guards who warded them wore uniforms different from those of their Italian counterparts, but no less functional. There was a gap between the cardinals and bishops on the one hand and Protector Pacelli and his . . . jailers on the other.

At last, the limousines bearing the representatives from the Muslim republics and constitutional monarchies and those of the Far East began to move as the procession stretched out to its full length. "So far, so good," Hisham said.

"The Ides of March have come, but they have not yet gone," Dawud said. The security man looked at him as if he had several screws loose. He condescended to explain: "It's from Roman times."

"Oh." Now Hisham just seemed disgusted. "I don't care about anything that happened before the Prophet—peace be unto him—lived."

Some Muslims remained as narrow-minded as any Christian. That was a shame, but what could you do? Hisham had to make a good security man, or he wouldn't be riding in this limousine. As long as he took care of his job, he was entitled to believe whatever he pleased.

Police and soldiers had set up a three-strand barbed-wire

perimeter to keep mourners back from the procession. They stood in front of it, some with rifles, others with nightsticks, to make sure it was respected. All of the mourners—men, women, and children—wore black from head to foot. Some of them waved Italian gonfalons as the bier rolled by: the only splashes of color in the gloomy scene.

Lorenzo was going to bury Cosimo in the Pantheon. Like so much of Rome, the building had gone up more than half a millennium before Muhammad lived. It was ancient when that long-dead Pope dedicated the column in the Forum that had so awed Khalid. He supposed that meant the Pantheon should awe him all the more, but it didn't. He didn't sneer at the Romans the way Hisham did, but Agrippa and Hadrian couldn't measure up to the Prophet for him.

The Pantheon stood northwest of the Palatine Hill. It had been a Christian church after it was a pagan temple, and a fortress after it was a church. Like so much of Western Europe, Italy had a crowded, bloody history. *And it's still got one like that,* Khalid thought uncomfortably.

Some of the people in the crowd were monks, whether Aquinists or of a different order Khalid couldn't tell. Were they mourning Cosimo or secretly rejoicing? *Render unto Caesar* was a Christian rule. *Rend Caesar with a bomb* wasn't, but they'd done it anyhow.

An obelisk stood in the square in front of the Pantheon. It was small, as obelisks went: not so tall as the domed and columned building behind it. Even after three thousand years and more, the hieroglyphs the ancient Egyptians had carved were still plain to see. Its base bore the papal arms in high relief, so that was recent, at least by Egyptian and even Roman standards. So was the verdigrised cross atop the obelisk.

The wagon stopped before the Pantheon's colonnaded entranceway. The great bronze doors were open and waiting. Italian soldiers in ceremonial uniforms—gaudy, to Khalid's eye—came out. One of them whisked the gonfalon off Cosimo's casket. With immense dignity, he folded it and stowed it between his left arm and his body. Beneath it, the coffin was covered in black velvet.

After a final salute, the remaining soldiers transferred the coffin from the wagon to their own shoulders. They began to carry it into the Pantheon. Khalid kept scanning the crowd behind the strands of barbed wire. A woman slid a handkerchief under her black veiling to dab at her eyes.

Someone not far from her started shooting right about then. He couldn't see who it was, only the muzzle flashes from an automatic weapon. "There!" he shouted, pointing.

People in the procession began falling, or perhaps going down of their own accord to keep from getting shot. If the dignitaries had even a dram's worth of sense, they would be wearing bulletproof vests under their finery. Of course, that wouldn't mean a thing if you got hit in the head.

Hisham and Muhammad swore horribly. So did Khalid. A split second later, bullets slammed into the limousine. One of the thick windows starred, but it didn't let the round through.

Both security men thrust their assault rifles out through firing ports and blazed away. A lot of the people they hit would be innocent bystanders, but they didn't let that worry them. Neither did any of the other men guarding the funeral procession, regardless of whether they served the new Grand Duke or his distinguished visitors.

Screaming mourners tried to flee. Some did. More were either shot or trampled one another. Here and there among the bodies, men lay down and returned fire. How many with weapons had infiltrated the crowd? *Too many* was the only answer that occurred to Khalid.

Some of them had grenades. They managed to set one limousine on fire—he couldn't make out whose. The helicopters swooped down to rake the crowd with machine guns and rockets. Khalid hoped all that ordnance went into the crowd, anyhow. If it tore up the procession, it was liable to do more harm than the Aquinists or whoever these attackers were.

"Well, I hope Grand Duke Lorenzo's happy," Dawud said.

"Happy?" Khalid wasn't sure he'd heard right. The assault rifles had stunned his ears even more than the bomb that murdered Lorenzo's father.

But Dawud nodded. "Happy," he repeated, louder this time. "He's got TV cameras showing the whole world what a wonderful realm he's ruling. Wouldn't *you* want to come see Italy after this?"

Hisham laughed harshly as he slapped a fresh magazine onto his rifle. "I didn't want to come to Italy before this," he said. "But they give you an order and you've got to go. Damned stupid cross-carriers!" He fired a short burst, at what Khalid wasn't sure.

Whoever the foes were, they kept shooting, too. More rounds hit the limousine. Again, none got into the passenger compartment. The firm that had armored the vehicle knew its business, all right.

Khalid peered over at the limousine carrying the Maghrib's underwazir for foreign affairs. It had a starred window, too, but not a holed one. Only a few bullets scarred its sheet metal. This car had done a tolerable job of shielding it.

He looked toward the Pantheon. Bullets and rocket fragments had scarred and chipped the marble from which it was made. But it had taken those kinds of wounds before. No rocket strike smashed the dome that must have made it one of the marvels of the ancient world. The Grand Dukes and other great lords who lay inside it still rested undisturbed.

"I think it's over," Muhammad said after a while. "Let's see what we can do for the poor bastards who went down."

He tried the door on his side, which faced what had been the sea of mourners. It wouldn't open. A bullet must have smashed the latch. He cursed. "Here," Dawud said, and opened the door on the side that faced the underwazir's car. Even though the shooting had died down, he made sure he had that heavy Italian revolver in his hand before he got out.

Khalid kept his automatic ready, too. Muhammad and Hisham were both as alert as if they'd gone into combat every day since their beards sprouted. Khalid did his best to imitate them. He crouched low to make himself a smaller target as he moved away from the shelter of the armored limousines.

"Oh, what a bloody mess," Dawud said when he got a good look at things. And that was about the size of it. The stench of gore filled the air, so thick it made Khalid's stomach want to turn over. With it came the sharper reek of smokeless powder and a vile latrine stink. People fouled themselves when they were very frightened— and when their bowels let go in death.

The Dauphin of France was down. The Prince of Wales knelt beside him, bandaging his wounded arm with cloth cut from a velvet robe. The prince's ceremonial sword lay on the ground next to him. By the way things looked, he'd used it to cut the robe. That took presence of mind. It also took a sword with a blade that had been sharpened even though it wasn't intended to leave the scabbard. Someone on the prince's staff paid attention to detail.

One Irish prince was binding up his own leg. Another lay ominously still, the blood pooling under his head even redder than his hair. However hard the assassins had tried, they hadn't slain Lorenzo III. The new Grand Duke shouted orders in Italian too fast and colloquial for Khalid to follow.

Pope Marcellus stared in horror from under the glassed-in bubble atop his armored vehicle. The thick glass bore plenty of fresh scars, but it had stopped everything that came his way.

Domenico Pacelli stared, too: up at the sun out of sightless, unblinking eyes. Khalid looked at him, then looked away. He'd taken so many bullets, he looked almost as much like a piece of chopped meat as like a man. When the shooting started, the guards must have blamed him for it. They'd paid him back the only way they knew how. If God willed it, the Corrector would be answering for his time on earth right now.

Warbling sirens and blazing red lights announced ambulances. Some of the emergency workers who jumped out of them made the sign of the cross at the carnage they faced. Then they got to work, as efficiently as their counterparts in the Muslim world might have done. They did tend to high-ranking victims and guards ahead of ordinary folk among the crowd. That might also have happened in the Maghrib or Persia.

One more shot rang out. Khalid whirled, bringing up his pistol. He lowered it again when he saw an Italian soldier standing over someone he'd just killed. "Son of a whore tried to grab for his rifle," the man yelled. "Now he can tell his story to Satan in hell."

"He should have tried to take him alive," Dawud said. "Then they could have questioned him."

"And found out what? That he was an Aquinist? That he's proud to be a martyr for his cause?" Khalid said.

His comrade sighed. "That's about it, I'm afraid."

An ambulance wailed away with the Dauphin of France and the wounded Irish lord. The Prince of Wales got to his feet. When he picked up the ceremonial sword, he held it with the air of a man who knew what to do with it. That was more than Khalid could say for himself. Catching his eye, the prince spoke in good if accented Arabic: "This is a terrible day."

"It is, sir," Khalid agreed. "You Europeans ought to do something about it, and about the people who cause such black days."

"Easier for you to say than for us to do, I fear," the Englishman replied. "Too many people in too many kingdoms will be dancing in the streets because of this. The only thing they will be sorry for is that more people who hope to bring us into the modern world did not die here."

"Then God—yours, mine, anyone's—have mercy on you," Khalid said.

He forgot about the Prince of Wales in the next moment, because Annarita Pezzola came up to look over the horrific scene. She waved away his worries, saying, "I was safe enough. I was far back in the procession. I am only a functionary, after all, and only a woman." Her mouth twisted. "I told Lorenzo he had to be mad to try to make a public ceremony out of burying his father."

"He should have listened to you," Khalid said.

"He wasn't sleeping with me." She didn't try to hide her bitterness. "Neither was Cosimo, but Lorenzo wouldn't believe that. He wouldn't pay attention to me. And so we have—this." She suddenly seemed to notice she was leaving bloody footprints. She doubled over and was sick on the sidewalk.

VI

A newsman scowled out of the television set. "By order of his Supreme Highness, Grand Duke Lorenzo, the vicious organization that calls itself the Monastic Order of Saint Thomas Aquinas is hereby proscribed throughout Italy. All its seminaries are to be closed immediately. All members of the so-called Aquinist Order who do not renounce their vows at once are subject to arrest and imprisonment and interrogation. Resistance will be punished by death without trial."

"If they'd done that thirty or forty years ago, when the Aquinists were just starting to make trouble, we wouldn't have this problem now," Khalid said in the hotel room he shared with Dawud. "Cosimo might still be alive, too."

"Or he might not, and we might still," the Jew answered. "You notice this fellow doesn't say anything about how the crackdown is going, or even if it is going anywhere outside of Rome."

Khalid sighed. "Italian television is like that." Italian TV showed what the Grand Duke wanted his people to see. How close a resemblance that bore to what was really going on was a function of the politics and personalities involved. Well, that was true everywhere, but it was much more true in Europe than in the Muslim world.

On the screen, helicopters like the ones that had flown over the funeral procession lashed the Aquinist Seminary in Rome with rockets. Smoke poured from the building. "Thus the Grand Duke punishes the enemies of the state!" the newsman shouted fiercely.

How many Aquinists were left in that seminary, though? Wouldn't it have emptied out after the assassination, and after Lorenzo seized Corrector Pacelli? The Christian fanatics were enemies, but they hadn't shown themselves to be fools.

"Reports of fighting in Bari and Naples and Bologna are strongly denied by the Grand Duke's Ministry of Information," the newsman went on. "And rail service between Milan and the Adriatic has *not* been interrupted. Construction on the line has led to a few unfortunate delays, but that is all."

Dawud looked at Khalid. Khalid looked at Dawud. They both sighed this time, on the same note. Whatever the Italian was denying, that had to be what was really going on. If a couple of foreigners could see as much, didn't he think his countrymen could, too?

Or maybe he didn't care. He was getting the official story out. When the official story was the only one the people were allowed to hear, getting it out was important business.

"In other news—" the Italian began. Before he could go on, an explosion shook the hotel. The windows rattled in their frames. One of them broke. Tinkling, sparkling shards fell in on the carpet. The broadcaster must have been in Rome, too, because his jaw dropped. *"Dio mio!"* he exclaimed, and started to cross himself, but caught himself before the gesture got very far.

"Well, well." Dawud ibn Musa sounded calm. He also sounded like a man working very hard to sound calm. "I wonder what that was. Nothing small, not by the noise it made."

"No, nothing small." Khalid also worked not to show how jittery he was. "I think it came from the direction of the Pantheon." Warm outside air full of tobacco smoke and auto exhaust started pouring into the room.

On the TV screen, a hand appeared and gave the newsman a scrap of paper. As the fellow read it, his bushy eyebrows jumped.

"That thump you may have heard even in this soundproofed building was a bomb gong off inside the Pantheon. It can only have been a time bomb, since security around the building has been impeccable since our beloved Grand Duke Cosimo was lain to rest there yesterday."

Why hadn't security at the Pantheon been impeccable *before* Grand Duke Cosimo was lain to rest there? *Because the Italians are a feckless lot*, Khalid thought sadly. They were Europeans. Despite long and close contact with the Muslim world, they remained as sloppy as anyone else in this backward corner of the world.

"The Pantheon is badly damaged, if not altogether destroyed," the newsman went on. "Thus Grand Duke Lorenzo's murderous enemies show their hatred for Italy's glorious Roman past. It is a shameful proof of how savage they are."

"I wonder what the Egyptians would do if one of their political parties blew up the Sphinx because it didn't like what the government was up to," Dawud remarked.

"Don't be silly," Khalid said. "In countries where you have political parties like that, they don't go blowing up people they don't like—or monuments from ancient days, either."

"Well, you're right," Dawud said, his plump features glum. "Which only goes to show Italy isn't a country like that. What a surprise!"

The hand passed the newsman another note. It was attached to an arm wearing a tight-sleeved Italian-style tunic. The newsman, by contrast, could have come from Alexandria or Baghdad or Seattle by his clothes: he had on a white robe and a keffiyeh.

"I am informed that, as a result of this latest outrage, Grand Duke Lorenzo has declared martial law throughout his domain," the newsman said. "All civil liberties are suspended for the duration of the crisis. Citizens are advised to comport themselves accordingly."

"Well, well," Dawud repeated, still sounding calmer than he had any business being. "Now we can wonder whether the Aquinists planted that time bomb or . . ."

He didn't go on. Khalid could see why. When the room was so likely to be bugged, Dawud had said quite enough. Too much, perhaps. If the Aquinists hadn't planted the bomb, who had? The other candidate who sprang to mind was Grand Duke Lorenzo himself. If he was looking for an excuse to declare martial law, why not hand himself one on a silver platter?

But Khalid shook his head. "I don't believe it," he said, both because he didn't want to believe it and because he did want to get his friend off the hook. "The fanatics must have done it. They don't care about pagan Rome, and they hate Lorenzo and his dynasty."

"You're bound to be right." Dawud must have realized he'd overstepped. He sent the lamp on the nightstand a genial smile.

On the television screen, the newsman was saying, "There will be a sundown-to-sunup curfew in place until further notice. Required workers will be exempt, but must have proper authorization from the police."

Without a doubt, the Aquinists would have people busy forging whatever papers "proper authorization" turned out to represent. Khalid wouldn't have been surprised if they got their documents before ordinary bakers and nurses and sanitation-plant workers and other folk who had to go out at night did. From everything he'd seen, the fanatics were more efficient than the Grand Duke's government.

The telephone rang. Khalid picked it up. *"Pronto?"*

"Annarita Pezzola here," said the voice on the other end of the line. "In light of everything that has happened, Grand Duke Lorenzo has decided he might be wise to confer with the two of you after all. Please come to the Palatine as soon as you can."

"We're on our way. Thank you," Khalid said.

"What makes you think I had anything to do with it?" she asked.

That was a question needing a long answer, and not one he wanted to give over a line probably tapped. He contented himself with saying, "Thank you for letting us know, whether you had anything to do with it or not." Then he hung up.

"Where are we on our way to?" Dawud inquired.

"Lorenzo's decided he *does* want to talk to us," Khalid said.

"Happy day. I'm not more than five-eighths sure I want to talk to him." But Dawud heaved his bulk up off the bed. Pausing only to light a cigar, he followed Khalid out of their room and toward the elevator.

Rome looked and felt like a city at war. Soldiers and policemen had sprouted on street corners the way toadstools popped up in a shady meadow after a rain. Unlike toadstools, the nervous-looking young men carried automatic weapons. Before too long, some of them would get the jitters and start shooting up cars and passersby for no good reason. Khalid hoped they didn't start on the taxi that carried him and Dawud to the Grand Duke's palace.

No, not to the palace. Toward it. Roadblocks made the driver stop several furlongs farther from the base of the Palatine Hill than they'd managed when they went to Cosimo's ill-fated banquet.

Khalid's legs wobbled with nerves as he approached the hard-faced men behind the roadblock. No nerves from them: only watchful waiting. They would have been Cosimo's elite guards, now serving a new master. He hoped his robes kept them from noting the wobble.

When he gave his name and Dawud's to a sergeant, the under-officer used a field telephone to check with the palace. Lowering the handset, the man nodded. "People by your names are expected, yes," he said. "Now I need to see your documents, and we'll frisk you."

The documents passed muster. The frisking . . . "If I were a woman and you did that to me, you'd have to marry me afterwards," Dawud said.

"If you were a woman and I did that to you, I'd enjoy it more," the sergeant retorted. They grinned at each other.

When the Maghribis actually got to the palace, a different set of guards checked their papers and searched them. They were as thorough as the first batch had been. At last, scowling like dogs that wanted to bite but were ordered not to, they let the investigators go on.

Along with a squad of soldiers, Annarita Pezzola waited inside the entranceway. "I will take you to his Supreme Highness," she said, first in Italian and then in classical Arabic. The foreign language made the soldiers scowl.

"*Grazie,*" Khalid said. At his Italian, the armed men in mottled uniforms relaxed as much as they were ever likely to.

This was the same entrance he and Dawud had used on their way to the banquet, but they went in an entirely different direction. Khalid began to get some notion of just how vast the Grand Duke's palace was. Some windows gave views of blooming gardens—paradises, the Persians would have called them. Then the hallways, though still crowded with art, stopped having windows. Were they dug back into the Palatine Hill? That was how it seemed to Khalid. How far into it? He didn't know, but if the ground above was shielded with lead and reinforced concrete a man might ride out a nuclear strike here.

Partly thinking along with him, Dawud said, "I'm glad I'm not the kind who worries about how much weight is pressing on the roof over his head." He used Italian, to keep from making Lorenzo's guards any more nervous than they were already.

That made *Signorina* Pezzola glance over at him. "You speak my language better than I thought you did," she said.

Dawud shrugged. If they checked, he'd given himself away at the roadblock. "Thanks," was all he said.

She started to say something more, then shrugged and let it go. After a few more turns, she stopped at an unmarked door. It might have been a broom closet, only a broom closet wouldn't have had more tough men with serious weapons standing in front of it.

Annarita Pezzola knocked on the door. There was no audible answer, but a little red light winked on next to the doorway. Seeing it, one of the guardsmen turned to work the latch.

Inside, behind an ornate, massive marble-topped desk that must have belonged to his father, sat Grand Duke Lorenzo III. His uniform carried fewer showy medals than the one Cosimo had worn. He didn't look at home in it the way the older man had, either.

As the door swung shut, he nodded to Khalid and Dawud. "You are the men from the Maghrib," he said. His Arabic was good enough, though not on a par with his father's or Annarita's.

"That's right, your Supreme Highness." The pompous title of respect tasted odd in Khalid's mouth. Such flowery honorifics had fallen out of fashion a couple of hundred years earlier on the southern shore of the Mediterranean.

"My father asked you to come here because he feared the rising tide of fanaticism," Lorenzo said. His mouth twisted. "He did not take fright soon enough, did he? What can you do to help me bring my realm back under my hand? There's madness in the air."

"How bad is it outside of Rome, sir?" Dawud asked.

"Worse than it is here. Quite a bit worse." Lorenzo didn't pretend not to know what the Jew was talking about. Khalid gave him points for that. The young Grand Duke went on, "In Rome, the army and the security forces and the police have things under control."

"They're sitting on things, you mean," Dawud said.

Lorenzo III nodded, unembarrassed. "That's right. I don't have so many loyal troops out in the provinces, and the police there. . . ." He looked as if he'd bitten into a piece of bad fish. "In the provinces, a lot of the constabulary would sooner follow the Aquinists than me. Milan is mostly behind me. Turin also—I think. Some of the other northern towns, I know they are screaming 'God wills it!' as loud as they can. And down in the south, they always listen to priests and monks before they pay any attention to the state. How is a man supposed to rule a realm like that?"

He meant it as a rhetorical question. Khalid answered it anyhow: "Carefully, your Supreme Highness."

Cosimo would have understood him. Cosimo had ruled Italy for more than twenty-five years. He'd spent most of that time nudging his country toward the modern world that beckoned from the far side of the Mediterranean. He'd gone step by step, sometimes digit by digit. When priests or Aquinist monks made his people raise an uproar, he'd taken a step back and waited. He wasn't in a hurry.

And what had it got him in the end? A tomb in the Pantheon, a tomb wrecked by a—probably—Aquinist time bomb. He'd moved Italy forward, but he would never see it become an ordinary country like the Maghrib or Arkansistan.

In France, King Jean XXIII played the same cautious game. His fundament still warmed the cushions on his throne. But his son lay in a hospital here in Rome. Both Jean and the Dauphin had to hope the guards in and around the hospital followed the Grand Duke, not the late Corrector.

Lorenzo . . . Lorenzo all but spat on the vast expanse of polished marble in front of him. "I am in no mood to be careful. My father was careful, and they killed him anyhow. If they want to play those games, they will see I can kill them, too. They will see I am not afraid to do it, either."

"Your Supreme Highness, what will a civil war do to Italy?" Annarita Pezzola asked. "Even if you win it, what kind of land will you have afterwards?"

"That *is* the question," Khalid agreed. An Italy where most of the people hated their modernizing Grand Duke? A ruler could make a desert, but these days he couldn't call it peace after he made it. He would never be able to stop watching his own back, lest he get what Cosimo had got.

An Italy like that also wouldn't keep its troubles to itself. It would help inflame the rest of Western Europe. And, because its economy would be ruined, swarms of young Italians would go looking for work in the Muslim world. How many of them would be Aquinists, or people the Aquinists could seduce? More than a few; Khalid was only too sure of that.

"If I lose the war, or if I cannot govern Italy, what kind of country will it be?" Lorenzo retorted. He eyed Annarita. "I see why my father listened to you. You worry as much as he did."

She bowed her head. "May I have your leave to withdraw, your Supreme Highness?" she asked in a low voice. The Grand Duke nodded brusquely. She walked from the room without looking back.

"Now we have only men here," Lorenzo said to Khalid and Dawud, as if that was important to him. "If we are going to knock the head off this adder, how do we go about it?"

"Making sure you can before you start to try may not be the worst idea I ever heard," Dawud answered.

Lorenzo looked at him. "*Et tu, Brute?*" he said sourly. The Latin meant nothing to Dawud, or to Khalid. Seeing as much, the Grand Duke threw his hands in the air in disgust and went back to Arabic: "It means 'You, too, Brutus?' It's what Julius Caesar said when he saw that Brutus, who he'd thought was his friend, was one of the men sticking knives in him."

"I don't want to stick a knife in you, sir," Dawud said. "I don't want any of the people you think are your friends to stab you, either. Or the people you know are your enemies. Anybody."

"I believe you," Lorenzo said. "The Maghrib had better want to keep me alive. You can be sure I won't sell Italy out to the Aquinists. Anyone else you get, you won't be able to count on him for that."

Not even your brother? Khalid wondered. But that was a question he didn't ask. He also didn't let his face show it had crossed his mind. When you were dealing with someone who'd gained power by right of birth, you had to remember he feared losing it every moment, not just when the next election rolled around. And to whom would he fear losing it more than to the man who stood next in line?

Wearing European clothes and broad-brimmed hats to help obscure their faces, Khalid and Dawud approached the Maghrib's embassy in Rome. The Italian policemen guarding the embassy scowled at them. Europeans were more likely to be dangerous than men from the Muslim world.

Their scowls deepened when Khalid used his bad Italian to say, "We have an appointment with the ambassador." He gave his name and Dawud's; they both displayed their papers.

Most literate men could read the Arabic alphabet, even if their language didn't use it. One of the policemen showed he could. After studying the travel documents and identity cards, he telephoned into the embassy. His Arabic was like Khalid's Italian: far from wonderful, but enough to get the job done. When he hung up, he nodded to the two Maghribis. "You can go in," he said, still in Arabic. He even held the entrance gate open for them.

Though the Italians hadn't searched them, their own country-men did. Only after they passed muster were they escorted into the presence of Umar ibn Abd-al-Aziz, the Sultan's envoy to the Grand Duchy of Italy.

Umar was short, slim, and balding. He had to be in his late fif-ties; his beard and the fringe of hair he still owned were going from gray to white. The pouches under his red-tracked eyes said he'd seen a good many complications, and expected to see quite a few more.

"Well, gentlemen, I heard you were in the country," he said. "How can we best steer Italy toward something this side of civil war?"

Khalid and Dawud exchanged dismayed looks. "We were hop-ing you'd tell us, your Excellency," Khalid said. "We had a meet-ing with Lorenzo yesterday afternoon. He seems ready to start one himself."

"Not just ready," Dawud said. "Eager." Khalid nodded, accept-ing the correction.

The ambassador looked pained. "I've heard the same thing. I was hoping you would tell me it was wrong. Doesn't he see that one of the risks of starting a civil war is losing it?"

"Sir, I would be amazed if that's crossed his mind," Khalid an-swered. This time, Dawud nodded.

Umar ibn Abd-al-Aziz sighed. "And doesn't he see that his fight may not stay a civil war?"

"You don't suppose he'd start something to get all the Italians, or most of them, behind him?" Khalid said in alarm. He supposed Lorenzo could. Sicily had belonged to the Maghrib for centuries, but plenty of people here still saw it as an unredeemed part of their homeland. Italian lords and lordlings had banged that drum before, more than once.

But Umar shook his head. "That isn't what I meant. With the Aquinists fighting Lorenzo here, they're liable to call for warriors of the cross from all over Europe to come give them a hand."

"Crusaders." Dawud ibn Musa spoke the word with distaste. Waves of them had invaded the Holy Land long before. Other waves drove the Muslims out of most of Spain. They'd fought against pagans, too . . . and, fairly often, killed Jews who got in their way for the sport of it.

These days, the disaffected young Christian men who crashed planes or blew up themselves and their neighbors in cities across the Muslim world often called themselves Crusaders. Like their long-dead coreligionists, they saw themselves as holy warriors, certain of heaven if they died fighting people they believed to be infidels.

"Can they call a Crusade against other Christians?" Khalid asked.

"I've been looking into that. I think they can," Umar said. "They've done it before, against people whose style of Christianity they didn't fancy. Some of their squabbles made the quarrels between Sunnis and Shiites seem like garden parties by comparison. . . . Are you laughing at me, Dawud?"

"Not very hard, your Excellency," the investigator answered. "Jews go after people they think are misbelievers, too. Who doesn't?"

"I haven't seen them bombing public buildings," Khalid said.

"Probably just a matter of time," Dawud said. "They can take lessons from the Christians, I'm sure. Why not? All those years ago, the Christians took lessons from us." He didn't say anything about Muslims' taking lessons from Jews. In his own strange way, he was a polite man.

"You've spoken with the Pope, haven't you?" Umar ibn Abd-al-Aziz said.

"Yes, your Excellency," Khalid replied. Whoever had briefed the ambassador had done a good job.

"If Marcellus condemns a Crusade against Lorenzo and Italy, that may help some," Umar said. "Some of the fanatics would sooner follow the Aquinists' preachers than the Pope, but not all of them. And I think—I hope—Marcellus would do that. For a Christian, he's a decent man."

"Marcellus would be a decent man if he were a Buddhist or a pagan," Dawud ibn Musa said. Perhaps because he wasn't fully a part of the Muslim world himself, he noticed condescension sooner than those who swam untroubled through those waters.

Umar coughed. "Well, I suppose he would be, yes," he allowed after a tiny pause.

Dawud went on as if the ambassador hadn't spoken: "Who knows? Marcellus might even be a decent man if he were a Muslim. You never can tell." He beamed at Umar with a childlike innocence they all knew wasn't real.

After another pause—this one longer—Umar managed to smile back. "I had heard that you enjoyed being difficult," he murmured.

"Ah, well," Dawud said airily. "You hear all kinds of things. What turns out to be true, that's a different story. It is a lot of the time, anyway, isn't it?"

Was he talking about the amount of truth in Judaism, Christianity, and Islam? If he was, no one could prove it. As far as Khalid was concerned, that was bound to be just as well. This time, Umar ibn Abd-al-Aziz smiled without having to work himself up to it. "I submit to your superior wisdom," he said.

Islam meant *submission*. Dawud grinned, acknowledging the hit. "So which important fellow did you offend with your wit, sir, to make them pack you off to Rome?" he asked.

"This isn't exile for me, even if it does seem that way sometimes," Umar answered. "For the record, I asked the Wazir to send me here. I hoped I could do some good. For a while, I thought I *was* doing some good. And then—"

As if on cue, a large explosion rattled the embassy. It wasn't so close as the Pantheon had been to the investigators' hotel. No glass fell from the windows. But it also wasn't the kind of noise that would reassure anyone about the gentleness of his fellow men.

"We fought bigger wars than this, your Excellency," Khalid said: the best consolation he could offer.

"Yes. We did." Umar sighed. "Have you run across any of the Aquinist broadsheets that admire Faruq al-Ghaznavi and say the Christians ought to adopt his methods?"

"Tell me you're making that up!" Dawud ibn Musa spoke before Khalid could find words.

"I only wish I were," Umar said. "The greatest murderer the world has ever seen, and the one who slaughtered all those Tamils for no better reason than that they *were* Tamils . . . The Aquinists want to be like him."

"Up till now, I had trouble stomaching Cosimo and Lorenzo," Khalid said. "Not any more. The difference between bad and worse is bigger than the one between good and better."

"Sometimes it's bigger than the difference between bad and good," Dawud said. "Most of the rest of the world ganged up on Faruq, and didn't worry about anything else till later."

"The difference is, once Faruq was beaten, his army surrendered and the war was over," Khalid said. "The Aquinists don't work that way. Taking out Domenico Pacelli won't make them all give up. It'll make some of them fight harder than ever. We'll have to keep watch against . . . Crusaders for another lifetime, maybe for another hundred years."

"I fear you're right," Umar ibn Abd-al-Aziz said. His sharp gaze swung toward Dawud once more. "You find something in all this that amuses you?"

"Only that I'd hate to be an investigator with nothing left to investigate, your Excellency." Dawud lit a cigar and puffed before finishing, "Doesn't look like I'll need to worry about that for a while, does it?"

The ambassador shook his head. "No. It doesn't."

Going through Rome in native costume showed Khalid how split the city was. Many people—probably most people—wanted nothing more than to go about their business. Here and there, they managed to do it. Some neighborhoods might never have heard that Cosimo was dead and the Aquinists in arms against his son and successor. Venders sold olives and mushrooms and tomatoes and pasta. The last wasn't much eaten in the Maghrib, though Khalid had liked it well enough when he tried it here.

A man who laid tiles was arguing with a housewife about how a floor should go and how much it should cost. Even more than it would have in Tunis or Algiers, that turned into street theater. Friends and neighbors came out to watch the fur fly and to stick in their own two coppers' worth.

Less than half a parasang away, a throng of pro-Aquinists—not quite a mob, but on the way—marched through the streets. "God wills it!" they bawled in ragged chorus. Police were trying to hold them back with shields and billy clubs. "God wills it!" the angry young men roared again.

One of the policemen roared, too, through a bullhorn: "Break it up! You are violating the Grand Duke's martial-law decree! This is your first, last, and only warning!"

Rocks and bottles flew toward him. "God wills it!" Yes, that was a mob now.

For a few seconds, the police fired into the air. Then one of them went down, hit in the face by half a brick or a cobblestone. At that, they opened up on the crowd. More makeshift weapons answered them. Some of those bottles were full of gasoline, with lighted cloth wicks to set it ablaze when the glass smashed. Some of the people in the crowd had firearms of their own, and shot back at the policemen.

When a bullet cracked by over Dawud's head, he said, "I don't want to stick around here any more."

"Now that you mention it, neither do I," Khalid said. They scurried back around a corner. Riots were interesting to watch from a safe distance, in the same way the quarrels of bears in a zoo might have been. When the distance you were watching them from turned out not to be so safe, and when there weren't any bars between the animals and you, hastening elsewhere looked like a great idea.

More policemen hurried forward to reinforce their comrades. "Let's see your papers, you two!" one of them growled at Khalid and Dawud.

"Here you are, sir." Khalid moved slowly and carefully. He didn't want the Italian to think he was reaching for a weapon. Dawud was just as cautious. Alarming a man who was pointing a submachine gun at you looked like a losing proposition.

The policeman stared at their documents. "I'm supposed to believe you assholes are from the Maghrib?" he growled.

"I hope you do," Khalid answered. "Could I speak Italian this bad if I grew up here?" That last should have been a subjunctive, but he couldn't remember how to make it.

"I ought to run you in and let my captain figure out what the devil you are," the policeman said. Then he thought about it; Khalid could all but see the gears meshing inside his head. He jerked his thumb away from the tumult ahead. "But I gotta help my *amici*. So go on—beat it. And stay the hell out of this part of town if you know what's good for you." He trotted away.

Khalid and Dawud hurried back toward the neighborhood where people argued about tiling a kitchen floor and not about God's will. "*Do* you know what's good for you?" Khalid asked.

"Well, I wouldn't mind a big house in Tunis, a pile of money in the bank, and a beautiful girlfriend who thought I was the sexiest man alive," Dawud said. "I'm not sure all that would be good for me, you understand, but I'd like to find out. How about you?"

"You could do a lot worse than that. Or I think so, anyhow," Khalid said. "Of course, if you asked an Aquinist, he'd tell you it was doing the things that got you into heaven and sending every-body who disagreed with you to hell."

"You didn't ask an Aquinist. You asked me," Dawud said. "Then again, if a lot of Aquinists had a big house and money and a girl-friend who thought they were great, they wouldn't be Aquinists any more."

"That's true." Khalid nodded. Europe's poverty and backward-ness went a long way toward turning people into fanatics. A long way, but not all the way. "The scary thing is, some of them still would be."

Behind them, a machine gun hammered out a long burst. Screams cut through the stutter of the murder mill. Khalid had trouble thinking of any ruler in the Muslim world who would turn machine guns on his own people. Then again, he had trouble think-ing of any ruler in the Muslim world who would need to.

When he said so, Dawud ibn Musa shook his head. "You never can tell," he said. "If trouble started in the European quarter of some of our cities, it might take machine guns to quiet things down."

Khalid thought about that. He didn't need long. "I hate to admit it, but you're right."

They took a roundabout route back to their hotel. Almost any route in Rome was roundabout. The streets weren't on any kind of grid. If Khalid had to guess, they followed cow tracks from the days before Rome first became a great city—or any kind of city at all.

Soldiers steered them away from one turn into a risky part of town they might have made. One of the soldiers snarled some-thing at them in a back-country dialect even Dawud couldn't follow. A sergeant cuffed the soldier the way a farmer might cuff a mean dog. How loyal to Grand Duke Lorenzo was that skinny young man? How close to yelling *God wills it!* was he? And to opening up on his squadmates? Khalid was glad he didn't find out then and there.

His feet hurt by the time they finally got to the hotel. He was surprised to see Annarita Pezzola sitting in the lobby reading a newspaper. He went over to her. "Does the Grand Duke need something else from us?" he asked.

"I don't know," she said, her voice expressionless.

"Huh?" Later, Khalid kicked himself for being slow on the uptake.

"I don't know," Annarita repeated. "I am no longer in the Grand Duke's service."

VII

"What? Why not?" Khalid couldn't believe his ears. "If he's canned you, he's . . . making a mistake." He almost said *He's too stupid to live*, but that wouldn't do, not where he might be overheard or recorded.

"He did not dismiss me," *Signorina* Pezzola said. "I offered my resignation, and he decided to accept it." She was also choosing her words with care.

"I'm very sorry to hear that," Khalid said. "You did his father a lot of good. You could have done more for him—he doesn't have the experience Cosimo did."

Annarita shrugged. "I'm afraid not. He did not care to listen to me. That being so, I saw no point to shouting into the wind, so to speak."

"I see." One of the things Khalid saw was that she was holding herself together by main force of will. He admired that; it was what someone from his side of the Mediterranean would have tried to do. Here, people were more inclined to let themselves go.

"Which brings us to the next interesting question." Dawud ibn Musa spoke with a certain somber relish. "What are you doing *here*? Why did you come to us instead of crying in your family's *vino*? I know that's two interesting questions, but you can do them together if you want."

"Dawud—" Khalid's voice had an edge to it.

But Annarita raised a hand and cut him off. "It's all right," she said. "I don't know if they're interesting questions, but they're important ones. Even if his Supreme Highness doesn't want to listen to me, I still may know some things he needs to hear. If they come from you, he has a decent chance of paying attention to them. For one thing, you're Maghribis. For another—"

"We're men," Khalid finished for her.

"That's right." She nodded.

"It still matters on our side of the sea, too," Khalid said. "Not as much and not as often as it does here, but it matters. It shouldn't, but—"

Now Annarita Pezzola interrupted him: "On your side of the Mediterranean, at least you see it shouldn't matter. Not here. Here they say things have always gone one way, so they should keep on going that way till the end of time."

"Congratulations," Dawud said. Khalid and Annarita gave him almost identical odd looks. After rolling his eyes at how dense they were, he deigned to explain: "Even if Corrector Pacelli were still alive, he couldn't sum up the Aquinists' program any better in one sentence."

"Oh," she said. "Thank you, but I could do without the honor."

"How about doing with some supper?" Dawud said. "I don't know about Khalid, but dogging fanatics all afternoon's given me an appetite."

"I could eat," Khalid said.

"I can always eat." Dawud patted his belly. He looked heavier in a tight European tunic than he did wearing the robes of the international style. He went on, "But by now I've got an appetite."

"Do the two of you mind if I order from what you would call the *haram* side of the kitchen?" Annarita asked.

Khalid shook his head. Dawud said, "Not even a little bit." His prohibitions weren't the same as Khalid's, though they had points in common. He followed or flouted them as he pleased, the way most people who belonged to the international civilization did, whether they were Muslims or not.

In the hotel restaurant, they got the waiter who'd tried to tempt them with forbidden food as if it were filthy pictures. The man smirked when Annarita chose slow-cooked pork ribs slathered in a sauce made of tomatoes and hot peppers from the Sunset Lands. Khalid ordered chicken. Dawud asked for spaghetti and meatballs.

"We can make those meatballs with ground pork, if you want." The waiter sounded as oily as any pimp ever hatched.

Dawud took it in stride. "Thanks, but don't bother," he said. "I like beef better."

They all ordered wine. That revived the waiter's sneer, but only a little. Some Muslims flicked out a drop before raising their glasses, so they could truthfully say they had not drunk one drop of wine. Khalid didn't waste the time or the wine. He worried about the hereafter less than the here-and-now.

"Peace be unto us," he said, and tasted his white.

"Unto us, peace," Dawud and Annarita echoed. They also drank. Annarita added, "The Grand Duchy needs peace."

"The whole world does," Dawud said. "How do we get it, though? Short of killing everybody who doesn't think the way we do, I mean. Faruq tried that, and it didn't work so well."

"No, you can't kill everyone who disagrees with you," she said. "But if the people who disagree with you want to kill you because you disagree with them, what are you supposed to do about that?"

"'Behold, how good and how pleasant it is for brethren to dwell together in unity!'" Dawud said. Annarita nodded. To Khalid, the Jew explained, "That's from the Book of Psalms in the Bible."

"Thanks." Not surprisingly, Khalid knew the holy book of the Jews and Christians less well than his own, and he wasn't anywhere close to being fully familiar with the Qur'an, either. He went on, "That would be good and pleasant, if only brethren could manage to do it."

Dawud wagged a finger at him. "If you're going to complain about every little thing . . ."

★   ★   ★

The guards who manned a perimeter outside the Aquinist Seminary in Rome these days belonged to the Grand Duke's army, not to the fanatical monastic order. The building itself had also changed since the last time Khalid and Dawud visited it. Most of the windows were shattered; shards of glass sparkled on the sidewalks and streets. Smoke streaked the outer walls. Here and there, rockets had punched holes in the building.

All the same, Major Badoglio said, "We took too many casualties clearing this place. We had to do it floor by floor, sometimes room by room. We didn't bring out many prisoners, either. The Aquinists fought to the death."

Khalid believed him. The stench of death still wafted out of the seminary, though most of the bodies had been cleared. He said, "I hope you got a big enough intelligence haul to pay you back for the lives you spent."

"We've made some finds," the officer from the Ministry of Information . . . agreed? How much of what they had found was the Ministry not sharing with the Maghrib? If Khalid was any judge of such things, Italy would hold back as much as it could.

"Didn't I hear that the Aquinists had a couple of time bombs in and under the seminary?" Dawud asked.

"Yes, that's true," Major Badoglio said. "Our disposal units got to both of them before they could go off." He smiled a thin smile. "Obviously, or the place wouldn't still be standing."

"Are they sure they found them all?" Khalid asked.

"I wouldn't be going in there with you if I didn't think they had," the major answered. Khalid had to be content with that—either be content with it or turn around and head the other way as fast as he could.

Having Badoglio with them helped get the Maghribis through the military checkpoints. Once inside the seminary, Khalid wrinkled his nose. The death smell was stronger indoors. It mingled with the chemical reek of burned paint and a more ordinary sour-smoke odor.

Soldiers had shot up the image of Saint Thomas Aquinas near the elevators. That of Christ stern in judgment next to it had taken only a couple of probably accidental bullets.

Major Badoglio and the investigators trudged up the stairs; the electricity in the seminary was out. Hallways far from windows were dark. Badoglio's flashlight pierced the gloom like a spear of brightness. Daylight reached into some of the hallways through open doors.

Inside one of those open-doored rooms, a young lieutenant was going through file cabinets. He looked disgusted at what he was finding. "The stinking Aquinists worked as hard at getting rid of their papers as they did at fighting our men," he complained.

That Aquinists had fought in the room, Khalid couldn't doubt. Bullet holes pocked and scarred the walls and ceiling. Heavy black bloodstains in one corner said a man had probably bled to death there.

The lieutenant went on, "Some of these, they set on fire. Some are soaked. Whether they did that or our people did it trying to douse the fire, I'm not sure. And some of the files have had fire extinguishers sprayed over them. That doesn't do the paper or what was on it any good, either."

"Files and papers in desks are like this all through the seminary," Giacomo Badoglio said. "It's one of the main reasons we haven't come up with more on the fanatics here."

"What might another main reason be?" Khalid asked. One that sprang to mind was Aquinists secretly working inside the Ministry of Information. How much of the incriminating evidence that did turn up disappeared before it saw the full light of day?

If Major Badoglio realized what he asked with the question, the Italian didn't show it. "Well, if you come up another couple of floors, you'll see one of the reasons," Badoglio replied.

Going up another couple of floors wasn't easy. The Aquinists had barricaded the stairway. Grand Duke Lorenzo's forces needed to blast them out of the way with rocket-propelled grenades. Those had been invented to kill tanks. They were also wonderful for things like smashing bunkers.

Again, smoke and blood stained the stairwell. Some of the grenades had wrecked the stairs along with the office furniture and file cabinets the Aquinists used to block them. Khalid could see that the records in those cabinets wouldn't be worth excavating. Grand Duke Lorenzo's sappers had had to lay metal ramps over the shattered stairs. Major Badoglio climbed them as gracefully as a mountain sheep. Khalid managed. Dawud made heavy going of it. Khalid reached out and yanked his colleague up the last cubit or so.

"I thank you." Dawud might not be graceful, but he hung on to his aplomb.

When they went out onto the fifth floor, just about all of it looked like the stairwell. Much of it was burned out. The Aquinists had set up more barricades at the corners in the hallway. Some of the walls between rooms had holes in them. The stink of smoke was stronger here. So was the stink of death. Until you'd seen the aftermath of modern war, you didn't realize how many chunks could come off a body or how hard it was to gather up all of them.

"Not much useful information here," Badoglio said, his voice dry.

"Yes, I can see that," Khalid answered. "But what are the top floors like? The ones where the Corrector and the other important Aquinists worked?"

"The rockets from our helicopters did more damage up there than lower down," Badoglio said. "We're still going through them, though. If you want to walk back to the stairs, you're welcome to see for yourself."

"We'll do that, yes," Khalid said. Dawud sent him a wounded look, but didn't complain out loud.

No sooner had they got back to the stairwell, though, than the bellow of a man on a bullhorn echoed up from below. "Clear the building!" the fellow shouted in Italian. "Everybody out! Right away! They've found another bomb down in the cellar!"

"Well, shit!" Dawud said. Major Badoglio crossed himself. Both responses amounted to about the same thing.

They went down much faster than they'd gone up. That was partly because they had gravity on their side. It was also because they had fear on their side. Dawud skipped down the metal ramp as nimbly as someone who did such things every day.

The foyer was crowded, with everybody trying to get out at once. Khalid caught an elbow or two and threw an elbow or two. He let out a long sigh of relief when he was out in the sunshine once more. Maybe the Italian bomb-disposal men could keep this bomb from going off, too. But he didn't want to find out they couldn't the hard way.

Soldiers around the Aquinas Seminary were already trotting away from it. Some of them were frankly running away from it. Khalid trotted along with Major Badoglio and Dawud. He wanted to break into a sprint. Until they did, though, he wouldn't. His fear of getting squashed like a cockroach under a sandal was somehow less than his fear of seeming a coward in front of men whose good opinion mattered to him.

He'd gone two or three hundred cubits when the ground lurched under his feet, staggering him. He'd been in earthquakes in Tunis. This reminded him of one of those. But it was at the same time smaller and more concentrated. Behind him, the Aquinist Seminary dropped, almost as neatly as if wreckers had used explosives to bring it down.

"*Dannazione!*" Major Badoglio shouted, before returning to calmer Arabic: "The Grand Duchy just lost some good men in there."

Khalid had done some dangerous things in his time. Trying to dispose of bombs? As far as he was concerned, that was nothing better than slow suicide. No doubt the world was a better, safer place because some men were brave or harebrained enough to think otherwise. But one of the rare ones who'd lived to retire to teaching the trade wrote a memoir he called *I Am a Fugitive from the Law of Averages.*

A wind full of dust and gravel shoved Khalid hard from behind. He staggered again, and almost fell. A chunk of concrete the size of his fist thumped down half a cubit in front of his right foot. Had its flight been only a little different, it would have smashed in his skull and stretched him out dead on the sidewalk. What made it go the way it did instead of the other way? He had no idea why. No one could have any idea why, save possibly God. Was it any wonder that writers sometimes spun stories around such might-have-beens?

Coughing, his eyes streaming, he lurched around a corner. That got him out of the worst of the windstorm from the fallen building. He saw he stood in front of a streetside coffee shop. The Italian who ran it stared, wide-eyed, at the chaos.

"Give me a glass of water, *Signor*, please," Khalid said. Automatically, the man did. Khalid drank some of it, swished it in his mouth, and spat it out on the sidewalk. The stream that came from his mouth was brown, which surprised him not at all. He poured the rest of the water into his eyes and over his face. If it got his clothes wet, he didn't care.

"That's a good idea," Dawud said. "*Signor*, let me have a glass, too." Major Badoglio nodded. The man handed one to each of them. They both imitated what Khalid had done. After a beat, the Italian man who ran the coffee shop rinsed out his own mouth.

"You said you didn't think the Aquinists would have put three booby traps in the seminary." Khalid spoke to Major Badoglio in accusing tones. Then he coughed again. He couldn't swish water around in his lungs.

Badoglio bowed his head. "My master will forgive me, I beg," he said in the most formal, flowery Arabic Khalid had ever heard from him. "No doubt my master, being among the wisest of all men ever born, has never once found himself mistaken."

Dawud chuckled. "He's got you, Khalid." Then he coughed, too.

"Hrmp," Khalid said. He had trouble meeting Badoglio's eye. "All right. You made your point. You put your neck on the line along with mine."

"And mine," Dawud added. Fresh crashes came from behind them as more of the Aquinas Seminary collapsed.

"Oh, who cares about a Jew's neck?" Khalid said. Dawud laughed. If Khalid hadn't been sure Dawud would laugh, he wouldn't have made the crack. Major Badoglio couldn't have got away with it. Friends could tell jokes that got acquaintances punched in the teeth. They could . . . as long as they didn't do it too often.

When Khalid imagined a European interrogation room, his mind conjured up something terrifying and medieval. Darkness. Bars on the door. Lice and fleas. Thumbscrews. Pincers heating in a brazier. Maybe even the horror of an Iron Maiden.

All of which only proved he'd watched too many bad movies. The interrogation room in which he sat in the Ministry of Information in Rome could have come straight out of the Bureau of Investigations' headquarters in Tunis. A plain table separated the suspect on one side from his questioners on the other: Khalid, Dawud, Major Badoglio, and a captain named Paolo Salgari. Suspect and questioners all sat on cheap, functional chairs.

Yes, the suspect was manacled. Yes, his feet were chained to the floor. That might also have been done with a dangerous man in Tunis. Yes, he was tonsured and wore the black robe of an Aquinist monk. Sadly, these days that also might have happened in Tunis.

Major Badoglio didn't walk to the far side of the table and start slapping the prisoner around. He just opened a notebook. "State your name for the record," he said.

"I am called Father Martino of Padua," the Aquinist answered. He showed no signs of having been abused before he was brought here.

Badoglio wrote it down—from left to right, of course. "State your birth name as well," he said.

"I was born Andrea Assarotti," Father Martino said. Badoglio wrote that down, too, along with his date of birth (which he gave in the Christian calendar, not the more widely used Hijra reckoning) and his birthplace: yes, Padua.

That done, Badoglio said, "All right. Let's get down to business. You are charged with plotting against the Grand Duchy of Italy and with rebellion against your lawful sovereign. With treason, in other words. We can take you out and shoot you anytime we please."

He wouldn't have been so blunt in Tunis. Even Aquinist monks had certain rights there. They could have a lawyer with them while they faced interrogation, for instance. They weren't required to answer questions that pointed toward their guilt. This room might look like its equivalent across the Mediterranean, but the medieval world lived on inside it.

Father Martino's answer sounded distinctly medieval, too: "I do not recognize your authority to judge me, or the authority of the Grand Duchy. I recognize only the superiority of my monastic superiors, and of God."

"You may not recognize the state, but the state recognizes you," Dawud said. "And the state is suppressing the Aquinist Order, so the people who were your superiors have no authority over anybody."

The monk's eyes blazed. "I don't have to listen to lies from a stinking Jew."

"As a matter of fact, you do," Dawud answered mildly. "And it's interesting you know I am one. Right this minute, though, I promise I smell better than you do. I'm not lying, either. I'm also not here because I'm a Jew. I'm here because what you're up to worries my country along with the Grand Duchy."

"How *do* you know this man is a Jew, Father?" Captain Salgari asked.

"How? One look at him and you can tell," Father Martino answered, adding, "I say that only because it's so plain, not because you have any right to question me."

"You say that because you think you can get away with lying," Khalid said in his clumsy Italian. "He looks not much different to—different from?—a Muslim Maghribi like me. He also looks not much different from Italians." He nodded toward Salgari, who was dark and had a beaky nose.

"Your lies come from the Father of Lies," Martino of Padua said. "I would sooner hearken to our Lord and Savior."

"Would you sooner hearken to our Holy Father, the Pope?" Major Badoglio asked.

Khalid dared hope Martino of Padua would say yes. The Christians had a much more formal religious hierarchy than Muslims used. Clerical officials owed obedience to their superiors, and Marcellus IX was superior to everyone else. But the monk cautiously answered, "What are you talking about?" He wasn't going to commit to anything sight unseen.

He didn't have to. Badoglio unfolded a sheet of stationery with the Papal arms embossed at the top. He passed it across the table to Father Martino. The Aquinist could use his hands to position it where he could read it. The major explained it anyway: "His Holiness commands all members of the Aquinist Order to obey and cooperate with the secular authorities in the Grand Duchy of Italy. The edict, as you will see, bears his signature and his seal."

Father Martino finished reading the document, then looked up at the security man. "This does not bind me. For one thing, I do not know that the signature and seal are genuine. For another, even if they are, that would only prove the Pope has lapsed into heresy. I am not obliged to obey a heretic. I put my soul in peril if I do."

"You put your body in danger if you disobey his Holiness," Captain Salgari said. "That gives us more reason to treat you the way you deserve."

"You have me. You will do what you will do," the monk said with bleak courage. "I can't stop you. All I can do is pray that God will grant me strength to bear what I must bear. In the world to come, I will see Him in heaven. Satan's demons will torment you in hell."

He sounded sure of himself, sure enough to send a small chill through Khalid. This wasn't the first fanatic's interrogation he'd been a part of—far from it. Sometimes they broke. Sometimes, in spite of everything you did to them, they wouldn't.

Major Badoglio steepled his fingers. "We know from others that you were involved in planting Maria Conti in the Grand Duke's palace." That was the name of the serving girl who'd blown herself up, and Cosimo with her.

"I deny it," Father Martino said.

Badoglio stood, walked around the table, and stopped next to the Aquinist. He slapped him in the face. You would not have seen that in an interrogation room in the Maghrib. Khalid shook his head. You should not have seen that in an interrogation room there. Investigators being human, it did happen now and again. The Italian major took it for granted. He slapped Martino of Padua again, harder. "Don't waste our time with lies. We will make you sorry."

"I *am* sorry—sorry you follow the godless ones. It will cost your soul endless suffering," the Aquinist said.

"We are not godless. Only a fool would say we are," Captain Salgari snapped.

"You are so godless, you have no idea how godless you are." As Father Martino spoke, a thin line of red dribbled down from the corner of his mouth. He went on, "You worship the Grand Duke. You worship the state. You worship howitzers and helicopters. You worship filthy films and foul music. You worship Mammon. You do not render unto God the things that are God's."

"Mammon?" Khalid whispered to Dawud.

"Wealth," the Jew whispered back.

Badoglio slapped the monk again. "We didn't bring you in here to make speeches. We brought you in here to find out what you know—and who you know. You would be smart to sing for us. We may go easier on you if you do."

He didn't say they would go easy on him. Khalid noticed that. So did Father Martino. "You'll kill me any which way," he said, which wasn't quite an admission that he'd helped put Maria Conti in the palace, but came close.

"You're right. We will," Major Badoglio agreed. "But if you tell us who helped you, we may do it fast."

"You cannot punish me as a righteous, vengeful God will punish you," Father Martino said. "Our cause shall prevail. God wills it!"

This time, Major Badoglio hit him hard enough to rock his head back. Blood streamed from the monk's right nostril. He snuffled when he breathed. Badoglio didn't wipe the blood away. If Martino choked or suffocated, the major didn't mind—or didn't let on that he minded. He also gave no sign that he enjoyed tormenting a prisoner. He was just a man doing a job. He might have been a mechanic putting a new battery in a Garuda.

Khalid wondered whether that made what he did better or worse. True, he got no kick from hurting someone else. But what did you call a man who hurt other people strictly in the line of duty? *A monster* was the first thing that came to mind.

It went on for a long, unpleasant stretch of time. After a while, Martino of Padua began naming names. Whether they were names of any value might be a different question. Captain Salgari wrote them down. Martino might have condemned more people to torment. No, not might have—he had. Khalid had to hope they would deserve it.

This was how investigators played the game here. Khalid and Dawud went back to their hotel and got drunk at the bar. Dawud seemed at least as eager to do that as Khalid. The way it looked to Khalid, that made his colleague seem better, not worse.

Everything had consequences. If you followed the Aquinists, you fell foul of the secular authorities. If you served in the Grand Duke's Ministry of Information, you tortured people because that was what functionaries in the Ministry of Information did. And if you got drunk over the course of an evening, you felt like a badly resurrected corpse the next morning.

Khalid woke up with evil jinni throwing fireballs at one another inside his head. Sometime while he was sleeping, a camel had shat in his mouth. Repairmen had slapped plywood over the window the Aquinists' bomb shattered. It was too bright in there anyhow.

"*Yisgadal v'yiskadash sh'may rabo*—" Dawud began, his voice harsh as a raven's croak and much too loud.

"What is that horrible racket?" Khalid's own voice sounded much too loud in his own ears, too.

"Prayer for the dead," Dawud answered.

"Oh." Khalid thought it over. Thinking also hurt. He nodded, which made his aching head want to fall off. He wished it would. "Well, you've got that right."

Dawud lurched to the sink and splashed cold water on his face. He was more urgent about it than he had been when the Aquinas Seminary was falling down behind him. Afterwards, he blew like a grampus. "Have you got any aspirins in your travel kit?" he asked.

"I think so. Let me see." Khalid bravely stood up himself. He didn't think he'd hurt himself this badly since some of the parties in his madrasa days in Egypt. He pawed through the little crocodile-skin case. "Here we go! Three for you and three for me."

He and Dawud swallowed the pills with as much alacrity as they'd gulped grappa the night before. The barman had sworn grappa was distilled from grapes. He'd left out the part about the thunder and lightning. They rumbled around inside Khalid's aching skull.

"Coffee," Dawud said. "Coffee and a little something greasy. After that, I'll just feel . . . bad."

"Maybe you didn't drink as much as I did, then," Khalid said. "Well, now I remember why the Prophet—peace be unto him—forbade Muslims from drinking wine."

"We weren't drinking wine. We were drinking dynamite. Something pretty much like it, anyhow," Dawud said.

"It's not even *haram* for you," Khalid said.

"Drinking that much ought to be *haram* for everybody," his friend replied. "A little every once in a while is nice. It makes you feel good. It makes you feel happy. But we weren't drinking to get happy last night. We were drinking to get the taste of Martino of Padua out of our mouths."

"That's about the size of it," Khalid said unhappily. "I felt as if I'd been slapping him around myself, as if I'd break the bathroom mirror here if I looked into it. Or if I didn't break it, I wouldn't want to see what was looking back at me."

"Sometimes you have to do these things. I keep telling myself that," Dawud said. "I keep telling myself the Aquinists are worse, too. We can work with the Grand Dukes and their people. We've done it for years, and we'll go on doing it. Work with the Aquinists? Good luck!"

"I've been telling myself all the same things. They're true. We both know they are." Khalid could hear that he sounded like a man trying to persuade himself. Well, that was the kind of man he was right now.

"Yes, we do." Dawud nodded, then looked as if he regretted the motion. Khalid sympathized with him there, all right. The Jew went on, "We went out and drank ourselves disgusting last night anyhow."

"So we did. Come on, let's go downstairs and see if we can spackle over some of the cracks," Khalid said.

The Italians brewed coffee as strong as what he was used to on the other side of the Mediterranean. They sweetened it less than Maghribis liked, but pouring in more sugar took care of that. Dawud ordered a plate of scrambled eggs and fried potatoes. That seemed like such a good idea, Khalid picked the same thing. Greasy food would help coat his stomach against the horrible things the grappa had done to it.

"Keep the coffee coming," Khalid told the waiter in Italian.

"Just as you say, sir," the man replied with a knowing smirk. "Did you and your friend hurt yourselves a little last night?"

"No," Dawud said before Khalid could answer. As the waiter raised an eyebrow, Dawud amplified that: "We hurt ourselves a lot."

"I see," the waiter said. "Coffee will help with some of that, yes. I'll get you some more right away." He hurried off.

Khalid wished he were back in Tunis, in a land that had come by modern civilization honestly instead of getting its nose rubbed in the stuff and hating the smell. Given their druthers, the Christian lords of Western Europe would have stayed the way they were before advancing science and engineering changed the whole planet. They didn't have that choice, not if they wanted to avoid being ruled by their Muslim neighbors to the south and east. But they and their countrymen still fought modernity every way they could. Why would so many of them keep on wearing their traditional, uncomfortable clothes if they really wanted to join the rest of the planet?

"What can you do?" Dawud said when Khalid came out with some of that. "They are the way they are, not the way we want them to be. If we get them to the point where we don't have to strip-search them before we let them on airplanes, that's about as much as we can reasonably hope for."

The waiter came back with the coffee. Khalid and Dawud poured it down. As it and the aspirins took hold, Khalid began to feel human again, in a melancholy way. And even thinking about being melancholy could make him melancholy in a new and different way. European doctors had clung to the theory of the four humors till only a little more than a century ago, hundred of years after the Muslim world found the evidence to show it was nonsense.

"Humors?" Dawud said when he remarked on that. "Well, if you say so. Not much funny about the way I feel, though."

"Something ought to be done about your sense of humors, all right," Khalid said. Both Maghribis managed wan grins.

When they talked with each other, naturally, they spoke Arabic. They didn't pitch their voices to carry. All the same, other people eating breakfast started glancing their way. Wearing robes wasn't enough to make them seem foreign. A fair number of forward-thinking Italians did choose the international style. Another language? That was a different story.

"Some of these people will be memorizing our faces and—" Khalid began.

"—and then throwing away their heads. I wish I could throw mine away right now," Dawud broke in. Khalid nodded. Of course, the Aquinists already knew they were here. That didn't mean they wanted extra notice, though. Want it or not, they had some.

VIII

Even walking along the streets of Rome turned risky. Almost every day, a car exploded somewhere in the city. Sometimes it would be one parked (often double-parked, given how traffic worked in Rome) on a busy thoroughfare and set off by a timer. Nearly as often, a fanatic would aim a rolling bomb at a group of policemen or soldiers and touch it off himself.

No doubt the Aquinist was sure he'd go straight to heaven while sending his foes to hell. Nobody came back from either place to let the fanatics know they were right. That didn't stop them, or even slow them down.

"You'd think, what with all the explosives they planted under the Aquinas Seminary, they'd be running low on them by now," Major Badoglio grumbled.

"Too much to hope for?" Khalid said.

"Too much to hope for," the Italian agreed. "This is a big town, and it's an old town. Too many places to hide things, too many ways to bring in more no matter how much we find."

"If they were sensible people, the idea of blowing themselves to charred couscous would wear thin after a while," Dawud ibn Musa said. He sighed and did an excellent job of mimicking Badoglio's tone: "Too much to hope for."

"The really horrible thing is how much damage a car bomb can do," Badoglio said.

"We've seen," Khalid told him. The Aquinists would put a couple of talents' worth of explosives in a car's trunk, and add more in the hard-to-inspect space between the front and back seats. When the driver joyfully flipped the switch that touched it off, all the steel and glass in the car turned to shrapnel. Gasoline and motor oil added liquid fire to the blast. Sometimes nothing at all was left of the man behind the wheel.

A bomb like that could kill dozens of people. It could blow out windows for half a parasang in all directions, and leave a hole in the roadway ten cubits wide and three cubits deep. Khalid had visited several bombings. One of the things the papers and television didn't talk about much was the horrible wounds sharp fragments of flying metal inflicted on people they didn't kill. Getting splashed with blazing gasoline was another horror not widely covered.

Khalid wondered whether that discretion made good policy. If people understood what a foul weapon a car bomb was, wouldn't they turn on the maniacs who used them?

"They might," Major Badoglio allowed when he asked the question. "Or they might decide to fear them instead. And they might decide that, if we can't stop those bastards, siding with them would make them quit."

"It's much harder to stop someone who wants to die than someone who wants to stay alive," Dawud said.

"Isn't it just!" Badoglio said. "If Maria Conti had cared about staying alive, Grand Duke Cosimo would still be with us, too."

The Jew rubbed his jowly chin in thought. "Could Pope Marcellus—would Pope Marcellus—declare that people who kill themselves to harm others go to hell, with no hope of heaven?"

"With Christ, there is always hope. So we are taught," Badoglio said. "But his Holiness might perhaps be persuaded to say something not far short of that." He scrawled a note to himself.

He seemed a normal, careful, competent investigator. Not at all the kind of man who would hurt a prisoner because the fellow didn't feel like talking. Which proved . . . what, exactly? That you couldn't tell by looking. And that not all the pieces of a man's life came out of the same puzzle.

A messenger hurried in and handed Badoglio a folded sheet of paper held closed by a blob of blue sealing wax. The major examined the seal and nodded to himself before breaking it. Wax was an old-fashioned way to secure a document, but still worked well.

After reading the message, Badoglio swore under his breath, crumpled it into a ball, and threw it into a wastebasket by his desk. "What's gone wrong now?" Khalid asked. Plainly, something had.

"Our people have arrested two more policemen at a checkpoint on the Via Cassia—the road down to Florence," the major answered. "They were letting the Aquinists smuggle things past them. Not even for a price, mind you, but because they believed. Well, the fanatics will get a surprise the next time they come through there."

"Good," Khalid said. After a polite moment, he added, "Not the first time that's happened, is it?"

"I only wish it were," Badoglio answered. "Too many traitors. Too many men who line up with the Grand Duke's enemies. You expect some of that in the police. Everybody knows you can pay a lot of them off. But we're getting reports of disloyal soldiers, too."

"That *isn't* good," Khalid said. Badoglio took the idea that policemen were for sale for granted. It happened on the other side of the Mediterranean, too. It was bound to happen everywhere. Some policemen were venal, and that was all there was to it. But they didn't take it for granted in the Maghrib, or in most of the civilized world. They fought it. Here, it was part of the way things worked.

How long had it been part of the way things worked here? The Romans built the Via Cassia centuries before the archangel Gabriel gave Muhammad the Qur'an. Did ancient Roman police prefects or whatever they called them let Christians slip past in exchange for some silver, or because they'd decided to follow Christ themselves? Khalid wouldn't have been surprised.

How many other pieces of the past survived in an old, backward land like Italy? Even the name of the highway to Florence hadn't changed in all those hundreds of years. How many people here could tell you who Cassius was and why he had the road named after him? How many people here thought of him as a great-uncle or something like that?

Dawud's mind was going in a different direction. He asked Major Badoglio, "If there's, ah, dissension among the police and the army, how do you know the Ministry of Information is free of it?"

"*Quis custodiet ipsos custodes?*" Badoglio answered.

It sounded like Italian, but it wasn't. "Sorry—I don't follow Latin, if that's what that is," Khalid said. He thought Dawud did, but the other Maghribi wasn't foolish enough to let on. The less they knew you knew, the better off you were.

"Yes, it's Latin. We don't use it just for things of the Church. Juvenal was a long way from a religious writer." The Italian grinned crookedly. "That bit means 'Who will guard those guardsmen?' He's talking about brothel guards."

"Is he?" Khalid's grin was crooked, too. "Well, who does keep watch on the Ministry of Information?"

"There are people—I know that," Badoglio said. "I don't know all the details, and I don't suppose I should."

"All right." Khalid could see he'd have to be content—or discontented—with that. The Maghrib certainly had people keeping a discreet eye on government agencies. Why shouldn't the Grand Duchy of Italy?

One reason that Italy might not was that it was a less sophisticated state than the Maghrib. But that didn't seem to be true. Plenty of Italians might hate the direction in which the world civilization was going. But they had their own long history of plots and coups and treachery. They saw they needed watchdogs. If Major Badoglio was to be believed—and Khalid found no reason to doubt him—they had them.

Dawud said, "If you can't count on your police or your soldiers against the Aquinists, will you come out on top in the end?"

"No, of course not." Badoglio sent him a sour look. "We're all giving up. I expect to start shouting 'God wills it!' any second now. And we've turned the fanatics loose so we can chuck your lot into jail to take their place."

If Lorenzo III wanted to do that, he could. It would horrify the Maghrib and complicate life over a much broader swath of the world. If a major European state aligned itself with the Aquinists, diplomacy and police work might not be enough to keep the lid on. It might take war.

For now, though, Major Badoglio was joking. Dawud's dry chuckle acknowledged that. "Well, you got me there," the Jew said. "Let's get on with things, then." And they did.

Grand Duke Lorenzo was furious. He didn't even try to hide it. "They found this, this filth in Milan and Turin! Even in those places!" He'd said the northern cities backed him. He slammed his fist down on the pile of crumpled broadsheets and posters on his desk. Maybe he'd been wrong.

Khalid nodded in sympathy. "Yes, your Supreme Highness. I've already seen some like those."

Medieval knights in chainmail or plate galloped on armored horses across the badly printed pages. They all carried a black shield with a red cross blazoned on it. On some of the posters, they were spearing a man who looked like a fat Egyptian banker. On others, they aimed their lance at a nasty caricature of Lorenzo. Still others had the knight making shashlik of both the banker and the Grand Duke.

CRUSADE! the posters shouted. GOD WILLS IT! Then they exhorted the people who read them to rid first Italy and then the world of God's enemies. *Kill Muslims and heretics!* one of them screamed. *Help bring the Kingdom of God on earth!*

"These aren't just in Italian, either," Grand Duke Lorenzo snarled. "We've got them in German, in French, in Catalan, even in English! If I leave even one Aquinist alive, nobody will make me believe *I'm* doing God's will."

"They aren't stopping at much, are they?" Khalid said. He'd seen a poster in a language that seemed utterly incomprehensible to him. Someone from the Ministry of Information told him it was Danish. All he knew about Denmark was that it was one of those places that grew blonds. Fanatics, too, evidently.

"They aren't stopping at *anything*, may their bones fry in hell for the next five billion years." Lorenzo looked and sounded ready to pick up an assault rifle himself and go gunning for black-robed monks. "They want people to come here from every corner of the world and kill Italians."

"Yes, sir. That's just what they want—and you can turn it against them." Khalid had hashed this over with Annarita Pezzola the night before. "If your subjects see that the Aquinists are bringing in foreigners who want to kill them and their kin, they won't like it."

"True!" Lorenzo's eyes glowed. He came around the desk and folded Khalid into a bearhug. For good measure, he hugged Dawud, too. Not quite idly, Khalid wondered if he'd ever embraced a Jew before. Lorenzo went on, "We'll make them see that, yes! You have a good notion of how things work here—better than I would have expected from a foreigner."

He didn't say *from a Muslim*. He didn't say *from a man who doesn't think anything like most Italians*. He didn't say any of those things, no. Khalid could hear them whether he said them or not.

"Thank you very much, your Supreme Highness," the investigator said. "I don't get all the credit, though. *Signorina* Pezzola helped a lot when it came to working out how to make the Aquinists sorry for this kind of propaganda." If he could do Annarita a good turn, he would.

"Did she?" The Grand Duke shrugged. Like a good many Italians Khalid had met, he owned expressive shoulders. He eyed Khalid. "Do you happen to know whether my father was sleeping with her?"

"She's told me he wasn't, sir," Khalid said in surprise: nothing but the truth there.

"Which may be true and may not. I don't suppose it matters much one way or the other," Lorenzo said. Khalid was about to agree with that when the Grand Duke went on, "She's too old for me. She might not have looked that way to Dad, though. He was even older than you are."

"A man in his forties doesn't think of himself as old . . . sir," Khalid said tonelessly. He didn't think of himself as old till some punk kid rubbed his nose in his years, anyhow. When the punk kid happened to be the hereditary overlord of an important country, you couldn't even call him out for it. Or you'd get yourself talked about if you did.

"No, eh?" Lorenzo chuckled, as if to say he knew something Khalid didn't. But, hereditary overlord or not, he had some manners concealed about his person. He didn't make any more gibes about Khalid's age.

He didn't say anything about Dawud's, either. Dawud was three or four years older than Khalid. Even in the egalitarian Maghrib, a Jew had to work harder than a Muslim, and didn't get the payoff a Muslim would. Had the Grand Duke sniped at him, Dawud would have been more likely to laugh than to show he was irked. He never seemed to care about his age. So his belly bulged? So he had a double chin? What were they but signs he'd enjoyed himself so far? The gray streaks in his hair and beard? He'd come by them honestly.

Now he asked, "How well are your borders sealed, your Supreme Highness? If these, ah, Crusaders"—the face he made showed what he thought of them—"start swarming into Italy, can you keep them out?"

"They won't come in at the usual crossing points. Well, only the really stupid ones will." Lorenzo III might be young, but he could see the obvious.

"Yes, sir. That's what I meant," Dawud said.

"I can hope for some help from the King of France. The Aquinists hate him almost as much as they hate me, so he won't give them free passage through his realm," Lorenzo said.

"He might not, but pro-Aquinists in his service may," Khalid said. "There will be some, the same as there are here."

"Bastards," the Grand Duke muttered. "Well, you're not wrong, even if I wish you were. But we still need to worry about Germany more. Every little prince and duke and archbishop up there is lord of his own domain, with a tinpot army and his own coins and postage stamps and customs inspectors. It used to be almost that bad here, till my family pulled this place together. The Emperors haven't been able to do it in Germany. So some of those people will like the Aquinists and help them along. Others won't."

"Some fanatics will get through, then. Some more will, I should say—some already have." Khalid gestured toward the sheets on the Grand Duke's desk.

"I'm afraid so." Lorenzo nodded. "I can't roll barbed wire all along the frontier—I haven't got enough of it. I can't send all my men to dig foxholes along the border, either."

They'd used that much barbed wire and dug that many foxholes in the last war between Persia and Baghdad. Men who'd flown in space said they could look down from on high and see how the old entrenchments still scarred the desert. They called that kind of combat a warning to mankind. To Khalid, it seemed more a proof that mankind didn't heed warnings.

Proving he didn't heed warnings himself, he said, "You know, sir, it's a shame you accepted *Signorina* Pezzola's resignation. She has a good view of things." He could have been more eloquent in Arabic, but even in Italian he got his meaning across.

Not that it did him any good. Lorenzo shook his head. "I don't want a woman trying to tell me what I should do. A man, you can see what he wants. But who knows with a woman? Is she saying something because she means it? Or because she's ambitious the way a man would be? Or just because it's her time of the month?"

A Maghribi politician or official who said anything like that would get hounded out of office in short order by his outraged constituents. Women wouldn't be the only ones outraged, either. Most men there knew better than to believe anything so stupid, let alone say it.

But who would tell the Grand Duke he wasn't supposed to come out with such things? Nobody. Nobody who didn't want to see the inside of an Italian jail, anyhow. Yet Lorenzo was the kind of man whom governments throughout the Muslim world wanted to work with. The way things were in Europe, he was the comfortable choice. The alternative to people like him? The Aquinists.

Bad and worse, Khalid reminded himself once more. That the Aquinists plainly were worse had to be a measure of their damnation.

Annarita Pezzola expertly twirled spaghetti with a fork and a tablespoon. Maybe *expertly* wasn't the right word for such a mundane task, but it came to Khalid's mind all the same. His own efforts at balling the squiggly noodles around his fork kept falling apart or shedding worms of pasta. Dawud did better, but not so well as Annarita.

She laughed when Khalid praised her skill. "I'll tell you what the difference is," she said. "I started doing this before I was three, and I doubt a week's gone by since when I haven't done it more than once. You don't eat so many noodles on your side of the sea."

"That's true," Khalid said. "We make porridges of wheat and barley instead."

"Well, there you are. You do plenty of things we don't, too." Annarita paused to half empty her wine goblet. "You treat women like human beings, for instance."

"Every once in a while. When we feel like it. If the wind is blowing the right way," Dawud said.

"It's not something to joke about," she said sharply.

He cocked his head like an overweight sparrow. "Why do you think I'm joking?"

Khalid said, "When we talked with the Grand Duke today, I tried to persuade him to bring you back into his service."

"It didn't work," she said: statement, not question.

"Well . . . no," Khalid admitted. "But barriers don't fall unless you keep trying to knock them over."

"You're lucky he didn't get angry at you. Or he probably did. You're lucky he needs the Maghrib too much to show it. At least he sees he needs civilized help."

Were *you sleeping with Grand Duke Cosimo?* Instead of poking at that question, Khalid drank from his own goblet. It gave him something to do, and the strong red wine took the edge off his troubles. As long as he didn't make a pig of himself, wine struck him as a good thing, no matter what the Prophet said about it.

While he and Annarita talked, Dawud finished his supper. He dabbed at his mouth with the linen napkin. Then he stood up. "Don't mind me, you two. I'm going back to the room to finish that evaluation I promised to Major Badoglio tomorrow."

Khalid opened his mouth. As far as he knew, Dawud hadn't promised Badoglio any evaluations. Then he closed it. He didn't know how far he knew. Dawud might be doing something like that. Or he might be giving his friend some time with an attractive woman and without a spare wheel. When you did something like that, you didn't add a line like *Now go jump on her!* You didn't if you were more than seventeen, anyhow.

Annarita watched Dawud stroll out of the dining room. "I never had much to do with a Jew till now," she said. "He's pretty much like anyone else, isn't he?"

"Anyone else with an odd sense of humor, yes," Khalid answered.

"You said that. I didn't." Annarita's voice took on a teasing edge. "What would he say if I told him you said it?"

"Probably something like 'Thank you,'" he answered.

That made Annarita laugh. "I believe it. He's your partner, so you take working with a Jew for granted, don't you?"

"Pretty much, though if he were a Muslim I'd likely be *his* partner. I was thinking about things like that a little while ago," Khalid said. "People in the Maghrib are free and pretty much equal under the law. Less so in fact, though we do try."

"But you don't mind?" she persisted.

"Not me." He shook his head. "I don't even mind coming to Italy and working with Christians."

The dining room was dimly lit, as dining rooms all over the world seemed to be, but it wasn't too dark for him to miss the flush rising from her neck to her hairline. "I walked into that, didn't I?" she said.

"I meant it," Khalid answered. "People are people, pretty much, no matter what they believe. More people in Europe take their religion very seriously than they do where I come from, but we have our share who don't want to believe animals and plants change through the ages—even a few who don't want to believe we go around the sun and not the other way around."

"In Italy, we do want to believe we still are the crowns of creation. The Romans were. They ruled the whole Mediterranean world for hundreds of years." Annarita sighed. "Then their empire fell apart, and then things . . . changed. You started exploring the natural world, and we argued about the nature of God. And argued. And argued. And we're arguing about it to this day—and buying the things we need and the things we want from the people who know how to make them."

Khalid waved to the waiter for another bottle of wine. "That's . . . part of Europe's problem," he said carefully.

Annarita waited while the man in the fancy costume—he might almost have been able to march in Cosimo's funeral procession—used his corkscrew, got Khalid's approval, and filled their goblets again. After he went away, she asked, "And the rest is . . . ?"

"You know as well as I do, I'm sure," he said. "I mean no offense, truly, but it's not only the Aquinists who are drunk on religion in this part of the world. In the Maghrib, someone as able as you wouldn't have to work through a man because you're a woman."

"We're trying to fix that, too." Annarita scowled and stared down at her wineglass. "We still have a way to go, don't we?"

"You would still be working in the Grand Duke's palace if you didn't," Khalid said.

"Yes. I would. Or maybe I would. Cosimo listened to me. He didn't always do what I suggested, but he listened. Lorenzo didn't want to. Maybe that was because I was a woman. But maybe he wouldn't have wanted to listen to me if I had a beard down to here." She gestured. Khalid chuckled. She added, "Sometimes people just don't get along, that's all."

"I suppose not." Khalid didn't believe that was the problem, not for a second. Instead of telling her so, he said, "You'd look silly with a beard even half that long."

She snorted. Then she tried to pretend she hadn't. That made her snort again. "Your sense of humor is as odd as the Jew's," she said.

"I doubt it," Khalid said. "Dawud makes foolishness look easy. Me, I have to work at it."

"You do pretty well," Annarita said.

"*Grazie*," Khalid replied. Her Arabic was better than his Italian, so they'd been using that language. He was glad for the chance to drop in a word of her birthspeech.

He did wonder once more why Cosimo had listened to her. Was that only because the late Grand Duke recognized ability when he heard it? Or had Cosimo had more basic human—more basic male—reasons for putting up with her, even if he hadn't necessarily done anything about them? Khalid picked up his goblet and sipped from it. No, it wasn't a question he could ask, especially not when the two of them were at the moment no more than acquaintances.

If they were ever going to turn into more than acquaintances, he'd have to do something about it. Ever since his divorce, he'd been leery of approaching each new woman who piqued his interest. He knew disappointment was too often the only thing waiting ahead. All the same, if you didn't bet, you couldn't possibly win.

And so he set down the wineglass and said, "In all the heaps of free time we have—and if the curfew lets up enough—could I ask you to a film or some music somewhere?"

She arched an eyebrow. Her reply wasn't altogether responsive: "I wouldn't think you cared much for European music. The musicians who play in your modes aren't likely to come here during our troubles."

"Some European stuff isn't bad," he said gallantly. "Or we could find a place to eat that isn't in the hotel, or just somewhere to have a few drinks and talk. However you please."

Annarita studied him. Was that amusement on her face? If it was, it quickly faded. "I've never gone out with a Muslim man before," she said.

"I dated a Christian girl for a while when I was at the madrasa in Egypt, but she was a Copt," Khalid said. "A little different." Copts were more than a little different from European Christians. They'd risen with, and within, the international civilization. They were part of it. They hadn't got left behind, the way folk north of the Mediterranean had. Still . . . "I'm not afraid if you're not."

"Well . . ." The amusement came back. "Why not? We can see what happens. If it doesn't work, it doesn't work, that's all."

"A bargain." Khalid lifted his goblet again and held it out. Annarita clinked with him.

Dawud was watching television when Khalid came in. Not news or anything important: a polo match from Alexandria. It was close. The stands were in a frenzy, Reds and Whites shrieking abuse at each other. "And?" Dawud asked without looking away from the screen.

"And what?" Khalid returned. The Reds scored—a pretty goal. The tumult from the crowd redoubled.

Unfazed, Dawud returned, "And should I pack up and move into a room of my own? Will you be needing this one for your love nest?"

Khalid used some Arabic street slang he hadn't hauled out for a long time. If you said that in a different tone of voice, the man you said it to almost had to try to kill you. Dawud only laughed. "And your mother's, too," he said. "You still didn't answer my question."

"Another room? You must be kidding! The garbanzo-counters who dole out our expense money would never let you get away with it."

"Oh, I don't know. Things are a lot cheaper on this side of the sea." Dawud was right about that. Maghribis often retired to the toe and heel of the Italian boot to take advantage of the lower cost of living here. Khalid wondered how many of them were packing up and heading for home right now to get away from the political and religious turmoil here.

But that had nothing to do with what they were talking about. "You don't need to move out, Dawud. Certainly not yet. We won't get stains on the sheets tomorrow night. We'll see what happens and go on from there. We'll see if anything happens."

"Not yet, eh? You could do plenty worse. She's pretty. She's smart." Dawud eyed Khalid. "The other question is, how much better could she do?"

"Blessings upon you for your boundless generosity, my master," Khalid said. Arabic could be snottiest when it sounded sweetest.

"Anytime," Dawud replied easily.

There were plenty of other questions, as they both knew perfectly well. Annarita was Christian. She was Italian. They weren't altogether certain she wasn't working for the Aquinists. Khalid thought that unlikely—he wouldn't have wanted anything to do with her if he hadn't—but he didn't know it for sure.

If the spark struck, he would have to worry about it more. In the meantime . . . Khalid pointed to the TV. "Nice to know the Grand Duke tries to keep his people interested in something besides grappa, Aquinism, and rebellion."

"They care about polo here. They care about it more than I do, as a matter of fact. I was just killing time till you came back—if you came back tonight." Dawud kept right on needling.

The Italians *were* maniacal polo fans. So were most Europeans. They hadn't invented the game, but they had latched on to it. Every town here had a team. Every city had several. European teams competed in international tournaments. They'd never won one, but they'd made some respectable showings.

"I'm here. I'm going to bed—by myself." Only with the last couple of words did Khalid react to his friend's teasing.

The next morning, the TV news and the papers were full of stories about German invaders. Italians and Germans had trouble getting along, almost the way Arabs and Persians did in the Muslim world. By calling all the Crusaders Germans, the news warned the locals not to trust them. Whether the locals went along with any of that was liable to be a different question.

"Of course it is," Dawud answered when Khalid said as much over breakfast. "If you'd heard mostly lies from your leaders for the past hundred years, would you want to believe them now?"

"How much truth would the Aquinists tell them?" Khalid asked.

"If we're very, very lucky, we won't have to find out," Dawud said.

Two days later, the Ministry of Information brought a handful of captured Crusaders down to Rome from the north. When Major Badoglio asked Khalid and Dawud if they wanted to question one of the men, they jumped at the chance. The prisoner was tall and fair and had a bandaged arm. His name was Gottlieb Schrempf.

"'Gottlieb' would be 'Amadeo' in Italian," Badoglio said helpfully.

"How about 'Schrempf'?" Khalid asked.

"I don't know. It sounds like a fart, doesn't it?" the major replied.

Khalid turned to the would-be Crusader. "What were you doing in Italy?" he asked in Arabic. Schrempf just shrugged. Khalid tried the same question in Italian. The German shrugged again. Khalid turned to Major Badoglio. "How are we supposed to talk to him?"

Badoglio eyed the prisoner. "*Loquerisne Latine?*" he asked.

Comprehension lit up the man's tired, blunt features. "*Sic. Hoc ille.*"

"He understands Latin," Badoglio said. "Another sign he's an Aquinist, of course. I learned it in the university—sort of like a madrasa—but he isn't likely to have."

"Ask him why he came to Italy," Khalid said.

Badoglio did. "*Deus vult!*" Gottlieb Schrempf replied. Khalid knew what that meant, all right.

"If God wills that he's going to win, why is he sitting here in an interrogation room? Ask him that," Dawud said.

Major Badoglio put the question into Latin. Gottlieb Schrempf answered in the same tongue. Badoglio translated his response back into Italian: "He says he must be here because he is a sinner. Even though he's a sinner, he's sure his side will come out on top in the end."

"What does he think we'll do with him?" Khalid asked.

More translations followed. Questioning this way was slow and clumsy, but you could do it. Through Badoglio, the Aquinist prisoner said, "I don't care. Whatever happens to me here on earth, I'm sure to spend eternity in heaven. Devils will torment you misbelievers till the end of time."

Khalid and Dawud looked at each other. Dealing with foes who intended to die and didn't care if they did was different from, and worse than, fighting people who wanted to go on living just as much as you did. The Crusaders would go after their enemies without worrying about what happened to them while they did it. How were you supposed to stop fighters like that?

Badoglio said something in Latin. Dawud coughed; though Khalid thought he knew the Christians' sacred and scholarly tongue, he didn't let on that he did. "Sorry," Badoglio said. "I asked him where he comes from and how he got into Italy."

"I am from the Archbishopric of Ochsenhausen," Schrempf said, not without pride. Khalid wouldn't have been so proud of it, not when he doubted whether anyone more than five parasangs from the border had ever heard of the place. Badoglio had to bring out a map of Germany to discover that the archbishopric lay in the southern part of the country, not far from the boundary with the Swiss cantons. It was, luckily, a large map. Ochsenhausen wouldn't have shown up otherwise.

"How did you get into Italy?" the major asked again.

"Oh, that was easy," Schrempf said. "In the cantons, all the Aquinist seminaries fed us and gave us beds. And plenty of people on this side of the border helped us through. The Grand Duke's heretics didn't know we were close by till we started shooting at them."

"Then they shot back." Khalid pointed at the Crusader's bandaged arm.

After Badoglio translated the comment, Gottlieb Schrempf shrugged again. "It happened, so God must have willed that it should happen. His will be done—amen!" He seemed content enough. That in itself was plenty to frighten Khalid.

IX

"Are you sure we want to do this?" Dawud asked as Khalid pulled the nondescript little Ochipway onto the street. Like the rest of Europe, the Italians imported their cars; they didn't make any themselves.

Rome's traffic flow wasn't much heavier than Tunis'; Tunis also predated the automobile by centuries. But Rome's drivers routinely did things only drunks and lunatics would have imagined in Tunis. They ignored signs and lights whenever they thought they could get away with it. They double-parked, even on narrow streets where any parking was against the rules. They pulled halfway onto the sidewalk to pick someone up or drop someone off. They refused to yield or to signal, and they leaned on their horns.

They stopped for security checkpoints only because they knew they'd get shot if they didn't. They complained so much, those stops took longer than they would have otherwise.

Once upon a time, Roman roads had been the finest in the world. Bouncing through Rome on his way to the Via Cassia, Khalid wondered whether they'd been resurfaced since the days of the Caesars. Once he got on the northbound highway, he discovered that long stretches of it *did* still have their ancient paving blocks. He hoped the Ochipway's suspension would hold up.

Dawud had other things on his mind. "I'm sure glad I went to the dentist not long before we came up here," he said. "Otherwise, I'd be wearing all my fillings in my lap."

"Fillings?" Khalid said, dodging potholes. "What about your teeth?"

"Well, those, too," Dawud said. "I was trying to give this wretched road the benefit of the doubt." Another jounce almost put him through the roof of the car even though he'd tightened his safety belt. That was one more thing the Italian drivers seldom bothered with. They seemed to want to let God's will be done on the highway. To an evolutionist like Khalid, if you didn't wear a belt, it was God's will that you were too stupid to live to reproduce.

The countryside was greener than it would have been most places in the Maghrib. It wasn't *green*, the way it would have been in France or England or Irokoyistan in the northeast of the Sunset Lands. Summer in Italy was the dry season, as it was on the other side of the Mediterranean. But the weather here was a little cooler and damper.

Italian cattle were of varieties different from those in the Maghrib. They were also smaller and skinnier. They hadn't been bred so systematically or for so long. They weren't just meat or milk machines. They were animals you could imagine living on their own. Every so often, one would shake a warning horn at another that might steal grass from it.

"I wonder if they still use oxen, or maybe donkeys, to plow here," Khalid said.

"That would be something to see, all right," Dawud agreed. "They wouldn't do the job as well as a tractor, or as fast, but they'd be a lot more fun to watch."

In the Maghrib, you couldn't tell a farmer from anyone else by his clothes. Here, the peasants—that seemed the better word to Khalid—often wore colorless homespun: baggy linen shirts over clinging wool trousers. Instead of using keffiyehs or turbans, they kept the sun off their heads with wide-brimmed hats woven from straw.

"I kind of like the hats," Khalid said. "They may do a better job than what we wear."

"They look stupid, though," Dawud said. "Unless they ever come into fashion back home, people would stare at you and call you names if you put one on." He paused to light a cigar. "I should wear one, not you. Everybody already knows I have no sense of style."

"You said it. I didn't," Khalid replied.

"Oh, I know I have no sense of style, too," Dawud said cheerfully. "The difference is, I don't care."

"If you say so." Khalid sounded distracted, and was. Another truck was racing up behind. Of course it would want to pass. He slid over to let it by, something few Italians would have done.

Pass him it did. A plume of stinking black smoke poured from its exhaust. "That smells worse than your stogie," Khalid remarked as he slowed to get away from the worst of it.

"I am affronted." Dawud didn't sound affronted. He didn't quit smoking the cigar, either.

The truck was elderly. In the Maghrib, it would have been junked years before. In Italy, it soldiered on for as long as it would run. It was piled high, higher, highest with what looked like sacks of beans or grain. Whoever'd tied them on did a haphazard job of it. The springs were so old and tired, the truck rode low. Khalid wondered why the chassis didn't strike sparks from the paving stones every time the truck hit a bump or a pothole.

Before long, they came to a checkpoint. Khalid was sure he saw the truck driver pass money to the men with guns. They waved him on. Khalid made a note of the numbers and letters on his plate. The numbers were in the European style, not the one he was more used to, but he could deal with them, as he dealt with the Latin alphabet.

"For now, we just have to hope he wants to go on, and that those sacks don't have machine guns and cartridge belts stashed in them," he said.

"That wouldn't be so good, would it?" Dawud said. "I don't

think the bribe was big enough to cover anything like that, though—it was only one bill."

"Ah, was it? Thanks. I didn't notice that. Probably just ordinary smuggling, then," Khalid said. Dawud might look sloppy—might, in fact, make a point of looking sloppy—but he didn't miss much.

The Italians manning the checkpoint gave the Maghribis' identity documents dubious looks. Seeing that they had a field telephone, Khalid said, "Call the Ministry of Information in Rome. Ask for Major Giacomo Badoglio. He will tell you who we are."

He wondered whether merely making the offer would be enough to intimidate the soldiers. But one of them spoke into the telephone in a dialect he couldn't begin to follow. Whoever was on the other end of the line must not have had any trouble with it, though. The man on the telephone here slammed down the handset in a hurry. He said something to his superior.

"Pass on!" that worthy said to Khalid.

"They're doing their job," Khalid said once they'd got out of earshot of the checkpoint.

Dawud nodded. "So they are. I wondered if they'd pretend to call Rome, tell us the Ministry of Information had never heard of us, and either shake us down for money or shoot us, depending."

"Urk!" Khalid said. "You come up with all kinds of pleasant notions, don't you?"

"I try." Dawud probably thought he spoke with becoming modesty. Khalid thought he laid it on with a trowel.

They stopped at a little town called Montevarchi for a snack and more coffee. Anywhere in the Muslim world, such a stop would have been as ritualized as a visit to a mosque. One or two of the leading five or six anonymous societies would have sold gasoline. There would have been a couple of low-end eateries out of the same number of possibilities, and one better one out of three or four. One of the three leading coffeehouses would have had an entry at the stop. You wouldn't get wonderful food or terrific coffee, but what you did get would be good enough. And you would know ahead of time just how good good enough was likely to be.

It wasn't like that in Montevarchi. The eateries and coffeehouse here didn't represent anonymous societies that stretched across continents, sometimes across the ocean to the Sunset Lands. They represented their owners, and Montevarchi. The pasta Khalid and Dawud got was plainly made at the eatery, and sauced and spiced differently from any they'd had in Rome. The coffeehouse, on the other hand, served hot mud.

"Can't win 'em all," Dawud said philosophically.

"At least it's got a jolt to it," Khalid said.

"Can't win 'em all," the Jew repeated. Khalid didn't need long to decide he was right. They got back into the Ochipway and headed on to Florence.

Rome was the center of the Grand Dukes' power. It was the capital of Italy. Being such a place, it was also more likely to be loyal to Lorenzo III than an ordinary provincial town. Things were bad enough in Rome. Khalid wanted to see how they were in those provincial towns.

One of the first things he saw, on the outskirts of the city, was a dead tank. It hadn't just caught fire from a gasoline bomb, either. The hole in its side armor half a cubit below the turret said it had taken a direct hit from a rocket-propelled grenade.

He and Dawud had to pass through two checkpoints before they got into the center of Florence. Red crosses were painted on walls and fences everywhere, sometimes with DEUS VULT! close by, sometimes not.

The great church—the Duomo—and the Old Palace dominated the skyline. Southeast of the Duomo stood the Church of the Holy Cross. Though formerly held by a different order, it had belonged to the Aquinists for more than two hundred years: ever since it became obvious that Europe was falling behind the more progressive parts of the world. Now it lay in ruins, smashed by what looked like artillery fire.

The hotel for which Khalid and Dawud had reservations was a

shabby little building. Plainly, it had been built before such refinements as electricity and running water reached Italy. The tub sat on green bronze lion's feet, in the ornate Egyptian style of a hundred years before. The lamps were converted from gas-burners.

"Well, it could be worse," Dawud said once he'd surveyed the room.

"How, exactly?" Khalid inquired.

"They've taken out the sconces that used to hold torches and wallpapered over the soot stains," Dawud replied after a visible pause for thought.

"Oh, joy," Khalid said. "The Ministry of Information's local headquarters is only two or three blocks away. That's why they put us up in this dump. Do you remember how to get there?"

"I think so. We can stroll the streets together—till people start shooting at us, anyhow."

He might have been his usual sardonic self. More likely, he was speaking the simple truth. Plywood and cardboard covered a lot of shattered windows. Bullets pocked plaster and scarred brick- and stonework. The air was sour with smoke; a faint whiff of decay lay under that smell. Everyone on the streets seemed nervous of everyone else.

Barbed wire and sandbags protected the Ministry of Information building. All by itself, that told Khalid a good deal of what he needed to know about how things were. If the Grand Duke's servants weren't worried about attack, they wouldn't have warded themselves so well.

A sergeant sent a private back into the headquarters to make sure the Maghribis were expected. Coming back, the private pointed his thumb up at the sky. "They're waiting for you, all right," the sergeant said. He unlocked the gate to the checkpoint, which was made from a plank frame with barbed wire nailed to it. "Step right in. Make yourselves at home."

"Ha!" Dawud said. It might not have been mannerly, but it squeezed a laugh from the Italian underofficer.

A captain named Enrico Pavarotti met them at the door. He was short and plump—fat, really—and owned a resonant tenor voice. "A privilege, my masters. A privilege," he said. He spoke fair Arabic, with the musical local accent. "We have coffee and little cakes. We can try some while we talk, if that should please you."

"That sounds fine," Dawud said. Like Captain Pavarotti, he was always ready for a snack.

They had more than coffee and little cakes. They had olives and dry sausages and salted fish and cheese and peppers that growled without quite snarling. With a spread like that, you could munch your way through the day and never worry, or even notice, you were missing regular meals.

As they were helping themselves, a machine gun started hammering off in the distance. *"Dannazione!"* Pavarotti said, falling back into Italian. With a frown that pulled his mouth into the same shape as the bushy black mustache bracketing it, he made himself return to Arabic: "That's one of the fanatics' guns."

"How can you tell?" Khalid asked.

"Hear how fast it fires? That's a Japanese model. They use them a lot in the German states, and in England, too. We buy most of our automatic weapons from the Sultanate of Delhi, and you can hear the difference."

Like Europe, Japan had done what it could to stand aloof from the rising tide of the world civilization. Then the Japanese decided that they had to adapt or go under. They'd adapted very well. Comics could always get a laugh by spoofing the way Japanese businessmen spoke Arabic. Japanese native costume was colorful. Those businessmen unfailingly chose gray or white robes and white keffiyehs, though.

Europe didn't feel like adapting or going under. It wanted to kick up its heels. Another machine gun answered the first. It did spit death at a slower rhythm. Khalid suspected it was suitable for all ordinary murderous uses, though. He asked, "How are things here?"

Pavarotti gestured theatrically. "Half the people in town don't think the Grand Duke—God bless him!—is a proper Christian.

Christ on His Cross, at least a quarter of the people in town don't think the Pope—God bless *him*, too—is a proper Christian. And we've got these Crusader madmen filtering down from the rest of Europe so they can go to heaven and send us to hell. It's a fine kettle of crabs. Oh, you bet it is."

"How can you hold things together if half the people are against you?" Khalid asked. He didn't know the Italian officer was right about that, but he hadn't seen anything to make him disbelieve it.

Pavarotti eyed him. The man looked tired and worried and very cynical. "You're the experts from the Maghrib. You're supposed to have all the answers tied up in pink ribbon for us."

"And then you wake up," Dawud ibn Musa said. "What are we? Just a couple of infidels."

"I wasn't going to say anything about that if you didn't," Captain Pavarotti replied. "I'm glad you had the sense to wear our clothes. People in robes get shot at a lot. Even Italians in robes get shot at a lot."

One of the machine guns cut loose with another burst. Khalid thought it was the one that belonged to the Grand Duke's men. It wasn't close enough to alarm him into asking. Instead, he said, "If your country falls to the fanatics, that won't make anyone's life better. Plenty of people's will get worse, but nobody's will get better."

"You know that, my master. I know that. Anyone with eyes in his head and a brain bigger than a wall lizard's knows that." Now Pavarotti just looked disgusted. "But all these fools, what they care about is going to heaven. You can beat 'em like donkeys while they're on earth, as long as they take the up elevator after they check out."

As he had with Major Badoglio, Khalid asked, "Would it help if the Pope said that backing the Aquinists was a sure ticket to riding in the other direction?"

"It might, with some people," Pavarotti answered. "Not with everybody. The ones who want to follow the Aquinists anyway, they still will. The Aquinists might say that his Holiness had shown he was a heretic and choose an Antipope for their own mouthpiece. The Church has gone through splits like that before. Nobody wants another one."

That was about what Khalid had heard from Badoglio. He decided he would do better not to push Marcellus IX against the Aquinists. As things were, the Pope had some influence over all of Western Europe. If he suddenly found himself with none over half of the volatile continent, things would only get worse.

"Can we see what it's like on the streets?" he asked.

Pavarotti eyed in him some surprise. "Are you sure? It's getting dark. Same as mosquitoes and rats, the Aquinists come out at night."

Well, we could wait till tomorrow morning. That was what Khalid wanted to say. What came out of his mouth was, "Well, we came up here to find out what things were like." Sometimes a sense of duty was a terrible thing to have. It was even worse when your sense of duty had you.

Captain Pavarotti kitted out the Maghribis the way he would have with replacements from his own service's ranks. He gave them uniform tunics and trousers that more or less fit, boots that were on the large side, and helmets and bulletproof vests. "The helmets are just for keeping fragments out of your brain pans," he warned. "Chances are they won't stop pistol rounds, and for sure they won't stop anything from a rifle or a machine gun. So don't get cocky."

"How about this vest?" Even in a uniform, Dawud looked untidy.

"Pistol rounds, probably," Pavarotti said. "Rifle? Well, maybe. If you're lucky. If it's a glancing hit. Don't count on it."

"Thanks for easing my mind," Dawud told him.

"Anytime." The Italian was putting on his own vest and tightening his helmet's chin strap. "If I get shot leading you around tonight, remind me not to be angry at you."

"I'll make a note of it," Dawud answered. Captain Pavarotti chuckled.

They left the Ministry of Information building by a side door that opened on an alley. The short hallway leading to the door was dark; it had another door at the opposite end, one that Pavarotti made sure to close behind them. Khalid appreciated the precautions. He might have wished them less necessary.

The bulletproof vest was heavy. So was the assault rifle he carried. Pavarotti had flat-out refused to let him and Dawud go out with no more than a pistol. With this thing, he could spray lead out to six or seven hundred cubits. In the daytime, he stood a decent chance of hitting what he aimed at from farther away than that.

Pavarotti murmured in Italian to one of the perimeter guards. As quietly as the man could, he opened the wood-and-wire gate and let the little party out into unsecured Florence.

As soon as Khalid tramped past the barbed wire and sandbags, he started trying to look every which way at once. The streets were dark, dark, dark, except where the gibbous moon poured down a little wan light. It kept going in and out of the clouds, which made the moon shadows seem to move. Since Khalid wanted to shoot anything that moved, he got even jumpier than he had been before.

Captain Pavarotti acted calm enough. So did Dawud—the Jew rarely showed he was rattled. Khalid had to hope he didn't look too nervous. *Be what you wish to seem*: advice that went back to the ancient Greeks. Socrates' followers had probably had just as much trouble following it as Khalid did.

From one of the deeper shadows that showed a blown-out window came a *click* and a *whoosh* and a thread of fire. A split second later, a rocket-propelled grenade slammed into the front of the Ministry of Information building.

"Down!" Pavarotti shouted in Italian. Khalid didn't blame him for losing his Arabic at a moment like that. A rocket that could punch through hardened steel also did a terrific job of housebreaking. Half the front wall fell in on itself.

Another grenade whooshed away from that window, trailing flame. Captain Pavarotti fired into it, not with a burst on full automatic but squeezing the trigger for each shot to be more accurate. You could still empty your magazine in ten or fifteen seconds doing that. An anguished shriek rewarded him.

But the second rocket-propelled grenade slammed into the Ministry of Information building even before the shriek rang out. More of it fell in and fell down. Flames started dancing in the ruins. They quickly grew and spread.

"We could have been in there," Dawud said. Khalid heard him as if from far away; the rifle fire stunned his ears. Dawud went on, "If we'd left a few minutes later, or if they'd fired a few minutes sooner . . ."

"It didn't happen," Khalid said firmly, as much to calm himself as to answer his countryman.

"Come on!" Captain Pavarotti hopped to his feet. He might have been round, but he was young enough to have stayed agile. "We've got to help them out!" He clapped a hand to his forehead. "All our records, going up in smoke!"

No bureaucrat from the Maghrib could have sounded more tormented at that thought. Maybe Italy had some touches of civilization after all.

Khalid and Dawud followed Pavarotti back toward his headquarters. The soldiers manning the perimeter had run back to aid their comrades. That left no one to open a gate for the men outside the wire. Pavarotti had a cutter on his belt. He snipped a gate well enough to squeeze through the gap. The Maghribis followed again.

People scrambled out of the burning building. Some used the side door by which Khalid and Dawud had left with Captain Pavarotti. Others chose the holes the grenades had torn in the building. Some helped injured companions get away. Some of the ones who did were injured themselves.

Pavarotti paused for a moment to order a few men, ones carrying weapons, back to the perimeter. "They'll use the firelight to shoot at us," he said. "Make the *cazzi* keep their heads down."

"*Cazzi!*" That wasn't a word Khalid's course in Italian had taught him.

"Pricks," Dawud said helpfully.

"C'mon!" Pavarotti shouted. "Bound to be people still in there. We don't want to let 'em cook." He plunged into the burning Ministry of Information building.

Khalid also didn't want to cook himself. But he wanted even less to hang back under Dawud's eyes and those of the Italians. As he clambered over the bricks that had come down, he thought, not for the first time, that much of what got called courage was really just unwillingness to look bad in front of other people. Flames and a few flashlights gave what light there was. The grenades had knocked out the building's power. A man lay groaning, his leg trapped and probably smashed under a toppled file cabinet. Khalid levered it off him with a length of wood. Dawud grabbed him and dragged him away. He left a trail of blood. That couldn't be good. But, even if they had to cut off that ruined leg, he'd probably live.

A man with a badly burned face staggered out. He had a hand clapped over his eyes, which also wasn't a good sign. "Here." Khalid took him by the elbow. "I'll get you away."

"*Grazie, amico,*" the Italian said. "I can't see."

"This way." Khalid led him to the biggest hole in the front wall. "Careful, now. There are bricks here."

"Hang on to me so I don't fall, then."

Khalid did. He had to hold the man up once or twice when he stumbled over a brick or a piece of brick. "All right," he said. "Now you're out." A bullet snapped past them. "And now you'd better get down. The fanatics are shooting at us."

"If I'm blind, they may as well kill me." But the Italian went to the sidewalk. He might say he didn't mind dying, but his body didn't believe him.

Khalid plunged back into the building. The flames were hotter now. He flung up an arm to protect his own face. Here came Pavarotti, with a wounded man on his back. "Where are the fucking fire engines?" he shouted.

"I wish I knew," Khalid said. "Are there more people back there?"

"Not live ones, I don't think," the captain answered. "You may as well get out. You've done all right, Mussulman."

After a beat, Khalid realized that meant *Muslim*. Real Crusaders had called his ancestors such names all those centuries before. Evidently, Europeans never got rid of any old ideas. Not even the Europeans who were supposed to be modern and progressive.

Something over his head creaked and shuddered. If the upper floor came down, he wouldn't get out in one piece, or at all. Coughing in the smoke, he hurried back the way he'd come.

Fire engines did scream up then. Some of the men on them shot back at the Aquinist gunmen. Captain Pavarotti eased his comrade to the ground. He paused long enough to light a cigarette, then nodded at Khalid. "All right," he said with a twisted smile. "Now you're here. Now you've had a look for yourself. How do you like things in Florence?"

Major Badoglio eyed Khalid and Dawud. "Good to see you both," he said. "I hear you had adventures in Florence?"

"A rest home," Dawud said, his voice bland.

"If you want to rest forever, that is," Khalid put in.

"If I'd known you would come so close to doing that, I never would have let you go," Badoglio said. "I didn't want to have to walk into your embassy and explain how I sent you to the place where you got killed. I especially didn't want the people there thinking I had sent you to Florence so you would get killed."

"Don't worry about it," Khalid said. "We didn't want that, either."

"Maybe for reasons different from yours," Dawud added.

"There are places where they keep order better than in Florence," Major Badoglio said. "There are also places, I'm afraid, where they don't keep it nearly so well."

"Any place where they don't, I'm afraid of that," Dawud said.

"Now that you mention it, so am I," Khalid said. "Florence just falls to pieces as soon as the sun goes down."

"We may be getting the upper hand there, though, in spite of the attack on the Ministry of Information headquarters," Badoglio said. "The Po Valley in the north, the country from Naples south . . ." He shook his head. "Not so much."

"You really want to be in control of your own country," Khalid said, remembering how Lorenzo had claimed the northern cities of Milan and Turin followed his lead. Maybe he'd been misled, or maybe he'd just lied. "If you're not, it doesn't belong to you any more."

Major Badoglio scowled at him. "I may be nothing but a backward European, Senior Investigator, but I can figure that out for myself without flying you in from the Maghrib to tell me."

Europeans had a touchy pride. You stepped on it at your peril. "Sorry," Khalid said, more or less sincerely. "Walking barefoot through the obvious, I suppose." He spread his hands, trying to look as harmless and apologetic as he could.

"Let it go, then." Badoglio still looked and sounded irked. But he didn't seem like a man on the point of exploding into a temper tantrum. "The main question is, how do we bring the country, and especially the towns, back under our control? This country doesn't belong to the Aquinists and the Crusaders."

"It does if your people think it does," Dawud said. "If they'd rather have the fanatics tell them what to do, and not the Grand Duke, his Supreme Highness has more trouble than he knows what to do with."

"Some of them do," the major said slowly. "How do we bring them back to their proper allegiance?"

"As I'm sure you already know, there are two main ways." Khalid did his best to make sure Badoglio didn't think he thought the Italian major was ignorant. "You can try to make them love Lorenzo, so they turn against his foes of their own accord. That's the better path. If it doesn't work, you can try to make them fear him so much, they don't dare back the Aquinists because they know what will happen to them if they do."

"With the second one, we run the risk of turning them all against the Grand Duke," Badoglio said. "That can work—one Roman Emperor's motto was 'Let them hate me, as long as they fear me'—but it's dangerous."

"Yes. That's what I said," Khalid replied.

Dawud said, "Caligula didn't last very long before they assassinated him, did he?"

"No, he—" Major Badoglio broke off in surprise. "I wouldn't have looked for someone from your side of the Mediterranean to know which Emperor it was."

Khalid certainly hadn't known. Dawud was the image of nonchalance. "Why not? He ruled over there the same as he did here," he said.

"Well, yes, but . . ." Instead of going on, Badoglio gestured toward Dawud's keffiyeh and robes.

"No, Caligula wasn't a Muslim. He wasn't even a Jew," Dawud said. "But I've got news for you, Major: he wasn't a Christian, either. And I promise you, sir, he didn't wear trousers."

"That's . . . probably enough, Dawud," Khalid said.

"It's all right. I think I had that coming," Badoglio said. "If you gentlemen will excuse me, I need to talk with my colleagues about how we can detach some of the people from the Aquinists. Those madmen should be hunted animals, not fish swimming safe in the middle of a school that makes them impossible to spot."

"You're right. They should." Khalid clasped hands with the Italian. "Always good to talk with you, Major." Again, he was more or less sincere.

"He's able enough. He's loyal enough. If Lorenzo had more like him, he'd do better for himself," Dawud said as they left the Ministry of Information and picked their way through the security arrangements around it. The Aquinists wouldn't have so easy a time attacking this headquarters as they had in Florence.

"That's true, that's true, and that's true, respectively," Khalid said.

"Of course, the Grand Duke does have one other thing going for him," Dawud said. Khalid made a questioning noise. The Jew went on, "Major Badoglio said it himself. The Aquinists are fanatics. They're maniacs. And one of the things fanatics and maniacs do is, they go too far and make the people with working brains hate them."

"Here's hoping," Khalid said.

Budding civil war or no budding civil war, Rome's traffic stayed as appalling as ever. Cars, buses, trucks, motorcycles, motor scooters, bicycles . . . They all jostled for position on winding streets that followed the tracks of ox carts and flocks of sheep in ancient days. There wasn't nearly enough room for all of them. The drivers' complete lack of manners only made things worse, or at least more crowded. Everyone blared away with his or her horn. There weren't many females behind the wheel—pious Christians frowned on their women learning such secular skills—but the ones who did drive were at least as nasty as the men.

Dawud pointed to a coffeehouse. "Let's stop," he said. "I could use a pick-me-up."

Khalid would rather have walked around the corner and headed back to the hotel. But his colleague looked so desperately decaffeinated that he gave in. "Oh, all right," he said. "Not for long, though."

The man who served them muttered when they both spooned plenty of extra sugar into their little cups. Khalid realized that marked them as men from the Muslim world. Dawud didn't seem to care. He knocked his back as if it were brandy and said, "I'd like another, please."

No sooner had the counterman handed him his reload than something around the corner exploded with a thunderous roar. "Jesus Christ!" the Italian shouted, and made the sign of the cross. Dawud gulped the second cup without sweetening it. Then he followed Khalid out of the place.

Staggering, bleeding people were coming the other way. "He yelled 'God wills it!'" a middle-aged woman said. "He yelled 'God wills it!' and he blew himself up!"

"Who did?" Khalid asked.

"That *stronzo* on the scooter," she answered. "Let me by. I've got to clean up." She had a cut on her forehead that would probably need stitches, but she didn't realize it yet. Khalid didn't know what a *stronzo* was, either, but he could make a good guess.

When he and Dawud rounded the corner, nothing much was left of the scooter or of the man who'd ridden it. Two smashed cars lay on their sides. Two or three others were on fire. People lay on the sidewalks. Some were still: unconscious or dead. Others writhed and wailed. The air was thick with smoke and the smell of blood.

"Fuck those Aquinists!" a man behind Khalid said. "Nobody here did anything to them."

Khalid hurried forward to give what first aid he could. As he tore a tunic into strips to make bandages, he thought about over-reaching.

X

A few Italians were part of the archaeological team excavating east of Naples. Most members came either from the Maghrib or from a madrasa in Arkansistan. The leader of the Maghribi contingent was an eager young fellow named Lisarh ibn Yahsub. "I wish we had more locals with us," he told Khalid and Dawud. "I especially wish we did because of the language issues. We slog through Latin, but for them it comes naturally. Their language is descended from it, and they even use it in their religious services."

"Yes, I know about that," Khalid agreed. "But why don't you? It's their country and their history, after all. Some of them know a good deal about it." He told how Major Badoglio had quoted Caligula.

"Did he? Isn't that interesting?" Lisarh said. "Well, he must be a secular man, and there aren't enough of them here. For too many Italians, anything that happened when the pagans ruled isn't worth remembering."

"Kind of like the idea of the *Jahiliyah*," Dawud put in.

"Well, yes, but *we* don't think of the days before the Prophet—peace be unto him—as the Time of Ignorance any more. Not all those days, I should say." The archaeologist eyed the investigator. "The *Jahiliyah* isn't exactly your people's idea, is it?"

"You mean because I'm a Jew? I'm part of the wider world, too, or I am whenever the wider world feels like letting me be one, any-how," Dawud answered.

"That's a commendable attitude. I wish more of the Italians had it," Lisarh ibn Yahsub said. "Some of the Italians who were here have packed up and gone home because of the political situation."

"The political situation. Yes. That's one way to put it," Khalid said. The archaeological dig had a barbed-wire perimeter strength-ened with sandbagged machine-gun nests that would have done credit to a Ministry of Information building. The men serving the machine guns and walking the perimeter were among the Grand Duke's most trusted troops. If they weren't, they might have turned on the archaeologists themselves.

"It's so frustrating!" Lisarh burst out. "We've known for almost two thousand years that there were two Roman towns buried under the lava here. One Roman writer, Pliny the Elder, came to the erup-tion site and died near here trying to get people away by boat. His nephew, Pliny the Younger, wrote about what he saw from farther away."

"Why didn't he go with his uncle?" Khalid asked.

"Nobody knows for sure. The best guess is, he didn't have the nerve," Lisarh answered. "And so he lived for another forty or fifty years, and had a fine career of his own. Not brave, maybe, but very sensible. His account has been available for centuries, but the Italians never did any digging of their own. The people from the madrasa at Tuskalusa deserve the credit. They started the project twenty-odd years ago, and we've found incredible things since."

"Arkansistan has even more oil than the Maghrib does," Dawud said. "More than it knows what to do with, almost."

"Not like the Faisalis who rule the holy cities and the Rub' al-Khali," Khalid said. "They don't have to share their money among so many people."

"They don't have to—and they don't," Lisarh said. "They get rich off the pilgrims who make the *hajj* every year, too. And it all piles up and piles up and piles up." The Faisalis had never been famous for generosity. One of these days, odds were they'd regret that. In an ever more open and democratic world, they were almost as tyrannical as some of the nastier European lords.

Dawud smiled, then coughed and pretended he hadn't. A reputation for stinginess clung to the Jews. The Faisalis might be the most pious of Muslims, but no one in the history of the world had ever squeezed a coin any tighter than they did.

"Nobody's give you any trouble here?" Khalid asked.

"No. Of course, having the soldiers around doesn't hurt," Lisarh ibn Yahsub replied. "But the farmers are friendly enough. They sell us olive oil and eggs and a lamb every once in a while. They aren't interested in what we're doing, though. It's sad, really."

"I'd say you're lucky," Dawud remarked. "If they thought you were digging up gold or something, you'd never get them out of your hair."

"Well, you're bound to be right about that. We've found some gold and silver coins—not a lot, but some," the archaeologist said. "Some jewelry, too. Step into my tent if you want to. You can see what I mean."

They did. The tent looked to have come from the Maghribi army, and had seen hard use. It still kept sun and wind off the people inside it. Coins, rings, necklaces, earrings . . . All were carefully labeled to show where they'd been discovered. Lisarh showed that they'd all been photographed in place, too, before they were collected.

"The trench that we've dug this season goes right into the heart of what was the Roman town of Pompeii," he said. "We've discovered body casts, where volcanic mud shows how someone fell and died all those years ago. Sometimes you can even make out a person's expression."

"What would happen if the volcano erupted again?" Khalid asked uneasily.

"Naples would be very unhappy," Lisarh said, which would do for an understatement till a bigger one rolled down the highway. But the scientist hadn't finished: "So would air travelers all over the Mediterranean. An eruption throws grit and crud thousands of cubits into the air." He grinned. "Don't you love those techni-cal terms? That's what it is, though. And airplane engines don't like sucking in all that grit and crud. Till it comes back to earth, either you go around where it is or you don't fly."

"That's an even more cheerful thought than some of the politi-cal ones we've been dealing with lately," Khalid said.

"It is, isn't it?" Lisarh nodded to himself. "It's so stupid, too. If they had themselves a leader who wanted to bring back the glory of the Roman Empire and they got all excited about him, I could just about understand that. When Vesuvius blew, Rome was the greatest country in the world."

"That isn't what the Aquinists have in mind, though," Dawud said.

Lisarh ibn Yahsub grimaced. "Believe me, I understand that. They want to bring back the *Jahiliyah*—not just for Italy, but everywhere. Everything we've learned, all the things we've made and the diseases we've stopped . . . They care more about God than about any of that. If they want to live that way, it's their business. But if they say everybody has to live that way—"

"*Deus vult!*" Khalid broke in.

"*Deus vult!*" Lisarh agreed sourly. "And they *do* say everybody has to live that way. And that turns it into my business, because I think I have the right to live the way I want to, not the way they want me to."

"Shows what you know, you dog of an infidel, you," Dawud said.

"You should talk," Lisarh retorted, and Dawud chuckled.

"One of the reasons we wanted to check up on you was to make sure the Aquinists hadn't learned you were out in the countryside *learning* things." Khalid made that sound as filthy as he could.

"Oh, we're learning things, all right," Lisarh said. "Let me show you a few more photographs. Some of the buildings under there are so perfectly preserved, even the paintings on the walls are as fresh as if they were done yesterday. The pictures in this folder are from a lupanar we found."

"What's a lupanar?" Khalid asked. Lisarh showed him and Dawud the photographs. Once he saw them, he had no doubt what a lupanar was. "Well, it doesn't look like we've learned a whole lot of new ways to do it over the past however many years."

"Funny—that's just what I said when we discovered the place. If the Aquinists knew it was there, they'd want to blow it up so it doesn't give ideas to people who already have them," Lisarh said.

"Are you worried about publishing what you've found, then?" Khalid asked.

"Not even a little bit," Lisarh answered. "One of the things I've found out is that the people who go around screaming 'God wills it!' aren't the kind who go to a madrasa library to check out an academic journal."

"Good. They should leave the juicy stuff for people who can appreciate it," Dawud said. The archaeologist laughed. He liked that so much, he pulled out a bottle of grappa and some more dirty pictures for the investigators.

Naples was even older than vanished Pompeii. It was the first place the Greeks had settled in Italy. At about the same time, the Phoenicians were founding Carthage, not far from modern Tunis. In different languages, both cities wore the same name: New Town.

When Dawud remarked on that, Khalid said, "I wonder how many Carthages there are in the Sunset Lands, Carthages and Damascuses and Jerusalems and Alexandrias and Cairos. . . ."

"Probably an Istanbul or three, too," Dawud said. "Who knows? Maybe even a couple of Romes. If they didn't keep the native names for the places there, they named them after places here."

"Or else they called them things like Little Rock or Riverside that showed what was in the neighborhood," Khalid said.

"That, too." Dawud nodded. Then he sighed. "I'll tell you—I wouldn't be sorry if we weren't right by Naples. I'd be even less sorry if we weren't inside this miserable place."

"Now that you mention it, so would I," Khalid said. "It's not even so much that I wonder whether every other man on the street is an Aquinist with a bomb strapped to his belly who wants to blow me to shreds. I do, but that's not it."

"No, that's not it." Dawud nodded again, more emphatically this time. "I'll tell you what it is. The last honest man who ever lived here starved to death five hundred years ago, and all the crooks who stayed behind have been laughing at him ever since."

"That's it!" Khalid looked at him with nothing but admiration. "That's just it! I hadn't put my finger on it so well."

"You can buy anything here, anything at all," Dawud said. "You only need cash and connections. And if you have the cash, tomorrow you can buy the trusting fool who sold you what you wanted today."

"If you've got the cash, it's a wonderful place. If you don't . . ." Khalid frowned. "If you don't, you have to sell yourself."

"In a way, though, that works to our advantage," Dawud said. Khalid made a questioning noise. Dawud explained: "The Aquinists don't care about money. They care about God. They seem just as stupid to the people who run things here as they do to us, even if it's for different reasons."

"Huh," Khalid said thoughtfully. "I'm glad to have you along, you know? I'm not sure I could be so cynical all by myself."

"Nice to know I'm good for something." Dawud sounded pleased with himself.

Instead of visiting the Ministry of Information building the next morning, Khalid and Dawud called at the central police station. The prefect of police was called Pietro Vaccaro. He understood the Italian the Maghribis used, but his own Neapolitan dialect was opaque to them both.

It turned out not to matter, because he spoke fair classical Arabic. "You want to see *whom*, my master?" he asked Khalid. Patiently, Khalid repeated himself. The prefect's eyes were red-veined and weary and shrewd. "What makes you think I know this Dino Crocetti fellow, or where to find him?"

While Khalid cast about for a polite way to answer that, Dawud stepped into the breach: "This is Naples. You're the police boss. He's the mob boss. Chances are you have dinner with him once a week, so you can keep each other up to date."

Prefect Vaccaro swung toward him. "Yes, this *is* Naples," he agreed. "People who talk to me like that are liable to have unfortunate accidents. How would you like to get fished out of the harbor six weeks from now? The crabs eat the eyes first, I hear."

"Yes, I've heard the same thing," Dawud said placidly. "Do you want to take the chance of putting the Grand Duke and the Maghrib after you at the same time? Isn't it easier just to tell us how to get hold of Crocetti?"

Vaccaro still glowered. "They say Jews talk too damn much," he rumbled. "I see they're right."

"My wife certainly thinks so," Dawud answered.

"You're staying at the Santa Lucia." The prefect did not make it a question.

"That's right," Khalid said along with Dawud.

"Get the devil out of my office. Go to the hotel. Don't come back here," Vaccaro said. "Someone will pay you a call. So just remember—if you meet the crabs in the harbor, I won't be the guy who introduces you."

"Well, it's a story." Dawud still sounded altogether at ease. He and Khalid left Vaccaro's office. Khalid imagined he could feel the daggers the prefect of police was looking at his back.

"You really know how to make officials fall in love with you, don't you?" Khalid said after they got out of the station. He hadn't been altogether sure they *would* get out, but they did.

"I try." Dawud's eyes glinted. "I'm sure they think I'm very trying."

The Santa Lucia wasn't far from the center of town. The furniture was old-fashioned, but each room had a television, a telephone, and a bathroom with hot and cold running water. Khalid and Dawud drank bottled mineral water, though. The stuff that came out of the taps in Naples could give a foreigner who wasn't used to it a nasty flux of the bowels.

They waited. They waited. They waited some more. When they were about to go downstairs for supper, someone knocked on the door. Khalid opened it. The man in the hallway was short, but stocky and tough looking. "Come on with me," he said.

Go with him they did. He bundled them into a green Pontiak, then slid behind the wheel himself. Traffic in Naples seemed more snarled than Rome's. Khalid could imagine nothing worse to say about it.

The driver eventually pulled up in an alley and pointed to a door. "Get out," he said. "Go in there."

It could have been an ambush. If it was, they couldn't do anything about it now. They went in. It smelled like old garbage outside. As soon as the door closed behind them, the odors turned heavenly. They'd walked into the back of an eatery, and plainly a good one.

A man in a white tunic with brass buttons addressed them in good Arabic: "You must be the Maghribis. This way, my masters, if you'd be so kind."

He led them into a small private room curtained off from the area where most people ate. The man waiting there was about sixty, and strikingly handsome. Good living had given him a double chin and pouches under his eyes, but he still seemed able to take care of himself. He wore a robe of elegant cut and a keffiyeh with restrained red stripes.

"Peace be unto you, my masters," he said in classical Arabic even better than the waiter's. "I am Dino Crocetti. Someone tells me you've been trying to get hold of me."

"I wonder who that might be," Khalid said dryly.

"It doesn't matter," Crocetti said, which might or might not have been true. He rose to clasp the investigators' hands, then waved them into chairs. The waiter reappeared with wine. It was as good as any Khalid had had in Italy. A plate of little fried squid whetted the appetite. Khalid thought they were delicious. So, plainly, did Dawud. Crocetti smiled, watching him eat. "Those are *haram* for you, aren't they?"

"We'd say *treyf*. It amounts to the same thing, only the rules are a bit different," the Jew answered. "But I like 'em, so I eat 'em. It's between me and my God. Nobody else needs to worry about it."

"I suspect the Aquinists would have a thing or two to say if they heard that from you," Dino Crocetti remarked.

That gave Khalid the opening he'd hoped for. "Well, *Signor*, that's what we wanted to talk about with you."

"Me?" Crocetti must have had practice at looking innocent or he couldn't have done it so well. "I have no idea why you would say such a thing. I am only a simple businessman, doing what I can to stay afloat."

"Right." If Khalid sounded disbelieving, he was. Dawud snorted. Even Dino Crocetti smiled, displaying teeth that had seen some expensive dentistry. Khalid went on, "If the Aquinists start running Naples—"

"If the Aquinists start running Italy," Dawud added.

"That, too." Khalid nodded. "If the Aquinists take over, what happens to your businesses, *Signor* Crocetti? They aren't what you'd call keen on brothels or gambling houses."

Before Crocetti could answer, the waiter stuck his head into the private room. The mob boss switched to rapid-fire Neapolitan dialect. Then he came back to Arabic: "I thought we would have *'o pigniatiello 'e vavella*—it's a soup made with fish and shellfish and octopus—and then *sartù di riso*, a rice cake with mushrooms and meat. Does that suit you, my masters?"

"Sounds good," Khalid said. This time, Dawud was the one who nodded.

"And to return to your question," Crocetti continued smoothly, "if the Aquinists take over, very little happens to my businesses. People always want to gamble. Men always want to lie down with women. God wills it, you might say." He smiled the amused smile of a man who'd seen everything more than once.

"You know that. We know that." Khalid couldn't match the mob boss' cynicism, but he could come close. "Do the Aquinists know it, though? Or would they shoot you or hang you to discourage the others?"

"It's possible. I haven't lost a lot of sleep over it," Crocetti said. "But what you are telling me is that you want me to support Grand Duke Lorenzo and not just wait to see what happens and then ride the horse whichever way it is going. Or am I wrong?"

"No, *Signor*, you're not wrong—as you know perfectly well," Dawud said. Crocetti smiled again, this time the self-satisfied smile of a man who knew he knew what he knew. The Jew continued, "But if you back him now, he'll owe you something later on."

"He will—if he wins," Dino Crocetti said. "But even if he does, will he pay it back? Princes—and Grand Dukes, as well—have sadly short memories when it comes to debts like that."

"You're wasted in Naples, *Signor*," Khalid exclaimed. "You should come to the Maghrib. In a year or two, you'd be our spymaster, or else running the underwazirate in charge of war."

"It could be." Whatever Crocetti's flaws, modesty wasn't one of them. He displayed those perfected teeth again. "But why on earth would I want less power there than I enjoy here?"

Khalid started to laugh. Then he realized the Italian wasn't joking. He wasn't just a high-ranking functionary here in Naples. He had the authority of a prince, if not the title.

Before Khalid could reply, the waiter brought in the fish soup. It was wonderful. Khalid had looked for nothing less. Crocetti knew what the best here was, and knew how to get it. Halfway through, Khalid said, "However you look at it, you aren't a natural ally for people who think having fun is sinful."

"I daresay not," Dino Crocetti answered. "I am not their natural enemy, either, though. I try to get along with everyone, from Prefect Vaccaro to people like you."

"Ah, but if they don't want to get along with you . . . ?" Dawud said.

"Then I adjust as needed." If anything fazed Crocetti, he didn't let on.

If you don't play along with our side, your life gets more com-

plicated. Khalid thought about coming out with it, but held his peace. Obvious threats would only make the Neapolitan scorn him. And Prefect Vaccaro was all too likely to warn Crocetti of any trouble blowing his way. If Lorenzo III started getting rid of police prefects as well as crime bosses, the ones he didn't get rid of would probably discover they'd been secret Aquinists all along. . . .

What he did say was, "This is fine, fine soup."

"I'm glad it pleases you, my master," Crocetti replied. That was the respectful politeness of Arabic, nothing more. He remained in effortless control of the situation here.

In due course, the rice cake with beef and mushrooms came in. It might have been even better than the soup. Before Khalid tasted it, he wouldn't have bet more than a copper that such a thing was possible. He wasn't sure it outdid the soup, but he also wasn't sure it didn't. More wine accompanied it, and Italian ice cream followed. Khalid found he had a much harder time disliking Dino Crocetti than he had before they ate together.

"Well, gentlemen, I'm glad you seem to have enjoyed Ciro a Santa Brigida," the Neapolitan said, which told the investigators where they'd been eating. Crocetti lit a cigar. Beaming, Dawud ibn Musa followed suit.

"Think about what we've had to say, that's all," Khalid told the boss.

"*Assolutamente,* my master," Crocetti said. "I do know which end is up, I promise you. Is there anything else, or shall I have Enrico drive you back to your hotel?"

"Give our regards to the prefect next time you see him," Dawud gibed.

"*Assolutamente,*" Crocetti said again. He blew a smoke ring up toward the ceiling. "It shouldn't be long."

On his home ground, he was more than a match for even the Jew's sarcasm. The investigators went back to the odorous alley. They got into the Pontiak. Enrico drove away with the sublime disregard for life and limb that looked to be every Italian's birthright. Why they didn't get back with a dented hood and with bicyclists draped over both front fenders Khalid couldn't have said, but they didn't.

"So much for that," he grumbled when they walked into their room.

"Hey, we got a demon of a supper out of it," Dawud said. "Dino was buying, too, so we don't have to put it on the swindle sheet. And whatever else he is, he's no dope. He can stay in business with Lorenzo. With the Aquinists, he takes his chances. I don't think he likes taking chances he doesn't have to."

"Here's hoping." That was the best Khalid could do.

"I hate those bosses," Annarita Pezzola said after the investigators returned to Rome and Khalid told her how things had gone in the south. Dawud was reporting more formally to Major Badoglio.

"You could do worse than Crocetti." Khalid hoped that wasn't the good food talking. He didn't think so, but how could you know for sure?

"You could do better, too," Annarita answered. "The bosses are almost as much a part of the past we need to break away from as the Aquinists are. They corrupt whatever they touch, and they touch everything in the country. As long as they can get their way with bribes and murders, Italy will never be honest and modern."

She spoke with great conviction. It wasn't that Khalid thought she was wrong, either. If greasing a palm could get you whatever you wanted or needed, your land wouldn't go forward as fast as it would if you could trust your officials.

But . . . "The bosses aren't trying to murder the Grand Duke and let the fanatics take over."

"Not right now, no," Annarita admitted reluctantly. "But they've risen against the Grand Dukes before. They want to be lords in their cities, not just crime bosses. And with the money they siphon away from the treasury through their gambling and their whores and their smuggling, they almost are."

"One set of enemies at a time." Khalid was a practical man.

Most investigators were, and had to be. "If you try to take them all on at once, you won't beat any of them."

"I know that here." Annarita tapped a temple to her forefinger. "But here"—she laid a hand on the sweetly rounded flesh above her heart—"I hate it. What kind of country are we when the only way to get anything done is to pay somebody off? It makes me embarrassed to be an Italian."

Italy, Aragon, Castile, Portugal, France . . . They were all notorious for corruption. Khalid gave Annarita what consolation he could: "It's even worse in the little German states, I hear."

"Oh, joy!" If she was consoled, she hid it very well. "This ought to be a country where things run as smoothly as they do on your side of the Mediterranean. If Cosimo had lived for another twenty years, if the Aquinists hadn't murdered him, it might have turned into one like that."

"Maybe." Khalid didn't want to argue with a woman he found so attractive, but he also didn't believe her. If the old Grand Duke had ruled for another twenty years, Italy would have been an honest, orderly place as far as his eye could reach, and not a digit farther. Out of his gaze, the bosses would have kept right on doing all the profitable but illicit things they did, and they would have kept crossing police prefects' palms with silver, too, to get them to look the other way. Italy had run like that since the Roman Empire collapsed, and probably had run like that back when Rome was strong.

"You think I'm crazy," Annarita said. For all his efforts, something in his voice must have given him away.

He shook his head, denying everything. "What I think is that you're wasted in Italy. I've told you so before. You could do much better for yourself in the Maghrib, especially now that Lorenzo's Grand Duke."

Now that your patron's dead, he meant. Italy ran that way. The crime bosses were patrons, too, big ones. That was part of the reason they were so hard to root out. Police prefects were also patrons. So were bishops.

To a certain degree, things everywhere worked that way. People with power helped other people they liked, and those people paid the favor back or else paid it forward. In the civilized world, though, law and custom put checks on the system. Not in places like this.

"I'd be a foreigner there. I'd still be a woman there, even if that isn't as hard as it is here," Annarita said. "And you have too many educated people there already."

"Not as many as we need. We never have as many as we need," Khalid said.

"We haven't got enough here. We especially don't have enough educated women here," Annarita said. "And I *am* an Italian. I want to be proud to be an Italian, not embarrassed. I want to make this a place all Italians can be proud of."

"Even the ones who don't want to pay any attention to you because you're a woman and the ones who don't think women have any business getting an education to begin with?" he asked.

"Even those," she said firmly. "I want to help make this a place where there aren't so many ignorant people like that."

"And the ones who yell 'God wills it!' want to make this a place where that kind of ignorance is king no matter who the Grand Duke is. They want to make Italy a place where it's illegal for women to get an education and illegal to listen to them if they do," Khalid said.

"I know. I'm not likely not to know, am I?" Annarita answered. "You can run away, though, or you can stay and fight to make things better. That's what I aim to do."

"And if you wind up in a country where the Aquinists *are* running things?" he asked. "They'll jail you or they'll hurt you or they'll kill you, and you won't have a chance to make things better."

"Maybe I'll be a martyr for the cause. That's not useless, either. Christianity had martyrs"—she used the Italian word this time, not the Arabic *shahid*—"before Islam did. Or maybe I'll see that I can't do anything then, and choose that time to leave."

"If you're able to," Khalid said.

"If I'm able to," Annarita agreed. "Life is full of different chances. You do what you do and you see what comes of it. Then you do something else, and you see what comes of that. What else can you do?"

"Well . . ." Khalid glanced at his watch. It was getting close to the twelfth hour of the day, the time when the sun went down. He plunged: "You could come to supper with me."

She studied him. She looked more amused than surprised, so she must have noticed that he'd noticed her. "All right," she said. "We can do that. But what happens next? You share your hotel room with the *Ebreo*. He's a funny fellow, but people don't always want company."

That was more forward than he'd expected her to be, more forward than some women from the Maghrib would have been. She took her modernity seriously. She took most of the things she did seriously. That was part of the reason she interested Khalid.

"We'll figure something out," he said. "Or if we don't tonight, maybe we will some other time."

Now she beamed at him. "Good," she said. "You always like to think someone wants to take you out for some reason beside what you have between your legs. That you're a person to him, not just a pussy."

No matter how the Catholic Church frowned on them, reliable ways to make sure you didn't plant a baby in a woman when you lay down with her had radically changed customs in the Muslim world over the past lifetime. Even there, though, most women still felt the same way Annarita did. Evolutionary biologists claimed there were sound reasons they did. Khalid didn't know about that. He did know he wouldn't have wanted women to be just like men. Half the fun would have gone out of the game if they were.

They went to an eatery not far from his hotel. It was crowded. Several people in the place were complaining about dining so early. They didn't appreciate Grand Duke Lorenzo's curfew. Neither did

Khalid, once he remembered it. If he went somewhere with Anna-rita after supper, he'd either spend the night there or take his chances dodging Lorenzo's patrols.

The same thing seemed to occur to her. "I think we'll have to find another time," she said. "Don't worry, though. I won't change my mind—unless I do, of course." Her eyes twinkled.

"*La donna è mobile*," he said in his indifferent Italian.

"I'm not nearly so fickle as half the men I know," Annarita said, and he believed her. She went on, "I do suppose I asked for that," so he knew he hadn't made her angry.

They were finishing their second course when something exploded in the distance. Sirens screamed through the streets. "That doesn't sound good," Khalid said, frowning.

"No. It doesn't," Annarita said. "It's from the direction of the Vatican, too. I hope his Holiness is all right."

Khalid hoped the same thing, perhaps even more than she did. Pope Marcellus saw that times had changed, and that Christianity needed to change to keep up with them. How could anyone guess whether his successor would feel that way, too?

After a few minutes later, the cook—who also seemed to be the owner—came out and said, "Ladies and gentlemen, the radio says two men in an auto blew themselves up at the edge of the Vatican. The streets were crowded—it killed people, and wounded more. His Holiness is safe, though, God bless him." He made the sign of the cross.

So did several of the diners and both waiters in the place. "Now," Khalid said, "the next interesting question is whether they were going after the Pope or only spreading terror around." *Only* spreading terror around? That was what had come out of his mouth, all right. There were worse things, even if he would have had trouble believing it before he came to Italy.

"No one from the Ministry of Information can question them now," Annarita said. "Satan will have to take care of it in hell."

"They think they're going in the other direction," Khalid said. That was, of course, part of the problem. Men drunk on the hope of heaven didn't care what happened to them in this world. It made stopping them much harder. Khalid feared death not least because he suspected this was the only life he had. The Aquinists truly believed in the world to come.

He couldn't even kiss Annarita good-bye after supper. He might have back in Tunis, but straitlaced Italy frowned on public shows of affection between the sexes. Feeling like a man from a bygone time, he squeezed her hand and walked back to the hotel alone.

XI

Dawud ibn Musa was watching television when Khalid let himself into their room. "Guess what?" the Jew said without looking away from the screen.

"You mean, besides the bomb at the edge of the Vatican a little while ago?" Khalid said.

"That's nothing. Those fools didn't get anywhere close to the Pope. They just killed a bunch of nobodies," Dawud said, his voice full of scorn. "But a couple of other Aquinists came *that* close to killing the King of France."

"They didn't do it?" Khalid asked.

"No. They didn't realize the lectern he was standing behind and the glass on it were armored. He's cut and bruised, and the news says he may lose the hearing in one ear, but he's not blown to shreds like Cosimo."

"A good thing, too!" Khalid exclaimed. King Jean, like the late Grand Duke, was trying to yank his country into the modern world by the ears. Khalid had seen the Dauphin, his son, at Cosimo's funeral rites, but had no way to judge how well the young man might follow in his father's footsteps, or even whether he would want to do that.

"It's good that they failed. It's bad that they tried, and worse that they almost did it," Dawud said. "One of the King's generals is dead, and a police official, too. More are injured. Not enough of the Aquinists with the bomb to bury."

He was right about that. The TV showed the town hall where the attempt took place. Red smears near the podium were all that remained of the would-be assassins.

Khalid flopped down on his own bed. He had more things on his mind than fanatics who blew themselves up for the greater glory of God. "Um . . . Dawud . . ." he said tentatively.

"What's up?" his countryman asked when he didn't go on right away.

"Remember how you teased me a while ago?" Khalid asked, still approaching things in a gingerly way.

"When?" Dawud asked, which was a fair question: he did it at any excuse or none.

"When you offered to take another room because I might want some privacy in this one."

"Well? What about it?"

"That . . . might not be such a bad notion after all." Khalid didn't like the idea of telling Dawud to clear out so he could use the room for making love. But he liked the idea of having nowhere to make love even less.

A grin spread across Dawud's fleshy face. "I'll move out, then. Just so you know, I've already cleared it with the people who order us around. They *will* spring for separate rooms, believe it or not."

"You told them you needed your own room because I've found a lady friend, and they went along with it?" Khalid had trouble believing him.

Well he might have, too. Dawud threw back his head and laughed. "I'm dumb, Khalid, but I'm not that dumb," he said. He was anything but dumb, as Khalid knew perfectly well. Laughing still, Dawud went on, "I told 'em it was for security reasons. If the Aquinists fire a rocket into our room in the middle of the night now, they can kill both of us. If we have separate rooms, they only blow one of us to smithereens. The other one can keep on helping Grand Duke Lorenzo. That, they went along with."

No, Dawud ibn Musa wasn't even slightly dumb. He knew how to talk to security higher-ups in their own paranoid language. Khalid got up and set a hand on his shoulder. "You're all right—you know that?"

"Maybe not too bad, for an ape or a swine of a Jew," Dawud said with no rancor Khalid could hear. He could cite texts from the Christians' section of the Bible, and from the Qur'an as well.

"Nobody with his head on straight takes those verses seriously any more," Khalid said. "Any holy book from a long time ago will have passages in it you wish it didn't. They thought differently back then, and you can't go along with everything in there if you've got a modern education and a modern way of looking at things."

"You understand that. I understand that. People like the Grand Duke and the King of France understand part of that when they're having a good day," Dawud said. "But the Aquinists, they don't understand that at all. They want the old days back again."

"Well, there are Muslims who want the old days back again, too," Khalid said. "They write books. They crank out letters to the newspapers. They hold marches. Sometimes they get into fistfights with modernists, or throw rocks at them. They don't shoot them or blow them up."

"It's the price we pay for civilization," Dawud said. "We don't get passionate enough about religion to want to kill each other on account of it." He made a small production out of lighting a cigar. "Not us! When we kill each other, it's because of politics. And politics is *important*."

"Er—right," Khalid said, a little uneasily. "By your logic, nothing is worth killing anybody else over."

"If somebody's trying to kill me, I'll kill him to keep him from doing it," Dawud answered. "Call me rude if you want to, but I think I'm entitled to go on breathing till I get sick and the doctors can't fix me or till I do something idiotic like walking in front of a train. I think everybody is."

"Shows what you know, doesn't it?" Khalid said.

"All right, call me a crazy optimist," the Jew replied. "But there haven't been any big wars in the civilized world for most of a life-time. We could do worse. They do worse here."

One of the reasons there hadn't been any big wars in the realm where modern civilization held sway was that countries there feared the consequences too much to risk them. When you worried more about this world than the next one, that was how you behaved. When heaven was what mattered, you'd do what you needed to do here and assume God would reward you in eons to come. You'd act like an Aquinist, in other words.

The Papal Guards searched Khalid and Dawud before admitting them into Marcellus IX's presence. They were thoroughgoing professionals. Had either Maghribi been carrying a weapon, they would have found it.

"You're clean," said the officer in charge of the detail. "You can go on."

"Captain Salgari told us to come unarmed. We already knew that, but he told us anyhow," Khalid said in some irritation. "Did you think we wouldn't listen?"

The officer gave back an impassive stare and an expressive shrug. "Maybe you're stupid, so you don't listen. Maybe you want to hurt his Holiness, and Captain Salgari doesn't know it. Maybe you really aren't who your documents say you are. So we go ahead and make sure."

He sounded like any security man worth his salary whom Khalid had ever met. Arguing with such people was more trouble than it was worth. Their nature and their training combined to make them what they were.

An ecclesiastical functionary waved the Maghribis to chairs in the antechamber to Pope Marcellus' private office. The man spoke to them in a language that sounded like Italian but wasn't. It had to be Latin. Dawud gave a low-voiced translation into Arabic: "He says the Pope is talking with someone else, but he should be done soon."

"Thanks," Khalid said, also quietly.

"Accept my apologies, my masters." The ecclesiastic might be dressed in odd robes of slightly faded velvet, but his command of classical Arabic was excellent. "I will use your tongue from now on." He eyed Dawud. "And how, ah, interesting that you should understand the language of the Vatican."

"I'd rather be interesting than boring," Dawud said, which might mean anything or nothing.

Khalid cautiously sat in one of the chairs. It creaked at his weight, but the wicker under his behind held. The chair's arms and legs had been gilded, but most of the goldwork had worn away, showing the oak from which the frame was made. Painters should have touched up the gilding. Had the Papacy been richer, they probably would have.

A modern intercom on the cleric's desk buzzed for attention. He picked up the handset, listened, murmured "*Sì, sì*," and put the handset back in its cradle. "His Holiness will see you now, my masters," he said, and hurried to open the door that led to the office. He might not have been young—no one in the Vatican except the guards seemed to be young—but he was spry.

Nobody but Marcellus awaited the Maghribis in the papal office. Whoever he'd been talking with before had left through a different door. Popes might need to keep visitors separate from one another. They made sure they could. In a more modern, efficient office, with only one way in and out, discretion would have been harder to preserve.

"Your Holiness," Khalid and Dawud said together, one in Arabic, the other in Italian.

"I greet you both, gentlemen," the Pope replied in his own good Arabic. "I must tell you that the state of the world, or at least of this part of it, has not improved since I first had the honor of making your acquaintance. Please sit, if you would be so kind. I do not bother with ceremony here. Getting away from it can be a relief."

Visitors' chairs in the chamber were good-quality office furniture. They wouldn't have been out of place in Calcutta or Qom or

Tallahassi. Neither would his own chair, which was the sort any prominent executive might have used. The antique desk and the bookshelves full of titles in close to a dozen languages, ancient and modern, told a different story, as did his regalia. He might not stand on much ceremony here, but he couldn't escape it all.

"No, things aren't better, your Holiness," Khalid said after settling himself. "That's why we wanted to speak with you again. The problem comes not least from the militant wing of your church."

"True. It does," Marcellus said sadly. "But people who want to eat fire *will* eat fire even if they have to kindle it themselves."

"You have the power to bind and to loose, though. That's what the New Testament says, isn't it?" Dawud said. Yes, he could quote other faiths' scriptures along with his own.

No doubt the Pope could, too, especially since Christians recognized the Old Testament as the foundation on which the New lay. But Marcellus chose not to here. "As I told you when we first met, what I may do in law is not the same as what I can do in the real world. If those I bind reject me, I have no army to force them to obedience. If they name an Antipope, they will deny I have any authority over them at all—and Christendom will be torn asunder. I cannot risk that."

"Not even if they blow up this great church of Saint Peter around your ears?" Khalid asked.

"I pray they will be able to do no such wicked thing," Pope Marcellus replied. "But if they should, I will echo our Lord and Savior when He said, 'Father, forgive them; for they know not what they do.'"

"Oh, they know what they're doing, all right," Dawud said. "They know much too well."

Before Marcellus could say anything more, the door that didn't lead out to the antechamber opened. A servitor walked in carrying a tray. It held small cups of strong coffee and sweet rolls fragrant with almond paste. "*Grazie,* Giorgio," the Pope told the man. He and the investigators ate and drank without talking till Giorgio left the office again.

"Very tasty," Dawud said then, licking sticky icing off a fingertip.

"*Grazie*," Marcellus said again.

"Your Holiness, if you can't see your way clear to ordering the Aquinists to disband or anything like that, could you issue an edict—" Khalid began.

"A bull. A Papal bull. That's what they call them," Dawud broke in.

Smiling, Marcellus said, "The *bulla* is the seal on the document. If it is gold, we call the document a chrysobull—Latin, borrowing from Greek."

Khalid didn't care why the Church called an edict a bull. He had a modern impatience with irrelevant details. He went on, "Could you issue a bull condemning violence that takes innocent lives? If you do even that much, the fanatics won't be so sure they're going straight to heaven after they blow themselves up in a public square."

"That . . . may be possible," the Pope said slowly. "I do not wish to do anything to touch off a schism in the Church. I will consult with the Curia—my council of advisors—and see if they feel I can safely issue such a bull."

"Please consult with Grand Duke Lorenzo, too, my master," Khalid said. "If the Aquinists kill him or overthrow him and grab hold of Italy, you won't have a comfortable time, will you?"

Marcellus was far from a young man. Even so, Khalid doubted that his thin, almost ascetic features could have shown so much pain very often. "I don't fear for myself," he said, and Khalid believed him where he would have doubted most men. After a moment, the Pope resumed: "That would not be good for the Church, though, and it would be dreadful for the Church's flock. It would mean war, wouldn't it? War with the Maghrib, I mean, and perhaps Egypt as well."

"It depends on what the Aquinists do next." Khalid picked his words with care.

"Seems pretty likely, though, doesn't it?" Dawud said. "They wouldn't stop with Italy. They'd figure it was just the first bite. They want to make over the whole wide world."

"Yes. They do," Pope Marcellus said. "As the civilization centered in the Muslim world has made the world over in its image through the past few centuries."

"Do you really want to fall back into the *Jahiliyah*, your Holiness?" Khalid asked. "That's what the Aquinists are after. They say 'God wills it!' but they mean 'We want it!'"

"You must know I have no love for ignorance, for obscurantism, for pretending the last few hundred years never happened," Marcellus said. "The world is as it is, not as one might wish it would be. One can, perhaps, turn back the hands of a clock. Once cannot turn back the leaves of a calendar. The Aquinists do not understand that, and they never will."

The world is as it is. Anyone who could see that had a running start at living in these modern times. Khalid nodded to the Catholic pontiff. "On that much, at least, your Holiness, we agree."

Dawud had a different way of looking at things. Or maybe it wasn't so very different after all. "We've got to keep you alive, your Holiness," he said. "You're too important to let those fools kill you."

"For which I thank you, though I doubt I deserve your generous praise," the Pope said. "The Aquinists have one thing right, at least. The future *will* be as God wills. It can be no other way. Unlike them, though, I don't think we can certainly know God's plan before we see it unfold. I also don't think we can use assault rifles to mold it into a shape we like. It will be as He wills, as I said—not as we will."

"You'd better be careful, sir," Dawud said. "If you don't watch yourself, people will start telling you what a sensible fellow you are."

"Oh, I don't think I'm in much danger there. Other dangers, possibly, but not that one." Did Marcellus' eyes twinkle behind his bifocals? Khalid thought so, but couldn't be sure. The Pope went on, "And now, my masters, if you will excuse me . . . I will seriously consider the bull you have urged on me, I promise. I expect I will issue it, though I am not in a position to pledge any such thing."

That side door opened. The servitor who'd brought in the coffee and rolls beckoned to the Maghribis. Out they went, through a corridor whose plaster walls showed water stains here and there. After the door closed behind them, Dawud spoke in Arabic to Khalid: "That, my friend, is what they call a *man*."

"He is," Khalid agreed in the same language.

"Well, you may be foreigners, but you aren't stupid foreigners." Giorgio proved to have better than decent Arabic of his own. Had he stood behind the door, listening to everything? He'd certainly known when to open it. Then again, Marcellus wouldn't not know he was there. That argued he was trustworthy—or at least that the Pope thought he was, which might not be the same thing.

After a few turns this way and that, the wanderers came to a side door with a stout modern lock and latch. The servitor opened it with a key from a ring he kept in a hidden pocket on his robe. Khalid and Dawud stepped out—and found themselves only a few cubits from the checkpoint where the Papal Guards had frisked them. One of the guards nodded pleasantly as they emerged.

Now speaking Italian, the servitor said, "God keep you, gentlemen. If you got here on your own, you should be able to make it back on your own."

Rome's street plan was even twistier than that corridor. The Grand Duke's patrols and strongpoints made things no easier. The investigators managed even so. *Maybe we're starting to learn our way around*, Khalid thought. That was a really alarming idea.

"Today," the Italian TV newsman said in portentous tones, "his Holiness, Pope Marcellus IX, issued a bull entitled *De necessitate pacis*, or *On the need for peace*."

The picture cut away from him and showed Marcellus reading in Latin behind a microphone. Khalid understood no more than a word here and there, when one chanced to sound recognizably like its Italian descendant. The old language was more rolling and sonorous than the new, just as classical Arabic seemed more majestic than the clipped dialects spoken at supper tables and in shops these days.

"In this bull"—the program cut back to the announcer—"the Pope stresses the urgency of resolving differences and disputes without violence. 'We are all brothers and sisters in our humanity, regardless of creed,' he states. 'Efforts to change people's views through violence and force fly in the face of the teachings of our Lord and Savior, Jesus Christ.'"

"That's about as strong a statement as he can make," Khalid said.

"Sure it is," Dawud . . . agreed? "Now for the next interesting question—whether anybody pays any attention to it."

They sat in the hotel bar, drinking red wine while they watched the news. The bar was crowded. The Italians and foreigners smoked and drank and ate salted nuts and olives and anchovies and other fare calculated to make them want to drink more. Some of them paid attention to the news. Others chatted among themselves or engaged in another age-old sport at dives plain and fancy: trying to pick up a barmaid.

If the Pope's edict impressed them, most of them hid it very well. They went on about their business as if his Holiness hadn't spoken. Khalid worried that the Aquinist fanatics would feel the same way.

Here was the handsome newsman again. "Grand Duke Lorenzo has announced his full support for the Holy Father's wise and compassionate bull," the man said. "He warns that those who continue to disturb order in Italy will face the most severe punishment in both this world and the world to come."

Khalid and Dawud looked at each other. They both took long pulls from their wineglasses. Pope Marcellus might be conciliatory. Lorenzo III seemed more ready to challenge the movement that had murdered his father. His worries and his approach were different from the pontiff's. *Not necessarily in a good way, either,* Khalid thought.

An arm reached in from off-camera to pass the newsman a sheet of paper. "This just in from the Corrector of the Aquinist Seminary in München, the capital of the Kingdom of Bavaria. Father Adolphus states, 'Our struggle continues. "I came not to send peace, but with a sword," our Lord says in Matthew 10:34. No one who fails to remember this can be a true Christian.'"

Sure enough, you could always find something in a holy book to support your point of view, whatever it happened to be. Father Adolphus hadn't needed long. Khalid sighed and drained his glass. The Corrector in München hadn't called for Marcellus' overthrow, but he had challenged the legitimacy of the Pope's beliefs. The difference was liable to matter only to people in the habit of splitting hairs.

"Well, we tried. The Pope tried," Dawud said, so his train of thought must have been rolling down the same gloomy track. "People who already believed we were right still do. Those who didn't, don't. Isn't it amazing?"

"That's one word for it." Khalid waved to the barmaid who'd been taking care of them. She came over right away. He and Dawud tipped well. They didn't get grabby or aim lewd propositions at her. "Another glass of the house chianti, *per favore,*" he said.

Dawud emptied his goblet, too. "And for me."

"I'll get them, gentlemen." She hurried off. Her rear view was pleasant. Khalid enjoyed watching without wanting to do anything more than watch.

"To life!" Dawud said when they got their refills. He and Khalid clinked glasses and drank. He lit a cigar.

"You'd live longer if you didn't do that so much," Khalid said.

"You keep telling me so," the Jew replied. "It would certainly seem longer. I can smoke and eat good food and die. Or I can do without them—and die anyway. I'd sooner enjoy myself while I'm here."

Khalid dropped it. He'd known plenty of people who talked that way . . . till their first heart attack, anyhow. Then a lot of them changed their tune—and their habits. A good many of the ones who didn't or couldn't didn't last long after that. But Dawud hadn't had to pay for having a good time yet. He might reach a ripe old age in spite of everything. Some did.

"Here is another facet of the Aquinist threat," the newsman said. "With me in the studio today is Dr. Giulia Cadorna, a surgeon on the staff at the hospital of San Agostino here in Rome."

Dr. Cadorna was in her late forties, with iron-gray hair severely pulled back and no-nonsense spectacles. She wasn't bad looking, but Khalid would have called her handsome rather than pretty. That might have been because she looked worried. She sounded worried, too: "If the Grand Duke—may God protect him—is overthrown and the Aquinists seize power, all the progress Italian women have made over the past lifetime will go up in smoke."

"Explain that, please," the newsman said.

"Certainly." She did: "It is possible now for a woman to think of being more than a wife or a mother or a nun. It is still not so easy as it should be. It is much harder than in the more developed parts of the world, I am sorry to have to say. But it is possible. I studied at the medical madrasa in Alexandria. Many of the students there were women, but very few, sadly, came from Italy or anywhere else in Europe. Still, women can get a fair education even here, and can find useful work, rewarding work, to do with it. They can now, I mean."

"But under the Aquinists . . ." he prompted.

"Under the Aquinists, women will go back to having babies and cooking and making coffee for their hung-over husbands. The men will beat them if they step out of line, and expect them to believe they deserve beatings for things like that. Any woman who does anything but fight the fanatics as hard as she can must be out of her mind. The same goes for any man who favors true equality between the sexes."

"Thank you very much, Dr. Giulia Cadorna. We'll be right back after these important messages." The messages were important only if you cared about which brand of sweetened carbonated water you drank. Khalid tried to ignore them—not easy, when they were made to tunnel from the eyeballs straight into the brain and stick there.

"You know what the scary thing is?" Dawud said. Khalid made a questioning noise. The Jew went on, "The scary thing is how many women in these parts don't want the chance to go to a medical madrasa or take charge of their own lives. They just want things to go on the good old-fashioned way."

"Look at the Muslim countries when change got fast enough to see in one lifetime," Khalid said. "Change does scare people. Plenty of the leaders who fought against letting women vote were women themselves. We've had generations to get used to the idea that things don't stay the same. We're ramming it down the Europeans' throats."

"And they're doing their best to spit it out again, too," Dawud said.

"I know. We wouldn't be here if they weren't," Khalid said with a sigh. "We just have to hope they finally swallow it."

Khalid and Annarita Pezzola met for lunch a couple of days after Pope Marcellus issued his bull. The eatery lay halfway between the Palatine and his hotel. They split an Italian-style cheese pie with anchovies, green peppers from the Sunset Lands, and fennel-flavored sausage. Khalid wouldn't have found anything like it in Tunis . . . unless he went into the Italian quarter there. It might have been strange, and hard to eat neatly, but it was good.

"Do you know Dr. Cadorna?" Khalid asked.

"Oh, yes." She nodded. "We worked together several times before the fanatics killed Cosimo."

"A woman did that," Khalid said, remembering what he and Dawud had been talking about in the hotel bar.

"I know." Annarita made a sour face. "A woman fooled by the Aquinists. They never have found out who let her serve that night, have they? That can only mean Lorenzo's security still has a hole in it."

"You're right." Khalid scrawled himself a note. "We still need to look into that—along with a million other things."

"I'd say we ought to sack everybody who had anything to do with the palace servants, except that would make the innocent people hate the Grand Duke," Annarita said.

"If there are any innocent people," Khalid said.

He wondered if his cynicism would shock her. More important, he wondered if it would put her off. But all she did was nod and say, "Yes. If."

Well, working closely with Grand Duke Cosimo probably would have turned a saint into a cynic. Not quite so casually as he wanted to, Khalid asked, "Do you have anywhere special you need to be this afternoon?'

Now Annarita shook her head. "The old Grand Duke would have expected me back as soon as I got done eating—and he would have expected me to eat fast. But here I am, on my own time. Lorenzo didn't want me around."

"The more fool him. Uh, he?" They were speaking Italian. Practice made Khalid's better, but he doubted it would ever be good. That was a shame, though—he had other things on his mind: "In that case, do you want to come back to the hotel with me?"

She didn't try to misunderstand him. "What about Dawud ibn Musa?" she asked.

"He took a room of his own on a different floor so the Aquinists would have to blow up the whole hotel to kill both of us." Khalid was glad he could—more or less—truthfully tell her Dawud had moved out for some reason other than to give him the chance to get her alone.

"Did he? How convenient." Annarita wasn't fooled. But she wasn't annoyed, either, for she went on, "Let's go, then."

They could have walked, but it would have taken twenty minutes or half an hour. Khalid waved for a cab. It stopped in the street to let Annarita and him slide in. People behind it blew a horn fanfare. The driver ignored the noise. As far as Khalid could see, you had to ignore noise if you were going to drive in Rome.

When they got to the hotel, he tipped the driver more than he usually would have. He tipped enough, in fact, to make the man go *"Grazie, Signor!"* and sound as if he meant it. In a place like this, where gratitude didn't grow on trees, that had to mean he'd over-tipped. Today, he didn't care.

He and Annarita rode the elevator up to his floor. By now, the hallway and the ugly, gaudy carpet were as familiar to him as if he'd lived there for years, not weeks. He opened the door to his room and put the DO NOT DISTURB sign on the knob. The message was printed in Italian, Arabic, and Chinese.

"Just a moment." Annarita disappeared into the bathroom. She stayed there a little longer than a simple call of nature would have needed. When she came out, she nodded to Khalid. "Now we don't have to worry that I'll get pregnant."

"All right. Good," he said. Even if Pope Marcellus was more forward-thinking than most of his predecessors, the Catholic Church still rejected contraception. Whatever the Church thought, Khalid already knew that plenty of Catholics held a different view of things.

They hugged. They kissed. They helped each other out of their clothes. Beneath her concealing European outfit, Annarita wore sheer, lacy international underwear. Her bra, in fact, came from the same Egyptian firm Khalid's ex-wife had favored. His fingers knew without thought how to slide it off her. If she noticed how smooth he was with the catch, she didn't say anything.

As they got down on the bed together, he said, "It's a shame to cover you up in that tent you had on. You're a lot more beautiful without it."

"I like the way you talk," she answered. Things went on from there. After a while, as if reminding herself, she said, "That's right. Muslims and Jews circumcise."

"Yes," he said. If she knew the difference, this wasn't her first time. Well, he hadn't imagined it would be.

She not only knew the difference, she proceeded to address it most pleasingly. Pulling back, she said, "I think it's neater this way."

"That's an interesting way to put it," he said, and soon returned the favor. She didn't trim away her bush, as women in the Muslim world would have. He thought things were neater without one, but it didn't matter much. He didn't say anything about it. He didn't want her to believe he believed her uncouth.

Then they went on to other things, which worked the same the world around. Afterwards, he mimed limp exhaustion. Annarita laughed. "I feel the same way," she said.

"Well, good. That's the idea." Khalid leaned over and kissed her.

"I wonder where we go from here," she said, and then answered her own question: "Probably back to business. That's what we get for doing this in the afternoon."

"Is *that* what we get?" he said. She poked him in the ribs. Taking no notice, he went on, "With the curfew, if we did it at night you'd have to sleep here and go home or to business in the morning."

"I know. It wouldn't do wonders for my reputation. I don't like that, which doesn't make it any less real. People here aren't as easy-going about those things as they are on your side of the sea." Annarita's laugh held little humor. "Of course, chances are the Ministry of Information and the Aquinists are both shadowing us. If I come to your room and stay for a while, they'll draw their own dirty pictures."

They would, too—it wasn't as if she were wrong. Khalid shrugged. "Right this minute, I don't much care." He took her in his arms again. He was past the age for quick second rounds. More often than not, he was past the age for any second rounds. He held her anyhow, held her and kissed her. He'd bedded several women after his marriage fell apart. This seemed a less casual coupling than most of those. He'd known even while he was enjoying those that they wouldn't go anywhere. This seemed as if it might.

He must have put some of what he was feeling into his caresses, because between kisses she asked, "What is it?" Fumbling for words in Italian, he went back to Arabic . . . and found he fumbled for words in his own language, too. He told her as best he could. She said, "I wouldn't be here if I didn't hope it would go somewhere. You never know before you try, but you need to hope."

"All right," he said.

She laughed at him. "I know about men," she said. "Men think about the good time first. If anything else happens, that's nice, but they still have the good time. With us, it's more complicated."

Which, like many things, was sometimes true and sometimes not so true. "Nothing wrong with a good time," Khalid said. He didn't ask if she'd had one. If you needed to ask, you wouldn't care for the answer. If she hadn't had a good time, she wouldn't go to bed with him again, and that was the long and short of it.

"No, nothing wrong at all," she said, "but that's not always the only thing going on. Or it shouldn't be." He couldn't disagree, not when he thought she was right again. He kissed her some more instead. That looked to be as good an answer as any, and better than most.

XII

Dawud ibn Musa eyed Khalid across the supper table in the hotel restaurant. "Wipe that grin off your face," the Jew said, as if he were a drill underofficer barking at new recruits in the Sultan's army.

"I don't know what you're talking about," Khalid said with dignity.

Dawud guffawed loud enough to make people all over the room turn and look at him. "The demon you don't!" he said. "If they could bottle the way you look and sell it, the Aquinists and the Grand Ayatollah in Qom would make peace tomorrow."

"That would be nice," Khalid said. Persia was a part of the modern Muslim world, but a prickly part. Persians looked down their noses at Arabs the way Italians looked down their noses at Germans—they'd been civilized longer and, if you asked them, better. They clung to their own language and to the Shi'a school of Islam to help keep from getting completely swallowed up by the larger community.

"It would," Dawud said. "But they can't bottle it no matter how much they wish they could, and the Aquinists will go right on being Aquinists."

"I'm afraid you're right." Following up on his own thought, Khalid went on, "At least they're still pretending to listen to the

Pope. If they broke altogether like the Persians, we'd lose a lever against them."

"That would be all we need, wouldn't it?" Dawud exclaimed. "Another Christian sect? As if the Europeans don't already have enough reasons to squabble among themselves!"

"As if," Khalid agreed. Wars between Sunnis and Shiites had torn up large stretches of Egypt, Mesopotamia, Arabia, and Persia in the early modern era. The idea that people should be free to go to hell in their own way rather than to heaven in yours had needed centuries to take root. The Persians still admitted it only grudgingly. The Aquinists aimed to pull it up and burn it.

"Well, you still look happy any which way," Dawud said. "That's good. You should look happy. People who always look like their granny just died aren't a whole lot of fun to be around."

Khalid paused with a piece of broccoli steamed in white wine halfway to his mouth. "I don't look like that all the time," he said, and then, more plaintively, "Do I?"

"No, not all the time," Dawud replied in judicious tones. "But you do look that way—or you did—more often than I liked to see. I hope Annarita is good for you."

Khalid reflected that Dawud didn't need to spy on him to know what he was doing. "Me, too," he said. "She hopes I turn out to be good for her. So do I."

"Worrying about how the other person feels makes a fair start." Dawud took a bite of eel that had been stewed in white wine and spices. The Italians often cooked with wine as well as drinking it. It made the cuisine exotic and intriguing to someone from the more abstemious side of the Mediterranean.

"I can see how it might, but why do you want to start with me when you give advice to the lovelorn?" Khalid asked. "Don't you think you could make more money writing a book or articles in the newspaper?"

"You should always start with somebody who isn't likely to throw rocks at you," Dawud said: the sort of pragmatic almost-nonsense he excelled at.

Someone somewhere outside fired a pistol—once, twice. The noise pierced the walls of the hotel, but no bullets did. A neat three-round burst from an assault rifle answered a moment later. Several people in the restaurant looked up. A few exclaimed or crossed themselves. No one stopped eating for longer than a few seconds. It wasn't as if the Romans hadn't heard noises like that before.

"You can get used to anything," Khalid remarked. He hadn't stopped eating, either.

"Is that a blessing or a curse, though?" Dawud asked.

"Probably," Khalid said.

Dawud sent him a reproachful look. "You've been hanging around with me too long." He stopped to think. "All right—that explains why you've been looking so gloomy all the time."

"Being in Italy and watching the whole country thrash like a snake you just stepped on has nothing to do with it, I suppose," Khalid said.

"Can't imagine why it should." When Dawud went off on a flight of fancy, he wasn't easy to call back to earth.

Another burst from an assault rifle, this one longer and more ragged, said the thrashing outside wasn't over yet. "If only Cosimo had lived, he could have kept this under control," Khalid said.

"If it were under as much control as he figured, he would have lived," Dawud answered. Khalid grunted. He hadn't thought of it like that. He should have.

"You know what the real trouble is?" Khalid said after a moment.

"Tell me. I'm all ears," Dawud said.

"The real trouble is, whether Cosimo died or not hardly matters." Khalid's voice sounded harsh even to himself. "Sooner or later, the Aquinists and the rest of the Europeans are going to have to come to terms with the problem we've been wrestling with ourselves for the past couple of hundred years."

"And which problem is that, O wisest of all men?" Dawud seemed to want to mock, but he couldn't quite bring it off.

"I'm not the wisest of men, and I know it as well as you do," Khalid said. "A good thing, too, or we'd all be in even more trouble than we are. But the problem's plain enough—it's how to live in a world where nobody's *much* wiser than you are, where men are all you've got to judge by because God gets less obvious the more you look at things."

"Oh." Now Dawud wasn't mocking. He was nodding instead. "Jews have been wrestling with that as long and as hard as Muslims have. We don't like our answers any better than you like yours. And we *really* don't like the idea that there may be no answer at all, not the way we used to think there was."

"I don't like that, either. It may be true, but I don't like it," Khalid said. "But we've been worrying about the question and worrying at it all this time now. Most of the Europeans haven't even started. They don't want to start. That's a big part of why they have so much trouble dealing with the modern world."

"Well, if the Aquinists win, they won't have to worry about it." Now Dawud tried to joke, but made heavy going of it. "They'll shout 'God wills it!' so loud, it'll be true for them. And they'll take the modern world out, tie it to a stake, and burn it so it won't bother them any more."

"And here we are, trying not to let them." Khalid thought of the two Grand Dukes, the live one and the dead; of Pope Marcellus; of earnest, capable Major Badoglio; and, last of all, of Annarita. He went on, "Not all the Europeans want to drop back to Aquinas' time or even further."

"We wouldn't have a prayer if they all did," Dawud replied. "Of course, considering what we've been talking about, having a prayer may not be so much of a much. We wish it were, because we remember how our ancestors thought. The Aquinists are sure it is, because they still think that way. And do you know what seeing who's right will prove?"

"Tell me," Khalid urged.

"It won't prove a damned thing," the Jew said. "What else have we been talking about?"

* * *

Major Badoglio had tacked a map of the Italian boot to a cork board on the wall of his office. Red pushpins, and a few green ones, showed where Aquinist trouble was brewing, and where the authorities had it under control or it had never got off the ground.

Eyeing the measling of red pins, Khalid remarked, "Things look better than this in the papers and on the TV news."

"Of course they do," the major replied. "Saying things are quiet can help keep them quiet. Saying things are terrible can help make them worse. People have a way of believing what they see and read."

Which only proves people can be fools, Khalid thought. Italy got the kind of news the people who worked for the Grand Duke thought it ought to have. Some here sang higher, some louder, but they were all part of the same chorus. In the republics of the Muslim world, every political faction could promote its views. Here, there was only one.

Well, there was only one official set of views, anyhow. The Aquinists kept right on spewing out malice against the Grand Dukes, the Pope, and modern civilization as a whole. Broadsheets and pamphlets full of red crosses and the phrase *Deus vult!* cluttered Badoglio's desk.

One of the broadsheets was a minor masterpiece of its kind, perfectly summing up how the Aquinists thought. In the background, ghostly lancers in funny-looking European armor thundered across the sky. In the foreground, similarly posed modern warriors carried assault rifles the same way. CRUSADE FOR CHRISTIANITY AND FREEDOM! the text said in big red letters. GOD WILLS IT!

Dawud noticed that one, too. Tapping it with his forefinger, he asked Major Badoglio, "Do you know who drew this one? For what it is, it's scary-good."

"Oh, yes, we know that chap. I wish we didn't," Badoglio answered. "He's a German, and he uses the name Mjölnir. In the pagan religion they had up there before Christianity came, Mjölnir was the hammer of the gods."

"I wouldn't be broken-hearted to see something unfortunate

happen to him," Khalid said. "Art like that can bring people over to his side."

"He lives in some little barony or archbishopric where the local lord is an Aquinist himself," Badoglio said unhappily. "If we're going to get rid of him, we'll have to assassinate him. What with the trouble that would stir up with all the other German rulers, we haven't thought it's worth the trouble."

"Well, I can see that," Khalid said, "but you may want to think again if you can find some way to do it without drawing too much notice to yourselves. How many men have picked up a rifle because of his broadsheets? How much harm have they done you?"

"It *is* a war, you know," Dawud added. "If Aquinists come down to Italy to hurt you, why shouldn't you go into Germany to hurt them?"

"Speaking for myself, I agree with you. But . . ." Badoglio touched the single star inside a rectangle on his collar tab. "I'm only a major. I don't make policy. I follow it when the people set over me have decided what it should be. If you want Mjölnir dead so much, you would do better to talk about it with his Supreme Highness than with me."

Captain Salgari walked into Badoglio's office. "Peace be with you, my masters," he said to Khalid and Dawud in Arabic. Returning to Italian, he spoke to Badoglio: "We just got word that the fanatics hit a convoy coming up the highway to Turin. They did a lot of damage."

"*Dannazione!*" Badoglio said. "That's the third time they've ambushed a column on that road. You'd almost think they knew our units were coming ahead of time."

"Maybe they do," Dawud said. "I mean no disrespect—please believe me—but some people in this country play double games. You might want to see who all knew ahead of time that these units were moving."

Badoglio and Salgari glanced at each other. "I have been looking into that, as a matter of fact," the captain said. "So far, I haven't come up with anything, but I keep digging."

"Good," Khalid said.

Major Badoglio stuck another red pin in the map just south of Turin. Scowling, he said, "We have to hold this city, and Milan, too. The Po Valley is home to most of our industry. It should be more progressive than the south. In a lot of ways, it is. But . . ." He paused the way he had when reminding the Maghribis of his middling rank.

"Part of the problem is that the Aquinists can easily bring men into the north from Germany and the Swiss cantons and maybe even from France," Khalid said. Major Badoglio nodded. The other part of the problem was that, while the Po Valley might be progressive, it wasn't always progressive in ways the Grand Dukes liked. It wanted more say in running its own local affairs. Cosimo hadn't been ready to let anyone reduce his own authority in any way. By all the signs Lorenzo III had shown, neither was he.

Mentioning such details wouldn't make the major or the captain any happier. They already knew how their sovereign felt. No one was likely to change his mind for him. Lorenzo seemed to change his mind even less readily than Cosimo had.

He did show enthusiasm for eliminating Mjölnir, when Khalid and Dawud put the idea to him. "Nothing I'd like better," he said, "as long as we can do it so it doesn't look as though my government is striking at him. If some of the German princes and clerics take that as an act of war, they'll help the Aquinists even more than they are already."

"You want it to look like a murder, not an assassination," Dawud said.

"That's right. That's exactly right!" The Grand Duke nodded. "If we send men after him, they can rob his house and steal his car and keep whatever they bring away with them." His smile was lopsided, the smile of a ruler who know how a particular kind of useful subject worked. "They'll hate that, won't they?"

"Of course, your Supreme Highness." Khalid sounded ironic, too.

"So they will; so they will." Lorenzo eyed him. "Are you and the Pezzola woman happy together?"

Sure enough, the Ministry of Information had been informing

the sovereign. "We are so far, sir," Khalid said. He saw no point to denying what Lorenzo plainly knew.

"Well, good. I'm glad to hear it. Nice to know she's settled, at least for now. She made me nervous—she still does. She was too close to my father. I don't know whether her ideas came out of his mouth or his still come out of hers."

"She's very able, sir. You should take her more seriously. She'd do you a lot of good," Khalid said.

"Not when she reminds me so much of my old man," Lorenzo said. Khalid didn't know how to respond to that, so he kept quiet. The Grand Duke went on, "Father wasn't always staring over *your* shoulder. Maybe that means you can be happy with her. Here's hoping. I'll tell you something else, too. If you want to take her back to the Maghrib with you when you go home, she won't have any paperwork problems. I promise you that."

"Thank you, your Supreme Highness. We'll have to see how things go. I don't know whether she wants to leave Italy, either. From some of the things she's said, she'd like to stay here and make things better for women if she can."

"If she can, yes. That's always the question," Grand Duke Lorenzo said. "But you're right. You—and she—don't have to decide right away. In the meantime, do you have any sneaky notions for disposing of this pestilential Mjölnir without leaving a trail that points back to Italy?"

"As a matter of fact, sir . . ." Dawud began.

After making love with Khalid, Annarita made as if to cover herself with the sheet. "The Ministry of Information probably has a camera hidden in the room," she said.

"Not much point to it if they do," he answered. "They already know we're together. They, or Lorenzo, let us know they know. That makes us hard to blackmail. And I doubt a camera would teach them much they hadn't figured out for themselves."

Her eyes sparkled. "Don't be too sure. The kind of people who plant cameras in bedrooms are liable to enjoy looking more than doing."

"Heh," he said. "I wouldn't be surprised. And just so you know, you intimidate Lorenzo even more than you thought." He summarized what the Grand Duke had said.

Annarita frowned. "I wasn't so close to Cosimo as he thinks. Cosimo didn't let anyone in that close."

"I can't speak to that. I don't know anything about it, though it does sound like the man I met and the man the Maghrib dealt with. But Lorenzo wouldn't be sorry to see you out of Italy, whether his reasons are good or bad."

Her frown deepened. "That only makes me want to stay more." Khalid nodded; he would have guessed she'd say that.

Recognizing her pride, he said, "You do need to think of what's best for you, not just how you can stick your thumb in Lorenzo's eye."

She glanced at her right thumb. The nail was long and sharp enough to do damage if she used it that way. By the look on her face, she would have loved to. But all she said was, "The other thing I need to think about is what's best for Italy. We lose too many people to countries with more chances for them as is."

"If you have no chance for yourself here, though . . ." Khalid let her draw her own conclusions instead of sketching them for her. When she'd had time enough to do so, he went on, "Even if the Grand Duke and the King of France and people who think like them win and the Aquinists lose, educated women are likelier to do well for themselves in the Muslim world than they are in Europe."

"Dr. Cadorna wouldn't agree with you," Annarita said tartly. "She's my hero. She's a hero to a lot of Italian women."

"I can see how she would be, but I think you're wrong." Khalid held up a hasty hand—Annarita looked furious. "Not wrong to have her for a hero. Wrong to say she wouldn't agree with me. You don't think it was harder for her to win a place at a hospital here in Rome than it would have been in Tunis or Alexandria or Damascus?"

"Well, yes, I suppose it was, when you put it that way." Annarita did recognize truth when she heard it: one more reason Khalid esteemed her. After a moment, she went on, "She's inspired so many to try to follow in her footsteps, though."

"To try to follow? Sure. Of course. But it's still as if a woman needs to throw a triple six with the dice to succeed here, where on the other side of the Mediterranean she can manage with—oh, I don't know—say, a five or higher on at least one die. Your odds are better."

"That makes doing well here mean more," Annarita insisted.

"I'm sure it does, for a handful of women who are lucky and talented, both. On the far side of the sea . . . I won't say anybody with an education and drive can do well. That's not always true, even for men. But we don't put so many roadblocks and ambushes in a woman's path, either. We've mostly got past that, the way we've mostly got past holding people back because of their religion."

Annarita raised an eyebrow. "What would Dawud ibn Musa say about that?"

"Ask him yourself next time you see him," Khalid replied. "If you're asking me, I think he'd say being mostly past that kind of discrimination doesn't mean we're all the way past it. If we were, chances are he'd outrank me. I know that. But I also know we know we have these problems and we need to work on them. Here, most people don't even see that they *are* problems. The Aquinists will tell you discriminating by faith and by sex is what God wants them to do."

"So it's not heaven on earth over there?" Annarita gibed.

"Of course not. We're people. We screw up. We do it all the time. We try not to do it the same old ways over and over. Sometimes that means we do better. Sometimes it just means we find new ways to screw up."

"You've got all the answers, don't you?" she said.

"Not me, sweetheart." Khalid shook his head. He didn't think he'd ever had such an intense conversation with a naked woman, not even when his marriage was falling apart around his ears. He continued, "The Aquinists have all the answers. If you don't believe me, just ask them. What we mostly have on the other side of the Mediterranean are questions."

"Questions," Annarita echoed. She seemed to weigh the word on scales inside her head. Slowly, she nodded. "Well, you could do worse, I think. The people who say they know all the answers are the ones who know the answers that keep folks they don't like in their place."

Once Khalid worked through the convolutions of that, he found himself nodding with her. "That's how it goes, all right," he said.

"And it's always gone that way, ever since the first tyrant made other people do things because he had some big fellows with clubs standing behind him," Annarita said. "It isn't fair. It isn't right."

"Not even close," Khalid agreed. "A republic where all the people can say what they want and do as they please if they don't hurt anyone else makes it harder for the bossy ones to order other people around. Not impossible—republics mess things up, too, believe me. But harder."

"I . . . need to think about that," she said slowly.

"Well, you've got some time. It doesn't look as though Dawud and I will be flying back to Tunis day after tomorrow." Khalid took her in his arms and kissed her. "I'm damned glad of it, too."

"So am I," she said. As far as he was concerned, that was definitely the right answer.

The map in Major Badoglio's office had acquired some new red pins south of Turin. The city wasn't quite under siege by the Aquinists, but it was hard-pressed. "The way the fanatics keep hitting our columns, they have to be getting word from a traitor about when we're moving," Badoglio growled.

"If we catch the son of a whore, we ought to string him up by his nuts to make any others think twice," Captain Salgari said savagely.

Khalid and Dawud exchanged glances. Khalid wasn't at all sure the young Italian officer was exaggerating. By the way Salgari sounded, he expected to be taken literally. The law in Italy was what Grand Duke Lorenzo said it was. The idea of a constitution and a legal system more important than the ruler's whim or will hadn't really taken hold on the north shore of the Mediterranean.

Things could have been worse, though. Instead of worrying about Lorenzo's whims, Italians might have been worrying about the iron doctrine of an Aquinist Corrector. When that occurred to Khalid, he reflected that things could almost always get worse.

"Maybe if we ride along with some of the Grand Duke's men, we can find out how they're getting betrayed," he said.

"Maybe you can get yourselves killed, too," Major Badoglio said. "Is that why you came to Italy?"

"We can get killed anywhere here," Dawud said. It was true, of course, but did he have to sound so blithe about it? "Somebody with a bomb under his clothes can blow us up on the street. A truck bomb can blow us up, too, and the street with us. An Aquinist in the hotel kitchen can poison our pasta. All kinds of interesting, entertaining ways to go."

"Entertaining?" Captain Salgari said. "Are you sure that's the word you're trying to use?"

"I'm sure the Aquinists would be entertained, anyhow," Dawud answered. Salgari threw his hands in the air.

Over the next few days, Major Badoglio was more helpful. He issued the Maghribis Italian Army uniforms, bulletproof vests, and helmets. The steel domes, painted a matte brown, looked martial enough but protected less of the head than the model the Maghrib used. The assault rifles Badoglio had them sign for weren't the same as the ones on the far side of the sea, but a good many Muslim countries also armed their troops with them. They were easy to handle and to field-strip, and lethal enough for all ordinary purposes.

The Italians' all-terrain vehicles came from Arkansistan. The Maghribis made their own. As with radar, though, the Grand Duchy preferred not to buy from its neighbors. Khalid could understand their thinking. He had no trouble driving this model. Gearshifts and foot pedals worked the same the world around. The Italians called the blocky, cloth-topped machine *the horse with wheels*. He liked that.

Off they went: horses with wheels, trucks full of soldiers, others full of supplies, and armored personnel carriers and light tanks to protect the soft-skinned machines.

Khalid and Dawud had driven up the Via Cassia as far as Florence. If anything, the horse with wheels had a rougher ride than the small car they'd taken before. It could do more than the car dreamt of trying, but couldn't do it nearly so comfortably. Comfort was a civilian virtue, not one the military cared about.

No one at the police strongpoints challenged the military column. Here and there, even on the Rome side of Florence, snipers plinked away at it. The armored personnel carriers and tanks fired back. The retaliation was overwhelming. Machine guns pockmarked houses and barns. Cannon rounds simply flattened a few. Livestock died. A chicken hit by a heavy machine-gun round exploded into a puff of feathers. Farmers and their families were none too safe, either. The soldiers seemed to have no idea whether they were killing any of the Aquinists who shot at them. They also didn't seem to care much.

"As long as the *strozzi* keep their heads down, that'll do," a lieutenant told the Maghribis as the column bivouacked just south of Florence. He tore open his ration pack, pulled the lids off tins, and poured hot water into pouches of dehydrated soup and instant coffee.

He ate with every sign of enjoyment. Khalid wished he could match the Italian's appetite, or perhaps his impaired sense of taste. Military rations could keep you alive for a long time. Eating them regularly would certainly make it seem like a long time, anyhow.

Dawud also found his supper less than delightful. He discovered ways to deal with it, though, that eluded Khalid's less agile mind. Holding up an empty plastic bag, the Jew said, "Look what I've got here."

"Air?" Khalid asked.

Dawud looked at him with mingled pity and scorn. His lip curled. "You don't know anything, do you? It's dehydrated water."

"Right." Khalid nodded toward the Italian lieutenant, who was still busily stuffing himself. In a low voice, he went on, "Don't tell him, or he'll want some, too."

"Wouldn't surprise me one bit," Dawud said. "Of course, you could pull the same trick on about a quarter of the junior officers in our army."

They slept in the little all-terrain vehicle, one wrapped in blankets on the front seat, the other in back. After the luxurious Roman hotel, it wasn't a grand way to pass a night. Getting wakened by two different fire fights, one before the moon rose and the other after, didn't make things any more restful for Khalid. The sentries were on their toes. No fanatics slipped past them and put the column in real danger.

North of Florence, the road wasn't called the Via Cassia any more. Instead, it went by the romantic name of A1. There were highways in the Maghrib with names like that, even if the Italians used a different alphabet. Sometimes being modern seemed a quest to drain everything even remotely interesting out of everyday life.

When Khalid complained about that, Dawud said, "If you're too attached to the past, you turn into an Aquinist. If you're not even attached to the present, chances are you won't."

"People need attachments," Khalid said. "They don't need to let the attachments strangle them."

The A1 went north to Bologna, then swung more nearly west till it got to Piacenza. At the madrasa in Cairo, Khalid had read the account of a traveler from Piacenza to Jerusalem, translated from Latin into Arabic. The traveler had been a Christian pilgrim who lived about a lifetime before Muhammad began to preach. If not for that, Khalid never would have heard of the town.

"You're one up on me," Dawud told him, "because I never did. I don't feel very deprived, either."

"It's not what you'd call an impressive place, is it?" Khalid said. Rome was the capital. Florence and Naples had been great cities once upon a time. Turin was a rising industrial center. Piacenza never had been much and never would be. It was a place where ordinary people lived ordinary lives. If you were in any way extraordinary, you escaped from a place like Piacenza as fast as you could. Or you turned Aquinist and did whatever you did for what you reckoned the greater glory of God.

The highway touched the coast at Genoa. In the days when European ships ruled the Mediterranean, Genoa had rivaled Venice as a port and a center for raiders and traders. That was long ago now. These days, the town seemed almost as much a backwater as Piacenza.

West past Genoa to Savona, and then north on the A6 to Turin. As the sea disappeared behind him and the column went up into the Po Valley, Khalid felt as if he were leaving the world he'd always known. The Po Valley had the feel of a more northerly land, one with as many affinities to Germany as to Rome. The people in these parts did still speak Italian, although with a nasal accent that reminded Dawud of French. But a surprising number of them—surprising at least to Khalid—were tall and fair. He knew there were lands where yellow hair and blue or gray eyes outnumbered the dark features common in the rest of the world. He hadn't looked for part of Italy to come so close to being one.

Oaks and apples and plums and pears grew in these parts. Many of them needed cold in the wintertime to flourish. That they grew here argued that they would get it.

Aquinists flourished in these parts, too. Bridge supports and culverts and walls seemed all but sure to have the Crusader cross and GOD WILLS IT! painted or chalked on them. Sniping had picked up as soon as the column rumbled out of Genoa. The men doing the shooting seemed more in earnest than their fellows had farther south. They killed several of the Grand Duke's soldiers, and wounded even more.

Here and there along the A6 lay the carcasses of wrecked trucks, personnel carriers, and horses with wheels. A rocket-propelled grenade had blown the turret clean off one tank. It lay upside down, a few cubits from the chassis, like an enormous steel ashtray that just happened to have a cannon sticking out of it.

A small town called Carmagnola sat just south of Turin and just west of the highway. Even from the road, Khalid could see that Carmagnola had been fought over, probably more than once. Every building taller than two stories had big chunks bitten out of it. At the moment, the Aquinists held the place. Instead of the Grand Duke's gonfalon, the black flag with the red cross flapped defiantly above the battered offices and blocks of flats.

Khalid had his assault rifle on his lap in the back seat, a round chambered and the safety off. Dawud, who was driving, laid his on the seat next to him. His right hand reached out to make sure he could grab it in an instant. "This is bound to be where things get lively," he remarked.

Before Khalid could answer, a bomb went off by the side of the road ahead of them. Some of the horses with wheels had been uparmored to give them a chance against such attacks. The machine in the lead was one of those. Uparmored or not, it flipped over and started to burn. The vehicles that could go off the road started to. Then a personnel carrier ran over a buried mine and brewed up. Leaving the highway was deadly dangerous.

So was staying on it. Aquinists opened up with assault rifles and rocket-propelled grenades. "Here we go!" Dawud shouted. He hopped out of the horse with wheels, got down on one knee behind the front fender, and started shooting back. Khalid joined him there, though he was far from sure that didn't give Aquinists on the other side of the road a clean shot at their backs.

Someone moved, there in the rubble on the outskirts of Carmagnola. Dawud's rifle barked. The Aquinist threw out his arms and fell down with his head and torso in plain sight. He kept wiggling and thrashing: one more proof of how hard to kill human beings could be. But he wouldn't cause the advancing column any more trouble.

A fanatic with a rocket-propelled-grenade launcher popped up and fired at a tank. The unguided rocket missed the turret by bare digits. The coaxial machine gun next to the cannon cut down the Aquinist. Then the tank clanked forward and shoved the burning horse with wheels out of the way. The commander popped up out of the cupola and waved the column forward.

Dawud and Khalid jumped back into their vehicle. Dawud put it in gear. Khalid sprayed bullets around to encourage their foes to stay under cover. They rolled on toward Turin.

XIII

Khalid soon discovered you could find almost anything in Turin. The town made—or had made, till chaos engulfed it—automobiles. A factory, one of the first of its kind, had turned out Pontiaks for the European market. It operated under license from the anonymous society in the Sunset Lands, which had been eager enough to take advantage of low Italian labor costs.

Now the factory stood idle. The Aquinists had attacked it with mortars and rockets. They didn't want any part of Italy hooked into the world-spanning modern economy.

But wizards and witches also advertised their services. For a fee, they would tell fortunes or predict the future. For a bigger fee, they would cast a spell to make someone love you or curse someone who already didn't. The fanatics had also given a few of them gruesome, old-fashioned ends.

"'Thou shalt not suffer a witch to live,'" Dawud quoted. "That's in the Old Testament. Seems the Aquinists believe in it anyhow. Christians have a way of picking and choosing when they go through our half of the Bible, or they could get a thrill out of eating pork, too, instead of just doing it."

"There are passages against sorcery in the Qur'an, too," Khalid said. "In the second sura, the one called The Cow, it says that people who buy spells won't reach paradise."

"For one thing, you don't expect the Aquinists to pay any attention to the Qur'an, do you?" Dawud returned. "For another, when was the last time anybody in our part of the world got punished for witchcraft?"

"It's been a while," Khalid said. "They take their holy book literally. Most of us don't take ours that way."

"Well, our laws don't, anyhow," Dawud said. "Start talking with farmers and peddlers in the Maghrib and you'll still find that a lot of them would be Aquinists if only they were Christians. Civilization's just a veneer. It isn't solid wood like my head."

Since he'd laughed at himself, Khalid couldn't do it for him. The senior investigator didn't try to tell his colleague he was wrong. Khalid did say, "We're working toward a solid civilization, not away from one."

"That's true," the Jew said. "The fanatics use the modern world's weapons, and printing and the radio, to try to turn back the clock to where it's not a clock any more—it's an hourglass."

"Too right, they do," Khalid said. "I wonder if they see the irony of that."

"One of the things they do when you become an Aquinist is inoculate you against irony," Dawud said . . . ironically. "They need to. The stuff's more dangerous to them than smallpox."

"You certainly missed *your* shot," Khalid said.

"Think so, do you?" the Jew answered. "Well, back in Roman times, someone asked a priest how he could get through his rituals without laughing, so the disease has been around for a while."

"Socrates had an even earlier case," Khalid remarked.

"Maybe, but maybe not. He didn't believe in the other Greeks' religion, but I think he did have his own."

Just then, a couple of the tanks that had fought their way into Turin opened up with their main armament. Greek pagans, even unorthodox Greek pagans, suddenly seemed much less interesting. Something not far from the barracks where Khalid and Dawud were stationed fell in on itself with a rending crash.

"One of those Roman historians was talking about how the

Empire conquered Britain," Dawud said. "The way he described it was 'They make a desert and they call it peace.' I wonder if Lorenzo's been reading Tacitus—I think it was Tacitus who wrote that."

Tacitus was only a name to Khalid. He was a more familiar name than Ssu-ma Ch'ien, but not nearly so familiar as al-Tabari. For that matter, Britain was hardly more than a name to him. Yes, England and Scotland and the Irish kingdoms had sent representatives to Grand Duke Cosimo's funeral rites. Yes, some of those states had enough offshore oil to be players in the great game of international finance. But the British Isles, off in their own backward corner of a backward continent, seemed much more exotic than the republics of the Sunset Lands, even if the Sunset Lands lay much farther away.

With an effort, Khalid wrenched his mind back to the business at hand. "Making a desert is all very well," he said, "but Lorenzo shouldn't need to do that to keep Turin loyal to him. Dammit, he's not the one who smashed up the Pontiak plant and threw all those people out of work. The Aquinists did. Remind the locals of that, and they ought to go after the fanatics with knives."

"Makes sense to me," Dawud said. "Of course, I can't do anything about it. You need to talk to the Italian commander here."

"Yes, I know," Khalid replied with a sigh. "I do need to talk to him. The problem is, he doesn't need to listen to me."

Major General Renato Procacci was one of Cosimo's veteran officers now serving under a new ruler. He was in his late fifties, with a bushy graying mustache under a plowshare of a nose that would have made an Armenian jealous. He understood Arabic, but spoke it worse than Khalid did with Italian. Each man used his own language in addressing the other, then, and hoped the other would get the gist.

"If I chase as many Aquinists as I can out of Turin and kill the rest, I won't have to worry about them any more." Procacci had all the virtues attached to straightforward aggressiveness. He also had all the vices attached to it.

"If you make the people here hate you, General, you'll spawn two fanatics for every one you get rid of," Khalid replied.

"We have plenty of ammunition," Major General Procacci said.

"Yes, but—"

"But what?"

They eyed each other in perfect mutual incomprehension. The general knew the inspector came from a country more powerful than his own and enjoyed Grand Duke Lorenzo's favor. But the responsibility for holding Turin was his, not Khalid's. He reminded Khalid of a meat-eating dinosaur: strong, slow, fierce, and stupid as the day was long.

As patiently as Khalid could, he said, "If you make people here hate the Aquinists, you won't have to kill so many of them. You may not even have to kill so many of the Aquinists." He made a point of *not* saying *If you make the people here hate the Aquinists worse than they hate your soldiers.* He was trying to make the major general not hate him. It was one of the more challenging assignments of his career.

"I don't care about the people here one way or the other," Procacci said. "It's the cursed foreigners I've got to get rid of. They're thick as fleas on a filthy dog."

"Yes, but you have homegrown fanatics here, too," Khalid said.

"Traitors," Procacci growled. "That's all they are, stinking traitors. When we kill them, they get what they deserve."

"But the point is not to make more men from Turin move against the Grand Duke, or it ought to be," Khalid said.

"No, the point is to punish the ones who do," the major general insisted. It wasn't just that he and Khalid were literally speaking different languages. They could have got around that if they were plotting strategy or the like. But they couldn't plot strategy, because their views of what it ought to be were so different.

Khalid took another stab at things: "We want the people who live in Turin to be happier under Grand Duke Lorenzo than they would be under the Aquinists."

"Happy?" Major General Procacci shook his big, square head.

"I don't care if they're happy or not. The only thing that matters is whether they do as they're told."

He wouldn't—more likely, he couldn't—look at it any other way. Khalid gave up on him and went to the Ministry of Information's headquarters, which was near the Chapel of the Holy Shroud. He didn't believe the shroud was genuine, which had nothing to do with whether Christians, and especially Aquinists, revered it. Khalid could understand as much. He was sure such a leap of imagination if not faith lay far beyond Renato Procacci.

A lieutenant colonel named Filiberto Juvarra headed up the local Ministry of Information staff. Unlike Procacci, he not only understood but spoke classical Arabic. He spoke it as well as an Italian was likely to, in fact. After listening sympathetically while Khalid poured out his troubles, Juvarra said, "Yes, that is a problem, my master, but what do you want me to do about it?"

"Ordering the stubborn fool not to antagonize the Grand Duke's subjects—his own countrymen—might make a good start," Khalid said.

"It might . . . if I could," Juvarra said, real regret in his voice. "But you need to remember: I am a lieutenant colonel, while he is a major general. He can give me orders. Much as I might like to, I can't give him any."

Put that way, the statement seemed obvious. Like a lot of things that seemed obvious, it wasn't. Yes, any flavor general outranked a lieutenant colonel. On the other hand, the Ministry of Information was a service nearer and dearer to the Grand Dukes' hearts than the Army.

So Khalid asked, "Are you saying that you can't give him orders or only that you won't?"

Juvarra eyed him. "You do find interesting questions, don't you? What I'm saying is, I can't give him any orders he is obliged to follow. Grand Duke Lorenzo may possibly be able to do so."

"Possibly?" Khalid said.

"Possibly," the officer from the Ministry of Information repeated. "As local commander, Major General Procacci enjoys a good deal of autonomy. Lorenzo would not have put him here if the hadn't expected him to exercise that autonomy."

"But he's exercising it so it helps Lorenzo's foes, not so it does them harm," Khalid protested.

"The major general would not agree with me if I told him so. From what you say, the major general does not agree with you," Juvarra replied. "Does he not have a right to his opinion, which may be as good as yours?"

"His opinion may be as good as mine. The only problem with that is, his opinion isn't," Khalid snapped. Lieutenant Colonel Juvarra just shrugged. Khalid had done his best to convince the Italian. Failing, he stormed out of the Ministry of Information building. Now he wondered whether, behind him, Juvarra was on the telephone to Procacci.

A great many people waited in line to get into the Chapel of the Holy Shroud. Khalid had to remind himself that not all of them would be partisans of the Aquinists. A man or woman might retain the simple piety of his or her youth and also retain the simple loyalty to the Grand Dukes learned with it. A man or woman might.

Or might not.

Khalid did assume that either Juvarra or Procacci or both of them had agents listening to the sermons the priests delivered when they celebrated Mass in the chapel. Which was good, as far as it went. Did it go far enough? He always worried about Aquinist infiltrators in the Army and in the Ministry of Information. If the priests declared that Lorenzo would burn in hell and so would anyone who didn't follow the Aquinist Correctors and the agents felt the same way, would their superiors ever hear about the seditious sermons? It seemed unlikely.

Who will watch the watchmen? Khalid remembered the meaning, but not the Latin Major Badoglio had quoted. Dawud would. He'd learned the Christians' language of prayer and cross-border communication. Khalid kept in his mind only the translation into the tongue the larger world used for the same purposes. It would have to do.

A man ran out of an alleyway tucking a can of spray paint inside his jacket. Khalid wondered whether he'd painted a red cross or DEUS VULT! or both. The man gave him a bared-teeth snarl—he was in uniform. He thought about chasing the Italian, but didn't. He hadn't come north to go after small-scale troublemakers like that.

Back forty or fifty years before, a Turk named Ablanalp had invented the valve that made such sprays possible. They had all kinds of uses, paint, cookery, and deodorants among them. From what Khalid had read, Ablanalp never dreamt how important they would be to graffiti scrawlers. Spraying your message was much quicker and easier than daubing it on with a brush.

Ministry of Information personnel were putting up posters of their own. These showed armored skeletons on horseback. Skulls stared out from under knightly helms. On their left arms, the skeletons bore shields showing the red cross. Instead of lances, they held bombs with burning fuses in their bony right hands. The slogan on the posters was short and to the point: TERROR KILLS!

Khalid nodded to himself. That was some of the best propaganda he'd seen from the Grand Duke's side. Not only did it get Lorenzo's message across, it also mocked the Aquinists' broadsheets. People who saw one of these posters might laugh because of it. The Aquinists wouldn't. God rarely issued fanatics a sense of humor.

An explosion a couple of blocks away was fierce enough to stagger Khalid and to blow glass out of a good many windows that had kept it till now. He ran toward the blast. One of that size was bound to leave wounded in its wake. Now he had a proper military first-aid kit on his belt. He might be able to do some good.

A bomb hidden in streetside rubble had smashed an armored personnel carrier. The vehicle burned merrily. It hadn't been armored enough. Ammunition inside cooked off with cheerful popping noises. Black, greasy smoke poured from the stricken machine. It stank of fuel and oil, of burning rubber, and, sickeningly, of scorched pork.

Sure enough, people in the street and on the sidewalk were down, too. Khalid knelt by a man pouring blood from a wounded leg. Bandaging it seemed hopeless. Thinking fast, Khalid pulled several safety pins out of his pockets and roughly closed the wound with them. Then he injected the man with morphine.

Ambulances screamed up. Attendants threw the injured man on a stretcher and hustled him into the back of one. Khalid dared hope the fellow would live.

An aid man beckoned to him. "Here—give me a hand with this guy, too. You look like you know what you're doing."

You're an optimist, Khalid thought. But he went, and helped the fellow who, with luck, really did know what he was about patch up a man with a belly wound and a broken arm.

Before long, the aid man discovered his Italian wasn't everything it might have been. "Where are you from?" the man asked.

"Tunis," Khalid said.

"You must have lived there a long time."

"I've lived there my whole life. I'm from the Maghrib. I'm a Muslim."

"Oh." When the aid man had a moment, he sent Khalid a curious look. "What are you doing here, then?"

"The same as you, *amico*—everything I can to keep the Aquinists from grabbing the reins."

"Oh," the man repeated. "You must think that's pretty important, then, huh? You and your government, I mean."

"*Sì.*" Khalid could answer in one short word, so he did.

"Good for you," the Italian said. "All those people want is to tell everybody else what to do, you ask me. Far as I'm concerned, they can eat shit salad with piss dressing."

Khalid had never heard it put that way before, which didn't mean he didn't like it. "Sounds good to me," he said. The aid man gave him a grin, then got back to work.

*   *   *

Major General Procacci summoned not only Khalid but also Dawud into his august presence. "You people are nuisances," the Italian said without preamble. "You're meddling in my affairs and trying to keep me from holding Turin under proper control."

"Close, sir, but not quite right," Dawud answered. "We're meddling in your affairs and trying to do a better job of keeping Turin under control."

Although the general was a swarthy man, he wasn't too dark to hide the angry flush that rose from his neck to his forehead. "And you think you know better than I do because . . . ?" he asked with what was meant for devastating sarcasm.

It failed to devastate, however. "Because that's why Grand Duke Lorenzo sent us here," Dawud said helpfully. "If you don't like what we're doing, why don't you complain to him?"

Major General Procacci opened his mouth. Then he closed it again. Telling your sovereign he hadn't had such a good idea was at best risky and at worst suicidal, at least if you ever hoped to become a lieutenant general. "Get out of my sight," he snarled.

"You do know how to endear yourself to everyone you meet, don't you?" Khalid said after they got out of the local commander's sight.

"Oh, he's even more lovable than I am," Dawud replied. "I thought so from the sweet way you talked about him. Now that I see for myself how delightfully he sings, of course I'll go out of my way to help him play in traffic."

"I think you put the fear of God in him for now." Khalid thrust out a warning forefinger. "And if you ask me 'Whose God?', I'll do something even you'd regret."

"Promises, promises," Dawud said. "But you're right. He may listen to reason for the next little while. Now if only we had some to spare."

"I know what I'd like to do," Khalid said.

"Which is?"

"I'd like to take the fight to the fanatics in the suburbs and out-lying towns instead of waiting for them to come after us."

"All by yourself?" Dawud said. "I know they make films about heroes like that, but in films they wash the blood off afterwards and nobody dies for real. Or are you showing off for your lady friend?"

Khalid exhaled through his nose. "Yes, *of course* by myself," he said. "Come on, who needs all the soldiers Procacci's in charge of?"

"By the way he uses them, he doesn't think anyone needs them," Dawud said.

"That's my point," Khalid said. The Jew was bound to know that perfectly well, but when he felt like being difficult you had to spell things out for him letter by letter. This seemed to be one of those times. Khalid went on, "If he doesn't feel like doing anything with them, maybe he won't mind somebody else borrowing them for a while."

"Anyone who doesn't speak Arabic for beans will mind if *you* borrow them." Yes, Dawud was being mulish. That didn't mean he was wrong. He was far too likely to be right. Europeans always resented it when people from the Muslim world stepped in and took care of things for them. They said it showed the Muslims lacked confidence in their ability to handle anything themselves.

Which it did. Some Europeans were capable enough. Others . . . A string of misfortunes over the past century or so showed that quite a few Europeans didn't want to bother taking the pains a complex technological situation required. Bridges run up on the cheap or not maintained, machinery not oiled or repaired, some-one who mattered drunk at the worst time, bribes instead of in-spections, minor mathematical errors that didn't get caught and ended up not being so minor—the list was long and depressing.

Thoughtfully, Khalid said, "I wonder how Lieutenant Colonel Juvarra feels about pushing out with the troops instead of holing up and waiting for the Aquinists to hit us."

"And if Procacci tells him to go hang himself?" Dawud in-quired.

"I don't know how the Army will feel about it, but I'm sure the Ministry of Information would be tickled to show off what fine officers it has," Khalid said. "Before I talk to Juvarra, I'll telephone Rome and get authorization to put him in charge here."

"The good news with that is, you know the Ministry of Information will fall all over itself doing what you want. Isn't playing politics fun?"

"Well, that's one word for it," Khalid said.

"It's fun if you do it well, and you sound like you're going to do it well." But Dawud hadn't finished: "The bad news is, the Aquinists will know that Juvarra's in charge and what he's going to do before Major General Procacci finds out. Or don't you think they're tapping the lines between here and Rome?"

Khalid sighed. "I would be, if I were in their shoes. But I'd rather do something than do nothing. We've had too much of that here already. The fanatics won't know exactly what we're up to, not from listening to me talk with Rome."

"No, not from that. But they'll have, ah, friends on Procacci's staff—and probably on Juvarra's staff, too." Dawud was full of truths Khalid would rather not have heard.

In spite of that, Khalid made the calls he needed to make. Sure enough, the higher-ups at the Ministry of Information were eager to let one of theirs give an Army general a black eye if he could. But they didn't have the authority to supplant Procacci. They had to get Lorenzo's approval first.

Major Badoglio was the man who called back. "It's authorized," he said. "I'm sure the Army will love you till the end of time. Someone else here in Rome is ringing up Juvarra. That way, the general won't be able to prove you had anything to do with the bayonet in his back."

"*Grazie.*" After a moment, that didn't seem like enough, so Khalid added, "*Mille grazie.*" A thousand thanks likely weren't enough, either, but he'd done his best. And, while Major General Procacci might not be able to prove anything, he wouldn't be in too much doubt. *Too bad*, Khalid thought. *He wouldn't have got dumped if he didn't need dumping.*

From the yelling and screaming and carrying on at the major general's headquarters when Procacci found out a mere lieutenant colonel—and a lieutenant colonel from the despised Ministry of Information, at that!—was replacing him in command, Khalid would have guessed a mortar bomb had smashed the building. Only the lack of an explosion before the explosion told him anything different.

Sure enough, Procacci didn't have to be a Turinese fortune-teller to divine who'd arranged his sacking. He stormed over to confront Khalid and Dawud as soon as he saw them. He was fearsome in his wrath—more fearsome, unfortunately, than he'd been against the Aquinists. Khalid had seen that he didn't speak much Arabic. He trotted out what he had, which included a good deal dragged straight from the sewers.

Khalid listened for a while. Procacci cussed him out in Italian, too. In his own language, he taught Khalid a few things the Maghribi hadn't known before. When the general showed signs of starting to repeat himself, Khalid said, "I am sorry, sir. I truly am. But you wouldn't take the fight to the enemy."

"Your mother's—" Yes, Procacci was repeating himself. For good measure, he added the gesture to avert the evil eye and the one the Italians called the fig. Then he stomped away.

"Now someone will have to make sure he doesn't go over to the Aquinists," Khalid remarked, with luck after the Italian was out of earshot.

"I don't know. I almost hope he does," Dawud said. When Khalid sent him a startled look, he explained himself: "Wouldn't it be nice to have at least one Aquinist commander who *didn't* hit us with everything he had?"

If that wasn't an epitaph for Renato Procacci's military career, Khalid couldn't imagine what would be. "You're right," he said, shoveling his own spadeful of dirt onto the career's grave.

* * *

As Khalid had seen before, Dawud ibn Musa contrived to look hopelessly unmilitary even in uniform, bulletproof vest, and helmet. The tunic and trousers were rumpled; they didn't fit well. He wore the helmet at a slight angle on his head, as if it were a jaunty Italian hat. He did seem to know what he was doing with the assault rifle he toted.

Eyeing Khalid, he said, "We'll be about as useful as a couple of impacted wisdom teeth, you know."

"Oh, yes." Khalid wasn't panting to shoot it out with fanatics half his age, either. "But the Italians need to see we think fighting the Aquinists is important enough for us to risk our lives, not just theirs, especially after we got their general sacked."

Cannons and truck-mounted rockets had been pummeling the fanatics in Candiolo, south of Turin, for three hours. Now batteries that had been masked opened up on Volpiano, northeast of the city. After fifteen minutes in which, with luck, the guns and rockets caught the Aquinists there by surprise, officers' whistles shrilled. The attacking force moved out of Turin. Khalid and Dawud trotted along with the Italian soldiers.

"Lorenzo!" the Italians shouted, and "The Grand Duke!" and "Italy!" Half of them had cigarettes dangling from their mouths. They were young enough not to get winded even so. Cigar-smoking Dawud also kept up. Khalid clumped along. Military boots felt as if they weighed a talent apiece.

As soon as Khalid got away from the built-up area in the center of Turin, he noticed how green everything was. In the Mediterranean world, where rain fell from late fall into early spring, this was the driest time of the year, with fields and hillsides bare and brown or yellow.

But the Po Valley wasn't part of that world by geography, even if politically and culturally it had been joined to the Mediterranean for millennia. Once upon a time, they'd called this land Gaul south of the Alps. Summer was the rainy season here, as it was farther north. And all the grass and trees and bushes seemed brighter and leafier than they ever got under the fierce Mediterranean sun.

One thing that meant was, they gave the Aquinists better cover than plants farther south would have. Bullets cracked past and over Khalid. He couldn't even spot muzzle flashes, much less the men who were shooting at him. He threw himself down on his belly. The luxuriant weeds gave him better cover than he would have got farther south, too.

"Forward!" the officers shouted. They blew their whistles over and over. "For Italy and Grand Duke Lorenzo!"

By now, in contact with the enemy, the soldiers mostly stayed quiet. A war cry might give away their position. The Aquinists kept still, too, except for occasional cries of "God wills it!"

Khalid scrambled up, dashed forward, and threw himself flat again. He found himself only a cubit or so from a fanatic who lay twisted in death. The man wore dungarees, a dark green wool tunic, and rubber-soled canvas shoes. It wasn't a uniform, but the clothes would do well enough in the field.

He did have a helmet: an Egyptian model, probably war surplus, that had to be older than Khalid. It might not protect as well as a modern helmet, but it was bound to be better than nothing. It hadn't kept him alive, not when the bullet that killed him tore out his throat like a wolf.

Up again. Forward. A bellyflop behind some bushes. Motion in front of him: big fair men in denim and wool and old-fashioned helmets. He fired a burst at them, then rolled over to a downed carport that offered some cover. They would shoot at where he'd been. Not staying there till they did seemed a good idea.

After some of the Italians dropped mortar bombs on the Aquinists, he advanced once more. He saw something he'd never seen before: a fanatic trying to surrender. Cradling a bleeding arm in his good hand, the Aquinist smiled like a beaten dog and said, "Kamerad!"

"Go back that way." Khalid jerked a thumb over his shoulder. If the fellow would talk, they might get something useful out of him. The man gabbled guttural thanks in a language Khalid didn't understand. He stumbled southwest, toward the rear.

A moment later, a shot rang out behind Khalid. He whirled, in case it was another fanatic who wanted to sell himself dear. It wasn't. An Italian soldier had plugged the would-be prisoner of war. As the Aquinist writhed in the grass, the soldier finished him with a head shot.

Khalid wanted to swear at the Italian, but knew he couldn't. If the soldier thought the Aquinist looked dangerous for any reason or none, he'd get rid of him. By the nature of things, giving yourself up was deadly dangerous. Not everyone who tried managed to do it. This poor bastard hadn't.

A few hundred cubits farther on, several Aquinists holed up in a house had no intention of quitting the fight. Their makeshift strongpoint gave them good fields of fire. A dead soldier who'd been careless lay stretched out partly behind a parked car. Thus warned, Khalid didn't show himself.

An Italian with a launcher for rocket-propelled grenades came up. So did another man carrying a canvas sack full of the grenades. He loaded one into the business end of the tube. The Italian carrying it went to one knee behind another parked car.

He pulled the trigger. With a hissing whoosh, the rocket zoomed toward the house. It blew out half the wall facing the shooter. Anything designed to slam through hardened steel made a demon housebreaker.

"Another one?" asked the soldier with the sack of reloads.

"Sure. Why not?"

The second grenade brought down the rest of that wall and part of the roof. Two or three fanatics ran away, doing their best to keep the ruins between them and the Grand Duke's men. Khalid hoped some Aquinists hadn't got away.

Someone fired from the house as Lorenzo's men started to approach it. They drew back. The soldier with the launcher gave it another grenade. It began to burn. When the soldiers did move up, no one was left to give them trouble.

Beyond the burning house, Khalid and Dawud bumped into each other again. The Jew was limping. "You all right?" Khalid asked.

"Fell over my own feet and twisted my ankle," Dawud answered. "I'm so graceful, I should have been a dancer."

A few glum Aquinist prisoners did shamble off into captivity, their hands clasped on top of their heads. "Satan will pay you back in the world to come!" one of them shouted.

An Italian soldier herding the prisoners along kicked the mouthy one in the seat of the pants. "Shut up, asshole," he said. "Worry about the next world when you're dead. You keep talking shit, that'll be pretty damn quick."

"Now there's a modern attitude," Dawud said.

"If that's what you want to call it," Khalid said. "You can do something about this world. The next one's out of your hands."

"That's a modern attitude, too," Dawud said. More firing broke out ahead. They hadn't subdued all the Aquinists in the suburb. Dawud grimaced. "Now they'll get another chance to hurt me or kill me. I'd sooner stick around in one piece, because I'm a lot surer about this world than the next one—which is also a modern attitude." Shaking his head, he jogged toward the fighting. The limp didn't slow him much, not least because he hadn't been fast to begin with.

Khalid trotted forward, too. He fired a four-round burst at an Aquinist who was looking in a different direction. The man went down with a shriek, clutching at his belly. You didn't want to think you'd caused somebody so much pain. On the other hand, the Aquinist probably would have cheered if he'd done that instead.

Some of the fanatics in Volpiano died. Some went into captivity. More pulled back to cause trouble elsewhere. Lieutenant Colonel Juvarra might not be another Julius Caesar or Amr ibn al-As in the making, but he'd won himself a victory here. In these hardscrabble times, you took what you could get.

XIV

Khalid pulled back the foil lid on a ration pack. The little sausages and pasta in tomato sauce were uninspiring. They'd do a decent job of plastering over the empty spot in his midsection, though. He shoveled a forkful into his mouth.

Dawud was digging into the same kind of entree. Between mouthfuls, he said, "I don't want to know what goes into the sausages."

"Neither do I," Khalid said with a sigh. "If it's a choice between eating what's probably pork and either going hungry or making a fuss, I'll eat it. If I don't know, I feel . . . a little less guilty, anyhow."

"It just comes to you in the line of duty. And you don't go out of your way to shove it aside," Dawud said. "You're also not going out of your way to look for it."

"That's right." Khalid nodded. "That horrible waiter at the hotel in Rome, pimping pork to Muslims on the prowl for something *haram* the way he'd pimp his 'nice, clean sister' in case they were looking for a girl . . . That's the kind of man I'd like to string up by the thumbs."

Dawud clucked in mild reproof. "You're not respecting his fundamental dignity as a human being, you know."

"*Kus ummak!*" Khalid came out with the same obscenity Major

General Procacci had fired at him a couple of days before. "That greasy bastard had no dignity to respect. And I wouldn't give you better than even money that he qualifies as a human being."

"He's just making a living, trying to get along the best way he knows how," Dawud said. "That's what he'd tell you."

"As if I'd believe anything he told me. He's nothing but another—" Khalid broke off, he hoped in the nick of time. He'd been about to say something like *He's nothing but another lying, cheating, thieving European.* Some of the Grand Duke's soldiers might be sprawled somewhere close enough to overhear, and might know enough Arabic to understand.

But that wasn't the only reason a man from the Muslim world shouldn't say or even think such things. Why were he and Dawud here on the outskirts of Turin at all? To help Italy, and eventually the other Europeans nations, out of their backwardness and fully into modern civilization. And to keep the Aquinists from imposing a fresh *Jahiliyah* on this backward, isolated fragment of the world.

If he was going to do that, or as much of that as one man could, it was hardly fair or right for him to stereotype Europeans the way so many people from the rest of the world did. Automatic contempt for everything and everybody on this side of the Mediterranean didn't do anybody any good.

But every time I see that filthy pimp of a waiter, I still want to punch him in the nose, Khalid thought. That, he told himself, wasn't stereotyping. It was reacting to one obnoxious individual. Europeans weren't all paragons, any more than Arabs or Persians or Chinese were.

As if to prove not all Europeans were paragons, the Aquinists up ahead opened fire on the Grand Duke's sentries. The loyal soldiers shot back. If there were any disloyal soldiers up there, they probably shot back, too. Nothing made you want to kill somebody like having him try to kill you. You'd do whatever you could to stop him.

An Italian soldier came up to Khalid and Dawud. Saluting, the man asked, "Sirs, you are the gentlemen from the Maghrib, isn't that right?"

Khalid wore a captain's rank badges, Dawud a senior lieutenant's. Being able to give orders to enlisted men without getting backtalk could prove useful. In the Italian Army, as in most European armed forces, officers came from higher social strata than the men they led and insisted on getting more deference than their counterparts in the wider world claimed.

None of that explained why both Maghribis hesitated before answering. The soldier might want to make sure he was delivering his message to the right people. Or he might be an Aquinist, itching to hose down some infidels with his assault rifle.

As Khalid said, "Yes, we're the Maghribis," Dawud unobtrusively picked up his own rifle. He might look as if he were about to start cleaning it, but he could open up in a hurry if he had to.

He didn't have to. The soldier only saluted again. "Sirs, if you'll please come with me, Lieutenant Colonel Juvarra would like to talk with you."

The man might be leading them into an ambush or a trap. It seemed more likely, though, that he just wanted to lead them back to the Italians' new commander. Grunting, Khalid got to his feet. Dawud did the same, a little more slowly. They both creaked; they carried too many years to be comfortable sleeping on the ground.

What had been a pleasant suburb, with the leafy greenness Khalid noticed so strongly, was now a place where a war had just happened. Explosives and fire and bullets and shell fragments had done their worst to buildings. A church that might have stood there for centuries was nothing but a pile of sooty bricks. A dead dog lay in the middle of the street, legs stiff and belly beginning to bloat.

The air stank of smoke and sewage. Men had relieved themselves in the open, wherever they could without getting shot. Some men, no doubt, had fouled themselves. Khalid felt lucky that he hadn't; he'd needed to clamp down tight more than once. And the smell of death was still faint, but it would grow.

Soldiers were tearing down the Aquinists' broadsheets and putting up the Grand Duke's in their place. Khalid nodded to himself. Juvarra could see that needed doing. Procacci might not have paid any attention to what he would have viewed as an unimportant detail.

Here and there, civilians came out of hiding. They stared in amazement at what the fighting had done to their peaceful town. Too many people who had lived in Volpiano would be staring up sightlessly at the sky. And this wasn't an especially fierce battle, or one that had lasted for long.

Occasional rifle fire echoed on the nearly empty streets of Turin. Aquinist holdouts were making nuisances of themselves. Chances were they hoped they could sneak clear before Lorenzo's men hunted them down and killed them.

Lieutenant Colonel Juvarra had moved his headquarters up near the polo field, in the direction of Volpiano. The only horses on the field at the moment were the ones with wheels: it was doing duty as a car park for them, tanks, and personnel carriers. Juvarra greeted the Maghribis as friends. Some of his staff officers, holdovers from Major General Procacci's tenure, were more reserved. One or two of them looked as if Khalid and Dawud, not the fanatics, were the enemy.

"Now that we've got Volpiano, we can swing left and clear some more of the suburbs," Juvarra said. The new commander sounded like a man who'd got the bit between his teeth. "As long as we keep pushing the Aquinists, they can't push us so much."

"That will be good," Khalid said. "You need to remember, though, the most important thing here is to make sure the people in these parts want to live under the Grand Duke, not the Aquinists."

"If we don't beat the God-cursed Aquinists, the people won't get to make that choice," Juvarra said.

"Even if you do beat the fanatics, if the people would rather see them in charge, you'll lose the war. It will take longer than if they whip you in the field, but you will," Dawud said. "Without the people behind you, all you have are guns. Most of the time, guns aren't enough by themselves."

Juvarra sent the Jew a thoughtful stare. "You play a deep game, don't you?"

"It's not just fighting," Dawud answered. "It's politics, too, and religion. If you don't keep an eye on all those things, you'll lose. Give the Aquinists credit. They understand that much. They wouldn't be so dangerous if they didn't."

"I can see why you wanted someone from the Ministry of Information in charge here, then," Juvarra said. "They don't train Army officers to juggle that many balls at once."

"No?" Khalid said. The lieutenant colonel shook his head. "Too bad," Khalid told him. "They'd better start, then, because they'll need plenty of people who can."

The column that went from Turin to Milan was smaller than the one that had come up from Rome to Turin. The journey was shorter this time, too. All the same, Khalid was glad to travel in the middle of the column, not up at the front. The fanatics harried it several times, but did it less harm than they must have hoped. The soldiers in the column were very alert, as they had reason to be. They sprayed roadside bushes and trees with machine-gun fire. Nothing blew up when they did, but the Aquinists who lived through those volleys wouldn't be in much shape to cause trouble.

Milan was a bigger city than Turin. Back when this was Cisalpine Gaul, it had gone by the name of Mediolanum. More than two thousand years had ground the name down a bit, but it might still have been recognizable to one of the Gauls forcibly yanked from his time into this one.

When Khalid remarked on that, Dawud replied, "I wonder if they'd started working on the Duomo back then."

He was joking. They couldn't have started on a Christian cathedral before Christ walked the earth. But they had started on it back in the late eighth century of the Hijra calendar: the late fourteenth century by the one Christians used. Now, more than six hundred years later, it remained incomplete. So many things in Europe moved slowly, when they moved at all.

"When we get to Milan," Dawud said, "I wonder whether the Aquinists will be shooting at us or it'll be the Army officers commanding the Grand Duke's garrison."

"There's a cheerful thought!" Dawud said. "We didn't get rid of Procacci because he belonged to the Army. We got rid of him because the only thing he wanted to do was catch whatever the Aquinists threw at him."

"You know that. I know that," Dawud replied. "The only thing the soldiers in Milan know is, we had one of their own sacked in Turin."

The commander in Milan was another major general, this one named Benito Dallolio. He made his headquarters in the shadow of the Duomo. Even unfinished, the cathedral was massive. It was in the style architects called Gothic. The tall, thin arches and spiky spires came from a building tradition altogether different from the mainly Muslim one that had spread around the world with modern civilization. You wouldn't find its like anywhere outside of Europe, as you wouldn't find a pagoda anywhere but in China or Japan.

Khalid didn't have as long to look it over as he would have liked. As soon as he and Dawud gave their names, the sentries outside the headquarters hustled them into Major General Dallolio's presence.

"Should I be pleased to meet you, my masters, or not?" Dallolio asked in reasonably good classical Arabic. Khalid gave him a point for being able to use the international tongue. Dallolio was younger than Major General Procacci, and leaner. He would have been strikingly handsome if not for a scar that made a badlands of his right cheek and jaw.

"We are not your masters, General." Khalid rejected the polite formula. "If we can help you, we will."

"Help me out the door, do you mean?" Dallolio said. "That's

what happened to poor Renato, eh? Did you two tell him you weren't his masters, too?"

"We have no problem with anyone who wants to go after the Aquinists, sir," Dawud said in his excellent Italian. Even if the general could speak Arabic, using his language in his country seemed only courteous. Dawud continued, "Major General Procacci seemed happier letting them come after him."

"I'd find your excuses easier to believe if you'd put another soldier in his slot, not one of those damned snoops from the Ministry of Information." No, Dallolio didn't want to keep things smooth.

"Lieutenant Colonel Juvarra looked to be the best man we could find in Turin." Khalid knew his own Italian would never be as good as Dawud's. It had got better with all the practice he'd had since landing in Rome. "He pushed the fanatics out of Volpiano. Now he's moving west from there."

"Renato Procacci could have done the same thing." Major General Dallolio stuck to Arabic. Maybe, as Khalid often did with Italian, he felt the practice would do him good.

"Yes, Procacci could have done it. No one's arguing that he couldn't," Dawud said. "But he *wouldn't* do it. That was the trouble."

"He might not have cared for taking orders from men who weren't in the chain of command," Dallolio said.

Dawud grinned impudently. "From filthy Muslim foreigners, you mean."

"I didn't say that," the commandant of Milan replied, his tone stiff.

"I didn't say you said it. I said you meant it," Dawud said. "But if he'd been taking the fight to the Aquinists when we got there, we wouldn't have had to tell him to do it. Everybody would have been happier then. Well, everybody except the Aquinists."

Benito Dallolio lit a cigarette. One thing smoking did was give you time to gather your thoughts. Beaming, Dawud drew a cigar from the breast pocket of his tunic. Dallolio offered his lighter. Dawud took it, lit the cigar, and puffed happy clouds of smoke.

After a few puffs of his own, Dallolio said, "I hope you will not have cause to doubt my military judgment."

"So do we. Believe me, sir, so do we," Khalid said.

"If you do doubt me, the Ministry of Information will hear about it. So will the Grand Duke." The general didn't sound like a man asking questions.

Dawud said, "Placed where you are, doing what you're doing, did you expect you *wouldn't* have anybody looking over your shoulder? At least you know we're doing it. How many officers and clerks on your staff and in town here send reports on you to other people you don't know anything about?"

With a quick, harsh gesture, Dallolio stubbed out the cigarette. The ashtray was made from the base of an expended artillery round. He lit another one even while the first still sent up a thin ribbon of smoke. "You ask intriguing questions, don't you?"

"That's one of the things we're in Milan to do," the Jew answered. "Sometimes people don't like it. They—"

"People like Procacci," Dallolio broke in.

"That's right," Khalid said.

"Questions bother some people," Dawud added. "Questions make them wonder if they ought to do things differently, not the way they and their father and their grandfathers always did them. Wondering things like that makes them uncomfortable."

"When you do things the way you always have, when you deal with people in the old-fashioned ways, you know where you stand and how everything ought to work," Dallolio said. "That keeps things simple. It keeps you from fussing and worrying a thousand times a day."

"It does if you're a general, certainly. Maybe not so much if you're a private," Khalid said.

Major General Dallolio blinked. Dawud warmed to the theme: "It does if you're a man. Maybe not so much if you're a woman. It does if you're a Catholic in Italy or a Muslim in the Maghrib. Maybe not so much if you're a Jew. One of the intriguing questions you can ask is, Why do we do it this way when that way would be fairer?"

"You want to turn Italy into a republic like the one you come from." The general made it sound like an accusation.

Yes, Khalid thought. "No," he said. "What we want to do is keep the Aquinists from dragging Italy back to the days when the Church and the state would kill you for thinking things like that, not just for saying them."

"That's what you want in the short term," Dallolio said. "In the long run, the Grand Duke is the same kind of roadblock to you that the Aquinist Correctors are right now."

Yes, Khalid thought again. Benito Dallolio was a man to be reckoned with. Not many people looked ahead so clearly. "For your lifetime and mine, sir, our interests go hand-in-hand," the investigator said.

"And if your grandson ends up buying and selling mine, that's just the turn of the card, eh?" Dallolio said.

"Would you rather your grandson were a serf who couldn't write his name?" Dawud asked. "That's your other choice, isn't it?"

Dallolio lit yet another cigarette. No wonder his right index and middle fingers had yellow stains. "I ought to hate you," he said. "I ought to hate you both. Instead, I've got to work with you. You're right—the other choice is worse. Life's grand sometimes, isn't it?"

Not far from the Duomo and Major General Dallolio's headquarters stood the Basilica of Saint Ambrose. That was a truly ancient building; it had gone up more than two centuries before the Hijra era began. Some of the inscribed stones outside the basilica were older still. Dawud pointed to one of them. "Look!" he said. "It mentions Pliny."

"Pliny . . ." Khalid knew he'd heard the name lately, but couldn't remember where. He'd had too many ancient Romans dropped on him at once.

Dawud snorted disdainfully. "The one who died trying to rescue people when Vesuvius erupted."

"Oh. Him." Khalid nodded. Now he knew which Roman Pliny was. He couldn't get too excited about knowing, but know he did.

They went inside. The paintings and mosaics surprised him. Christianity didn't ban portrayals of human beings, the way Judaism and Islam did. Neither the eldest faith nor the youngest took the prohibition seriously any more, but neither was likely to use such images inside a synagogue or a mosque. Christianity took them for granted. Christian painters had been the world's finest till Muslim artists, armed with geometrical perspective, passed them by.

A sarcophagus was carved with crowds of round-faced, curly-haired people. "That's got to be late Roman," Dawud said.

"It does?" The nuances of Roman art were also lost on Khalid.

"It does," Dawud answered firmly. A moment later, he found a card describing the sarcophagus. "Ha! Told you so. This was Stilicho's. He was a German general who helped prop up the Roman Empire around Ambrose's time."

"If you say so."

Under the church were catacombs where distinguished people had lain for century after century. One desiccated corpse, no more than a bit of skin and hair over bone, wore a bishop's golden miter and robes of fresh maroon velvet.

Again, Dawud found the card. "Thought so," he grunted. "That's Ambrose himself—or they say it is, anyway."

"Looks like he's been here long enough," Khalid said. "He was a little tiny fellow, wasn't he?" Ambrose couldn't have been more than three and a third cubits tall.

"People in those days tended to run smaller. They didn't get the nutrition we do now." But, having said that, Dawud eyed the saint's body again. "He'd still be the runt of the litter, chances are. He did it with brains—he didn't have to be built like a wrestler."

"I suppose not," Khalid said. Some small men pushed extra hard to compensate for the bad dice roll fate gave them. Maybe Ambrose had been like that. Or maybe he would have had the same driving personality if he'd been a cubit taller and towered over everyone.

As they left the basilica, Dawud said, "You know, I felt funny about uncovering my head in a house of worship. Jews do the opposite."

Khalid laughed. "With me, it was leaving my shoes on when we walked inside. Sometimes customs are just different, not better or worse."

"Whatever customs you find, you'd better go along with them when you can," Dawud said. "If the locals think you're mocking them, odds are you'll end up dead."

A tram rattled by. Its windows must have been of safety glass; two of them bore spiderweb-shaped bullet scars. "You can end up dead around here even if you do follow customs," Khalid said.

"Too right you can," Dawud agreed.

Instead of dining—if that was the word—on army ration packs, they ate with Major General Dallolio at an establishment a captain on his staff recommended. Seafood and saffron-perfumed rice improved on those sausages of unknown origin. Wine and grappa were better than the muddy instant coffee that came in the ration packs, too.

Khalid patted his belly. "No wonder so many officers come here." Enlisted men weren't likely to show up, not at these prices. But when the Maghribi embassy or the Ministry of Information paid the bills . . . The expense account was a wonderful, a *civilized*, invention.

"No wonder at all." The commandant of Milan lit an after-dinner cigarette. The ashtray—cut crystal, not expended brass—was full of during-dinner butts. He smoked a lot even for an Italian, which was saying something. After a puff or two, he added, "We will see what we can do about clearing the fanatics out of town. I've ordered a push starting at sunrise tomorrow."

"Good," Khalid said. Sometimes knowing people kept an eye on you was enough to get you moving.

"What you need to remember is, you'd better not drive the Milanese into the Aquinists' arms," Dawud said. "Some of them will back the fanatics anyhow, but you don't want your soldiers making most of them think the lunatics who yell 'God wills it!' are a better bargain than the Grand Duke."

"Believe me, I understand that." Dallolio sounded like a man working hard to hold his temper.

"I'm sure you do, sir." Dawud ibn Musa, by contrast, seemed to be trying harder than usual not to irritate an important local. "Your men have to get it, too, though. This is their own country they're fighting in. Even some of the Aquinists are Italians—"

"Rotten traitors to his Supreme Highness," Dallolio broke in.

"Yes, sir. But still Italians. After Lorenzo wins this fight"— Dawud didn't suggest that the Grand Duke might lose it—"they'll be his subjects again. Some of them—with luck, a lot of them— will make loyal subjects once the squabbling's over . . . as long as you don't make them hate you while you're knocking down the revolt. Of course you have that in mind. Your men need to think about it, too."

"Ah." The major general scratched that disfiguring scar with his forefinger. "I see what you're driving at. And I'm starting to see why the two of you shitcanned poor Renato. That isn't the kind of thing he'd worry about. I'll spell it out so even a conscript peasant off a farm his family sharecrops can't get it wrong."

"*Grazie*," Khalid said. He knew, as Dallolio doubtless did as well, that it remained quite possible to get such orders and not follow them. All it took was ill will. But the commandant here did sound as if he was doing what he could. In a world populated by human beings, you couldn't ask anybody for more than that. Khalid raised his glass in salute and gulped fiery grappa. Dallolio drank with him.

"Do we get combat pay for this?" Dawud asked as he worked the bolt on his assault rifle. The soft, oiled *snick!* chambered the first round in the magazine.

"You know, I'll bet we can," Khalid answered. "It just depends on whether the money's worth the trouble of filling out all the paperwork we'll need."

He already had a cartridge in the chamber of his own rifle. The sun wasn't up yet. He could see shapes. Pretty soon, he'd be able to make out colors. He and Dawud waited with a swarm of Italian soldiers near the Basilica of Saint Ambrose. Some of the men smoked. Some tossed down small cups of coffee. Some gulped from their canteens, which might hold water or something stronger. Some simply stood and waited.

That *whump!* was a flare pistol going off. The sky was still dark enough to make the blue flare look more impressive than it would have by daylight. "Come on, boys!" an officer shouted. "For Lorenzo and for Italy!"

"For Lorenzo! For Italy!" the soldiers echoed. Their boots thudded on concrete, on asphalt, here and there on cobblestones that concrete and asphalt hadn't yet swallowed. They were going to clear the enemy fighters from the district south and west of the basilica. They'd try to do that more than once before, but the Aquinists kept filtering back in.

The fanatics were ready to make a fight of it now. They opened up with their motley assortment of weapons. Every man on the other side had to be his own quartermaster sergeant: one of the disadvantages to a force made up of fighters who came to the conflict with whatever they could get their hands on.

The advantages to that kind of force . . . "God wills it!" the Aquinists roared. They fought from shops and blocks of flats and from behind parked cars and from any other places that gave them a little cover. A sniper in a tree wounded two soldiers before the rest realized when the rounds came from. That Aquinist didn't get a chance to surrender.

Neither Khalid nor Dawud said a word when the Grand Duke's men killed him. A criminal who fired from that kind of hideout in the Maghrib wouldn't have got a chance to give up, either. A police spokesman would go on TV and talk about "an officer-involved shooting." No one but his kin would miss the late gunman. They might not, either, considering the disgrace he'd bring down on his family.

Few Aquinists seemed to want to surrender, anyhow. Some had in Volpiano, but not many. Even fewer here in Milan gave up as long as they had a rifle and cartridges to use in it.

Lorenzo's men couldn't just blast all the buildings where the Aquinists were hiding, either. General Dallolio did understand that much. Plenty of innocent people, not all of them fanatics, lived and worked in those buildings. Blow them up without caring who got killed and you'd make the survivors hate you. The Aquinists understood the game, too. They didn't use civilians for human shields, not openly. They did fight from crowded places.

So the Italian soldiers had to try to clear away ordinary people to get at their foes. It wasn't easy. Men who spoke only German or French were likely Aquinists, yes. Men who spoke Italian with the local accent? That wasn't so obvious.

Women . . . The soldiers didn't even worry about them till one blew herself up as they were herding her to what they thought was safety. She killed several of them and several other women along with herself. After that, the women got frisked as thoroughly as their menfolk. It would breed ill will, but getting blown to bloody fragments had bred ill will in Lorenzo's troopers.

"We should have known something was up," said the sergeant who told Khalid and Dawud the story. "She was smiling like Christmas before she touched off the bomb, like she was already looking at heaven or something."

The two Maghribis exchanged glances. "We saw the serving maid who murdered Grand Duke Cosimo," Khalid said. "She had that same kind of look on her face." *Exalted* was the word he was digging for, but he couldn't find it in Italian.

"They're martyrs," Dawud said. "They see themselves that way, anyhow."

"Martyrs, my dick!" The Italian sergeant spat in disgust. "It's a coward's way to fight."

Soldiers always called their enemies cowards. It made the foe seem easier to face. How true it was might be a different question. Didn't blowing yourself to bits to hurt the opposition take something that might be called courage? It seemed that way to Khalid, anyhow. He didn't argue with the sergeant. What point, when he knew he wouldn't convince him?

Men from the Ministry of Information replaced Aquinist propaganda with the Grand Duke's flavor, as they had in Turin. Khalid hoped it would do some good. It wouldn't hurt. At the very least, it would show that the government cared enough to get its own version of the truth in front of the people.

Dawud put that better: "The country that lies together, tries together."

"Poetry," Khalid said, his voice dry. A helicopter gunship roared by overhead, only a few cubits above the rooftops. It poured rockets and machine-gun fire into a park where the Aquinists had a strongpoint. The fanatics fired back a rocket-propelled grenade. It missed the copter, but the machine zoomed away. Its crew liked shooting at the enemy a lot better than getting shot at. Well, who didn't?

Little by little, Lorenzo's men pushed forward. They had more in the way of heavy weapons than the Aquinists did. The Aquinists countered that with zeal. It worked, more or less, but it was expensive. With better arms, they would have spent fewer men.

And women. Normally, Khalid would have been horrified to watch soldiers on his side groping women. When they'd already taken casualties because they'd kept their hands to themselves, though . . . In an ideal world, they would have had women with them to do those searches. Women did serve in the Maghrib's armed forces, and in most throughout the Muslim world. Equality between the sexes had yet to reach Europe, as Annarita could have testified.

An Aquinist showed himself in a second-story window, fired a quick burst, and ducked back into the office or whatever it was. From his own spot behind a colandered Garuda, Khalid drew a bead on the window. If the fanatic was foolish enough to pop out again . . .

He was, which probably showed he didn't have much combat experience. He never got any more. Khalid's first shot took him square in the chest. The second, as the Aquinist slumped, blew out the back of his head. He fell from the window and thumped down onto the sidewalk as bonelessly as a cloth doll. Cloth dolls, though, didn't bleed.

"Hey! Well shot!" a soldier called to Khalid. He gave the Maghribi a thumbs-up, a gesture that dated back to the arena in Roman days. Khalid waved back carefully, so as not to expose his arm to other fanatics in that building. The man he'd just killed had got his last thumbs-down.

No supper at the fancy eatery tonight. A ration pack was all the more uninspiring when compared to what he'd eaten the night before. Enlisted men had to down this stuff all the time. No wonder Lorenzo needed conscription! Or maybe getting a full belly every day drew volunteers. Soldiering always looked better when other work was hard to find.

The Aquinists tried a night counterattack. It made for wild confusion. Men on both sides shouted their battle cries and fired in the direction of people shouting cries they didn't like. In the darkness, rifles and machine guns and grenades counted for more than artillery and rockets. So did knives and entrenching tools. Whoever led the Aquinists knew what he was doing. He got the most he could from his fighters when the Grand Duke's men couldn't use big chunks of their firepower.

"God wills it!" yelled someone not far away. Khalid and Dawud both fired in that direction. Then they rolled away from where they had been.

Shrieks said some of the bullets had struck home—or that the fanatics were quick-witted enough to bluff. Bullets cracked through the place where the Maghribis' muzzle flashes said they'd been. Khalid shot at the flashes he saw. He rolled again. You couldn't stay where you'd fired from.

"Oof!" he said—he'd just rolled off the curb and into the gutter. The water in it was cold and smelly. He didn't want to think about all the nasty things mixed with that water.

Someone launched a white star flare up into the dark sky. It lit up several blocks as brightly and as harshly as a photographic flash. Khalid froze into rigor mortis while the flare slowly, slowly descended under its parachute. If he didn't move, they might not notice him. Or they might think he was dead if they did.

Nobody shot him. Nobody even shot at him. When the flare finally fell, the night seemed blacker than it had before—his pupils had contracted against the burning glare. Everyone must have suffered from the same trouble: firing didn't pick up again for several minutes.

Finding Lorenzo's men alert, the Aquinists pulled back. They might have overrun the government forces if they'd caught them by surprise. Major General Dallolio and his junior officers deserved some credit. So did the ordinary soldiers who took nothing for granted.

"I'm not sure the Grand Duke is winning up here, but I'm pretty sure he isn't losing," Dawud said.

"That's about how it looks to me, too," Khalid replied.

XV

When the sun rose the next morning, the fighting rose again with it. Grand Duke Lorenzo's men kept pushing the fanatics back. They could do it, when they had a resolute commander to make sure they did. In the third hour of the day—halfway between sunup and noon, more or less—Khalid asked Dawud, "Do you think we've seen what we needed to see?"

"Yes, pretty much," the Jew answered. "Shall we go back to headquarters? As long as we've done our job, we don't need to hang around waiting to stop something. Or isn't that what you meant?"

"Who, me?" Khalid said. They both laughed. They'd taken their chances alongside the Italian soldiers. Even more to the point, they'd been seen taking their chances alongside them. They hadn't come to the Po Valley to drive the Aquinists away by themselves. They'd satisfied their honor, and the Maghrib's.

Some of the soldiers waved to them as they started back to Major General Dallolio's headquarters. "You guys are all right!" a man called to them. "That Aquinist the one of you finished, that was good hunting!"

"Thanks." Khalid wasn't thrilled about killing the man. If you got stuck in a war, though, you had to do things like that. The Aquinist wouldn't have sobbed into his *vino* if he'd potted Khalid instead. And it had been good hunting. He'd waited for the fanatic's mistake, and he'd shot faster and with better aim.

Behind the line, civilians trickled back to their flats and workplaces. Some seemed happy. They were the ones whose homes and shops hadn't got blown up or burnt down. Others wailed and wept and hid their faces in their hands. "I lived in this building for thirty years!" a woman cried, pointing to what were only charred ruins now. "Everything I had—everything in the world—was in here! What am I going to do now?"

The best you can. Khalid didn't say it. It wasn't the kind of answer that made anyone feel better. The woman probably would have sworn at him. But she'd have to go on somehow. Disasters happened all the time. Maybe she had relatives who'd be able to help her . . . if their blocks of flats weren't also wrecked.

Benito Dallolio stood outside his headquarters, talking with three or four junior officers, sending out runners with orders, and grilling others who came back to tell him what was going on. Every few seconds, he would grab a radio handset away from the operator and either listen or bark more orders into it. He was a man who could keep track of a good many things at the same time, in other words—a good thing for a high-ranking officer to be able to do.

He waved to Khalid and Dawud as they started across the square toward him. He had to have sharp eyes to recognize them at that distance . . . although Dawud, who looked about as unsoldierly as an armed man in uniform could, did stand out.

Yet another Italian enlisted man loped up to Dallolio and waited to be noticed. He didn't have to wait long. The general liked questioning runners. He was the kind of officer who would have been at the front himself if he hadn't understood he was more useful farther back.

The courier told Major General Dallolio whatever he had to tell him. Khalid was still too far away to make out what it was. Dallolio nodded and asked the man something. The soldier answered. Dallolio nodded again. Then, quite calmly, the runner pointed his assault rifle at the general and opened fire.

Dallolio threw up his hands and fell over. "God wills it!" the runner yelled, and shot down two of Dallolio's subordinates while they were still staring in astonished horror. The radio operator grabbed his pistol and shot the assassin. The runner choked out "God wills it!" one more time before he crumpled.

"*Allahu akbar!*" Khalid exclaimed. He and Khalid sprinted over to the scene of the sudden, unexpected bloodbath.

It was all over by the time they got there. Dallolio had taken three or four rounds in the chest and belly. The blood pooling under him reminded Khalid of how much a human being held. One of his aides was also dead, with two bullets in the left side of his chest. The other officer still twitched, but he wouldn't for long, not with the left side of his head smashed like that.

And the murderer was down and dying, too. The radio operator's pistol round had caught him just above the bridge of his nose. That was either a lucky shot or a very cool one. Khalid wondered whether even the radioman knew which.

An aide who hadn't stopped any bullets kept crossing himself over and over. "Jesus, Mary, and Joseph!" he choked out. His eyes almost bugged from their sockets. His face had gone the color of newsprint.

"Now we have to find out whether this son of a whore"—Dawud stirred the killer's corpse with his boot—"was an Aquinist in one of Lorenzo's uniforms or a real soldier who decided he was playing for the wrong team. Which do you suppose would be worse?"

As usual, he had a knack for finding the . . . intriguing questions. That one was so very intriguing, Khalid had no idea how to answer it. He came up with a question of his own: "Who takes command here now that Major General Dallolio is gone?"

"That would be Colonel Locchi," answered the man who'd been crossing himself. Anything involving rank and the chain of command was important enough to him to make his wits start working again.

Khalid was sure he must have met Colonel Locchi here in Milan. He couldn't dredge up a face or a voice to go with the name, though. That didn't seem like a good sign. Someone who was a leader of men should have made himself memorable in some way. Major General Dallolio certainly had.

Even if Colonel Locchi had the wizened soul of a bookkeeper, Khalid dared hope him a competent bookkeeper. The world wouldn't end if some hairy-chested major had to inspire the troops in his place. As long as the man at the top kept them moving in the right direction, things might work out.

Or some other soldier might go gunning for the new commander. How could you do our job if you couldn't trust the men you allegedly led not to murder you? With that uncomfortable thought, Khalid realized he *did* have the answer to Dawud's question. If would be worse if the assassin proved a soldier.

More and more officers and other ranks came to stare at the gruesome tableau and exclaim over it. Dawud tapped Khalid on the arm. "There's Colonel Locchi," he murmured, nodding toward a man who, but for his rank badges, seemed to own no distinguishing features.

A captain pointed at the dead assassin. "*He* did it? Mother of God! He's in my company. His name is Ungarelli. No, Ungaretti. He was a pretty good soldier—I was going to put him up for lance-corporal once things here calmed down a little."

Dawud's mouth twisted into a frown. "Well, now we know," he said.

"Now we know," Khalid agreed glumly.

Colonel Locchi spoke for the first time: "We shall have to carry on as if Major General Dallolio were still here to lead us. And we shall have to make a full report to the authorities in Rome." Everything he said was true—and about as inspiring as a bus schedule.

Since no one else seemed to have thought of it, Khalid pointed to the radio operator and said, "This man deserves a commendation—a medal, more likely. Without his quick thinking and good shooting, the murderer would have done even worse than he did."

"Yes. Yes, indeed." Locchi nodded. "What is your name, soldier?" he asked the radio operator.

"I'm Luciano Gentile, Colonel," the man answered.

He should have known that, Khalid thought. The radioman was at the headquarters all the time. Khalid would have bet that Dallolio knew his name—and whether he was married, and how many children he had if he was. The Grand Duke's forces in and around Milan were losing something along with their murdered commandant.

Colonel Locchi pointed first to Khalid, then to Dawud. "I hope you foreign experts will not go back to Rome until we have had time to consult."

"We are at your service, Colonel, of course," Khalid said. He hoped Locchi wouldn't lean too much on their expertise. Too many Europeans had a way of doing that when men from the wider civilization were available. They didn't trust their own abilities and judgment the way they should have.

Dawud added, "We'll need to make our own reports to the Ministry of Information and to the Grand Duke's palace. Phone or radio will do, but the phone would be better: harder for the Aquinists to tap."

"Just as you like, of course." Locchi licked his lips. He might give in, but he would have been happier saying no—so his manner declared. He could browbeat his own officers into putting things in a way that made him look good. He was in no position to intimidate the Maghribis, though. They could say whatever they pleased.

"You want to do the same things Major General Dallolio did: drive the fanatics away from Milan and make sure the people here stay contented with Grand Duke Lorenzo," Khalid said.

"Yes. Yes, naturally!" By the surprised way the colonel said it, he hadn't worried about why Dallolio was doing what he did. Only now had Locchi had a whole big jug of *why* spilled in his lap. How well he cleaned it up would go a long way toward determining whether he became a brigadier or got cashiered because he was fighting out of his weight.

Right this minute, Khalid didn't think Locchi was shaping any too well. The colonel might pull himself together. Khalid hoped he did. He wouldn't have bet more on it than a lunch at a cheap roadside diner, though.

"No, I'm sorry, my master, but you cannot speak to Major Badoglio now," Captain Salgari said into Khalid's ear. "He is on compassionate leave—his father had a small stroke yesterday. The doctors expect him to get better, but you can never be sure with those things."

"That's true. I'm sorry to hear the news," Khalid said. With something like that, they wouldn't have been sure of a recovery in the Maghrib, either. "I hope everything goes as well as it possibly can. Shall I tell you about what's going on here in Milan, then?"

"Yes, I'm cleared to hear those reports," Salgari answered. "We got the first word about Major General Dallolio a little while ago. Terrible! Do you know whether the killer was a soldier or a fanatic masquerading as one?"

"He was a soldier," Khalid said flatly. Was that confusion down in Rome just the usual uncertainty that came with fast-breaking news, or was Colonel Locchi trying to put the best face on things he could? Khalid went on, "We were close by when it happened. A captain who rushed up just afterwards said the assassin served in his company. He gave the man's name, too, so he definitely knew him."

"I . . . see." Even over the telephone line, Khalid heard Captain Salgari sigh. After a moment, the Italian continued, "That tells me more than I knew. I think it tells me more than anyone here knew. It's, ah, unfortunate, isn't it?"

What? That you can't trust your own soldiers not to open up on the men who tell them what to do? And that you don't want to admit it to your own bosses? Yes, I'd call all of that unfortunate! Aloud, Khalid said, "I'm afraid it is."

"I will pass on your report, in every detail, to Major Badoglio when he returns to duty," Salgari said.

"Good. Thanks," Khalid said. "I do hope his father recovers."

"So do I. As I told you, the prognosis is good. I'll send along your good wishes when I see the major, too. And I'll send your news to the palace. As I also said, you've let me have some details we didn't know of down here. I can't do anything about that myself, but his Supreme Highness may want to give the Army officers there a piece of his mind. If they don't tell us the true situation, how are we supposed to know what we need to do?"

"You can't know that if they don't," Khalid answered. Having people try to hide bad news or news that made them look bad was a human problem, not just an Italian one. But it got worse in a place like this, where more decisions depended on individuals and fewer on what policies and regulations ordained.

"You understand that. Colonel Locchi and his staff officers seem to have some trouble with it," Salgari said in frigid tones. After a moment, he asked, "When do you and your comrade, the *Ebreo*, plan to come back to Rome? Have you seen all you need in the north?"

"Pretty much so, yes," Khalid said. "We won't be staying much longer. If Major General Dallolio hadn't got killed, we might have driven back today. Now, though, we'll probably hang around another day or two and quietly make sure things are going all right."

"That sounds sensible. If being quiet about it doesn't work, make as much noise as you think you need. Colonel Locchi strikes me as being a trifle hard of listening."

Khalid chuckled. Some of that was bound to be Ministry of Information scorn for a mere soldier. Some . . . wasn't. "I hate to say so, but you may be right," the Maghribi replied.

"Ring me again when you do head south, *per piacere*," Captain Salgari said. "I will give that information to Major Badoglio and to the Army, so you won't run into any needless trouble or delay at the checkpoints.

"That would be wonderful, if you can manage it," Khalid said. "Very kind of you. Dawud and I will do something nice for you, too, once we get back to Rome."

"You don't need to bother. It's my privilege to help," the Italian said, but he sounded pleased.

Because he did, Khalid told him, "No bother at all." A dinner, some fine liquor or some cigars from the islands in the Caribbean— something like that, to show the Maghribis did appreciate the trouble he took. Doing something along those lines would have been appropriate even in the bureaucratic world on the other side of the Mediterranean. Here, where the personal element counted for so much more, showing your gratitude came closer to vital.

They said their good-byes. Khalid rang off. He told Dawud what Salgari had said, and how he'd responded. The Jew nodded. "Good for you," he said. "Got to keep him sweet, you know?"

"Just what I was thinking," Khalid said. "Oh—the other thing is, from what he told me, Locchi and his men tried to cover up that it was one of the soldiers who killed Dallolio."

"They think that makes them look bad. They aren't exactly wrong, either, are they? But all the same . . ." Dawud rolled his eyes. "You'd wish they had better sense, wouldn't you?"

"You would," Khalid said. "I'm pretty sure officers in the Maghrib wouldn't sweep anything that big under the rug, espe-cially not when they could see the word would get out whether they hushed it up or not."

"Covering things up is one thing," Dawud said. "Being stupid when you do it—you ought to know better."

"If they find out I blabbed to Captain Salgari, they'll probably arrange an 'accident' for us on the way down to Rome." Khalid laughed to show he didn't mean it. Dawud laughed, too, to show he knew Khalid didn't.

"Yes, we'll take the A1 to Rome," Khalid told Salgari. Dawud made hurry-up motions. Khalid nodded. He went on, "We're just leaving now. I'll see you when we get there. *Ciao.*" He gave the field-telephone handset to the soldier who carried the battery pack on his back.

"Safe trip," he heard the captain say before the soldier hung up.

A moment later, Colonel Locchi told him the same thing. Locchi added, "Be sure to let the people in Rome know we have the situation here under control."

"I will be sure to tell them you said so." Khalid hopped into the horse with wheels and drove away before the new commandant of Milan realized he hadn't promised exactly what was asked of him.

Dawud grinned. "That was naughty of you."

"It was, wasn't it?" Khalid said, not without self-satisfaction. "Sometimes the worst thing you can do to someone is tell him the truth."

"A lot of the time," Dawud said as they hit a pothole. He shook his head. "The rest of the time, the worst thing you can do is drive on one of these so-called roads."

They weren't in a column this time. They were by themselves: two rumpled men in rumpled uniforms piloting their little utility vehicle south down the badly paved highway. Khalid hoped any Aquinists lurking in the hills or skulking in the nearer bushes wouldn't bother wasting a rocket-propelled grenade on what looked like a worthless target. As they had on the way up, they both kept their assault rifles handy.

Khalid knew the drawback to that. Dawud also had to. It wasn't hard to figure out; even Colonel Locchi might notice it. They were out on the road, in the open. Anyone shooting at them would do it from the bushes, or from behind a stone wall, or from inside a barn or a farmhouse.

That shepherd off in the distance, now . . . Was he only watching his sheep? Or was he keeping an eye on the A1, too? All he had to do was duck behind a chestnut tree and use a little radio. Then the fanatics a few parasangs down the road would know something juicy was coming. The Ministry of Information couldn't monitor all frequencies all the time. Even if it could, any simple code would keep eavesdroppers in the dark long enough.

They passed an armored recovery vehicle bringing a damaged personnel carrier in for repairs. The damage looked to be to the engine compartment. That might mean the soldiers in the carrier hadn't got hurt. Or it might not. They'd already gone by a couple of roadside graves next to vehicles too badly smashed and burned to be worth salvaging.

They'd also driven by more red crosses and DEUS VULT! graffiti than Khalid wanted to contemplate. The Aquinists might not be more popular than the Grand Duke, but they were better at convincing the world about how popular they were.

For a while, going through checkpoints helped reassure Khalid. Lorenzo held the roads. He mostly held the cities in spite of the fanatics' best efforts to seize them. Then the Maghribi remembered what had happened to the late Major General Dallolio. Just because a man wore the Grand Duke's uniform, that didn't necessarily mean he was loyal.

"Thanks for cheering me up," Dawud said when he came out with what he was thinking. "I was feeling really gloomy till you reminded me about that."

More often than not, such a crack would reduce Khalid to spluttering incoherence. Today, he had a comeback ready: "I wanted to make sure you were as happy as I am."

Dawud glanced over at him. The horse with wheels started to slew sideways till the Jew straightened out his track. "You've been hanging around with me too long," Dawud said. "You're starting to talk the way I do. We might as well be married."

"I could have more fun with you if we were married," Khalid said. "I could divorce you when I got sick of you, too."

"You *are* starting to talk the way I do," Dawud said. "But you can't divorce me till we get back to Rome. The only way we could split up this car is Solomon's way, and it wouldn't run real well after that."

"Solomon's way?" Khalid asked. Dawud explained. When he got done, Khalid nodded. "There are stories about Solomon in the Qur'an, too," he said, "but that isn't one of them. Jews and Christians may know it. Muslims don't, I'm afraid."

"Ah, well," Dawud said, and not another word. Khalid understood what he meant as easily as if they had been married. If a tale circulated among Jews and Christians but not among Muslims, it didn't become part of the main current of world culture. It remained an eddy, a backwater, something you had to explain to most people. Dawud knew that. He also knew he couldn't do anything about it.

They stopped in Parma for lunch. Soldiers patrolled the streets, but the town seemed quiet. It didn't have the shot-up look of Turin and Milan. What had been the Aquinist Seminary there now had Ministry of Information men scurrying in and out. With luck, the fanatics had left interesting tidbits in their files.

Parma had a name for cheese and a name for ham sliced thin to the point of transparency. Both Khalid and Dawud steered clear of the ham. "I don't know why we bother," Dawud said. "After the sausages in those ration packs, our accounts with God are way in the red."

"Well, yes," Khalid answered. "But we didn't have much choice with the rations. Plenty of other things to eat here. The cheese *is* good." Dawud nodded. Grated over pasta, the cheese was excellent. It wasn't so sharp as what they made in Rome. Khalid preferred the milder stuff. By the way Dawud made his lunch disappear, he did, too.

The soldiers at the first checkpoint south of Parma waved on the horse with wheels after the briefest, most basic search. As long as no one in a vehicle had I AM AN AQUINIST! tattooed on his forehead in big letters, they'd let it pass. Khalid made a note of that. The men at the checkpoint needed to be more alert. Short of being dead, they couldn't have been much less alert.

At the next checkpoint, two soldiers were unhappily messing around under the hood of a utility vehicle. The others started to salute Khalid and Dawud. Then they checked the Maghribis' identification documents and discovered they weren't dealing with a couple of Italian officers after all. Their attitude quickly changed.

"Can we borrow your horse with wheels to take something down the road?" one of them asked. "Ours is shot." He jerked a thumb at the one that didn't work. "Soon as we get back, you can go on, swear on the Virgin's holy name." He signed himself with the cross to show how sincere he was.

Curious, Khalid asked, "Suppose we say no?"

"Well, we'll just have to check you out *real* careful-like then," the Italian answered. "You'd take longer getting on your way like that than if you went ahead and let us use the machine."

"What will you be hauling?" Dawud sounded amused.

"*Amico*, if you pretend you didn't ask that question, I'll pretend I didn't hear it." The soldier sounded amused, too, but in a less friendly way. "So what'll it be?"

He and his pals had the whip hand. They hadn't raised the gate. There were quite a few of them, and they were all armed. Khalid and Dawud nodded to each other. They got out of the horse with wheels together. "You talked us into it," Khalid said.

Two soldiers from the checkpoint jumped into the utility vehicle. Two more manhandled a large crate into the back seat. All the men were laughing and joking. Khalid didn't think they would act that way if they were, oh, selling the Aquinists weapons. He also didn't think he would get a straight answer if he asked. If he was wrong, he might get a bullet instead.

He didn't say anything. He just stood there and watched. He tried to smile, as if he thought the whole business was funny, too. It was funny business, all right—no doubt of that. Dawud puffed on his cigar. He also knew better than to ask any more awkward questions.

The checkpoint wasn't busy. The uprising or civil war or invasion or whatever you wanted to call it had crimped travel up and down the Italian boot. The soldiers swung aside the metal barrier and let the horse with wheels roll down the A1, off to . . . well, off to wherever it was going. They whooped and waved as it shrank in the distance.

Here, the highway ran straight and flat. Perspective pinched the sides of the road in toward each other. They didn't quite touch at the horizon, but you had the feeling they would if they kept going just a little longer. The utility vehicle went from full size to a toy a child could ride in to a toy a child could play with to a bug to. . . .

To a fireball. Two rocket-propelled grenades, one launched from east of the road, the other from the west, tore into it within half a second of each other and blew it to pieces. Khalid hoped the two Italian soldiers who'd commandeered the little car died fast. Die they surely did.

Their comrades back at the checkpoint screamed prayers and curses. Some were separate, some commingled. The men ran down the A1 toward the blazing horse with wheels. Khalid and Dawud ran with them. Khalid was too stunned to do anything but run. Words boiled inside him, but a stuck valve somewhere inside his head wouldn't let them out.

"That could have been us," Dawud panted, the cigar still in his mouth. "That should have been us."

"I know," Khalid said. Those were the words, all right.

No one fired at the soldiers as they neared the utility vehicle. Bushes grew by the roadside. Farther back, stone fences marked farm boundaries. A couple of the farms had little almond groves. A regiment could have hidden in plain sight. Certainly, no one was visible. The fanatics who'd smashed the utility vehicle had made their getaway.

The horse with wheels burned and burned. Khalid wasn't sure the gasoline in the fuel tank could have accounted for so much fire. Maybe whatever was in that crate the soldiers put aboard the vehicle added to it. Looking at their stricken faces, Khalid still didn't have the heart to ask them about it.

"Poor Luigi! Poor Piergiorgio! Not even enough left of them to bury!" one of them said. Tears streamed down his cheeks. He crossed himself again and again, hardly seeming to know he was doing it. Another soldier worked the beads on his rosary.

Dawud coughed apologetically. "Gentlemen, I hate to remind you of this, but we were on our way to Rome when you, ah, borrowed our car. How are we going to get there now?"

"If you can bring the bastard at the checkpoint back from the dead, you're welcome to it," answered the man who'd invited them out of their own machine. He shrugged an expressive shrug. "If you can't, before too long somebody heading that way will come along. You'll be able to snag a ride."

Khalid would have starved as a mechanic. Dawud had all kinds of tricks up his sleeve. Maybe that was one of them. If it wasn't, the Italian had a point. One way or another, they'd get back to the capital. In the meantime . . .

In the meantime, a truck grumbled up from the south. The man in it wasn't a military driver. He was carrying, in fact, a load of chickens in wood-slat cages. As he slowed to a stop, their feathers drifted down onto the badly paved highway like oversized snow-flakes. He leaned his head out the window and called to the sol-diers on his side of the road: "Can you guys let me by, please? I think I got room to squeeze past the wreck."

When you had a job to do, you tried to do it regardless of what got in your way. When trying to do it involved asking a favor of angry-looking men carrying assault rifles, you were as polite as you knew how to be. Grudgingly, the soldiers stepped aside. The driver waved his thanks. He put the truck into gear. Trailing a gray-black exhaust plume and more feathers, it went on its way.

As Khalid and Dawud and some of the Grand Duke's men walked back to the checkpoint, the Jew pointed to the disabled util-ity vehicle and asked, "What's wrong with it?"

"Doesn't want to go," a soldier answered, which wasn't the most precise diagnosis Khalid had ever heard. After a moment, the man added, "It tries to turn over when you hit the starter, so I don't think the battery's buggered up."

That was something, anyway. "Well, I'll check the carburetor first," Dawud said. He bent so he could work under the hood. After a few minutes of fiddling, he pulled back, straightened up, and nod-ded to Khalid. "Give it a try."

Khalid leaned into the passenger compartment. He punched the starter button by the wheel. The engine growled, coughed—and caught. The Italians exclaimed in admiration. Dawud came from an industrialized country. They took it for granted that he'd have a way with machinery. "What did you do?" one of them asked him.

"The needle valve in the float circuit was clogged. I cleaned it out, and we were good to go," he said with becoming modesty.

One or two of the soldiers seemed to have some idea of what he was talking about. As far as Khalid was concerned, he might have been speaking Kechwa or Nawatil or one of the other strange, obscure languages of the Sunset Lands. He might not understand the explanation, but he couldn't deny the results.

Before he got into the horse with wheels, he told the Italians, "We're sorrier than we can say about your friends."

"That's right." Dawud wiped his greasy hands on his trousers.

"You're lucky it wasn't you," a soldier said.

"God was with us," Dawud said. The Italians nodded. They would have nodded just as solemnly had the Maghribis refused to lend their vehicle, gone down the A1 themselves, and met the fanatics with the grenade launchers. Then their countrymen would have been the ones God was with. You could always say it. You could never prove it.

You could never prove He wasn't around, either. More and more, though, as science elbowed its way into province after province that had been religion's, it looked as if He wasn't. Those lives got more comfortable as knowledge grew, which also made God and religion seem less important.

Saint Thomas Aquinas had foretold all that. It was why he refused to reconcile Aristotle and the Christian Scriptures. He'd been right. He'd been absolutely right. And Europe had paid the price for accepting his rightness down through all the centuries since his time.

The soldiers who'd stayed by the burning horse with wheels waved as Khalid and Dawud drove past. The Maghribis waved back. Dawud, who sat in the back seat for this leg of the trip, saluted the Grand Duke's men. "That should have been us," he said once more.

"Tell me about it," Khalid replied. "We were lucky, that's all." Which was what the sophisticated modern man said instead of *God was with us.* As far as Khalid could see, though, one meant about the same as the other. A scholar at a madrasa might be able to define the difference. He couldn't begin to.

Both of them tried to look every which way at once as they went down to Rome. Khalid had no idea whether seeing an Aquinist who fired a grenade at the horse with wheels would let him do anything about it, or whether he would only get a moment of dreadful anticipation till the shaped charge smashed the vehicle to blazing scrap metal. Almost better to be taken by surprise, to die before you knew it.

Almost. Even if the chance of doing anything was tiny—and it was—you wanted to grab it if you could. Khalid did, anyhow. By Dawud's jumpiness, so did he.

Nothing happened. The rest of the drive was quiet. No one fired off anything anywhere near them. The blasted utility vehicle might have been a nightmare, an illusion. If he weren't behind the wheel of a different one now, Khalid could have thought it was.

As traffic got heavier on the outskirts of Rome, he said, "I'm going to drive to the embassy. Our people need to hear what's going on in the north."

Dawud nodded. "Good idea."

By what would do for a miracle in these secular times, he slipped into a just-vacated parking space a block and a half short of the embassy. The building was draped in black crepe streamers. The Maghrib's flag flew at half-staff above it. "Who died?" Khalid asked.

He asked the same question of the guard to whom he and Dawud presented their identity documents. The man gaped at them. "Who died?" he echoed. "You did—both of you."

XVI

Umar ibn Abd-al-Aziz gave Khalid and Dawud a careful inspection, careful enough that it irked Dawud. "Do we pass muster, your Excellency?" he asked pointedly.

"Oh, yes," the ambassador said. Like everyone else at the embassy, he kept staring at them. "It's just that I've never talked with dead men before. I've certainly never had them answer me before."

"Who told you we were dead, sir?" Khalid asked.

"Why, Captain Salgari did," Umar answered. "He said he was devastated, but he'd just got word the Aquinists had blown up your vehicle south of Parma. He said it went up in flames—there was no chance anyone inside it could have lived."

"He'd just got word. . . ." Khalid said slowly.

"They blasted that horse with wheels, all right," Dawud said. "We weren't in it, but they didn't know we weren't."

"He'd just got word . . ." Khalid said one more time, as the pieces started to fit together inside his head. "He didn't get word from the Army. The soldiers at that checkpoint knew we were alive. He got word from the people who thought we were dead. From the people who thought they'd killed us."

"From the Aquinists," Dawud agreed. "That *really* should have been us, then. If not for those smuggling Italians and their car that wouldn't start—" He shuddered.

Another piece fell into place. "No wonder he wanted me to call him before we left Milan. He was setting up the ambush!"

Umar ibn Abd-al-Aziz's eyes bounced from one of them to the other. "You *are* the talkiest dead men I ever met. Are you telling me Captain Salgari is playing for both sides at once?"

"Afraid so, your Excellency," Khalid said. "A captain in the Ministry of Information—in the part of the Ministry of Information that's been busy fighting the Aquinists—would be just what the fanatics want."

"Yes, I can see how it might be." The ambassador had a talent for understatement.

"Could you ask Salgari to come here, your Excellency?" Khalid said suddenly. "He could tell you all about what fine men we were . . . till we walk in to thank him in person."

"I like that!" Dawud said. "We can hang on to him until we let Lorenzo know what's going on, too."

"Under the strict usages of international law, we shouldn't," Umar said. "But, considering that Lorenzo would throw me out of Italy if we didn't, I think we can bend those usages a little."

He telephoned the Ministry of Information. When he got through to the captain, he asked if Salgari could possibly come over to give him more information about the deaths in person. A film star couldn't have given a better performance.

Hanging up, the ambassador reported, "He'll be here in half an hour, he says. Now I have to let the people up front know, so they don't give anything away."

Salgari was late. That might have been because appointment times on this side of the Mediterranean were statements of hope, not intent. Or it might have been because Roman traffic was horrendous. Umar ibn Abd-al-Aziz received the Italian officer in a room with a side door. Khalid and Dawud stood with their ears pressed to the other side of it.

"Yes, a tragedy. They were fine men, dedicated men." Captain Salgari didn't make the worst actor himself. He sounded tired and mournful. "It sucked the spirit out of me when I heard they were gone."

"How did you get the word?" Umar asked.

"From a checkpoint south of Parma," Salgari said. "They had identified themselves there, and they hadn't got out of sight before two grenades slammed into their vehicle, one from either side of the road. Nothing was left but a ball of flame. I am more sorry than I know how to tell you."

It could have been true. By all the signs, it should have been true. He'd had the attack set up just the way he described it. It had worked just the way he described it, too. The only problem—to Salgari's way of thinking—was that Khalid and Dawud weren't in the horse with wheels when it rolled past the assassination team.

"I see. Thank you." Umar must have leaned back in his chair; Khalid heard the creak. Another creak a moment later said he'd leaned forward again. "Then how do you explain—this?"

Dawud turned the knob. He and Khalid stepped into the room with the ambassador and the Italian. Both investigators carried their assault rifles, to make sure Salgari didn't do anything foolish. For a split second, the captain from the Ministry of Information showed complete and utter dismay. Very few people can hold their faces still when caught by surprise. But Salgari quickly rallied. "It is a miracle!" he said. His mouth twisted into a pretty good wry grin. "Or, perhaps more likely, I was somehow misinformed. I am very glad to see I was."

"You were misinformed, all right," Khalid said. "And you misinformed his Excellency about who told you we were bound for heaven or hell. It wasn't the men at the checkpoint. It was the Aquinists."

Salgari's laugh was pretty good, too, but only pretty good. "This is ridiculous!" he said. "Why would I do that?"

"I'm sure Grand Duke Lorenzo will want to know the same thing," Dawud said. "Now lie down on the floor, on your belly, legs spread, hands clasped on top of your head. Don't do anything stupid, either. If you do, we may try to shoot you in the legs and keep you from bleeding to death. But if you rush us, chances are we won't bother."

Salgari hesitated. "This is ridiculous!" he repeated. Was he trying to nerve himself for martyrdom? If he was, he seemed to discover he didn't have it in him. Numbly, like a man in the grip of a nightmare from which he could not wake, he did as Dawud told him.

Umar ibn Abd-al-Aziz stepped out of the room. Khalid stood a couple of paces away from Salgari's head—too far for the Italian to reach him with a lunge. Dawud did the frisking. He didn't find anything obviously incriminating. Well, Salgari would have been a fool to have something like that on him. He wasn't a fool—not that kind of fool, anyhow. He'd just made the mistake of believing what he heard from someone else.

The ambassador came back as Dawud was finishing. "Take him to the secure room," he said. "We'll keep him there till we decide what to do with him."

"You have no right to do anything to me. I'm not a citizen of the Maghrib. I'm an officer of the Grand Duchy of Italy," Salgari said from the floor.

"That's one of the things we need to work out," Umar said smoothly.

"You'll have to guide us to the secure room," Khalid said. "We haven't been there before." Dawud nodded.

Guide them Umar did. The room had no windows, no furniture, and a door that could be barred from the outside. Someone had put a bucket in one corner. "How civilized!" Salgari said when he saw it.

"Just go in," Dawud told him. As soon as the Italian had, Khalid closed the door. It was thicker and sturdier than the one behind which he and Dawud had listened; no sound would get through. Umar lowered the bar into place himself.

Once it was down, he let out a sigh. "Now I can tell you," he said. "I spoke to Lorenzo. He is *most* interested in finding out everything Captain Salgari knows. He's sending a squad of men whose loyalty he is sure of to take him off our hands."

"He may be sure of their loyalty, but is he right?" Khalid asked.

"That's his worry, not ours," Umar answered. "Any which way, I won't be sorry to see Captain Salgari gone from the embassy."

"Well," Dawud said, "no." Khalid nodded. He couldn't have put it better himself.

Giacomo Badoglio bobbed his head to Khalid and Dawud in turn. "Yes, my father's much better. Thank you," he said. "He's still a little clumsy on one side and sometimes he has trouble finding the word he wants, but the doctors say that will fade with time."

"Good. Glad to hear it," Khalid said. Badoglio was a solid enough man. *If he's really on the Grand Duke's side, he is,* Khalid thought. He'd had the same view of Captain Salgari, a view that turned out not to be true at all. But you had to trust somebody. You couldn't go through life without trust, not unless you found a cave out in the middle of nowhere and spent the rest of your days as a hermit.

"How is our caged bird?" Dawud had to be thinking of Captain Salgari, too. "Is he singing?"

"He's singing, all right," Badoglio answered grimly. "The Inquisitors had to singe his feathers a bit before he opened up, but he's singing now."

"All right." Dawud didn't sound altogether convinced it was. Khalid wasn't, either. In Italy, you had whatever rights the Grand Duke said you had. If he said you didn't have any, that was your hard luck. In the Muslim republic and constitutional monarchies, laws limited what the government could do to its citizens. Not in a place like this.

"Anything especially juicy?" Khalid asked.

"He says the Aquinists have men in Pope Marcellus' guard force," Badoglio replied. "His Supreme Highness is checking that as quietly as he can. So is his Holiness."

"That's the kind of thing he would say whether it's true or not," Dawud remarked.

"I know. So does the Grand Duke," Badoglio said. "It's the kind of thing where investigating stirs up trouble. That may be why Salgari came out with it. Or they may have squeezed him till he coughed up some truth. They're good at what they do, but no one is perfect."

Of course they're good at what they do. They get enough practice. Khalid didn't say it. Police and government investigators in the Maghrib sometimes used strongarm tactics. He couldn't think of a place on earth where that didn't happen once in a while. Police and investigators were human beings, too. But the Maghrib didn't keep torturers on the government payroll. There was a difference.

There was a difference now. But some of the outrages the Aquinist immigrants from Europe had perpetrated in the Maghrib and other republics and constitutional monarchies made even civilized people clamor for more limits on their civic rights. Some of the things civilized governments did to block the fanatics weren't pretty, either.

If we end up looking like these European kingdoms and grand duchies, haven't the Aquinists won? Khalid wondered. It wouldn't be the same kind of victory as if they made everyone turn Christian and forget the modern world. They might not recognize it as a victory themselves. One of the things they were after, though, was killing freedom wherever they found it. They were doing all too well with that.

"What else does Salgari say?" Dawud asked. "Does he know who sneaked that new girl into Cosimo's reception?"

"I wish he did. But they pushed him hard on that, as you can understand, my master, and he showed no sign of it." Major Badoglio sighed. "All in all, he knows less than we'd like. The Aquinists are careful. He mostly gets his instructions without knowing who gives them to him, and he can give orders without knowing the men who get them. Their spycraft is good, damn them."

Dawud's chuckle was sour. "I have a picture of an Aquinist Corrector with a pile of trashy espionage romances translated from the Arabic, or maybe even in the original, picking out the bits that ought to work."

"It could be true—you never know," Khalid said.

"It could be, yes," Major Badoglio said. "A better bet, though, is that some spies are Aquinists, too, and pass on what they know."

That struck Khalid as much too likely. Spear-carriers for the Aquinists needed only fanaticism. The people who ran the movement might be misguided, but they were a long way from dumb. They wouldn't have been so dangerous otherwise. An astringent intelligence like Corrector Pacelli's would have risen to the top in whatever line the man chose.

Badoglio found a question of his own, perhaps in the line of duty, perhaps not: "Is your lady friend glad to see you back in one piece"

"She is," Khalid replied. "She hadn't heard we were supposed to be dead, though, so that was all news to her. The ambassador told me he was going to call her, but he hadn't got around to it when we showed up at his door. He hadn't had the heart, he said. That once, putting things off worked out better."

"I know she met Salgari," Major Badoglio said. "Did she say anything about suspecting him?"

"Not a word," Khalid said. "She was as surprised as we were."

"He didn't have a sign on his back that said I'M REALLY ON THE OTHER SIDE," Dawud said. "The sign is what gives most spies away."

"Let me make a note of that." Badoglio did pretend to write it down. Khalid and Dawud both laughed for real. Someone from the other side of the Mediterranean might have made that comeback— Dawud might have done it himself. To a large degree, people were people regardless of where they came from or which religion they professed.

To a large degree, but not altogether. People who insisted on ramming their faith down everyone's throat took advantage of the toleration they got from those to whom religion was only a small thing. Tolerance needed to run both ways. When it didn't . . . *I wouldn't be in Italy if tolerance ran both ways*, Khalid thought.

"What did the Pope say when he found out the Aquinists might be infiltrating his guards?" he asked.

"He said it sounded like a logical thing for men with those beliefs to do," Major Badoglio answered.

"I should be so cool at news like that," Dawud said.

"He's not an excitable man. Excitable men don't last when they carry Saint Peter's keys," Badoglio said. "Then there was the one cardinal—I think it was about three hundred years ago—who died of joy when he found out he'd been elected."

"Does he count as a Pope?" Khalid asked, intrigued in spite of himself.

"Officially, yes. The Holy Spirit pointed to him."

"If you say so." The answer seemed arbitrary to Khalid. But a no from the Italian would have seemed arbitrary, too. Khalid had enough trouble believing in and following the tenets of the faith he'd been born into. He couldn't remember the last time he'd fasted by day all the way through Ramadan. He sometimes wished he were more pious, but it didn't seem to be in him. So penetrating the mysteries of this different religion felt like too much work.

Dawud said, "Joy? That's the way I'd like to go, preferably at the age of a hundred and three."

"You could do worse," Major Badoglio said. "Most of us will."

"Yes, that's so." The Jew sobered. Like Khalid, he was bound to be remembering that Badoglio's father had just had his brush with whatever lay on the far side of this world. And he was bound to be remembering the Maghribis' own brush with the unknowable. If those Italians hadn't had a utility vehicle they couldn't fix, Captain Salgari might be commiserating with Badoglio right this minute about what fine fellows the Muslim and the Jew had been.

They said their good-byes. Major Badoglio's father would stay in the knowable world a while longer. So would they.

★   ★   ★

"This is a different room," Annarita said when Khalid opened the door and waved her in. "The same floor, but a different room."

"That's right. After Dawud moved out, the garbanzo-counters at the embassy finally put me in a smaller one myself. They didn't see any reason for one man to rattle around all by himself in an expensive two-person suite." Khalid took out a notebook and scribbled in it: *Chances are this one is bugged, too.* He tore out the page and handed it to his lady friend.

She nodded, crumpled up the note, and walked into the bathroom. A flush said it was gone for good. When she came out, she turned on the television. The noise it made might give snoops trouble.

A chorus of women was singing the praises of a particular brand of pasta. The pasta box danced in time to the music with animated arms and legs. Annarita made a face. "Your advertisements can't be this stupid," she said.

"That's what you think," Khalid answered. "They all go for the lowest common denominator, and you can't get much lower than that."

"They can't get much lower than *that*." Annarita pointed to the gyrating box. "I'll never touch that brand again."

"You can think for yourself. You aren't the target audience," Khalid said.

"My cat wouldn't be the target audience for that!" she said.

He nodded. "Of course not. What do cats care about noodles?"

She poked him in the ribs. He took off his shoes and lay down on the bed. Annarita lay down beside him. His arm slid around her. She moved closer. Maybe after a while they'd turn off the television and do something else. Or maybe they'd leave it on while they did something else. When you figured you had people listening to you, confusing them was part of the game.

Another commercial came on, this one from a firm that took tourists to Jerusalem. That kind of pilgrimage wasn't required of Christians the way the *hajj* to Mecca was for Muslims, but it was still popular. "Our excellent security arrangements will make sure your journey stays perfectly safe!" the announcer said.

"No Aquinists." Khalid translated from advertiserspeak to ordinary language. "None they know about, anyhow." There had been incidents in what Christians and Jews called the Holy Land. Some fanatics took the idea of Crusading literally. Most of those were dead, along with an unfortunately large number of locals. The rest wouldn't see the outside of a prison cell for a long time, if they ever did.

After one more ad—this one for a cold medicine that claimed to cure better than holy water—the news came on at last. Khalid wondered if Captain Salgari's treachery would lead it. But the well-groomed man reading his well-groomed script said not a word about that. Grand Duke Lorenzo wanted to keep the Aquinists guessing, then.

What the news showed did nothing to reassure Khalid. Riots and insurrection had broken out in the European quarters of major cities throughout the Muslim world. The camera showed police and troops battling Europeans in a town that looked familiar to him.

Sure enough, the newsreader said, "This footage is from Algiers, in the Maghrib. But it could come from Rabat or Tunis or Alexandria or Cairo or Damascus or Baghdad or Istanbul. It could even come from Manahatta or Seattle or Tenochtitlan in the Sunset Lands."

"This is terrible!" Annarita exclaimed as a gasoline bomb sent a horse with wheels up in flames. Khalid couldn't have put it better himself.

When the picture cut back to the newsman, a scholarly-looking older fellow was sitting beside him in the studio. "With me is Professor Gianfranco Albertazzi, an expert on the Aquinist movement and international relations. Professor Albertazzi has a position at the Ducal University. Welcome, Professor."

"Thank you." Even in responding to a greeting, Albertazzi sounded like a man who chose his words with care.

"How likely do you think it is that all these uprising should have begun at the same time?" the newsman asked.

"That depends on how you define 'likely,'" the professor said—yes, he was cautious, all right. "If you mean, is it a coincidence that they all erupted together, I would find that highly unlikely. If you mean, was there planning to make them all start simultaneously, that seems much more probable."

"Planning by the Aquinists, you're saying." The newsreader didn't make that a question.

Professor Albertazzi's nod was measured, too. "Yes. In foreign lands as in our own, they seek to disrupt however they can. Chaos is a means to an end for them. It is almost an end in itself. They care very little about what happens to the people they lure away from good order."

That was how Khalid saw the Aquinists. He found it interesting that a European—presumably, a Catholic Christian—academic saw them the same way. Of course, with a different view Albertazzi wouldn't have found himself on the Grand Duke's television station.

"Europe's international reputation, and Italy's in particular, can only suffer because of this, wouldn't you say?" the newsman asked.

"Certainly." Albertazzi gave another measured nod. "The wider world will only see us as bloodthirsty barbarians. These riots live down to the stereotypes foreigners already hold about us."

"Thank you, Professor." The newsreader looked straight into the camera. "We'll be right back with more news, and with the weather and sports, after these important announcements."

That meant the station returned to huckstering. Capitalism in Italy was rawer and less sophisticated than in places where it had held sway longer. Some of these advertisements were much worse than the prancing pasta box, and would have made people in the Maghrib laugh themselves silly.

Khalid didn't want to pay attention to them anyway. Turning to Annarita, he said, "The Aquinists have a longer reach than I thought they did."

"They have a longer reach than anyone thought they did," she answered. "That someone in a German archbishopric, say, could touch off riots in Baghdad and Seattle at the same time—" She broke off, shaking her head.

"I wonder how long they've been putting this together," Khalid muttered, more than half to himself. The Aquinists might—did—hate modern science and technology for transforming the world and man's perspective of it. That didn't keep them from using technology's products when they came in handy. Plainly, the rioters had more and more potent weapons than they would have if they hadn't been stockpiling them. Just as plainly, modern communications made sure all the insurrections began together.

"All they want to do is tear things down," Annarita said. "Nothing else matters to them."

He leaned over and kissed her. It wasn't a kiss of passion: more a kiss of gratitude. "You really ought to come back to the Maghrib with me," he said. "You're wasted here."

"Come back with you as what? Your concubine? No, thank you." She didn't seem angry, only sad and matter-of-fact. "Besides, how long will it be before Europeans are welcome there again?"

"Sooner than you think," Khalid answered. "We need workers. There wouldn't be so many Europeans there now if we didn't. As for the other . . ." He paused. That was the important one, as he understood. "You could marry me, you know."

Her eyes widened. "Do you mean that? I'm not just someone to keep you happy while you're stuck in this barbarous country?"

"Yes, I mean it. You're about the least barbarous person I ever met," he said. "In case I never mentioned it, I was married once before. It didn't work, but I think I know—I hope I know—some things not to do now. I've grown up a good deal since then."

"We don't . . . break up marriages so casually here," she said slowly. "'Wherefore they are no more twain, but one flesh. What therefore God hath joined together, let not man put asunder.' That's the rule we live by."

"Different customs. I know. I think our way is better. It saves people from being stuck in unhappy marriages."

"And it means they walk away at any excuse or none," Annarita retorted. "I'm not going to stop believing what I believe even if I love you."

"I wouldn't want you to. You wouldn't be you otherwise. I won't try to convert you, and I don't expect you to try to convert me. We can get along the way we are." Khalid hoped living in a secular constitutional monarchy like the Maghrib would eventually make her take a more relaxed view of her faith. He didn't know that would happen with her, but he had seen the like with other bright, well-educated Christians. He kissed her again, this time in a different way. "And I do love you, you know."

"You must. Either that or you've gone crazy." But she kissed him back.

The commercials ended. The weather report came on. The sports followed. Neither Khalid nor Annarita paid any attention to them.

Black masks hid the faces of the soldiers in the narrow, high-walled courtyard. They carried old-fashioned, bolt-action rifles. One of them worked the bolt to make sure it functioned smoothly. A nod said the mechanism satisfied him.

Major Badoglio nodded to Khalid and Dawud. The officer from the Ministry of Information seemed pleased with himself. He sounded pleased, too: "I'm very glad I could arrange for you to be here this morning."

"Thank you for taking the trouble." Khalid could have done without Badoglio's diligence. He knew what was going to happen. He understood that it or something like it was necessary. He didn't want to watch it, but he knew declining would have insulted the Italian who'd got permission for him to come.

Dawud said nothing at all. There were occasional advantages to being a junior investigator.

Bugles blared a fanfare. A man with iron lungs shouted, "His Supreme Highness, the Grand Duke Lorenzo!"

Everyone stiffened to attention as the Grand Duke and his bodyguards walked into the courtyard. "As you were, friends," Lorenzo said. The men relaxed. Lorenzo came over to Major Badoglio and Khalid and Dawud. "He's getting what he deserves, eh?" he said. To the Maghribis, he added, "Getting what he would have given you."

"Yes, sir." Khalid nodded. Italians took revenge seriously, the way people in the Maghrib had back in the days before the world changed. This whole macabre ceremony seemed a tunnel through time to a bygone age.

A shout rose: "Bring in the prisoner!"

A door opened: not the one through which the Maghribis and Major Badoglio or the Grand Duke and his bodyguards had entered. In came Captain Salgari, escorted by three guards who also wore black masks. Salgari's hands were tied behind his back. He wore a uniform from which every insigne and decoration had been stripped.

The guards led him to a pole at one end of the courtyard. One of them tied his feet to the base of the pole. Another fixed the rope biding his hands to it. The third offered him a blindfold. He shook his head. The guard shrugged and put the strip of cloth back in his pocket.

"You have seen a priest and made your final confession?" the guard asked, plainly for the record.

"I have." Captain Salgari's voice wobbled, but he managed a nod.

Again for the record, the guard said, "Have you any last words? Be brief."

"I am a Christian man," Salgari said. "I did what a Christian man should do. I will go to heaven when I die, and all of you will burn in hell."

Lorenzo said, "You were a traitor to your country. You were a traitor to your sovereign, to *me*." He jabbed a thumb at his own chest. "You get what you deserve in this world, and you'll get what you deserve in the next one, too." He nodded to the squad of riflemen. "Carry out the sentence!"

"Load your weapons!" ordered the lieutenant in charge of the squad.

As the soldiers each chambered a round, Major Badoglio spoke in a low voice: "One man has a blank cartridge in his piece, so each can hope he did not fire a killing round."

Their faith is full of rituals. So is the way they execute a man, Khalid thought. On his side of the Mediterranean, executions were very rare, though treason could cause one there as well. In the Maghrib, they were handled quickly and quietly, with everyone doing his best to pretend nothing was happening. Not here. Here they turned death into a ceremony.

"Ready!" the lieutenant called. The men brought the rifles to their shoulders. "Aim!" he said, and the barrels all swung toward Captain Salgari's chest.

At the same time as the lieutenant ordered "Fire!", Salgari cried "God wills it!" A split second later, the rifles thundered as one. Salgari slumped against the post.

Out of the corner of his eye, Khalid saw that Lorenzo's bodyguards had unobtrusively slid between the firing squad and the Grand Duke. They took no chances on one of the black-masked soldiers' being a secret Aquinist. The precaution went for nothing, but they didn't know ahead of time that it would.

The lieutenant in charge of the firing squad drew his pistol and walked around behind Salgari. Though red splashed the wall there, he checked Salgari's pulse. If he had to finish the traitor, he would.

He straightened and slid the pistol into its holster. "He is dead. It is over," he said formally, and then, "Squad—dismissed!"

His men saluted him, shouldered their rifles, and marched out by the door Captain Salgari had used to come in. The lieutenant and the guards who'd tied Salgari to the post followed.

Lorenzo scowled at the dead man. "I'd like to chuck that carrion in the Tiber, but his Holiness would have something sharp to say if I did. I hate to waste Italian dirt on him, though."

"What he did when he was alive won't matter to the worms, sir," Dawud said.

"Ha! Well, you're right about that." The Grand Duke was still scowling, though. "I wish he'd known how the fanatics got the bomb through to my father. That would have given me a little peace of mind."

Even in the Muslim world, sultans and wazirs had bodyguards to keep them safe from the occasional maniac. Here in Europe, the maniacs weren't so occasional. If they'd managed to murder your father, of course you would worry your turn was liable to come next.

"May I suggest something, your Supreme Highness?" Khalid glanced at the Grand Duke's guards. Yes, Lorenzo trusted them near his person. Even so . . . There were spies as well as assassins. "In private?"

Lorenzo thought for a couple of seconds: no more. Then he nodded. "Step aside, *ragazzi*," he said. "This fellow's safe if anyone is."

They looked unhappy, but they obeyed. Obeying was what they were for. Khalid stepped close to the Grand Duke. In a voice not much above a whisper, he said, "You might let it be known that Salgari told you who'd helped plant that serving girl, but that you need a little more proof before you start seizing people."

"But—" Lorenzo stopped. He'd been about to say something like *But he didn't tell me that*. He was no fool, though. He saw what Khalid was driving at before his own sentence was well begun. The chuckle that followed was distinctly predatory. "And we see who takes the bait, you mean?" he said, also in soft tones.

"That's right, sir."

The Grand Duke chuckled again. "I just may give that a try. Yes, I just may. Whatever happens, it won't hurt anything. And it may do some good." He slapped Khalid on the back. No Maghribi would have done anything like that. Leadership in Italy was personal all kinds of ways.

More than a little to his surprise, Khalid found he liked it. You knew where you stood with the Grand Duke. He wouldn't smile and say nice things about you while he slid a knife between your ribs. *Not unless some from the Maghrib suggests it to him first*, Khalid thought uncomfortably.

Sometimes, though, you had to do what you had to do. If telling a lie to panic an enemy was a sin, Satan was toasting every politician since the dawn of time on his hottest griddle.

Dawud, Major Badoglio, and the bodyguards all watched Khalid as he walked away from the Grand Duke. Lorenzo and his guards left the courtyard. The Maghribis and Badoglio waited till a couple of jailers or whatever they were came out with a wheeled cart to take charge of Captain Salgari's corpse. After they were out on the street again, Badoglio sent Khalid another curious look. But he asked no questions. He said his good-byes and went on his way. He was a professional. He understood that he didn't need to know.

Once they were surrounded by ordinary Romans and away from snooping ears, Khalid did tell Dawud. "I like that," the Jew said. "I wish I'd thought of it myself—that's how much I like it."

"It may not work," Khalid said.

"It deserves to work. It's too pretty not to," Dawud said. They exchanged lopsided grins. Both of them knew how pretty a scheme was had nothing to do with what you got from it. Dawud added, "Don't tell your lady friend about it."

"Yes, Mommy. I probably shouldn't even have told you."

"Maybe you shouldn't. But I worried more about the bugs in the room than about her," Dawud said. Khalid nodded. You needed to worry about things like that . . . dammit.

XVII

If Khalid had been back in the Maghrib, he would have been doing everything he could to put down the Christian uprisings in the big cities. Instead, he watched other people trying to deal with them on Italian television. Because he also visited the embassy every few days, he knew more than Lorenzo's subjects. Knowing more didn't necessarily make him feel better.

"We're trying to keep cameras away from the fighting," Umar ibn Abd-al-Aziz told him. "The fanatics thrive on publicity. They wouldn't be doing any of this if they didn't want to show the world they could."

"You're telling me things are worse than most people realize," Khalid said.

"I'm afraid so," the ambassador replied. "One shopping center in Algiers will never be the same. The Aquinists there wanted to be martyrs. They were, but not on television. That was a very bad bit of business."

From everything Khalid had seen, Umar didn't exaggerate. He understated. "How bad is bad? Do I want to know?"

"They killed Muslims because they were Muslims. They murdered hostages. They wrecked as many shops as they could. They fought as long as they could, and killed themselves when they couldn't fight any more. Some of them booby-trapped their bodies before they killed themselves, so they could try to hurt us even after they were dead."

"They went in expecting not to come out, then," Khalid observed.

"It seems that way, yes." Umar nodded. "They wanted to die— the fighters there, I mean. They intended to be martyrs. They got what they wanted, too, but not on television."

"That's something. Not much, but something," Khalid said.

Umar ibn Abd-al-Aziz nodded again, even more gloomily than before. "I am told—unofficially, because it also didn't get publicized—that something a lot like Algiers happened in a suburb of Cairo where a lot of Europeans live. And in Istanbul the Aquinists tried to blow up the bridge across the Bosporus."

"*Allahu akbar!*" Khalid exclaimed. "They don't think small, do they? That would have been—what's one step worse than a disaster?"

"What we have right now," Umar answered. "That would have cut traffic between the Seljuks' Asiatic and European provinces. And if the fanatics had dropped the bridge into the water the way they hoped, they would have blocked shipping between the Mediterranean and the Black Sea, too, probably for years. The Turks stopped that, anyhow."

"I don't recall seeing anything about it on television or in the papers—I suppose because they did stop it," Khalid said.

"I'm sure you're right. Something that doesn't happen isn't news," Umar said. "Plenty of bad things *did* happen in the Seljuks' realm. The Aquinists didn't just go after Muslims there. They attacked Christians who aren't of their sect, too. Greeks and Armenians and Serbs and Bulgarians and such folk don't acknowledge the Pope, you know, and to the fanatics that makes them fair game."

"It's all foolishness." Khalid knew Islam hadn't been free of such squabbles. Sunnis and Shiites remained rivals to this day. The two groups argued with each other. Sometimes they insulted each other. They hadn't tried slaughtering each other for a good many years, though—not because of religion.

"Of course it is." Umar ibn Abd-al-Aziz smiled a small, sad, cynical smile. "Nowadays we march off to war in the name of nationalism, not faith. Haven't we come a long way?"

That fit much too well with what Khalid was thinking. He said, "Your Excellency, we're going to keep fighting. I wish I could believe anything else, but I can't. If we pile the old reasons on top of the new ones, we'll fight even more than we do already."

"I'd like to say I thought you were wrong. The trouble is, I think you're right." The ambassador rested his chin in his hands for a moment.

"Maybe, just maybe, the fanatics will see they can't win this way, because they're making everyone else hate them." That was as hopeful as Khalid could bring himself to be.

"Maybe so. All groups change over time. They have to." Umar might also have been trying to sound hopeful. He reached his limits even sooner than Khalid did, though: "I doubt the Aquinists and other Christian fanatics will give up in our lifetimes. They may not give up in our children's lifetimes."

"I haven't got any," Khalid said.

"High time you did, then," Umar told him. "One reason so many Europeans move to our lands is that we have fewer than we used to."

Khalid laughed under his breath, even if it wasn't really funny. For a couple of generations, demographers had worried that advances in medicine and farming and the mechanical arts generally were putting more people on the earth than it could sustain. Lately, contraception made population growth in the Muslim world and China slow and almost stop.

But the demographers didn't get to breathe a sigh of relief. Europeans kept right on breeding. Their countries were young and crowded and restless. That spawned extremism at home and emigration with it. Conservative politicians in Muslim lands stoked fears of being overrun by a pale, Christian wave from the north. They'd been screaming about cutting back on the number of immigrants long before this latest Aquinist explosion. Without a doubt, they'd scream louder now.

No matter how loud they screamed, though, work that prosperous people didn't want to do still needed doing. Without the Europeans—and, to a lesser degree, without blacks from south of the Sahara—who would do it? French, Italian, Castilian, German . . . Those were the languages of gardeners and carpenters and construction workers and dishwashers and prostitutes from Teheran to Tenochtitlan.

And Khalid had another reason for laughing. "Well, your Excellency, it is possible that I may end up with descendants after all," he said. "I wouldn't have thought so a few months ago, but it is."

Umar ibn Abd-al-Aziz nodded, unsurprised. "That Italian woman who was Cosimo's aide." It wasn't a question. He added, "You certainly could do worse for yourself."

When Khalid had worried about bugs in his hotel room, he'd worried about the Italian Ministry of Information and the Aquinists. Maybe he should have added his own embassy to the list. Or maybe not—another possibility sprang to mind. "You've been talking to Dawud," he said.

"Revealing my sources would be bad form," Umar answered primly.

Try as Khalid would, he couldn't get angry. His affair with Annarita was something the ambassador needed to know about. It could affect his judgment; chances were it already had, if not to any great degree. He did say, "Nothing definite yet. She's still making up her mind whether she wants to spend the rest of her life on the other side of the sea."

"The civilized side of the sea, the way we look at it. The way we look at it, anybody from this side of the sea ought to jump at the chance," Umar said.

"Dawud says she likely would if it didn't involve living with me." Khalid tried another probe.

"Dawud says all kinds of things," Umar replied, which could

mean anything or nothing. But he went on in a more serious vein: "Because we look at things that way, we forget that the Europeans have a civilization of their own, and that it has traditions older than Islam. They know they're backward now, but they're proud anyway. They're even proud *because* they're backward. Until you understand that, you don't understand anything about them."

"Oh, yes." Now Khalid nodded. "The Aquinists wouldn't be so popular if that weren't so."

"Well, all right. I should have known I didn't need to preach to you." The ambassador clucked in self-reproach. "I hope she does say yes. She'd be happier—the Maghrib will suit her better than Italy does. And you'll be happier, too. Nothing wrong with happiness, believe me."

"I'd like to try it one day." Khalid was joking, and then again he wasn't.

Annarita and Khalid walked through the Forum. Somewhere not far from here, he'd first set eyes on her, and taken her for somebody from his side of the Mediterranean. Now she was in European costume, more covered than she had been then. In these troubled times, Khalid saw fewer women wearing the international style. It was as if they didn't want to draw attention to themselves. No, not as if. That had to be just what they had in mind.

Khalid didn't want to talk about that. He'd seen how Annarita didn't care to acknowledge she'd given any ground to prejudice. He could have pointed it out and used it as an argument to help persuade her she could come to the Maghrib. His guess, though, was that she would have liked him less, not more, if he did. Sometimes you needed to know when to keep your big mouth shut.

Instead, he said, "I've seen Roman ruins in the Maghrib. But seeing them here in Rome . . . It's different here."

"The Maghrib—Africa and Numidia and Mauretania, they called the provinces then—was like an arm in those days," Annarita answered. "This, this was the beating heart of the Roman Empire. The Empire's gone, but the feeling lingers."

"It does," Khalid agreed. The vanished city of Leptis Magna had Roman remains as grand as these, and better preserved. But Leptis Magna, nowadays, mattered only to tourists and archaeologists. Its ruins were so well preserved because it was so long deserted. Rome remained an important city to this day, even if it wasn't the capital of the world the way it had been centuries before the Prophet preached.

Annarita was thinking along different lines. "If Carthage had won the Punic Wars, all the wonderful remains would be on your side of the sea," she said.

"I suppose they would. I never looked at it that way," Khalid said. "Back in those days, Tunis was just a little outlying town. Carthage was the city that counted in that part of the world. Even the Roman Emperor Heraclius came from there to Istanbul—"

"To Constantinople." Annarita broke in with the old name.

"To Constantinople." Khalid inclined his head to her, accepting the correction. "He was still ruling when Muhammad—peace be unto him—passed away. The Muslims conquered Carthage a lifetime later, but the city fell into ruin after that."

Annarita didn't say anything, which was bound to be politeness of a sort. If you looked at history from a European perspective, or from a Christian one, a lot of things fell into ruin after the rise of Islam. As Umar ibn Abd-al-Aziz had reminded Khalid a few days before, these people remembered greatness. And what could be harder than remembering greatness when you saw you didn't have it any more?

What survived of the ancient temple of Castor and Pollux, for instance, were three columns about twenty-five cubits tall. The explanatory signboard in front of them said they were of the Corinthian order, and that the modern Romans called them the Three Sisters. A jackdaw on top of the marble blocks surmounting them chirped squeakily.

Annarita looked up at it as if it were telling her something. She stopped in front of the signboard, but didn't read it. As if out of the blue, though it surely wasn't, she said, "Yes, I will marry you, Khalid." She might have been answering a question he'd just asked her.

The way his heart stuttered in joyful surprise said she wasn't. "Thank you!" he exclaimed, and took her in his arms. He kissed her, too. Public shows of affection weren't always taken for granted here, but he didn't care. She'd said yes! "I'll do my best to make you happy," he promised.

"I believe you," Annarita said. "If I didn't believe you, I would've told you no, wouldn't I?"

"I'm glad you said yes." He left it there. She'd taken longer to make up her mind than he would have liked. But she had a lot to think about. He came from another country. He came from another religion. He came from another civilization, one that lorded it over the culture she'd grown up in. Not all the changes she'd have to make in her own way of life would be simple or easy. Even so . . . He squeezed her again. "I love you, you know."

"I believe you," she repeated seriously. On this side of the sea, arranged marriages to join family interests remained common. Romantic love was gaining here, too, though. In most of the wider world, it had swept the old ways before it. Couples went into marriage happier than they had in days gone by, even if, as Khalid knew too well, they didn't always stay that way.

He and Annarita found a little café off the Forum and toasted each other with red wine. Khalid hoped Annarita didn't expect to live happily ever after without working at it. She'd never been married before, so she might. But if they stayed friends as well as lovers, they stood a chance.

And if you worry about whether it'll work just after she's said yes . . . you stand a chance of being someone who's gone through a divorce, he thought. If you didn't, if you couldn't, sit back and enjoy life once in a while, you didn't deserve a happy marriage.

"What will Dawud say when you tell him?" Annarita asked.

There was a good, distracting question. "Probably that if he'd been in your shoes, he would have thought even longer," Khalid answered. Annarita snorted. He held up a finger to show he hadn't finished. "And that he expects to be a groomsman. He'll wonder how a wedding between a Christian and a Muslim could possibly do without a Jew in it somewhere."

Annarita snorted again. "That sounds like him, all right. If he were a rabbi, he'd insist on marrying us, too."

"I wouldn't be surprised." Khalid wondered what kind of ceremony they would end up having. Whatever it was, it wouldn't be Jewish. Christian? Muslim? Christian and Muslim? Civil? Any or all of those were possible. He found a question of his own: "What will your family think?"

"They'll be glad I'm getting married—most of them are sure I'm doomed to die an old maid," she answered. "They won't be so glad I'm marrying a foreigner. They thought I was too forward when I got an education and started working for Grand Duke Cosimo. What about your kin?"

By *marrying a foreigner*, no doubt she also meant *marrying a Muslim*. Khalid couldn't dwell on that, though. He had to find his own response. "They'll be surprised I'm marrying a Christian," he said, which was bound to be true. "But they'll like you fine once they get to know you. Who you are will count for more than what you are." That was also true.

"My family won't think that way. I'm sorry," Annarita said.

"I love you anyhow. I *do* love you anyhow," Khalid said. To his relief, that seemed to be the right answer, or at least a right answer.

"Let me see." Dawud ran a hand through his badly combed hair, as if to stimulate the brain it covered. "When you hear news like that, you congratulate the fellow who's going to be the groom and you send your condolences to the poor girl who's stuck with him. I think that's how it goes."

"I'll tell you how to go, and where." Khalid made as if to throw a roll at his colleague. Rolls and coffee were the Italian notion of breakfast. Khalid was used to something more substantial to start the day, but he could cope with this.

"You'll need to invite me, you know," Dawud said. "Any wedding with two religions in it ought to have three."

Khalid laughed out loud. "Ha!" He stabbed a triumphant forefinger at the Jew. "I told Annarita you'd say that! How do you like being so predictable?"

"As long as it's you and not the Aquinists doing the predicting, I don't mind . . . too much." The qualifier showed that Dawud still wasn't overjoyed.

Before Khalid could reply, their waiter came up and said, "Excuse me, but is one of you gentlemen Khalid al-Zarzisi?"

"I am," Khalid said, wondering what had gone wrong.

"I have a telephone call for you, *Signor*, at the cashier's station," the waiter said. "If you will please come with me . . ."

Come with him Khalid did, however little he wanted to. Telephone calls at odd hours, in his experience, were unlikely to be good news. Had a relative in the Maghrib died or been hurt? Or had Annarita changed her mind and not had the heart to tell him to his face? That didn't seem like her, but you never knew for sure, not till the moment struck.

He had to tip the waiter for bringing word he was wanted. He picked up the handset like a man taking hold of an adder. "Al-Zarzisi here," he said harshly.

"*Buon giorno*. This is Major Badoglio." Sure enough, Khalid recognized the officer's voice. Badoglio went on, "When I rang your room, no one answered. So I tried down here, and I had good luck. Can you and your friend come to the Ministry of Information as soon as is convenient?"

"What's up?" Khalid asked.

"I'd rather discuss it in person, not over an unsecure line," Badoglio said.

That was reasonable. Khalid muttered under his breath all the same. "We'll be there shortly," he said, and hung up.

"What's gone wrong now?" Dawud asked when he got back to the table.

"Just what I was thinking," Khalid answered. "Giacomo wants to see us right away." The waiter hovered behind him. *Major Badoglio* might well mean something to the man. *Giacomo* was less likely to. No guarantees, of course, but you did what you could.

"Oh, he does, does he?" Dawud gulped his coffee and stuffed half a roll into his mouth. Blurrily, he inquired, "Did he say why?"

"He didn't want to, not over the telephone." Khalid drained his cup, too. He needed coffee more than food.

Fifteen minutes later, they were going through security at the Ministry of Information. The men there knew who they were; they'd checked them any number of times. They were as careful as if they'd never set eyes on the Maghribis before. Italy might lie outside of civilization's mainstream, but bureaucratic routine had found a home here.

Major Badoglio met them just inside the security checkpoint. "*Ciao, amici,*" he said. "Come back to my office with me, and I'll tell you what I know." Even here, in a place that was supposed to be secure, he didn't want to say too much. After Captain Salgari, he had good reason for caution, too.

After Dawud had closed the door behind them, Khalid said, "Well?"

"Well, gentlemen, Fabio Lancelotti has disappeared—fled," Badoglio said in portentous tones that, unfortunately, held no portent for Khalid. Seeing as much, the major explained: "He is—was—the first assistant to the Minister of the Interior."

"Oh-ho!" Dawud saw right away where that was going. He was a beat ahead of Khalid, in fact. "So when he heard Salgari'd sung before he met the firing squad, he believed it, did he?"

"That seems to be the way to bet," Major Badoglio answered. "And it's the way to bet not least because Cardinal Svetozar Boroevic has also vanished off the face of the earth, or at least from the Vatican."

"Cardinal who?" Khalid said. "What kind of name is that?"

"Cardinal Boroevic," Badoglio repeated. "He's a Croat. Their principality is on the other side of the Adriatic. The Croats are close kin to the Serbs in the Seljuk domain. Only don't tell them that, or the Serbs, either. They hate each other."

Who in Europe doesn't hate his neighbors, especially when they're related to him? Khalid wondered. Seeing no chance of getting a meaningful answer to that, he contented himself with asking, "And what does—or rather, did—Cardinal, uh, Boroevic do in the Vatican?"

"Among other things, he was second-in-command over Pope Marcellus' guards." Major Badoglio eyed the Maghribis, then nodded in somber approval. "I see this doesn't amaze you."

"If you'd told me he was the Pope's chief gardener, *that* would have amazed me," Dawud said.

"Are these two . . . officials traveling separately or together?" Khalid asked.

"We don't know." Badoglio sounded unhappy at admitting that, and well he might. Less happily still, he went on, "If they had false papers, they could have flown out of Rome to, well, anywhere in the world. Or they could have driven over the border to France or the Swiss cantons or one of the German states or even Croatia."

"They could be hiding inside Italy, too," Khalid said. "It's not as if the Aquinists don't still have friends here."

"I could wish you were wrong," Badoglio said. "But if I were either one of them, I'd want to get out of the country if I had any chance at all. Believe me, they won't enjoy themselves if Grand Duke Lorenzo gets his hands on them."

Khalid did believe him. No legal framework limited the kind of revenge Lorenzo could take if he caught the man who'd planted the serving girl who'd blown herself up—and Cosimo with her. Svetozar Boroevic might not have done anything to the Grand Duke himself, but Lorenzo also wouldn't love anyone who'd compromised the moderate Pope's safety.

"Without them—" Dawud broke off, as if wondering how optimistic he dared to be. He continued like a man shoving in money in a big dice game: "Without them, Lorenzo may be able to get the upper hand on the Aquinists, at least for a while."

"Sometimes buying time is the most important thing you can do," Khalid said. "People see that the fanatics are only stirring up trouble—they aren't fixing anything or making anything better. That's when their support starts slipping."

"That's when we hope their support starts slipping," Dawud put in. He couldn't stay very optimistic very long. He'd spent too long as an investigator and seen too much optimism come to nothing.

"Giving the people a chance to see that Lorenzo has Italy in his grasp, the way his father did before him, can only help him," Major Badoglio said. He nodded to Khalid. "From what he told me, planting the rumor was your idea. You had a good one there."

"Someone else would have thought of it if I hadn't," the Maghribi replied uneasily. He'd been raised to think modesty a virtue. One more thing that made him feel out of place in Italy, where people tooted their own horns as loud as they could.

"Someone else *might* have thought of it if you hadn't," Dawud said. "If his Supreme Highness feels like giving you the credit, take it."

Badoglio nodded. "Good advice!"

Was it? Khalid didn't care much one way or the other. Yes, Lorenzo was a better bargain than Aquinist fanatics running Italy would have been. But the Grand Duke wasn't his overlord, for which he thanked the God in Whom he indifferently believed. His main wish was for things to calm down enough so Lorenzo would send him and Dawud home. Then he could get on with his own life and see what kind of new one he could build with Annarita.

As if pickpocketing his thought, the Italian major said, "And I hear you're kidnapping Cosimo's assistant. Congratulations! I hope the two of you are happy together."

"*Grazie*," Khalid said. "I hope we are, too. That's what you can do—hope and try your best."

"She'll get along better in the Maghrib, I think," Badoglio said.

"Women who're that sharp make men here nervous. They're more used to it on your side of the sea, aren't they?"

"Yes." Khalid hoped he was right. His countrymen wouldn't scorn Annarita's talents because she was a woman. Because she was a Christian woman, an Italian woman? That might be a different story. He hoped it wouldn't, but it might.

He didn't plan to say anything about that to Annarita. Why borrow trouble? The Maghribis might just respect what she could do, the same as they would for a man born in Tunis. They prided themselves on judging a person for his or her abilities rather than his or her origins. Sometimes they did the latter anyhow, though. Not always. Only sometimes.

"His Supreme Highness has announced that the state of emergency declared for Italy is being relaxed." The Italian newsman sounded as proud as if he'd given the order himself instead of reading what Lorenzo had decreed. "Curfew hours will be shortened. Most travel restrictions will be lifted. According to the Grand Duke, this reflects our progress in the struggle against Aquinist fanaticism and foreign invasion."

The television screen switched from the studio to a prisoner-of-war camp somewhere in the north of Italy: the watery light told Khalid this was nowhere close to the Mediterranean. Glum-looking men, many of them blond and pale-eyed, mooched around inside the barbed wire. Some wore tattered camouflage coveralls; more had on equally frayed European civilian clothes. Faces stubbly or shaggily bearded made the prisoners look even more unkempt than they would have otherwise. Several men sported bandaged wounds.

By contrast, the Italian soldiers guarding the captives were clean shaven except for some neat mustaches or chin whiskers. Not a one that the camera showed had so much as a missing toggle on his uniform. Their assault rifles gleamed with machine oil and purpose. And, most important of all, they were outside the barbed wire, while the prisoners languished within.

"Once people from beyond our borders learn that we can and must tend to our own business, full peace will return to our beloved fatherland," the newsman declared.

"I wonder what he thinks when he isn't mouthing words off the prompting machine," Khalid said to Annarita.

"I wonder if he thinks when he isn't mouthing words off it," she answered. That was another good question. Some of the things Khalid had seen on Maghribi television—when the news crew had to ad-lib in the face of a breaking story, for instance—made him have his doubts, too.

But that wasn't the first thing on his mind right now. "I hope you haven't had any trouble with your passport and your emigration documents."

"No." Annarita's head was on his shoulder. He felt her shake it. "Everything's gone much more smoothly than I dreamt it would. I know our clerks can make a hash of things. I ought to—Cosimo used to complain about it all the time. Not with me, though."

"Good," Khalid said. "Lorenzo promised me anyone who gave you any trouble would end up envying what happens to Aquinists. People seem to think he wasn't kidding."

"I'm sure he wasn't," she answered. "He won't be sorry to see me go—not even a little. I'm taking Cosimo's secrets with me, and I won't spill them here."

"That might be part of it, but he does owe me something, too," Khalid said. "So does Umar ibn Abd-al-Aziz, as a matter of fact."

She laughed. "No wonder everything's so easy on that end, then! I thought the Maghribis would figure any Italian was an Aquinist until she could prove she wasn't. And I thought whom you knew was less important than what you knew on your side of the Mediterranean." Her classical Arabic was more precise and grammatical than a native speaker's would have been.

"Who you know counts for a lot everywhere." Khalid hardly noticed breaking the rule she followed; if she hadn't followed it, he wouldn't have noticed at all. He went on, "It may matter less in the Maghrib than it does here, but it matters, all right."

"I shouldn't be surprised," Annarita said, more to herself than to Khalid. "Anyone would think there were human beings on the far side of the sea, not the always rich, always happy demigods who enjoy pointing their fingers at the foolish things the mortals here do."

There were people in the Maghrib who looked at Europe the way visitors to the zoo looked at the monkey house. They found the antics here, both political and religious, funnier than anything in the cinema. The difference was, monkeys didn't think you ought to believe the way they did. And monkeys hardly ever reached for assault rifles to make you believe the way they did.

"Oh, we're human beings, all right," Khalid said. "We can be just as stupid as anyone else. We aren't always stupid the same ways people here are, but so what? Quarreling about ideology and about the economy instead of theology? It's like eating peaches instead of pears."

She hugged him. "I like the way you look at things."

"Well, good, but I was only getting started," he replied. "In all the little things, the things people do, not governments or religions, we *are* stupid the same ways in the Maghrib. Men cheat on women. Women cheat on men. Somebody gets drunk and slugs somebody else—or shoots somebody else. Sometimes somebody's just mean and doesn't need to get drunk first. People lie. They steal. We have police. We need them."

"How did you get to be an investigator, anyway?" Annarita asked.

"I'd graduated from the madrasa. I'd studied literature, mostly, but I didn't want to teach and I'm not a good enough writer to make a living at that. My Uncle Masud was an investigator for the city of Tunis. He knew some people, and—"

"Ha!" She poked him in the ribs.

"Well, he did," Khalid said. "He's dead now, but he helped me get started. I turned out not to be bad at it. I'll never get rich enough to support four wives, but—"

Annarita poked him again. "You'd better not!"

"Hardly anybody does, these days. Rich men buy big cars and houses and boats instead to show off how much they've made, and keep concubines on the side."

"You'd better not do that, either," she said darkly.

"If you're happy where you are, there's not much point. I expect I will be." Khalid kissed her. Again, he seemed to have found the right answer, or at least part of it. He went on, "Where was I? Oh— the other thing is, every once in a while I end up doing something worthwhile, not just going through the motions. In a lot of jobs, I couldn't say that. And I meet interesting people." He kissed her some more.

"How do you mean that?" she asked after a while.

"I don't know. How would you like me to mean it?"

By all the signs, she liked the way he meant it fine. When they got around to noticing the television again, the news was over. A quiz show was on instead, with a host who cracked rapid-fire jokes in a dialect Khalid had trouble following. His assistant, a statuesque young woman, looked alluring even when covered from head to toe.

"Is she distracting you?" Annarita asked.

"I wasn't distracted," he replied. "I was just noticing how you can do, um, interesting things in spite of the customs here."

"Is that what you were noticing?"

"Of course," Khalid said, as innocently as he could. "I noticed you a little while ago, and you were wearing quite a bit less than she is. You still are, as a matter of fact." He set a hand on her bare hip.

"So you noticed that, did you?"

"Dear, if I don't notice you, they can wrap me in a shroud and shovel dirt over me, because I'll be dead. And if I look at other pretty girls once in a while, who cares where you get your appetite as long as you eat at home?"

"Hmm. I'm not sure I like that." Annarita thought about it for a few seconds. Then she nodded. "I suppose I can put up with it. I suppose I'll have to. As far as I can see, men *are* going to stare at women, and you can either put up with it or go out of your mind.

That's one point to the women's clothes we wear here: they make men stare less."

"Or just use our imaginations more," Khalid said. Annarita made a face at him, but then she laughed. He cupped her breast in his hand. She purred. He went on, "I don't need to use my imagination now. I've got the real thing here with me. If that doesn't make me the luckiest man in the world, I don't know who would be."

"Flattery will get you somewhere. Oh, wait." She paused. "It already did, didn't it?" This time, they laughed together.

XVIII

Khalid and Dawud walked down an Italian street not far from their hotel. Khalid couldn't see any soldiers. The air didn't stink of smoke. No nearby gunshots made him dive for his life—or stole it.

The locals were taking advantage of the peace and quiet. Open doors invited customers into shops and eateries and taverns. WELCOME! signs shouted in big letters. SALE! they screamed in even bigger ones.

Most of the Aquinists' broadsheets were torn down. Few people dared sneak out at night to paste up new ones. By contrast, Grand Duke Lorenzo's young, handsome face stared at passersby from every wall and post and fence. THE GRAND DUKE PROTECTS HIS PEOPLE! was his latest slogan.

"It's quieted down," Khalid remarked.

"It has, hasn't it?" Dawud agreed. "A good thing, too, or this country might have fallen to pieces. If the fanatics grabbed control here, right across the narrow sea . . ." He shook his head. "That wouldn't have been good at all."

"No, it wouldn't." Khalid tried to see in his mind what might have sprung from such a disaster. "We probably would have had to invade to clear them out, either by ourselves or maybe with Egypt. Either way, can you imagine how the rest of the European countries would have screamed?"

Dawud threw back his head and screamed himself. A couple of Italians eyed him in alarm and edged away. "About like that," he said. "Or maybe even louder. Want me to try again?"

"No, don't bother," Khalid said quickly.

"Oh, be that way." Dawud sounded sulky. "But all the Europeans would have screeched about how we violated Italy's sovereignty and how we didn't respect them and on and on. Now they won't get the chance. I bet some of them are disappointed, too."

"I wouldn't be surprised. You're right, though—they won't get the chance," Khalid said. "Instead, we get the chance to go home."

Dawud laughed at him. "That breaks your heart, doesn't it? Just smashes the poor thing all to pieces. Now you'll have to go and marry your pretty Italian. I'd say she was a smart Italian, too, only she went and told you yes. So how smart can she be?"

"Never can tell with women. *You* got somebody to say yes, for instance," Khalid said.

"Sarah wanted to stay inside the faith, so she had fewer choices," Dawud said. "Chances are I wouldn't have been so lucky if she'd been able to look around a little more."

Khalid knew that was nonsense. Dawud knew he knew it was. The Jew and his wife had been a happy couple for many years. By all the signs, they'd stay a happy couple for many more. Whatever it was that made two people fit together, they had it.

"Annarita and I should find that kind of luck," Khalid said.

"Well, I hope you do," Dawud said. "Sarah and I were both sad when your first one fell apart. Those things happen—I know they do. You never like it when they happen to somebody you care about, though."

"Hrm," Khalid said. It wasn't as if he didn't know his share of couples whose members had been sure they would live happily ever after . . . and who now lived apart from each other. One of the things that followed upon marrying for love was breaking up when that love, whatever the reason, failed to stay the course.

He wanted to think that wouldn't, that couldn't, happen to him this time around. He wanted to, but it wasn't easy. He and his first wife had broken apart after coming together. What guarantee did he have that he and Annarita wouldn't go the same sorry way?

He had no guarantee, as he knew too well. But he'd made some mistakes the first time around that he didn't think he would make again. Some people did learn by messing up; he could hope he was one of them. And Annarita wasn't the same as his first wife. He thought she was more easygoing, more tolerant of foibles. If he hadn't thought it *could* work, he wouldn't have asked her to marry him.

When he and Dawud walked into the hotel lobby, Major Badoglio sat there waiting for them. He wore civilian clothes, presumably so he wouldn't alarm or alert other people going in and out. He stood up when he saw the two Maghribis. "Peace be unto you, my masters," he said in Arabic.

"And to you also peace," Khalid answered automatically.

"What's gone and fallen into the chamber pot now?" Dawud asked: exactly the question filling Khalid's mind as well.

But Major Badoglio only smiled. The expression pulled his thin face in unfamiliar directions. "Nothing . . . Nothing I know of, anyhow." Yes, he would be one to qualify that. After a moment, he went on, "I have a car in the parking garage down the street. If you'll come with me, the Grand Duke would like to give you his thanks and his farewells."

"How can we say no?" Khalid murmured. If you told a European ruler no when he wanted to hear yes, you needed to have force ready to back it up. The Maghrib had that kind of force when it dealt with Italy. Khalid and Dawud didn't when they dealt with Grand Duke Lorenzo.

Badoglio drove them to the ducal palace on the Palatine Hill. Security there had always been tight, even if, once, it hadn't been tight enough. It was no looser now. Still, the soldiers seemed less jumpy than they had at the height of the Aquinist uprising. They were ready for trouble, but they weren't looking for it to leap up and bite them in the leg.

A butler with some of the bushiest eyebrows Khalid had ever

seen led him and Dawud and the major to a small reception chamber. Lorenzo waited there with some of his aides and some women who might have been wives or concubines (Christianity frowned on them, which didn't mean there were none in Europe) or ornaments.

Khalid bowed to the Grand Duke. "Your Supreme Highness," he said. Beside him, Dawud went through the same unrepublican rigmarole. So did Badoglio, whose bow was more practiced and better polished.

"No ceremony needed today," Lorenzo said. He waved to a very ornamental woman with a tray of drinks. "Help yourself to whatever you fancy. You can have a glass of wine, too." The serving girl squeaked.

"I like that one, sir," Dawud said. Laughing, Khalid nodded. Even with no ceremony required, a Grand Duke's joke would be funnier because of who told it. Still, Khalid had heard plenty worse.

Annarita walked in a few minutes later, escorted by another officer—this one uniformed—from the Ministry of Information. She dropped Lorenzo a perfect curtsy. Khalid had seen the gesture only in Europe. In the wider world, women bowed like men, though sometimes more deeply.

The Grand Duke also told her no formality was needed. Then, in more public tones, he said, "We're here today to honor and thank our friends from across the sea. They came to help my father—God bless him—cope with the Aquinist fanatics and murderers. Though they couldn't save him, they stayed to work with me. And they gave me the lead I needed to flush out the villain who betrayed Cosimo. Ladies and gentlemen, here are Khalid al-Zarzisi and Dawud ibn Musa!"

Everyone applauded. Khalid and Dawud both bowed. The applause got louder. Khalid felt foolish. This kind of acclaim belonged to singers and polo heroes. More to the point, people like that basked in it. It just embarrassed him.

Along with bowing, Dawud grinned and waved. He might have been soaking up ovations his whole life. If he hadn't, his attitude said that he should have been. He'd always been better at enjoying himself than Khalid was.

Annarita stepped up and kissed Khalid on the cheek. That set off more cheers. Since they were the last things he wanted, he almost got mad at her. Then he saw how proud she looked. Finding that expression on the face of someone he loved made his annoyance melt like snow in the desert.

"Italy and the Maghrib have always been united in the fight against the fanatics," Lorenzo said. "When Khalid goes home, though, the countries will be joined together in a different, more personal way, because *Signorina* Pezzola here will be going with him."

That drew more applause and cheers. Some of what the Italians shouted sounded risqué. Khalid was glad he didn't speak the language perfectly, or he would have understood more of it. As long as Annarita kept smiling, he didn't worry. People in the Maghrib would have been calling out the same kinds of things, only in Arabic.

Dawud cheered along with the Grand Duke's aides and their ladies. Khalid sent him a look that meant *Do you have to?* The Jew's answering chuckle said *Yes, of course I do, you spoilsport.*

"We will continue the fight until the Aquinists are smashed, crushed, and utterly defeated," a man in major general's uniform told Khalid.

"I hope we do, sir," Khalid answered. He didn't expect that to happen anytime soon, if it happened at all. A man could always hope, though.

"Smashed!" the major general said. By the way he talked, he was busy getting smashed himself. His uniform sparkled with medals and ribbons and gold braid and scarlet piping. From everything Khalid had seen, the fancier a general's uniform, the worse the ordinary soldiers in that army would perform. Maybe Maghribi military men could quietly mention that to their Italian comrades in arms. It wasn't his place, so he kept quiet.

He drank more wine. The buffet offered little sandwiches and olives and fried squid rings and anything else a hungry man might want. Almost anything . . . "I don't see any dormice in honey," Dawud said, as if he'd been looking forward to that particular delicacy for weeks.

Maybe he had. You never could tell, especially with Dawud. But when Annarita said, "You know that was an old Roman dish, not a modern one," her unspoken message plainly was *Don't be more difficult than you can help.*

"I do?" Dawud sounded so innocent, Khalid knew he was responding to what she hadn't said.

The reception went on longer than Khalid would have liked. He and Dawud got one more round of applause when Lorenzo presented them both with the Order of Service to the Grand Duchy, Second Class. The medals were gaudy enough to have made the Italian major general jealous (after that thought crossed Khalid's mind, he noticed that the officer was wearing the same medal with an even more splendid ribbon—the Order of Service, First Class). Lorenzo should have given Annarita some kind of award, too, but he didn't.

At last, assisted by Major Badoglio, Khalid and Dawud made their getaway. *Pretty soon we'll get away from this whole country, too,* Khalid thought. He'd drunk a bit himself, but that only made him more sincere—and more eager.

From the walls of the casbah, which had been Tunis' citadel in the old days but was now reduced to the more mundane role of city hall, Khalid threw his arms wide. The casbah sat on a height, and gave a fine view of Tunis as a whole. "This is *my* town," he said proudly. "What do you think of it?"

As was her way, Annarita gave it a careful inspection before answering "Everything looks so clean, so new, and so white."

"Plaster—and the local stone is mostly white, too," Khalid said. "We don't paint it much. It fights the heat better if we leave it alone." He didn't comment on her other two remarks. Tunis *was* cleaner than Rome. It had had modern sanitation much longer, and the local authorities here cared more about cleanliness than they did on the Christian side of the sea.

Some of the tall buildings in town were glassy rectangular prisms that could have gone up anywhere in the Muslim world— or even in Rome or Turin, though they would have stood out more there. Others looked like larger versions of the old local structures, at least on the outside. Within, they would enjoy all the modern conveniences.

Annarita pointed out past the Bab-el-Bhar: the Sea Gate. No modern skybusters there, only small buildings huddled too close together. Even from this distance, you could see how cleanliness faltered in that part of town. You could guess the area had been grimy even before fire swept through it and soot spotted and marred so many walls. A little sadly, Annarita asked, "That would be the Christian district?"

"I'm afraid so," Khalid answered. "The markets there remind me of the ones I saw in Rome and Naples. If you get homesick for something and you can't find it in the big stores, chances are they'll have it there." He paused and looked down at his sandals. "You might want to wait a little while before you go exploring. Till things calm down some more, I mean."

"I understood you," she said. "I have my faith in common with the people down there, but that's about it. I came here because it's a freer, more open way of life than the one I left. They came to make money, but otherwise to hang on to how things are in Italy."

"That's about the size of it, I'm afraid. The ones who try to fit in here find they can. There aren't so many as we'd like, but there are some," Khalid said. Out in the harbor, a freighter's deep whistle pierced the hum of loud traffic noises. A dredged channel through the salt lake northeast of the city that led out to the Gulf of Tunis made this a port of call for ships from around the world. To the southwest, suburbs spread across what had been a soggy salt marsh.

"Shall we go back inside? I don't have to look at everything at once," Annarita said.

"Whatever you want." Khalid took her hand. She squeezed his when he did. Smiling, he went, on, "How much do you bet Dawud's already waiting for us?"

"I won't touch that one. And if we're even a minute late, he'll let us hear about it, too." But Annarita was also smiling.

In through the sliding glass doors they walked. Before Khalid went up to Italy, the police officers who served in the casbah had been some of the most bored men in the world. They looked much more alert now. The Aquinists had attacked here. Khalid was hazy on the details, but he knew it had happened.

Fluorescent tubes set into the ceilings behind frosted glass replaced Tunis' bright, harsh sunlight. Conditioned air, cool and as bland as if it weren't there at all, took the place of the hot, sea-smelling stuff outside. *More comfort but less flavor*, Khalid thought. Well, nothing wrong with comfort.

People sauntered or bustled through the hallways, heading for whichever office they needed. Signs and arrows on the white-painted walls told them where to go and how to get there. A janitor with a broom and a wheeled garbage can sang softly to himself in French.

MARRIAGE BUREAU—ROOM 227 was part of the list on one wall, with an arrow pointing to the left. Khalid had gone back to reading the familiar alphabet and to letting his eyes travel from right to left rather than the other way round with enormous relief. To him, figuring out Latin letters while reading in the wrong direction felt like wading through mud backwards.

He liked the old, ordinary numerals, too. The European variations on the theme, even though they ran the same way as the ones he was used to, had always looked funny to him. He couldn't just recognize them; he had to pause and translate them inside his head.

"Left," Annarita said.

She'd been using Arabic more and longer than he'd worked with

Italian. Educated people around the world communicated with it. If an Irishman needed to talk to a Japanese, that was the tongue in which they were sure to do it. Naturally, children learned their native tongues at home and studied them in school. If they acquired a second language, it would be classical Arabic.

The next arrow directed them to the right, the one after that to the left again. The inside of the casbah was a maze. "When I was a little girl, my mother told me a fairy tale about a boy and a girl lost in the woods," Annarita said. "They put down a trail of bread crumbs so they could find their way back."

"That sounds smart," Khalid said. "Did it work?" They didn't tell that story on this side of the sea.

She shook her head. "No. Birds flew down and ate the crumbs, so the kids stayed lost. They got into all kinds of trouble. They got out again, too."

"No birds in here, except every once in a while a sparrow that flies in by mistake," Khalid said. "Only that janitor with his can and his broom."

They rounded a last corner. There was room 227—and there was Dawud, leaning against the wall by the doorway. He looked annoyed: not because they were late (they weren't) but because a large sign across the corridor from the Marriage Bureau warned NO SMOKING UNDER PENALTY OF FINE.

"Wonderful world we live in," the Jew grumbled. "The government makes you be healthy whether you want to or not. I should move back to Italy."

"Especially if the Aquinists win," Khalid said. "Then you can smoke as much as you please—and the government will make you be Christian whether you want to or not."

"Do you suppose you can wait until you've served as our witness?" Annarita asked in sugary tones. "Please?"

"Well, since I got all dressed up to come over here," Dawud said. By *all dressed up*, he meant wearing a reasonably clean robe. That was as much as anyone could claim for it. It had more wrinkles than a block of flats full of ninety-year-olds. The cloth on his keffiyeh hung down so it was on one shoulder and off the other. He had indeed come over to the casbah, though.

They went into the room. Half of it was devoted to issuing licenses. Khalid had already been there. Unless he was completely misremembering, the fee had more than doubled since the first time he'd got married. He'd barely carried enough cash to cover it.

Clerks in the other half of room 227 performed civil marriage ceremonies. One of these days, Khalid and Annarita might have a religious ceremony, or a couple of religious ceremonies. At the moment, they cared more about making things official.

Annarita walked up to the closest unoccupied clerk: a mousy little man of about fifty, with a neat beard going gray. "You can marry us, sir?" she asked.

He bowed politely. "I sure can, my mistress, so long as you have all the required paperwork."

Khalid handed the man his identity card, his license, and a physician's attestation for each of them. Annarita presented her passport, which contained the endorsements from Grand Duke Lorenzo and from Umar ibn Abd-al-Aziz. Dawud, the least essential of the three, merely displayed his own identity card.

"Well, well." The clerk cocked his head to one side like a curious bird as he inspected Annarita's documents. "You have some high-powered friends, my mistress."

"Acquaintances." Yes, she was precise.

"For acquaintances, they seem to have gone out of their way to expedite your move down here." The clerk shrugged. "None of my business, I know." He filled in whatever forms he had to complete. "A Muslim groom, a Christian bride, and a Jewish witness. Modern times." He smiled.

"God wills it," Khalid said, deadpan. The phrase seemed far more innocuous in Arabic than it did in Latin.

"Yes, but whose God?" The clerk didn't even notice the slogan that had spawned so much trouble, some of it right here in Tunis.

"For us, they're all the same," Khalid said. Annarita and Dawud both nodded.

So did the clerk. "I happen to agree with you, my master. And that we do agree there, that's another sign of modern times. Even nowadays, you'd get an argument from some folks."

"They can have the arguments later. They didn't come here for one. They came here to get married," Dawud said.

"You're right, friend. Well, I can probably arrange that." The clerk bobbed his head to Khalid and Annarita. "Repeat after me, if you please. 'I'—state your name—'do hereby take'—state your spouse's name—'to be my lawfully wedded'—state wife or husband—'and agree to our union under the laws of the Republican Sultanate of the Maghrib, in the presence of a witness and of an authorized official of the aforesaid Republican Sultanate.'" He shoved another form across the desk at them. "I need your signatures on the lines that say *Groom*, *Bride*, and *Witness*."

They signed. Annarita wrote her name first in the alphabet she'd grown up with and then, switching directions, in Arabic script. "I'm still getting used to this," she remarked, tapping the pen on the Arabic version.

"Your hand is very neat, very readable," the clerk said, which was true—Khalid had noticed the same thing. The little man went on, "And, with those signatures, you have completed all the requirements, and you are husband and wife in the eyes of the state. Congratulations! May your union prove happy and prosperous."

Khalid kissed her. Though that might have been shocking in Italy, it wasn't here. Other couples at other desks had done the same thing. Annarita must have seen as much, because she kissed him back with no hesitation.

Dawud tipped the clerk before they walked away. That wasn't required, but it was good form. And the man had been nice enough, in a dry way.

"I've got a hotel room reserved for the day—" Khalid began.

"Probably won't want a witness to what goes on there," Dawud interrupted.

Nodding to him, Khalid went on, "And then you'll run us to the airport tomorrow morning. We're going to spend ten days in Agadir, on the Atlantic coast. All these years in the Maghrib, all this time by the Mediterranean, but I've never seen the real ocean."

"Neither have I," Annarita said.

"And you know what?" Dawud said. "Chances are you won't see much of it now, either."

Annarita squeaked. Khalid said, "Can't do that *all* the time, no matter how much I wish I could." He eyed his friend. "I won't be sorry you're a few hundred parasangs away—I'll tell you that."

"Oh, Khalid! You say the sweetest things!" Dawud trilled. They all chuckled.

"You can watch the sun sink into the water from the west coast of Italy," Annarita said, reclining on a lounge on the beach at Agadir. "I've done it often enough."

"I did it once or twice myself." Khalid lay back in his lounger, too. He sipped from an iced glass of wine flavored with fruit juice.

"The Atlantic seems big enough to take it, though. The Mediterranean never did." Annarita had an iced glass, too. "It's probably just my imagination, but—"

"That's a wide horizon," Khalid said. A strip of sand in front of him, then endless blue water meeting endless blue sky. The sun didn't hiss as if quenched when it went into the water, but Khalid still thought it should.

Two naked little boys ran down the beach, yelling at each other. They were very brown, partly from the sun and partly from birth. They shouted in the local Berber dialect, of which Khalid understood not a word. They would pick up Arabic in school but used their own tongue between themselves.

"This is a nice place. I can't think of anywhere better to honeymoon," Annarita said. Any minute now, the sun would kiss the Atlantic. It was so low in the sky, she and Khalid could look at it without hurting their eyes. She went on, "It's out of the way, but it's modern. If you ask me, it's more modern than Tunis, and that's saying something."

"It probably is," Khalid said. "There was a big earthquake here fifty years ago—something like that, anyway. A *big* earthquake, big enough to level the old town. They had to rebuild Agadir from scratch."

"They get earthquakes in Italy, too. The old town falls down . . . and then they argue about who's supposed to put it back together and how they're going to pay for it. And the people in the town, the ones who live there, patch up the ruins as best they can and stay in them. The money that's supposed to pay for repairs lines somebody's pockets instead."

From what Khalid had seen in Italy—especially in Naples—he believed her. Corruption happened everywhere; corruption was part of a world that involved human beings. But there was a difference between trying to hold it to a minimum and throwing up your hands and letting it become part of the system. The Italians had thrown up their hands centuries before.

In a way, Annarita had thrown up her hands, too. She didn't sound angry about repair money that never made repairs, the way a Maghribi would have. She just seemed resigned. Things in Italy worked that way. They always had. As far as she could see, they always would.

Khalid hoped she was wrong. He hoped that, as modernization finally came to Europe (if modernization ever caught hold in Europe), people there would develop a social conscience, the way they had in the Muslim world. It didn't always work like that. China boasted a modern economy. Even so, it ran on greased palms and getting away with whatever you could. The Chinese were trying to clean things up, but they were having a tough time.

He took another sip from his iced, fruity wine. None of this was worth getting excited about on a honeymoon. Maybe he'd remember bits and pieces when he went back to work. Or maybe he wouldn't. He doubted the earth would spin off its axis either way.

The sun touched the ocean, then sank into it. Sometimes, on a clear evening with an unobstructed western horizon, you saw a green flash at the moment the last of the sun's disk disappeared. You couldn't find a horizon much more unobstructed than the one here. No green flash, though—only the beginning of twilight.

Khalid got to his feet. He didn't grumble about the missing flash, any more than he grumbled about the evils of corruption. He didn't feel like grumbling about anything. He couldn't remember ever being happier—which was, after all, the point to a honeymoon.

"Let's go to supper," he said. He reached out to help Annarita up from her lounger.

She took his hand. There wasn't a literal spark when they touched—no static electricity or anything like that. He felt one just the same. By the glow in her eyes, so did she. After supper, he expected they'd go back to their room and enjoy honeymooning some more. Then they'd sleep soundly, and probably sleep late.

The hotel eatery featured tagines—stews simmered slowly in earthenware bowls. Annarita chose one made from fish: sardines cooked with herbs and tomatoes. Khalid picked one with chicken falling off the bone, pitted olives, and oranges and citrons. She ate an iced dessert. He declined. "Can't get too full," he said seriously.

"Oh? Why's that?" Annarita sounded as innocent as Dawud might have.

"Ha! You'll find out!" Khalid did his best to put a leer in his voice. He also did his best in their room a little later. Annarita seemed to think it was pretty good. Khalid did sleep soundly. He slept late, too. When he woke up, Annarita was still almost-snoring beside him. He smiled a lazy smile and wondered what he could manage after she opened her eyes.

Only one trouble with a honeymoon: you couldn't stay on it for the rest of your life. Eventually, you had to go back and pick up the threads of the everyday world. The concierge at the hotel telephoned a taxi. The bright orange Pontiak took Khalid and Annarita to the airport outside Agadir.

They got there two and a half hours before the flight back to Tunis was scheduled to take off. Because of the Aquinists' unrest, air-travel authorities had boosted security to its highest level. Everything and everyone got searched, and then searched again.

Eyeing his fellow passengers as they waited and after they finally got to board, Khalid didn't see anyone who seemed likely to want to blow up an airliner for the greater glory of God. He didn't see anyone who looked both European and fanatical, in other words. Yes, he was stereotyping the rest of the travelers, but not, he judged, unreasonably. Aquinists didn't always look the way they were portrayed in films and on television, but a lot of the time they did.

It was three hundred or three hundred fifty parasangs to Tunis: two hours for the jet. He and Annarita had spent longer waiting in the airport than they would on the flight. He did grouse about that. "It's still faster than if we drove or took the train," Annarita said.

"It's not as fast as it ought to be," he answered. Each of them aimed a severe look at the other. Then they started to laugh. What else were you going to do when you were both right?

Mountains and deserts unscrolled, thousands of cubits below them. The Maghrib's fertile coastal strip looked all the greener when contrasted with that brown and yellow. Off in the distance, Khalid sometimes got glimpses of the wine-dark sea. He didn't need to grope for Homer's term now, the way he had when he and Dawud flew from Tunis to Rome to give Grand Duke Cosimo a hand against the Aquinists. Chances were he would never need to grope for it again. From now on, it would jump into his mind whether he wanted it to or not.

"We're on our descent into Tunis," the pilot announced over the intercom. "Please straighten your seats, then close your trays and latch them. Thanks very much, my masters and mistresses. We'll be landing soon. This flight is right on time."

Annarita checked her watch. She nodded in happy surprise. "It *is* on time! Nothing in Italy is—nothing much, anyway."

"I noticed," Khalid said. "You're not in Italy any more."

"One more reason to be glad I'm not." She set her hand on his arm for a moment. He felt a smile on his face, wider than any he was used to wearing. So far, marriage agreed with him.

The plane touched down as smoothly as he could have wanted. Along with the rest of the passengers, he and Annarita filed off. Then they headed to baggage claim to pick up their suitcases and to meet Dawud. He would drive them back to Khalid's flat, where they would set up housekeeping till they found a bigger place they liked.

Annarita kept looking around. "Is it my imagination, or is the airport full of Jews?" she asked in a low voice.

"I was just thinking the same thing," Khalid said, also quietly. A lot of Jews looked and dressed like anyone else, or they would have if so many hadn't worn six-pointed stars on chains around their necks to mark themselves off. Several in Western European costume used the same signal. And some from Eastern Europe wore long black coats and wide-brimmed hats of black felt or fur . . . and the six-pointed stars. They would start to melt as soon as they left the air-conditioned terminal.

At the carousel, Dawud waved. He pumped Khalid's hand and hugged Annarita. "And they said it wouldn't last!" he exclaimed.

"Funny man," Khalid said. "What are all your tribesmen doing here?"

"You don't know?" Dawud clucked. "It's been on the news."

"We haven't cared about the news lately," Khalid reminded him.

"Oh? Why would that be?" Dawud was rarely ashamed to laugh at his own jokes. Once he had, he continued, "Anyway, the world gathering of the Jewish Nationhood Society is in Tunis this year. Hotels are bulging like you wouldn't believe. It'll pump all kinds of money into the economy."

"The Jewish Nationhood Society? What do they want?" Annarita asked.

"What the name says. A national home, the way the Persians have Persia and the Italians have Italy."

"Where would they put it?" she wondered.

"Wherever they can, basically," Dawud said. "Palestine is the first choice, but there might be others. . . . Whoops! Is that one yours?"

It was. Khalid grabbed it. Annarita asked the question that was also going through his mind: "What do you think the chances are?"

"Slim," Dawud answered frankly. "We've been talking about it since the Romans smashed the Second Temple. Jews like to talk—you may have noticed. But I don't suppose it'll ever amount to anything."

I sure hope not, thought Khalid, who could imagine any number of problems the Nationhood Society was probably ignoring. Since he was too polite to risk hurting his Jewish friend's feeling by saying that, he tried something else instead: "Why don't you take us home?"